PHONOGRAM Vol. 3,
THE IMMATERIAL GIRL

March 2016
ISBN: 978-63215-679-2
Published by Image Comics Inc.
Office of publication: 2001 Center St,
Sixth Fl, Berkeley, CA 94704.

For information regarding the CPSIA on this printed material call: 203-595-3636 and provide reference #
RICH – 668847. Representation: Law Offices of Harris M. Miller II, P.C. (rights.inquiries@gmail.com).

This book was designed by Sergio Serrano in Edmonton, Canada. The text face is Futura Std.
The paper is Liberty 60 matte.

KIERON GILLEN
WRITER

JAMIE MCKELVIE
ARTIST

MATTHEW WILSON
COLOURIST

CLAYTON COWLES
LETTERER

CHRISSY WILLIAMS
EDITOR

SERGIO SERRANO
DESIGNER

DEE CUNNIFFE
FLATTER

PHONOGRAM

THE IMMATERIAL GIRL

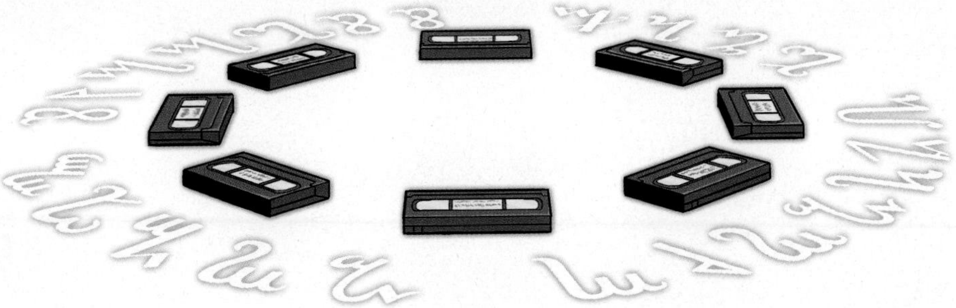

GILLEN McKELVIE WILSON COWLES

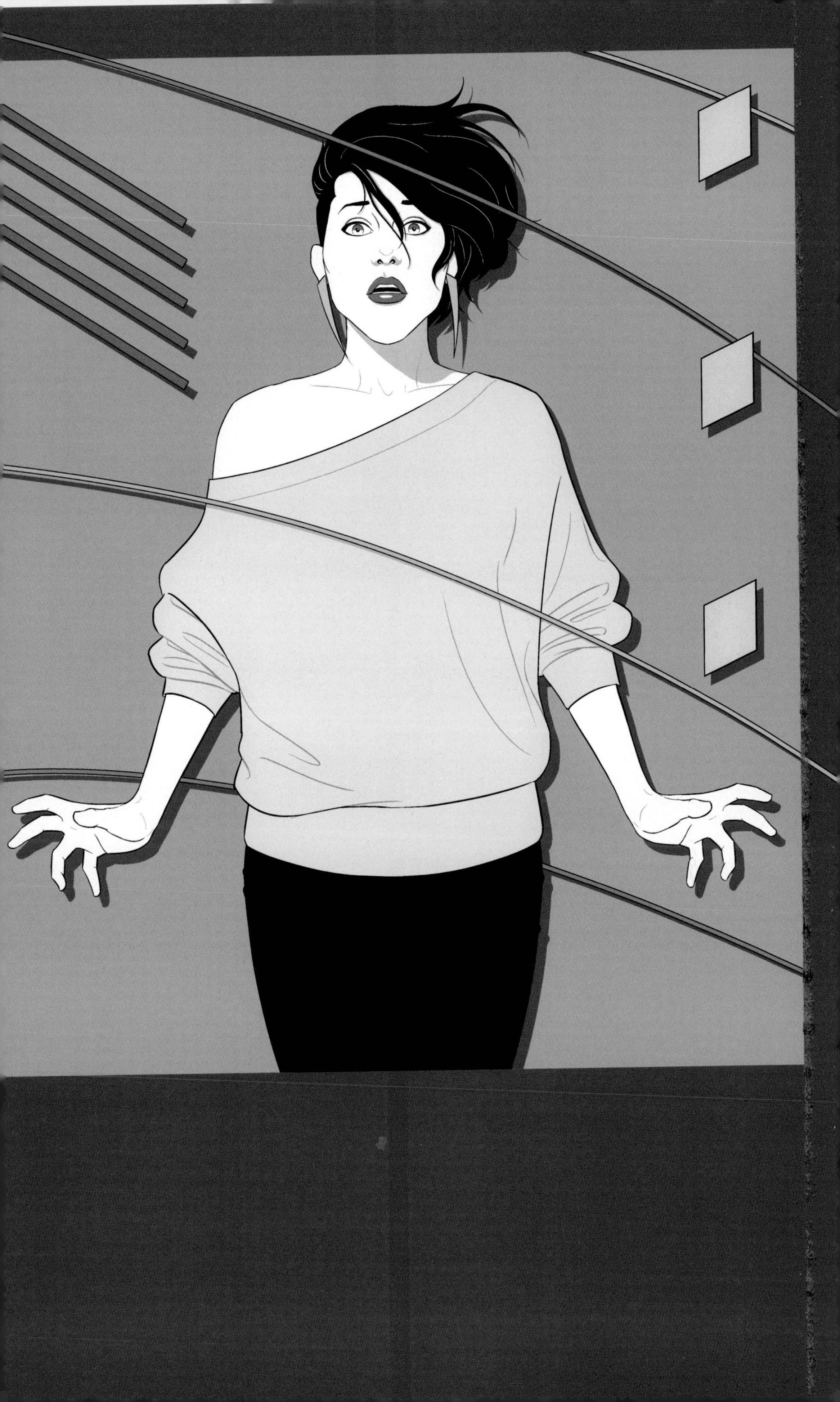

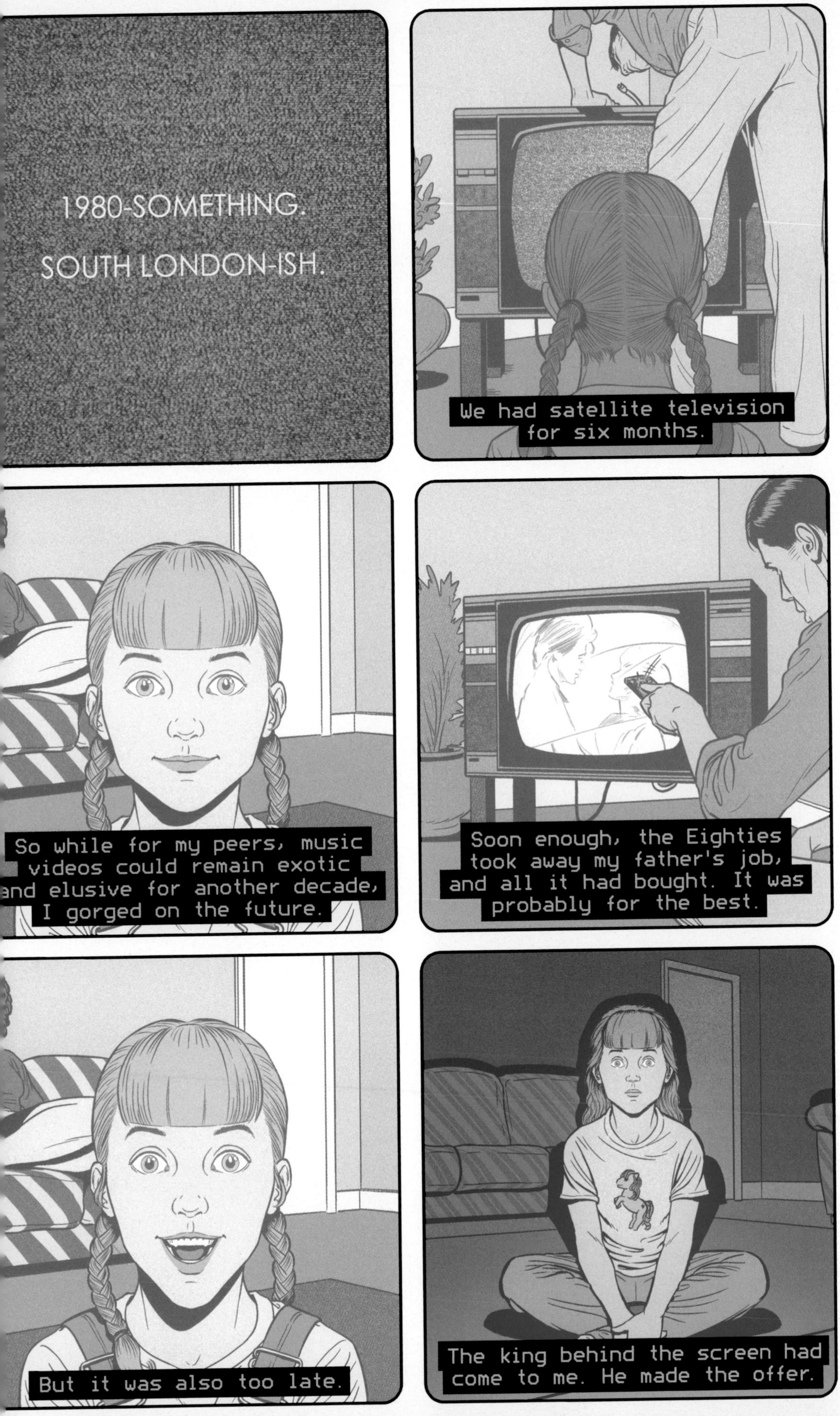
1980-SOMETHING.
SOUTH LONDON-ISH.
We had satellite television for six months.
So while for my peers, music videos could remain exotic and elusive for another decade, I gorged on the future.
Soon enough, the Eighties took away my father's job, and all it had bought. It was probably for the best.
But it was also too late.
The king behind the screen had come to me. He made the offer.

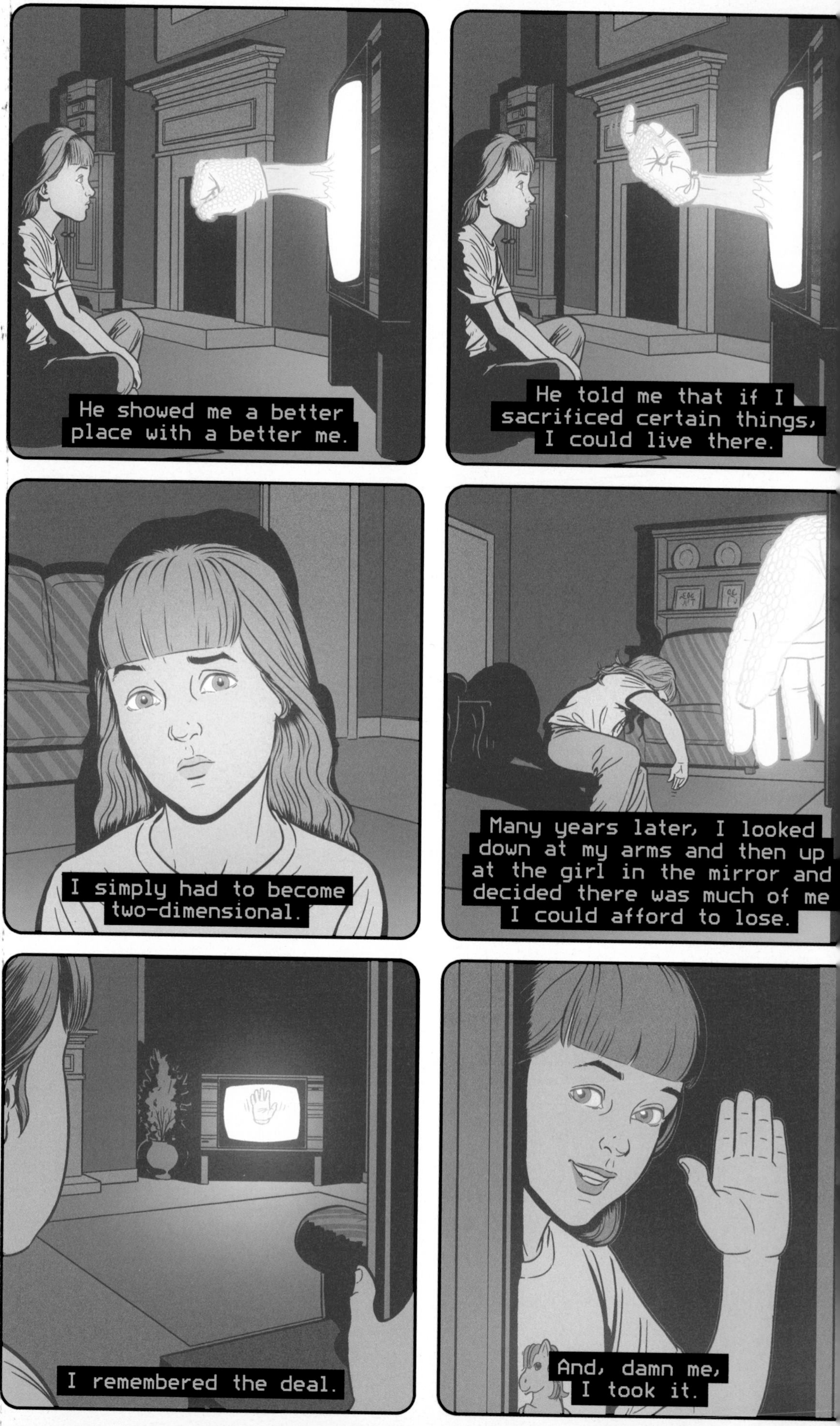
He showed me a better place with a better me.
He told me that if I sacrificed certain things, I could live there.
I simply had to become two-dimensional.
Many years later, I looked down at my arms and then up at the girl in the mirror and decided there was much of me I could afford to lose.
I remembered the deal.
And, damn me, I took it.

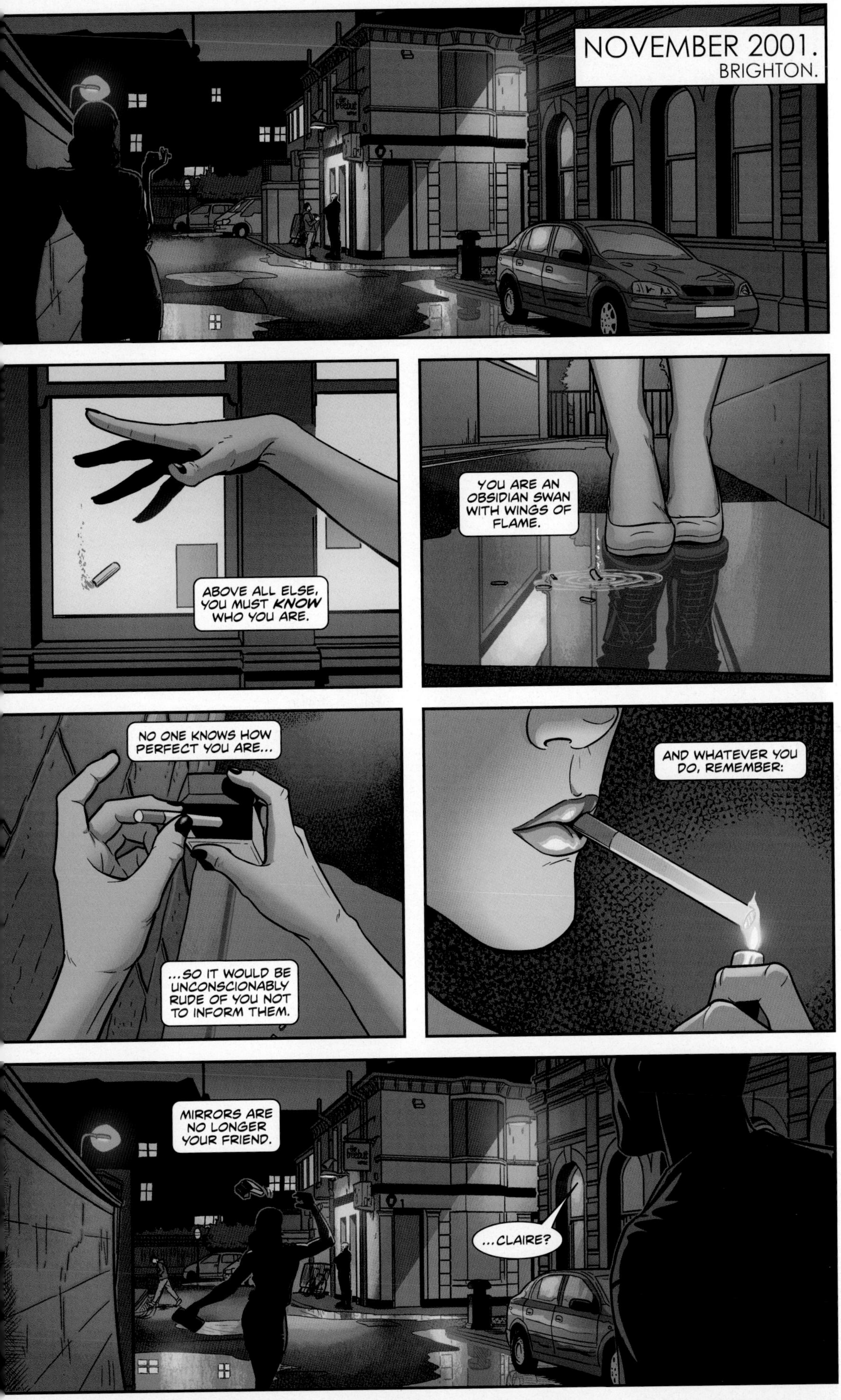
NOVEMBER 2001.
BRIGHTON.
ABOVE ALL ELSE, YOU MUST KNOW WHO YOU ARE.
YOU ARE AN OBSIDIAN SWAN WITH WINGS OF FLAME.
NO ONE KNOWS HOW PERFECT YOU ARE...
...SO IT WOULD BE UNCONSCIONABLY RUDE OF YOU NOT TO INFORM THEM.
AND WHATEVER YOU DO, REMEMBER:
MIRRORS ARE NO LONGER YOUR FRIEND.
...CLAIRE?

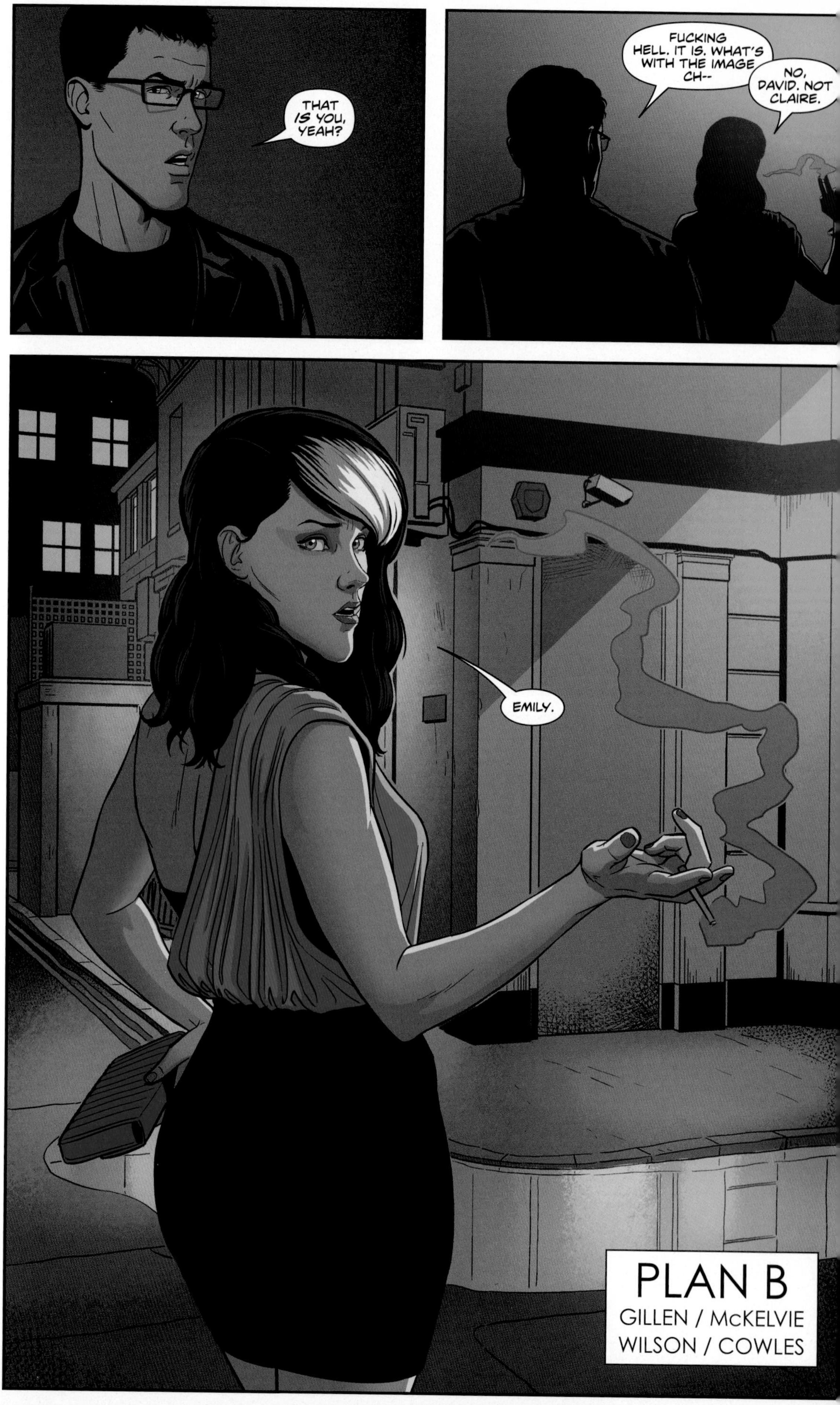
THAT IS YOU, YEAH?
FUCKING HELL. IT IS. WHAT'S WITH THE IMAGE CH--
NO, DAVID. NOT CLAIRE.
EMILY.
PLAN B
GILLEN / McKELVIE
WILSON / COWLES

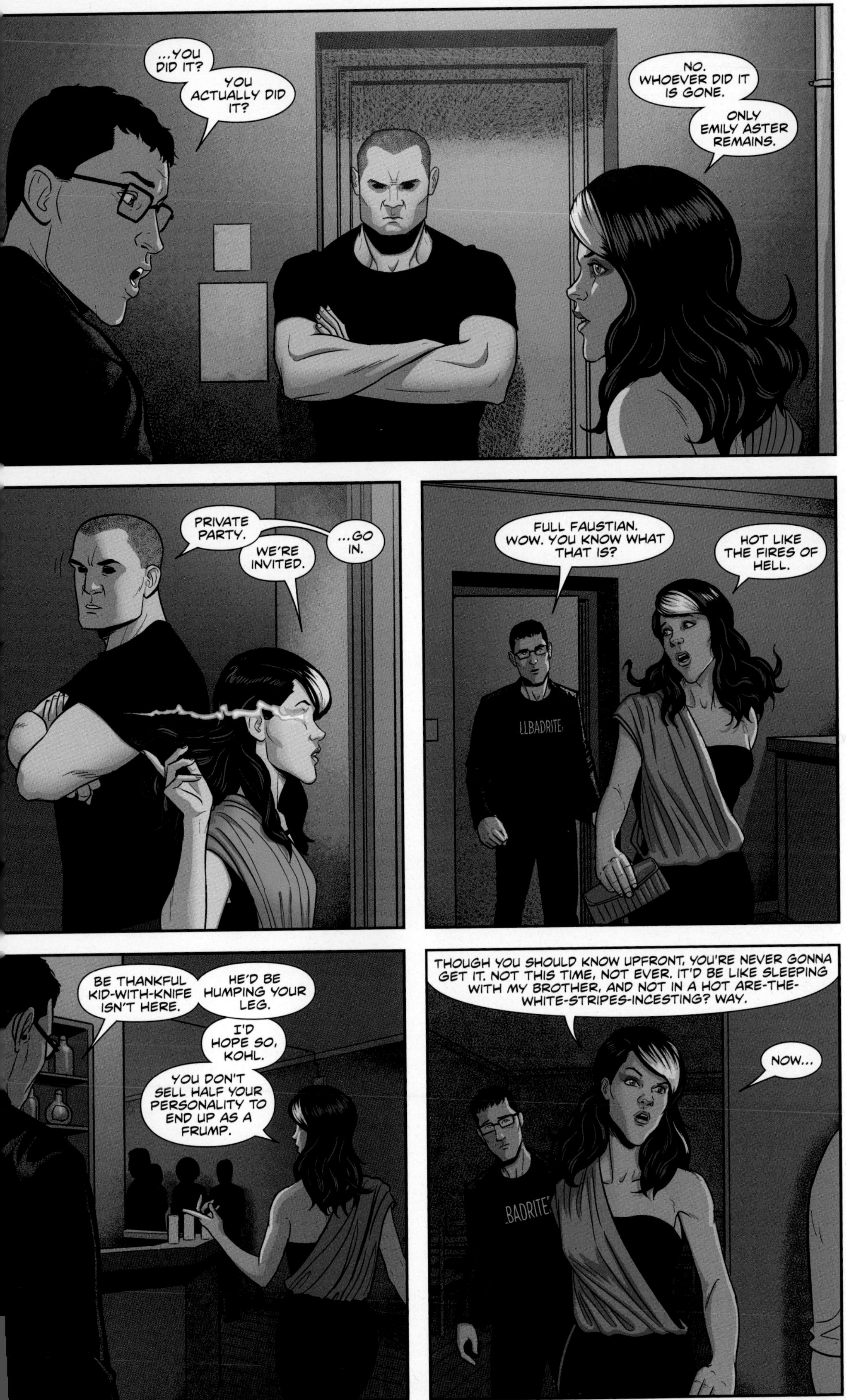
...YOU DID IT?
YOU ACTUALLY DID IT?
NO. WHOEVER DID IT IS GONE.
ONLY EMILY ASTER REMAINS.
PRIVATE PARTY.
WE'RE INVITED.
...GO IN.
FULL FAUSTIAN. WOW. YOU KNOW WHAT THAT IS?
HOT LIKE THE FIRES OF HELL.
BE THANKFUL KID-WITH-KNIFE ISN'T HERE.
HE'D BE HUMPING YOUR LEG.
I'D HOPE SO, KOHL.
YOU DON'T SELL HALF YOUR PERSONALITY TO END UP AS A FRUMP.
THOUGH YOU SHOULD KNOW UPFRONT, YOU'RE NEVER GONNA GET IT. NOT THIS TIME, NOT EVER. IT'D BE LIKE SLEEPING WITH MY BROTHER, AND NOT IN A HOT ARE-THE-WHITE-STRIPES-INCESTING? WAY.
NOW...

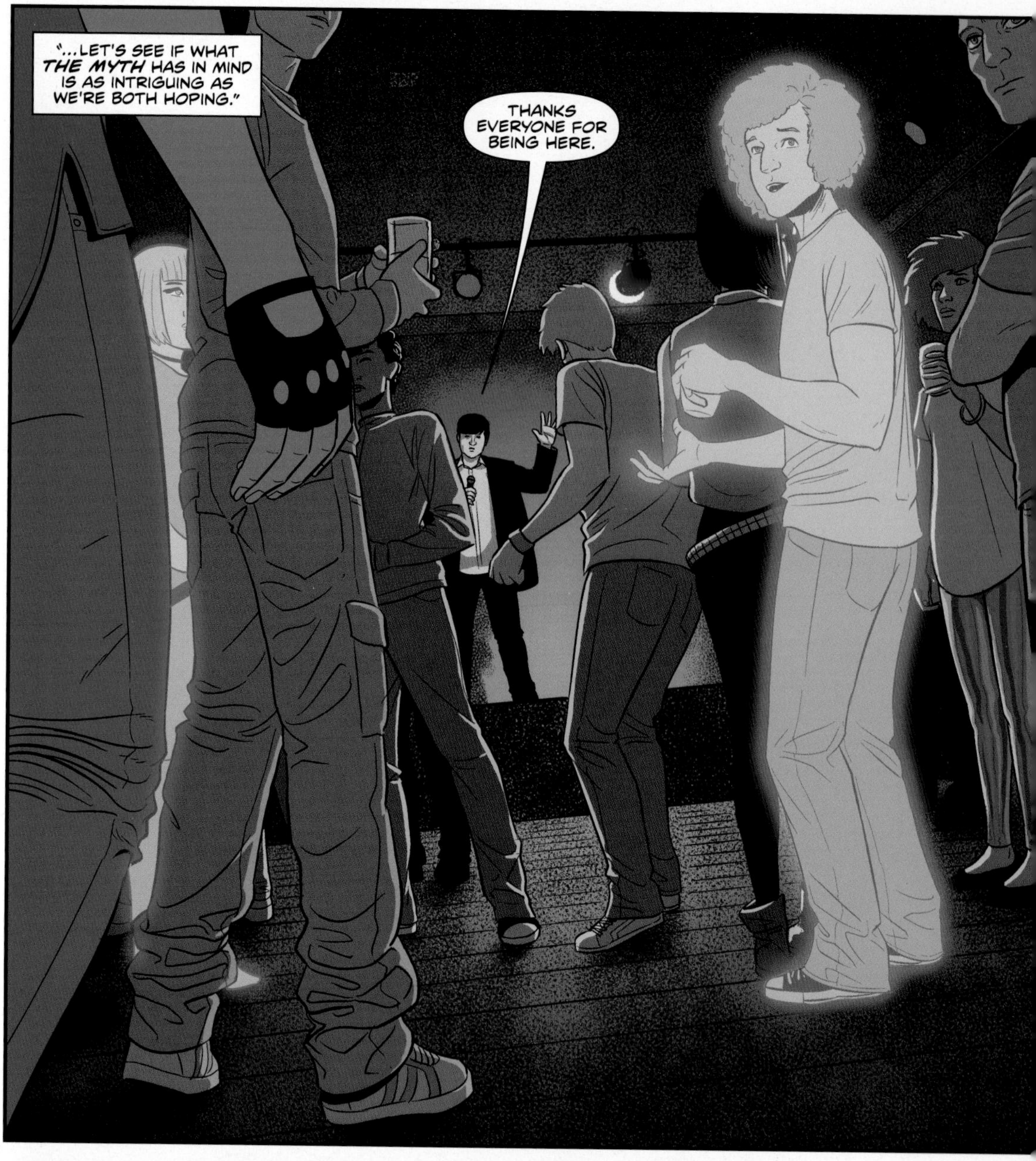
"...LET'S SEE IF WHAT *THE MYTH* HAS IN MIND IS AS INTRIGUING AS WE'RE BOTH HOPING."
THANKS EVERYONE FOR BEING HERE.

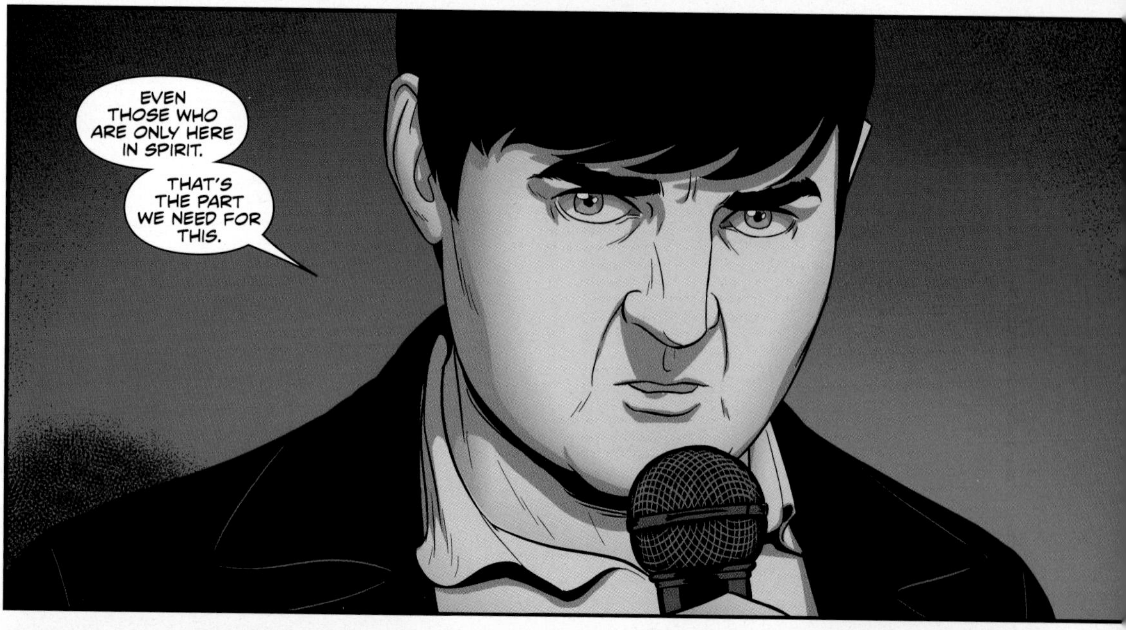
EVEN THOSE WHO ARE ONLY HERE IN SPIRIT.
THAT'S THE PART WE NEED FOR THIS.

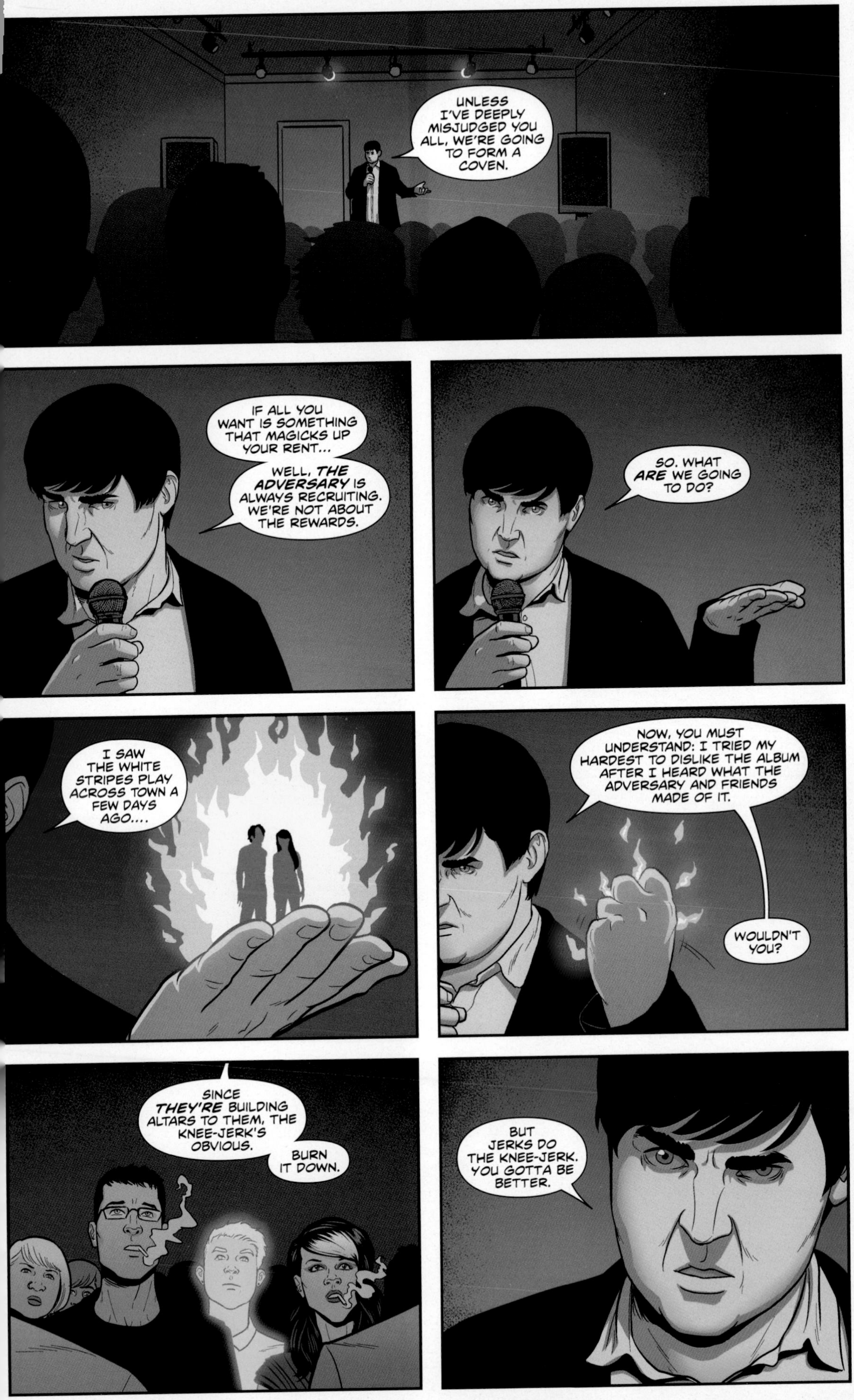

UNLESS I'VE DEEPLY MISJUDGED YOU ALL, WE'RE GOING TO FORM A COVEN.
IF ALL YOU WANT IS SOMETHING THAT MAGICKS UP YOUR RENT...
WELL, *THE ADVERSARY* IS ALWAYS RECRUITING. WE'RE NOT ABOUT THE REWARDS.
SO. WHAT *ARE* WE GOING TO DO?
I SAW THE WHITE STRIPES PLAY ACROSS TOWN A FEW DAYS AGO....
NOW, YOU MUST UNDERSTAND: I TRIED MY HARDEST TO DISLIKE THE ALBUM AFTER I HEARD WHAT THE ADVERSARY AND FRIENDS MADE OF IT.
WOULDN'T YOU?
SINCE *THEY'RE* BUILDING ALTARS TO THEM, THE KNEE-JERK'S OBVIOUS.
BURN IT DOWN.
BUT JERKS DO THE KNEE-JERK. YOU GOTTA BE BETTER.

SO THE ADVERSARY'S AFFECTION HASN'T STOPPED ME CARVING MY OWN LITTLE ALTAR. I THINK WE NEED MORE PEOPLE MAKING MORE ALTARS BECAUSE THEY WANT TO. BECAUSE THEY *NEED* TO.

OUR COVEN WILL BE A PLACE TO DO THAT.

NONE OF YOU AGREE. I DON'T WANT ANY OF YOU TO AGREE.

I JUST WANT YOU TO BE HONEST.

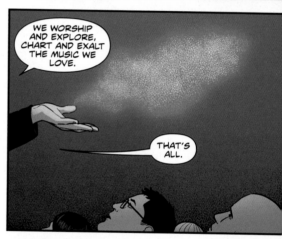

WE WORSHIP AND EXPLORE, CHART AND EXALT THE MUSIC WE LOVE.

THAT'S ALL.

AND WE'LL DESTROY ANYONE WHO THINKS OTHERWISE.

WE'LL DESTROY THEM BY BEING BETTER.

UNDERSTAND? GOOD.

TIME TO TURN THE MUSIC UP.

WHATEVER IT MEANS TO YOU, I WANT TO SEE YOU ALL ON THE DANCEFLOOR.

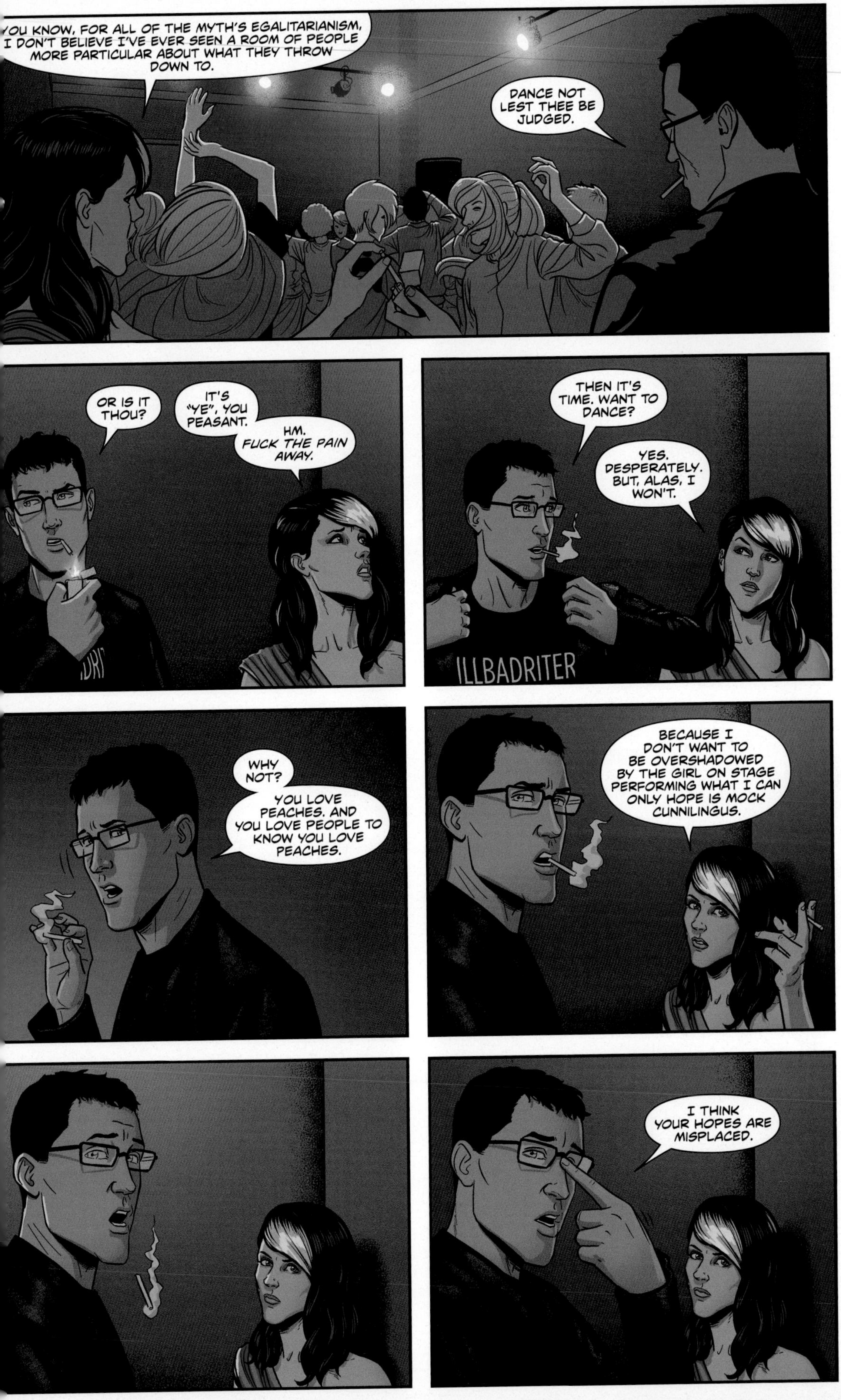
YOU KNOW, FOR ALL OF THE MYTH'S EGALITARIANISM, I DON'T BELIEVE I'VE EVER SEEN A ROOM OF PEOPLE MORE PARTICULAR ABOUT WHAT THEY THROW DOWN TO.
DANCE NOT LEST THEE BE JUDGED.
OR IS IT THOU?
IT'S "YE", YOU PEASANT.
HM. FUCK THE PAIN AWAY.
THEN IT'S TIME. WANT TO DANCE?
YES. DESPERATELY. BUT, ALAS, I WON'T.
ILLBADRITER
WHY NOT?
YOU LOVE PEACHES. AND YOU LOVE PEOPLE TO KNOW YOU LOVE PEACHES.
BECAUSE I DON'T WANT TO BE OVERSHADOWED BY THE GIRL ON STAGE PERFORMING WHAT I CAN ONLY HOPE IS MOCK CUNNILINGUS.
I THINK YOUR HOPES ARE MISPLACED.

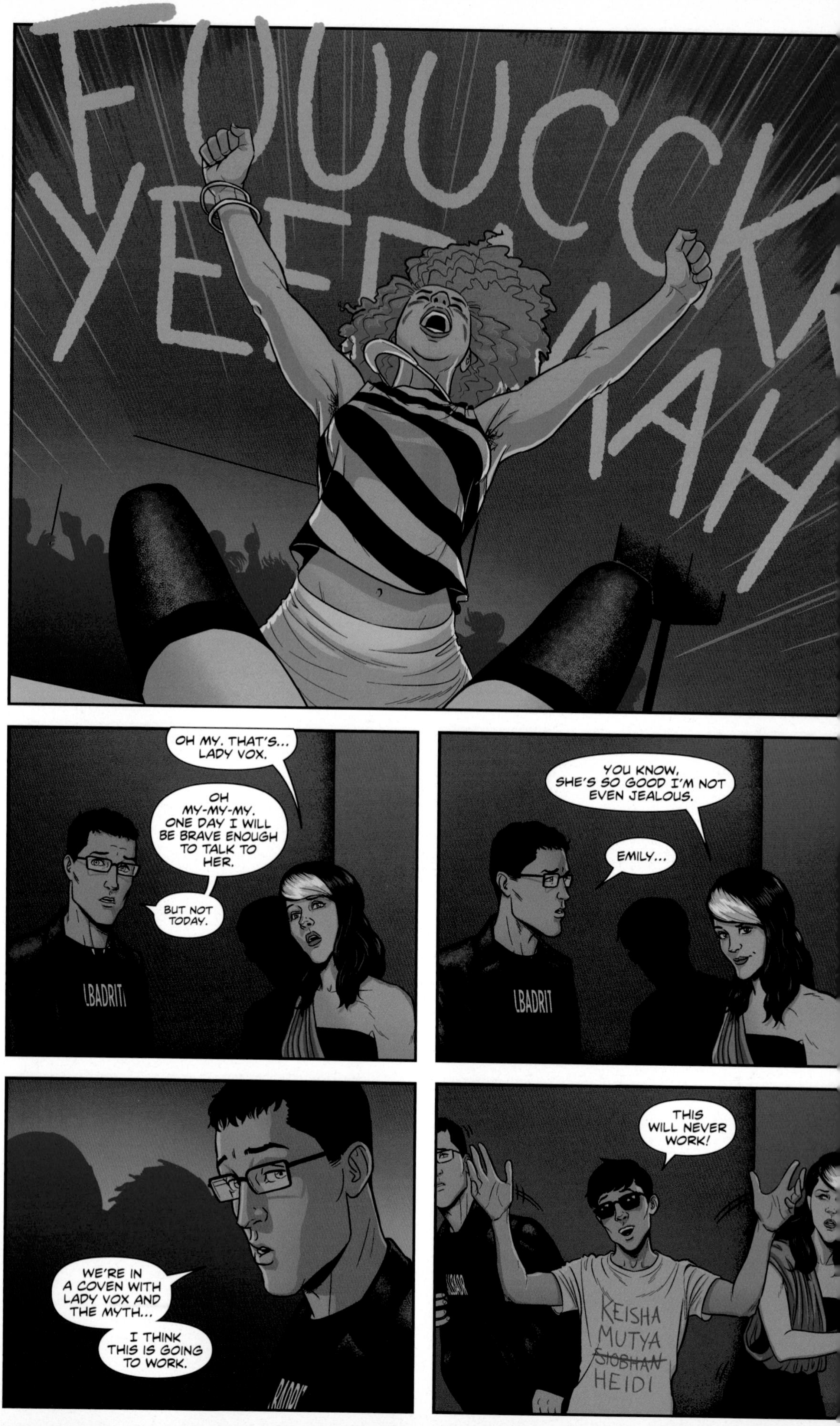
FOUUCCK YEEAAH
OH MY. THAT'S... LADY VOX.
OH MY-MY-MY. ONE DAY I WILL BE BRAVE ENOUGH TO TALK TO HER.
BUT NOT TODAY.
LBADRIT
YOU KNOW, SHE'S SO GOOD I'M NOT EVEN JEALOUS.
EMILY...
LBADRIT
WE'RE IN A COVEN WITH LADY VOX AND THE MYTH...
I THINK THIS IS GOING TO WORK.
THIS WILL NEVER WORK!
KEISHA
MUTYA
SIOBHAN
HEIDI

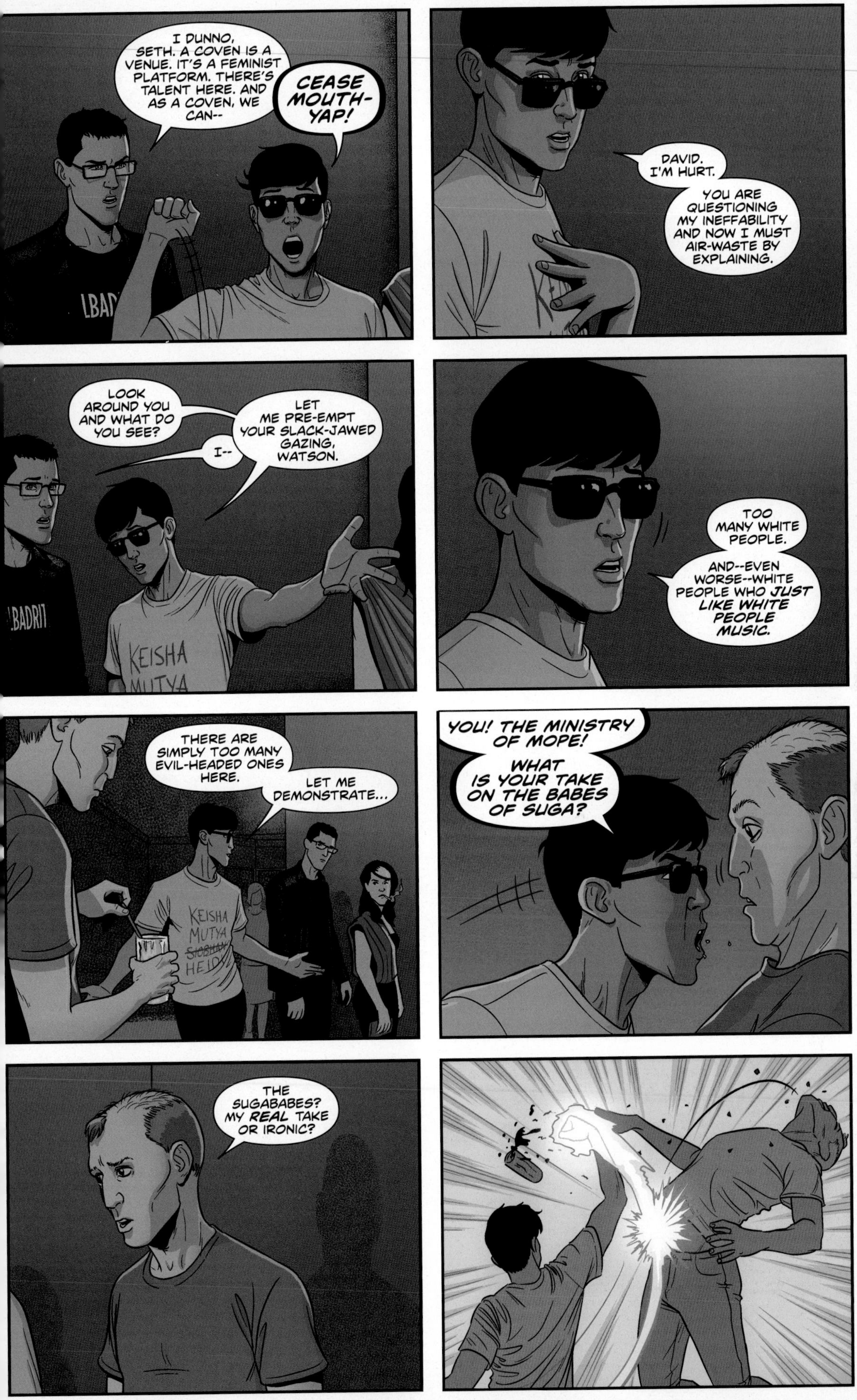
I DUNNO, SETH. A COVEN IS A VENUE. IT'S A FEMINIST PLATFORM. THERE'S TALENT HERE. AND AS A COVEN, WE CAN--
CEASE MOUTH-YAP!
LBAD
DAVID. I'M HURT.
YOU ARE QUESTIONING MY INEFFABILITY AND NOW I MUST AIR-WASTE BY EXPLAINING.
LOOK AROUND YOU AND WHAT DO YOU SEE?
I--
LET ME PRE-EMPT YOUR SLACK-JAWED GAZING, WATSON.
LBADRI1
KEISHA MUTYA
TOO MANY WHITE PEOPLE.
AND--EVEN WORSE--WHITE PEOPLE WHO JUST LIKE WHITE PEOPLE MUSIC.
THERE ARE SIMPLY TOO MANY EVIL-HEADED ONES HERE.
LET ME DEMONSTRATE...
KEISHA MUTYA SIOBHAN HEIDI
YOU! THE MINISTRY OF MOPE!
WHAT IS YOUR TAKE ON THE BABES OF SUGA?
THE SUGABABES? MY REAL TAKE OR IRONIC?

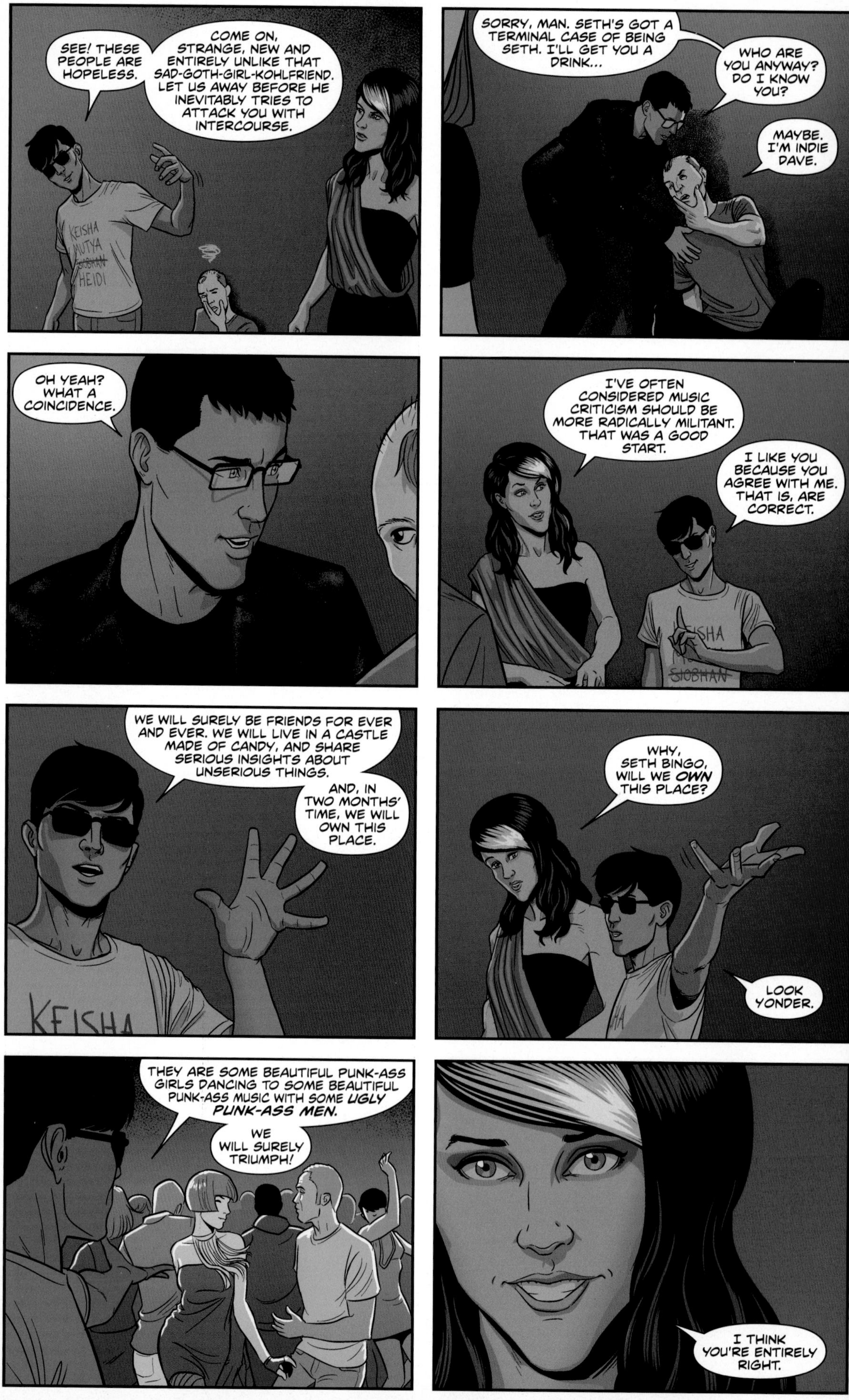

SEE! THESE PEOPLE ARE HOPELESS.
COME ON, STRANGE, NEW AND ENTIRELY UNLIKE THAT SAD-GOTH-GIRL-KOHLFRIEND. LET US AWAY BEFORE HE INEVITABLY TRIES TO ATTACK YOU WITH INTERCOURSE.
KEISHA MUTYA SIOBHAN HEIDI
SORRY, MAN. SETH'S GOT A TERMINAL CASE OF BEING SETH. I'LL GET YOU A DRINK...
WHO ARE YOU ANYWAY? DO I KNOW YOU?
MAYBE. I'M INDIE DAVE.
OH YEAH? WHAT A COINCIDENCE.
I'VE OFTEN CONSIDERED MUSIC CRITICISM SHOULD BE MORE RADICALLY MILITANT. THAT WAS A GOOD START.
I LIKE YOU BECAUSE YOU AGREE WITH ME. THAT IS, ARE CORRECT.
WE WILL SURELY BE FRIENDS FOR EVER AND EVER. WE WILL LIVE IN A CASTLE MADE OF CANDY, AND SHARE SERIOUS INSIGHTS ABOUT UNSERIOUS THINGS.
AND, IN TWO MONTHS' TIME, WE WILL OWN THIS PLACE.
WHY, SETH BINGO, WILL WE *OWN* THIS PLACE?
LOOK YONDER.
THEY ARE SOME BEAUTIFUL PUNK-ASS GIRLS DANCING TO SOME BEAUTIFUL PUNK-ASS MUSIC WITH SOME *UGLY* ***PUNK-ASS MEN.***
WE WILL SURELY TRIUMPH!
I THINK YOU'RE ENTIRELY RIGHT.

OKAY. GET THIS. HOLD ONTO YOUR CLIT IN CASE IT JUST FUCKING EXPLODES.

ARE YOU HOLDING ON?

YES, VOX. I AM.

HOLD ON.

TRUST ME. MY CLIT IS SUFFICIENTLY BRACED TO RESIST WHATEVER TRAUMA YOU HAVE IN MIND.

HIT ME.

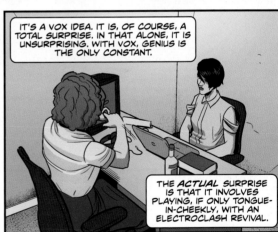

IT'S A VOX IDEA. IT IS, OF COURSE, A TOTAL SURPRISE. IN THAT ALONE, IT IS UNSURPRISING. WITH VOX, GENIUS IS THE ONLY CONSTANT.

THE *ACTUAL* SURPRISE IS THAT IT INVOLVES PLAYING, IF ONLY TONGUE-IN-CHEEKLY, WITH AN ELECTROCLASH REVIVAL.

ISN'T THIS A LITTLE RETRO?

TOTALLY. FOR FUCK'S SAKE, ARE YOU SLOWING DOWN, EMILY?

IT'S THE 21st CENTURY. ALL REINVENTIONS ARE EQUAL. ANY OF THOSE MOVEMENTS HAVE BEEN PLAYED OUT TWICE OR THREE TIMES OVER.

IT WOUND UP THE RIGHT PEOPLE THEN AND IT'LL WIND UP THE RIGHT PEOPLE NOW. LOW EFFORT, HIGH PAYOUT, MASSIVE GIGGLES. ALSO, ORGASMS. GREAT, HEAVING ORGASMS...

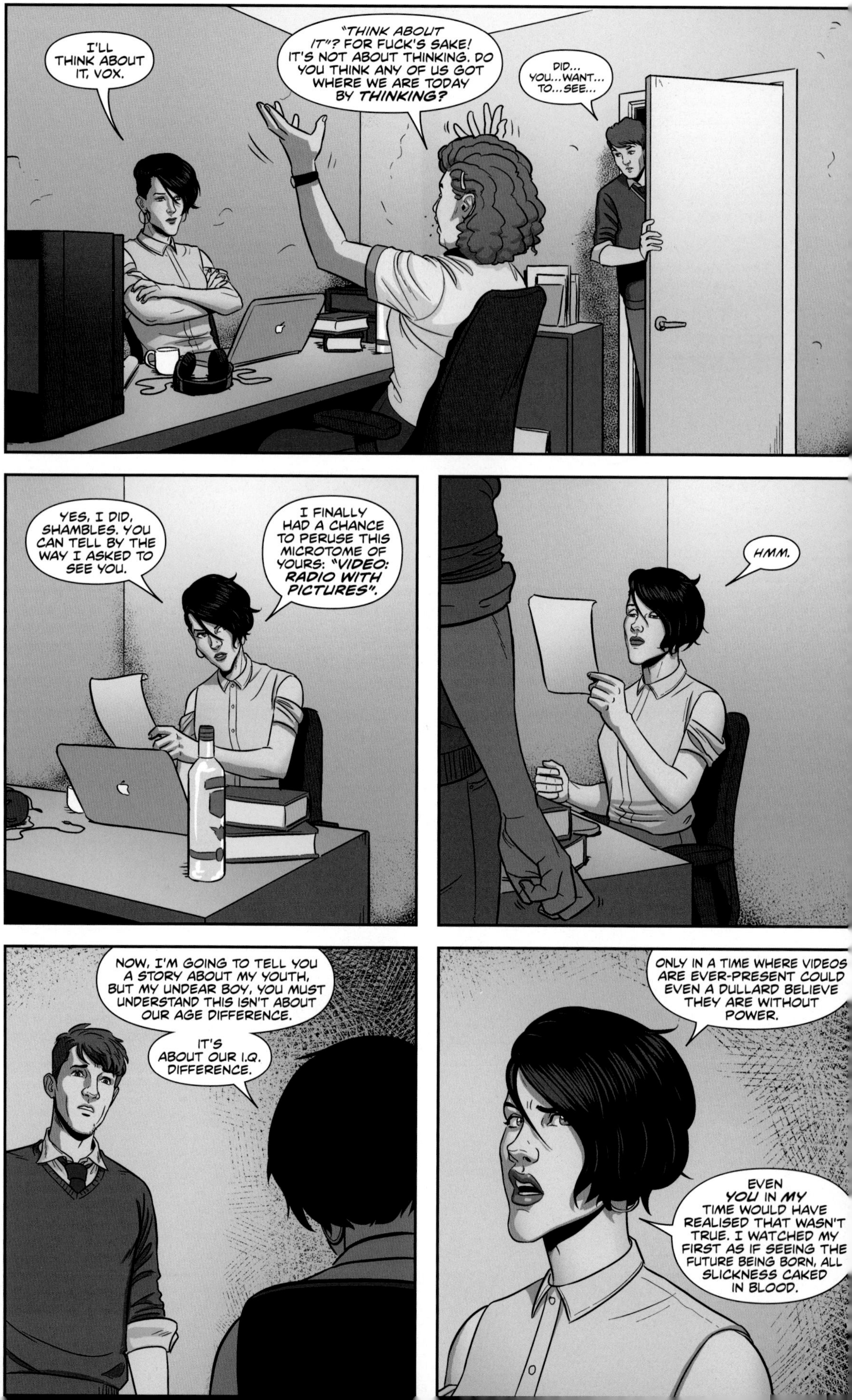
I'LL THINK ABOUT IT, VOX.
"THINK ABOUT IT"? FOR FUCK'S SAKE! IT'S NOT ABOUT THINKING. DO YOU THINK ANY OF US GOT WHERE WE ARE TODAY BY THINKING?
DID... YOU...WANT... TO...SEE...
YES, I DID, SHAMBLES. YOU CAN TELL BY THE WAY I ASKED TO SEE YOU.
I FINALLY HAD A CHANCE TO PERUSE THIS MICROTOME OF YOURS: "VIDEO: RADIO WITH PICTURES".
HMM.
NOW, I'M GOING TO TELL YOU A STORY ABOUT MY YOUTH, BUT MY UNDEAR BOY, YOU MUST UNDERSTAND THIS ISN'T ABOUT OUR AGE DIFFERENCE.
IT'S ABOUT OUR I.Q. DIFFERENCE.
ONLY IN A TIME WHERE VIDEOS ARE EVER-PRESENT COULD EVEN A DULLARD BELIEVE THEY ARE WITHOUT POWER.
EVEN YOU IN MY TIME WOULD HAVE REALISED THAT WASN'T TRUE. I WATCHED MY FIRST AS IF SEEING THE FUTURE BEING BORN, ALL SLICKNESS CAKED IN BLOOD.

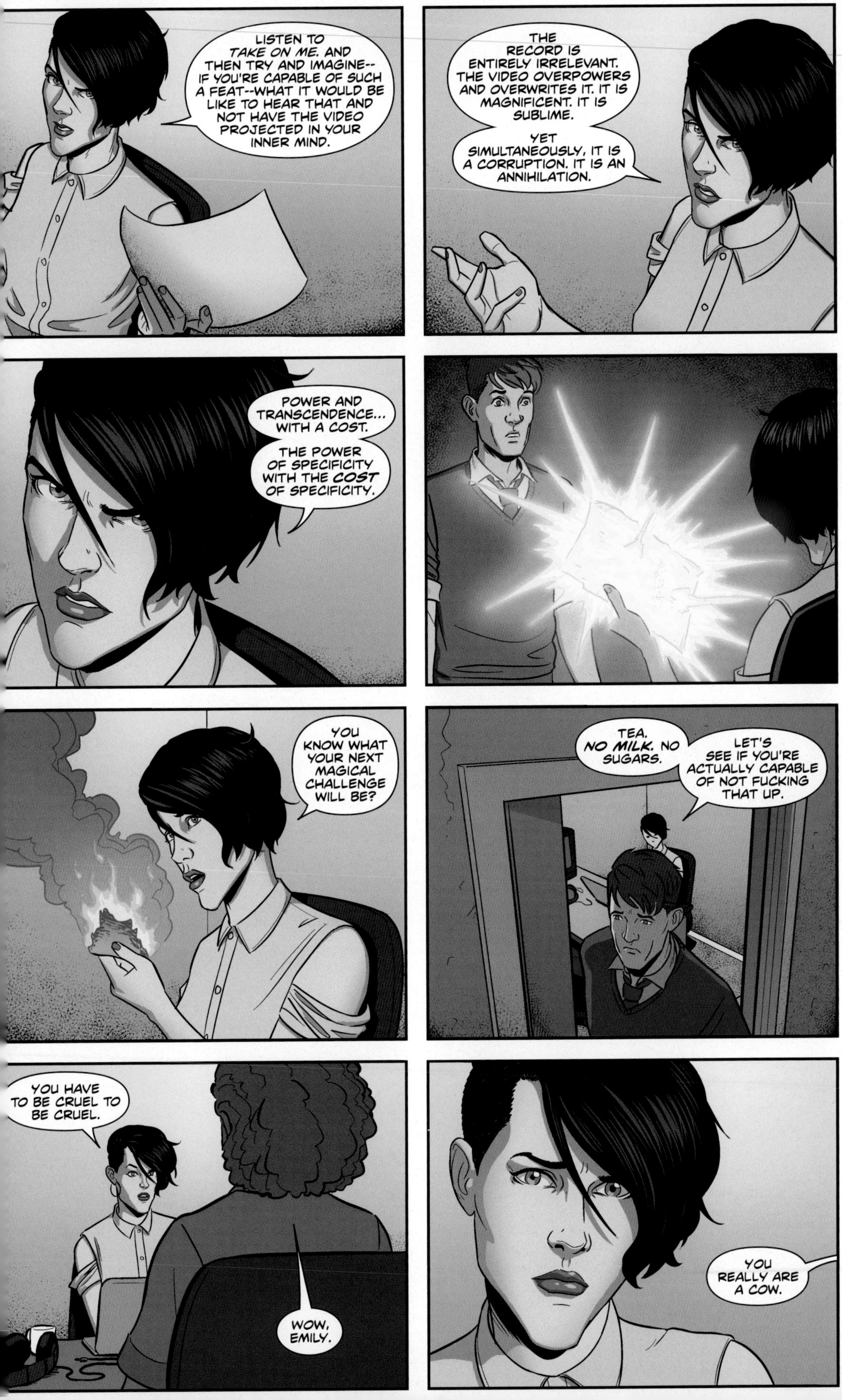

LISTEN TO *TAKE ON ME.* AND THEN TRY AND IMAGINE--IF YOU'RE CAPABLE OF SUCH A FEAT--WHAT IT WOULD BE LIKE TO HEAR THAT AND NOT HAVE THE VIDEO PROJECTED IN YOUR INNER MIND.
THE RECORD IS ENTIRELY IRRELEVANT. THE VIDEO OVERPOWERS AND OVERWRITES IT. IT IS MAGNIFICENT. IT IS SUBLIME.
YET SIMULTANEOUSLY, IT IS A CORRUPTION. IT IS AN ANNIHILATION.
POWER AND TRANSCENDENCE... WITH A COST.
THE POWER OF SPECIFICITY WITH THE ***COST*** OF SPECIFICITY.
YOU KNOW WHAT YOUR NEXT MAGICAL CHALLENGE WILL BE?
TEA. ***NO MILK.*** NO SUGARS.
LET'S SEE IF YOU'RE ACTUALLY CAPABLE OF NOT FUCKING THAT UP.
YOU HAVE TO BE CRUEL TO BE CRUEL.
WOW, EMILY.
YOU REALLY ARE A COW.

BEHIND THE SCREEN.

SOMETIME DURING FOREVER.

Far away and all too near, in a place with no time except what lies between ad-breaks, there sits a girl.

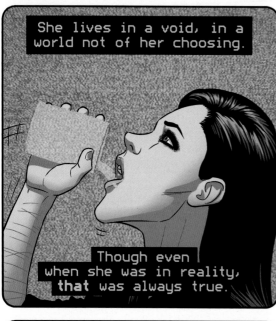

She lives in a void, in a world not of her choosing.

Though even when she was in reality, **that** was always true.

She thinks of herself as an immaterial girl.

Though she thinks of other-her as one too.

She waits.

The deal was for half of a girl's personality.

You may see a loophole.

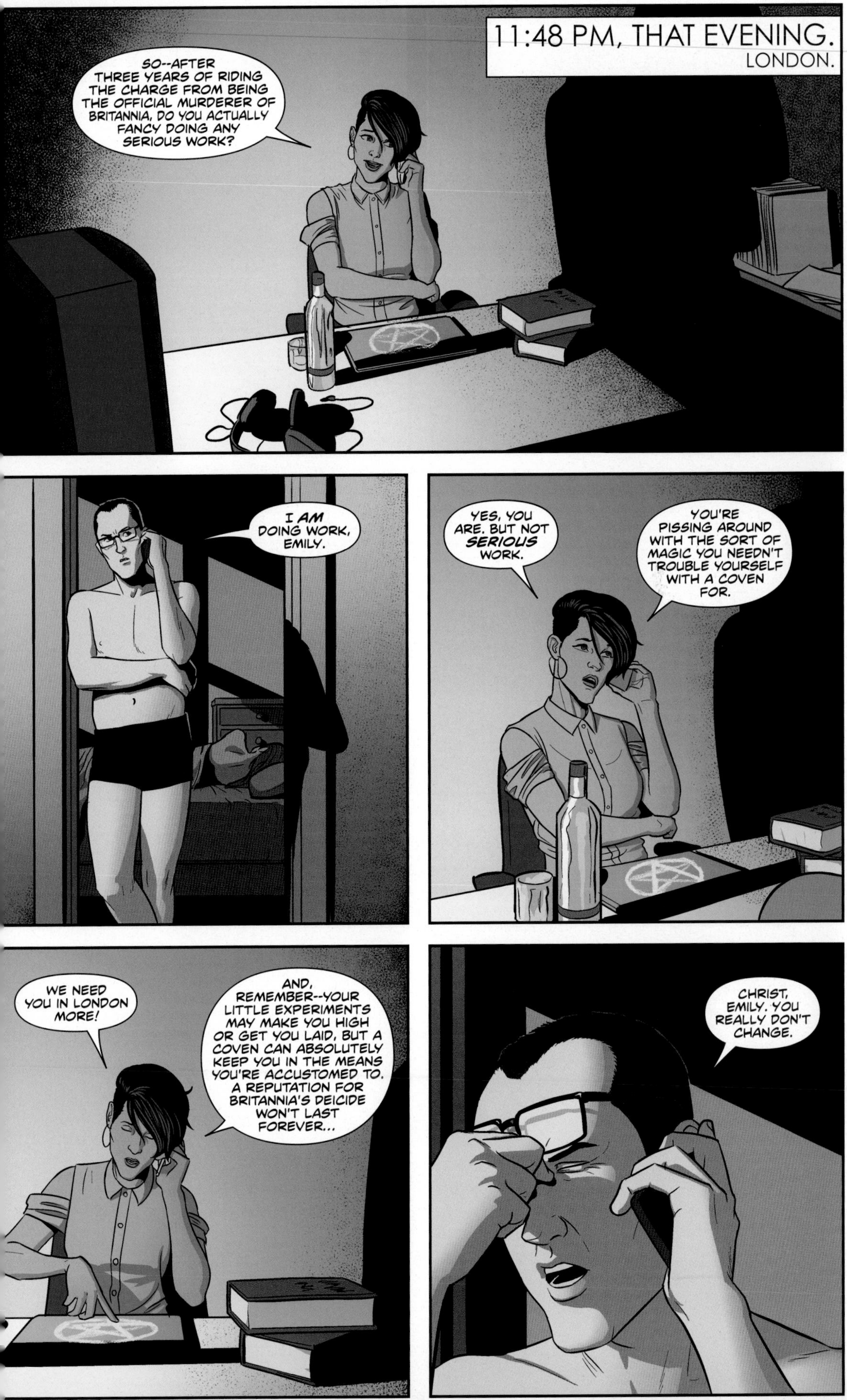
11:48 PM, THAT EVENING.
LONDON.
SO--AFTER THREE YEARS OF RIDING THE CHARGE FROM BEING THE OFFICIAL MURDERER OF BRITANNIA, DO YOU ACTUALLY FANCY DOING ANY SERIOUS WORK?
I *AM* DOING WORK, EMILY.
YES, YOU ARE. BUT NOT *SERIOUS* WORK.
YOU'RE PISSING AROUND WITH THE SORT OF MAGIC YOU NEEDN'T TROUBLE YOURSELF WITH A COVEN FOR.
WE NEED YOU IN LONDON MORE!
AND, REMEMBER--YOUR LITTLE EXPERIMENTS MAY MAKE YOU HIGH OR GET YOU LAID, BUT A COVEN CAN ABSOLUTELY KEEP YOU IN THE MEANS YOU'RE ACCUSTOMED TO. A REPUTATION FOR BRITANNIA'S DEICIDE WON'T LAST FOREVER...
CHRIST, EMILY. YOU REALLY DON'T CHANGE.

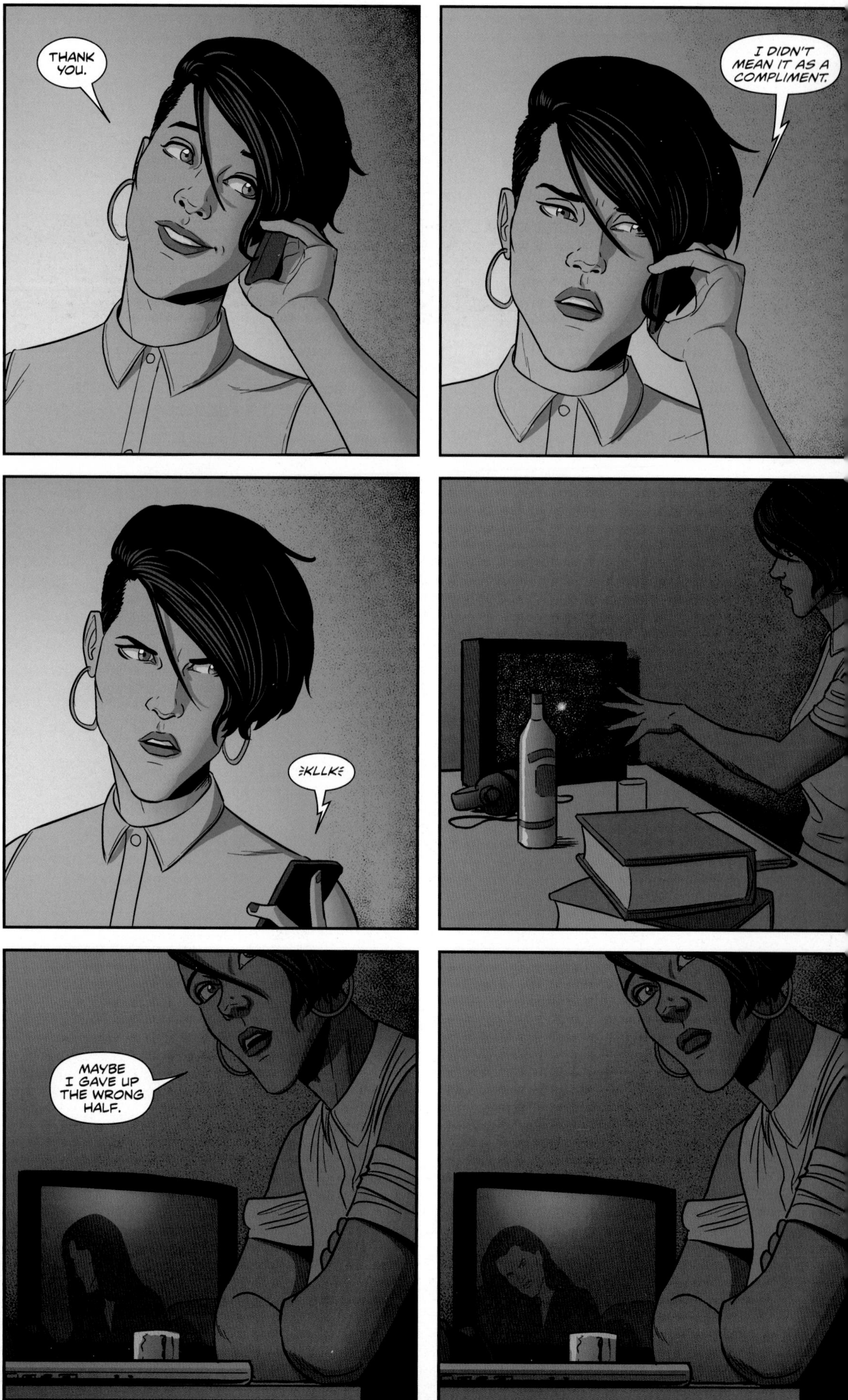
THANK YOU.
I DIDN'T MEAN IT AS A COMPLIMENT.
KLLK
MAYBE I GAVE UP THE WRONG HALF.

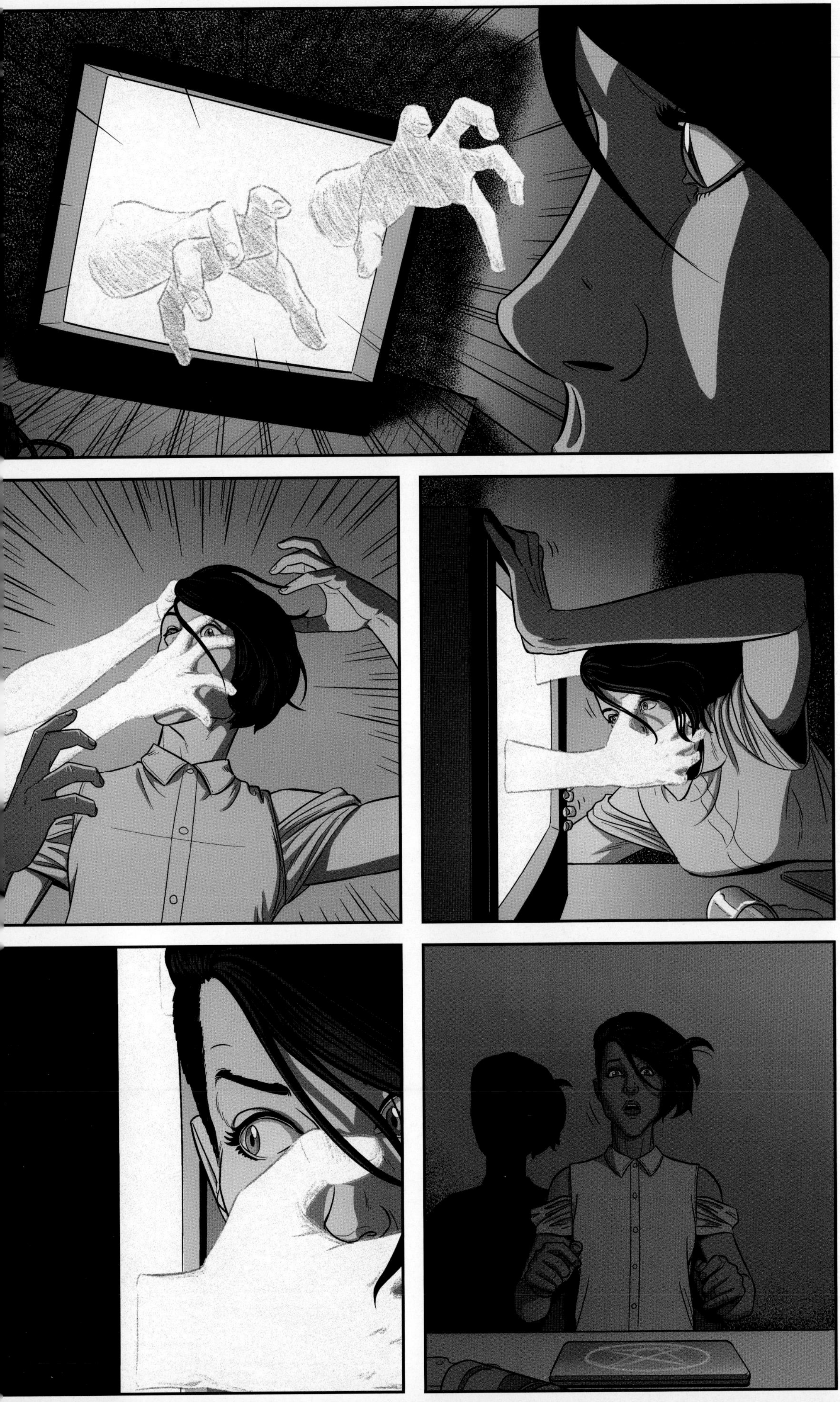

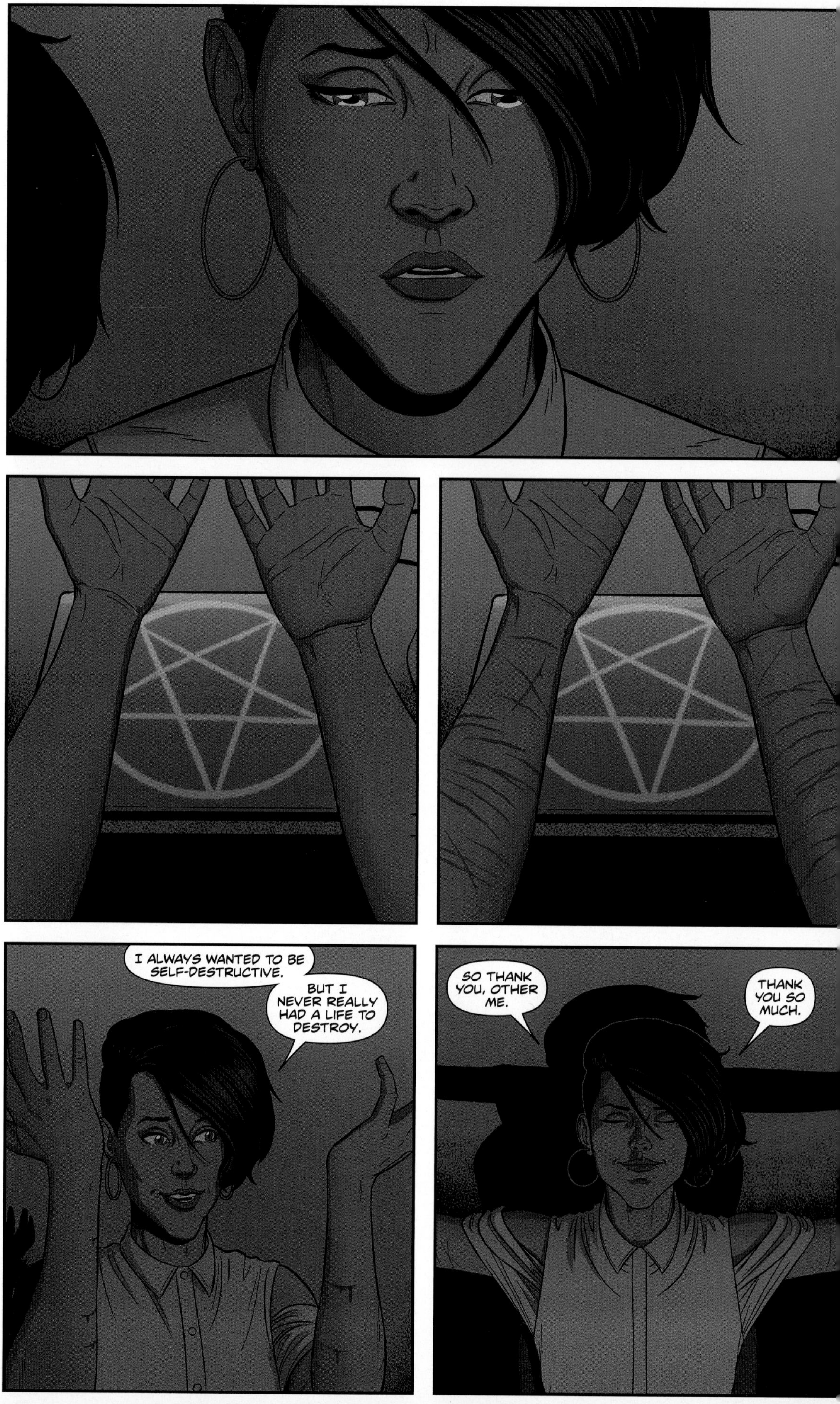
I ALWAYS WANTED TO BE SELF-DESTRUCTIVE.
BUT I NEVER REALLY HAD A LIFE TO DESTROY.
SO THANK YOU, OTHER ME.
THANK YOU SO MUCH.

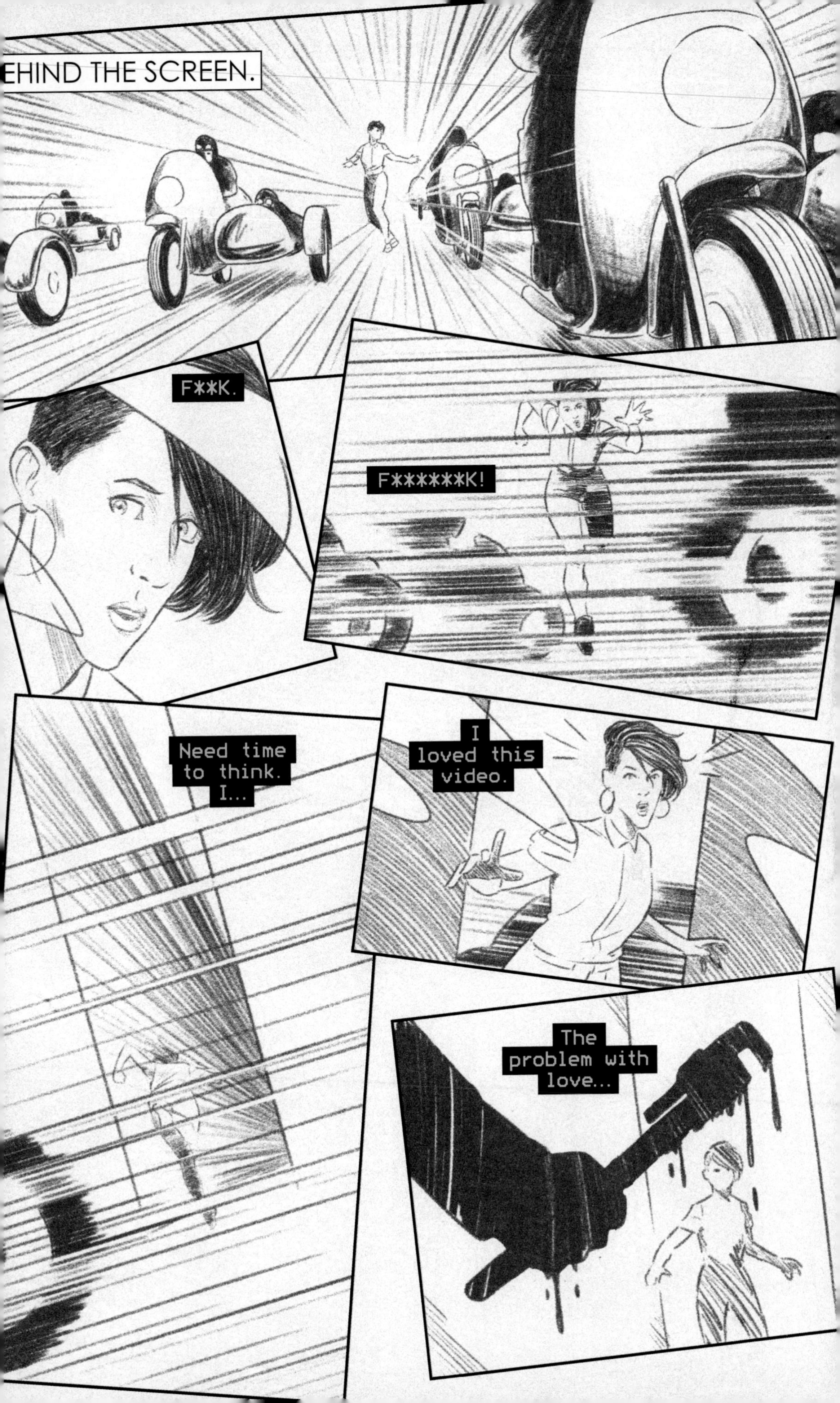
EHIND THE SCREEN.
F**K.
F******K!
Need time to think. I...
I loved this video.
The problem with love...

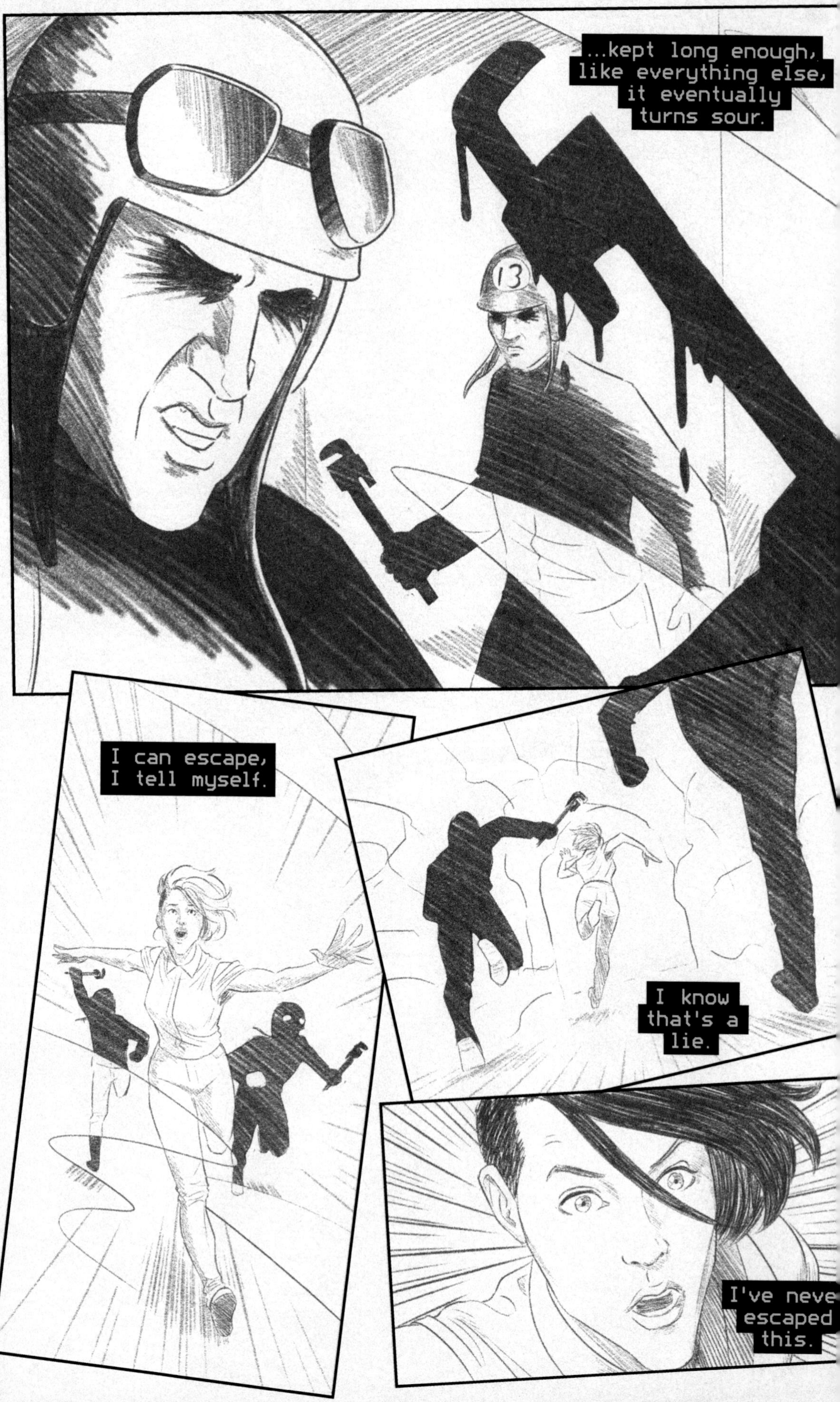
...kept long enough, like everything else, it eventually turns sour.
I can escape, I tell myself.
I know that's a lie.
I've neve escaped this.

PHONOGRAM

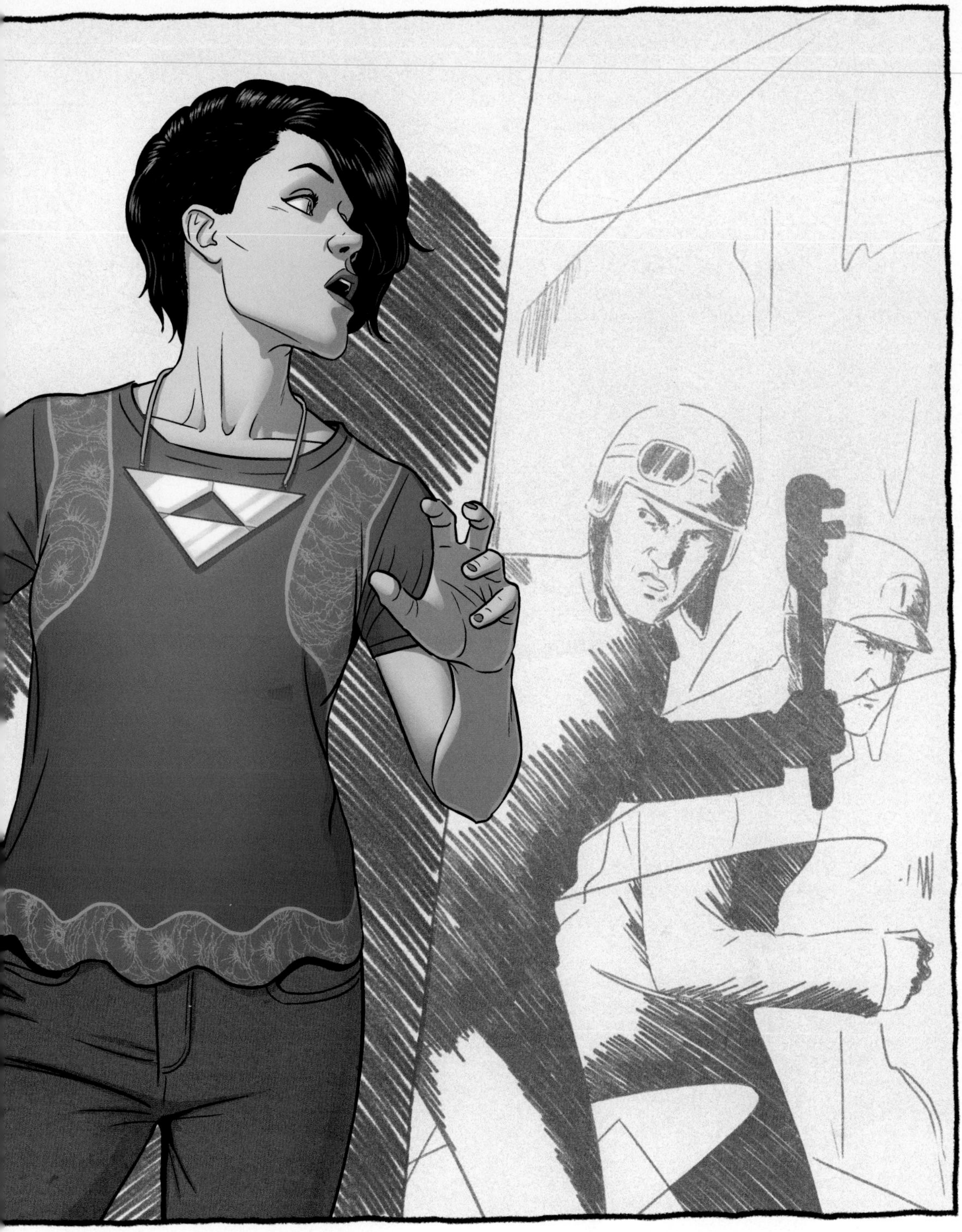

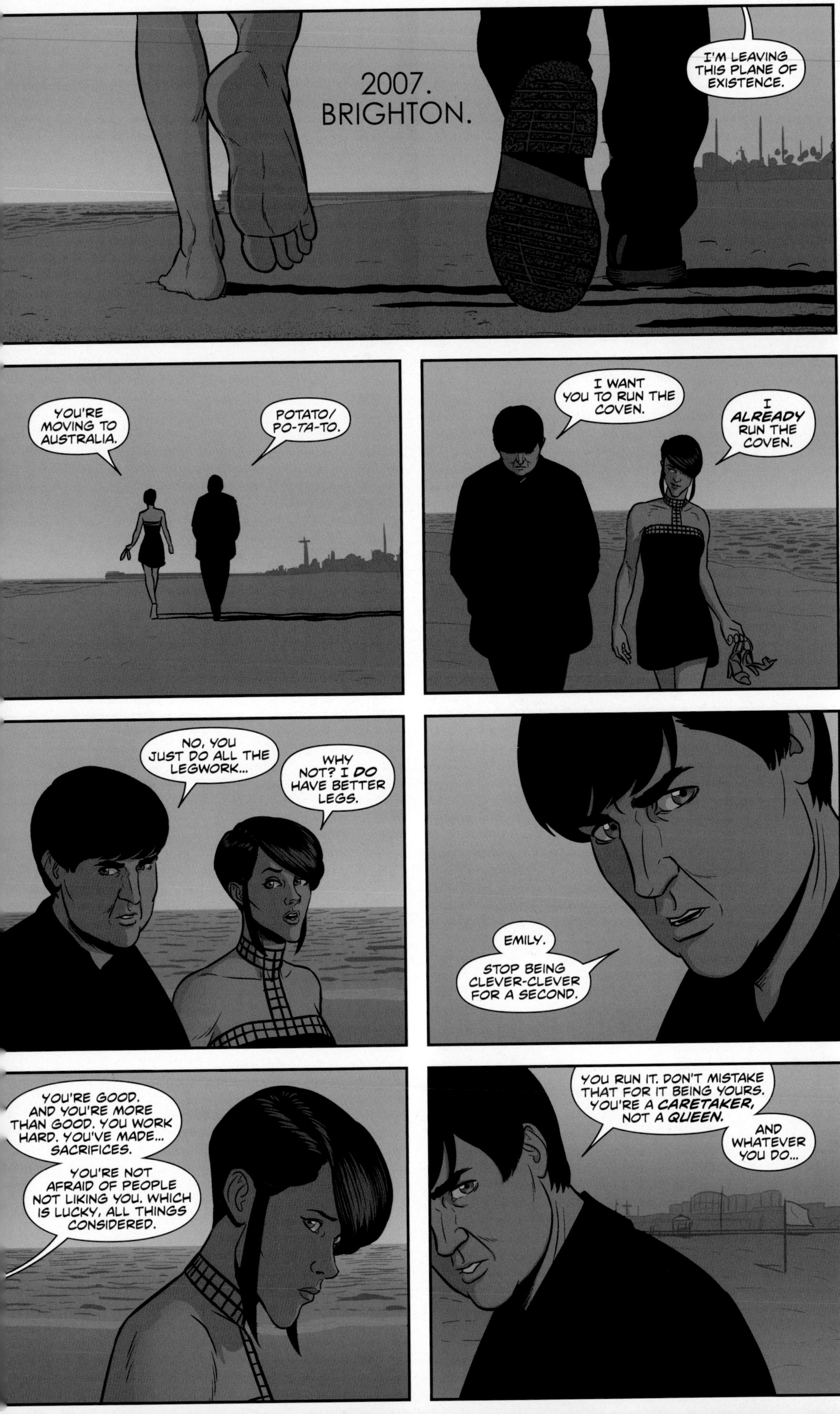
2007. BRIGHTON.
I'M LEAVING THIS PLANE OF EXISTENCE.
YOU'RE MOVING TO AUSTRALIA.
POTATO/ PO-TA-TO.
I WANT YOU TO RUN THE COVEN.
I ALREADY RUN THE COVEN.
NO, YOU JUST DO ALL THE LEGWORK...
WHY NOT? I DO HAVE BETTER LEGS.
EMILY.
STOP BEING CLEVER-CLEVER FOR A SECOND.
YOU'RE GOOD. AND YOU'RE MORE THAN GOOD. YOU WORK HARD. YOU'VE MADE... SACRIFICES.
YOU'RE NOT AFRAID OF PEOPLE NOT LIKING YOU. WHICH IS LUCKY, ALL THINGS CONSIDERED.
YOU RUN IT. DON'T MISTAKE THAT FOR IT BEING YOURS. YOU'RE A CARETAKER, NOT A QUEEN.
AND WHATEVER YOU DO...

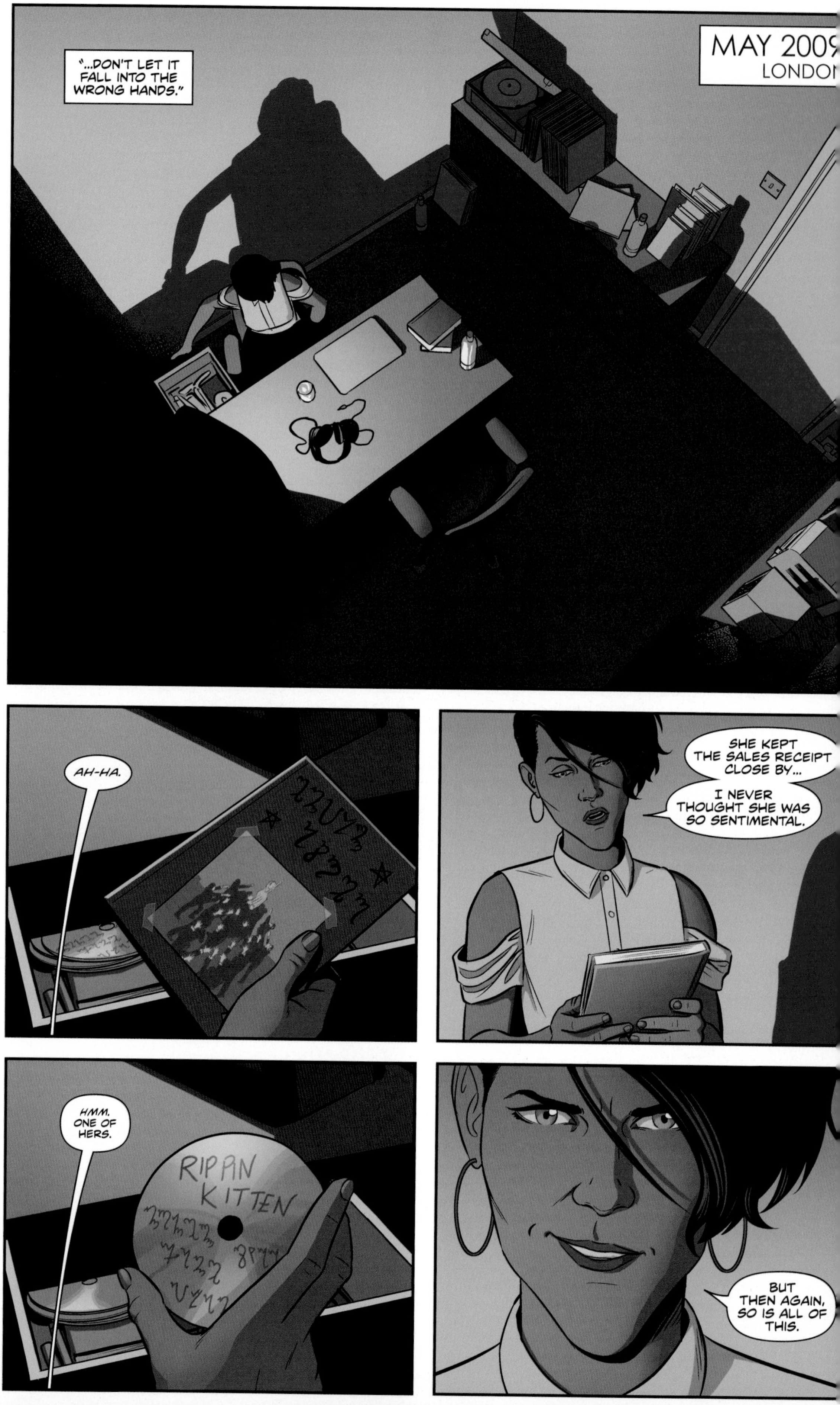
MAY 2009
LONDON
"...DON'T LET IT FALL INTO THE WRONG HANDS."
AH-HA.
SHE KEPT THE SALES RECEIPT CLOSE BY...
I NEVER THOUGHT SHE WAS SO SENTIMENTAL.
HMM. ONE OF HERS.
RIPPIN KITTEN
BUT THEN AGAIN, SO IS ALL OF THIS.

AND I'VE GOT TO MAKE EVERYTHING THAT WAS HERS, MINE.

I LOOK LIKE A SLUT.

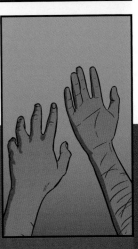

I LOOK LIKE *HER*.

PROBLEM... SOLVED.

THERE YOU ARE.

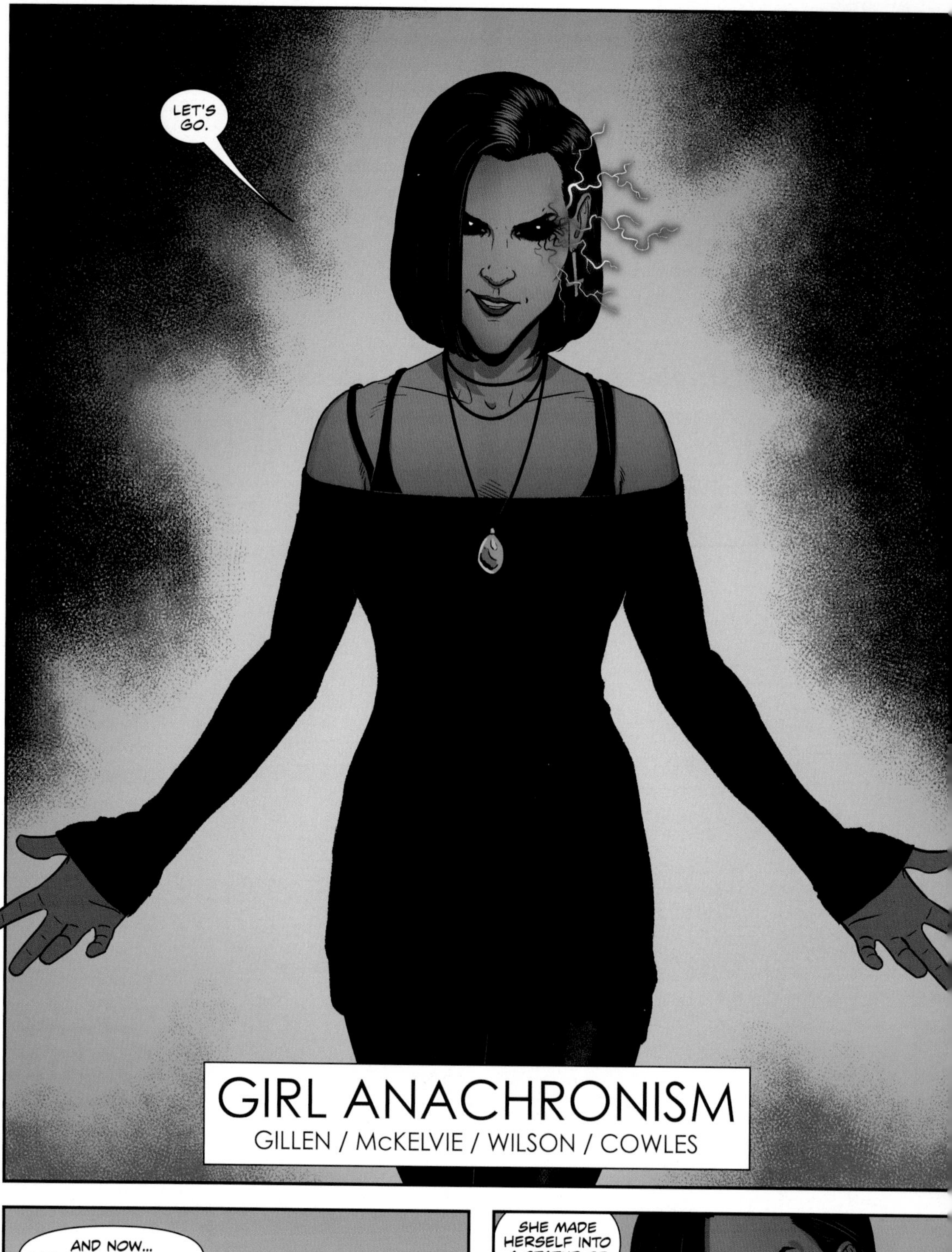
LET'S GO.

GIRL ANACHRONISM

GILLEN / McKELVIE / WILSON / COWLES

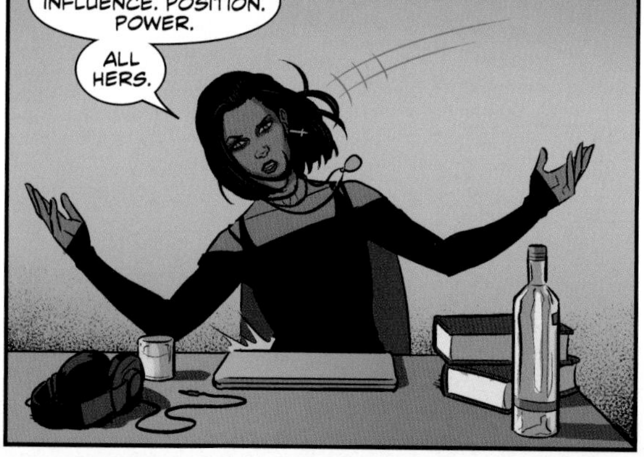
AND NOW... INFLUENCE. POSITION. POWER.
ALL HERS.

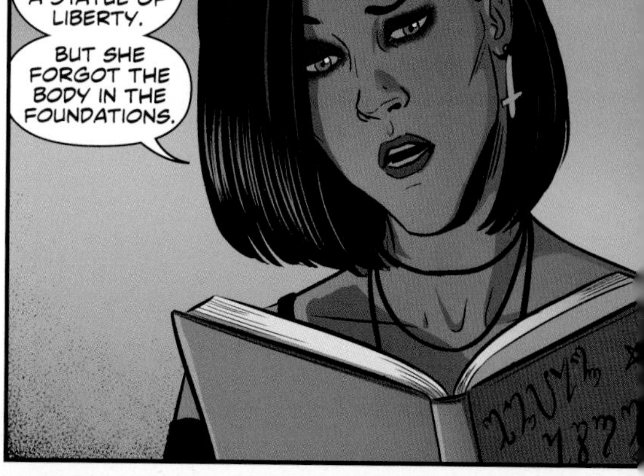
SHE MADE HERSELF INTO A STATUE OF LIBERTY.
BUT SHE FORGOT THE BODY IN THE FOUNDATIONS.

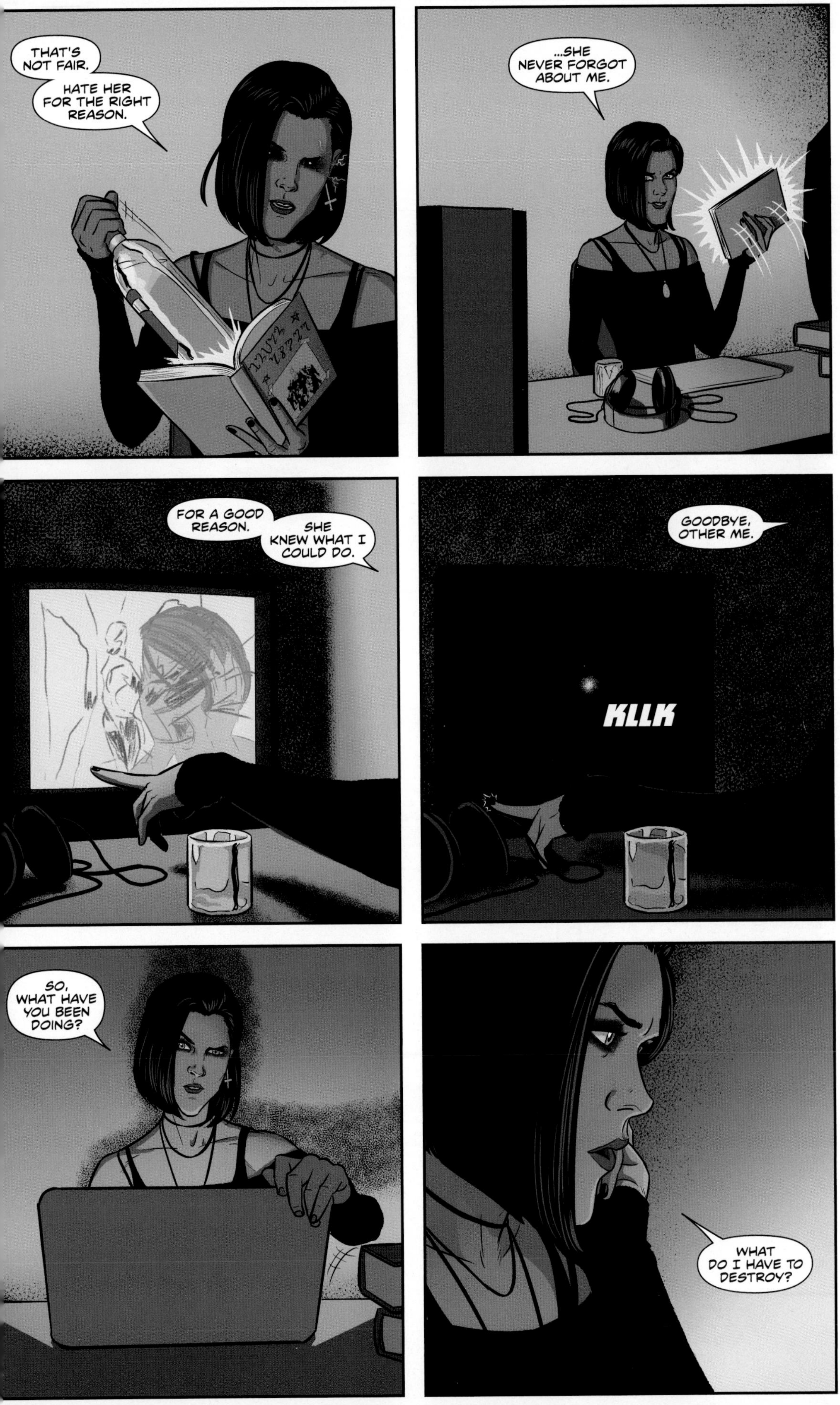
THAT'S NOT FAIR.
HATE HER FOR THE RIGHT REASON.
...SHE NEVER FORGOT ABOUT ME.
FOR A GOOD REASON.
SHE KNEW WHAT I COULD DO.
GOODBYE, OTHER ME.
KLLK
SO, WHAT HAVE YOU BEEN DOING?
WHAT DO I HAVE TO DESTROY?

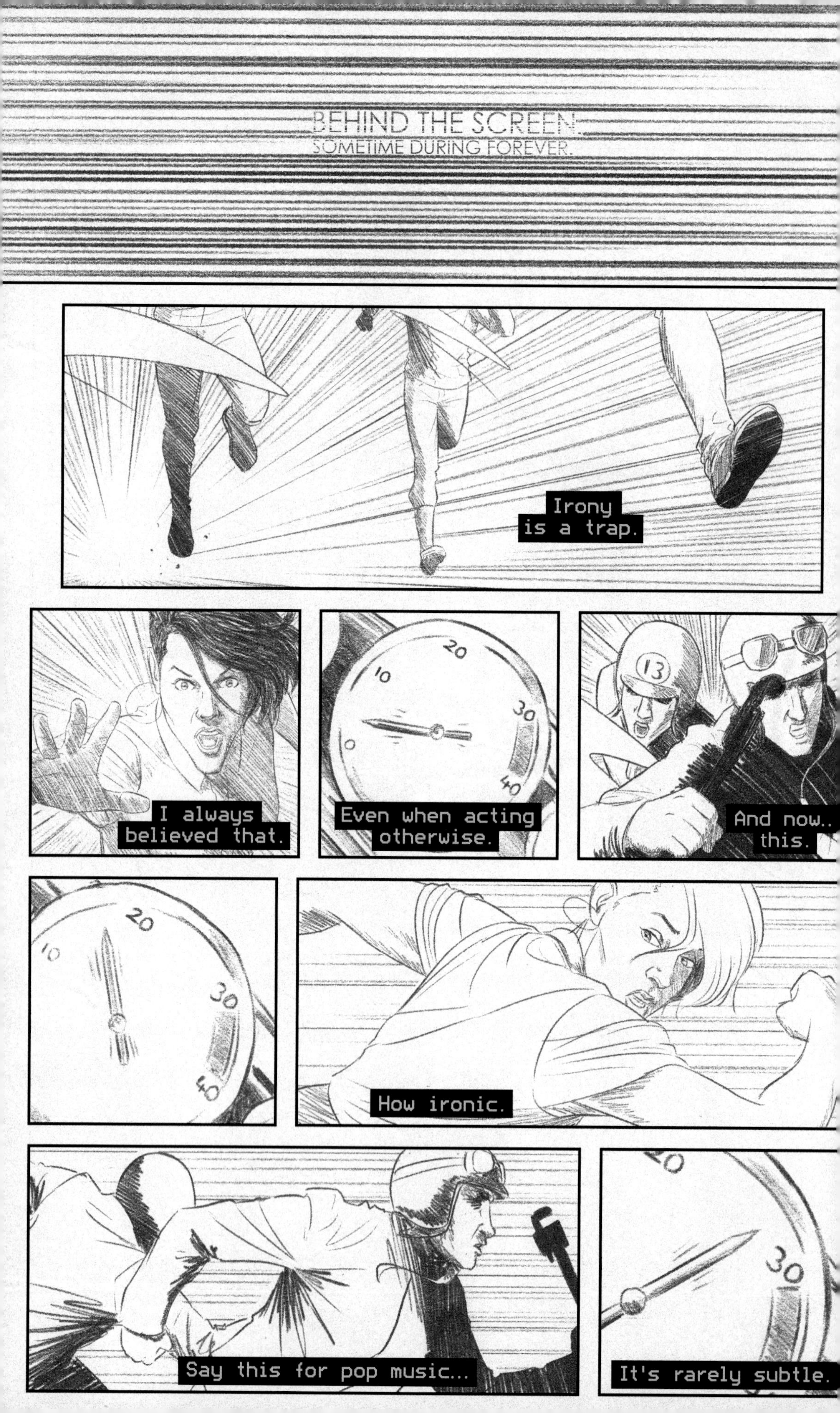
BEHIND THE SCREEN.
SOMETIME DURING FOREVER.
Irony is a trap.
I always believed that.
Even when acting otherwise.
And now.. this.
How ironic.
Say this for pop music...
It's rarely subtle.

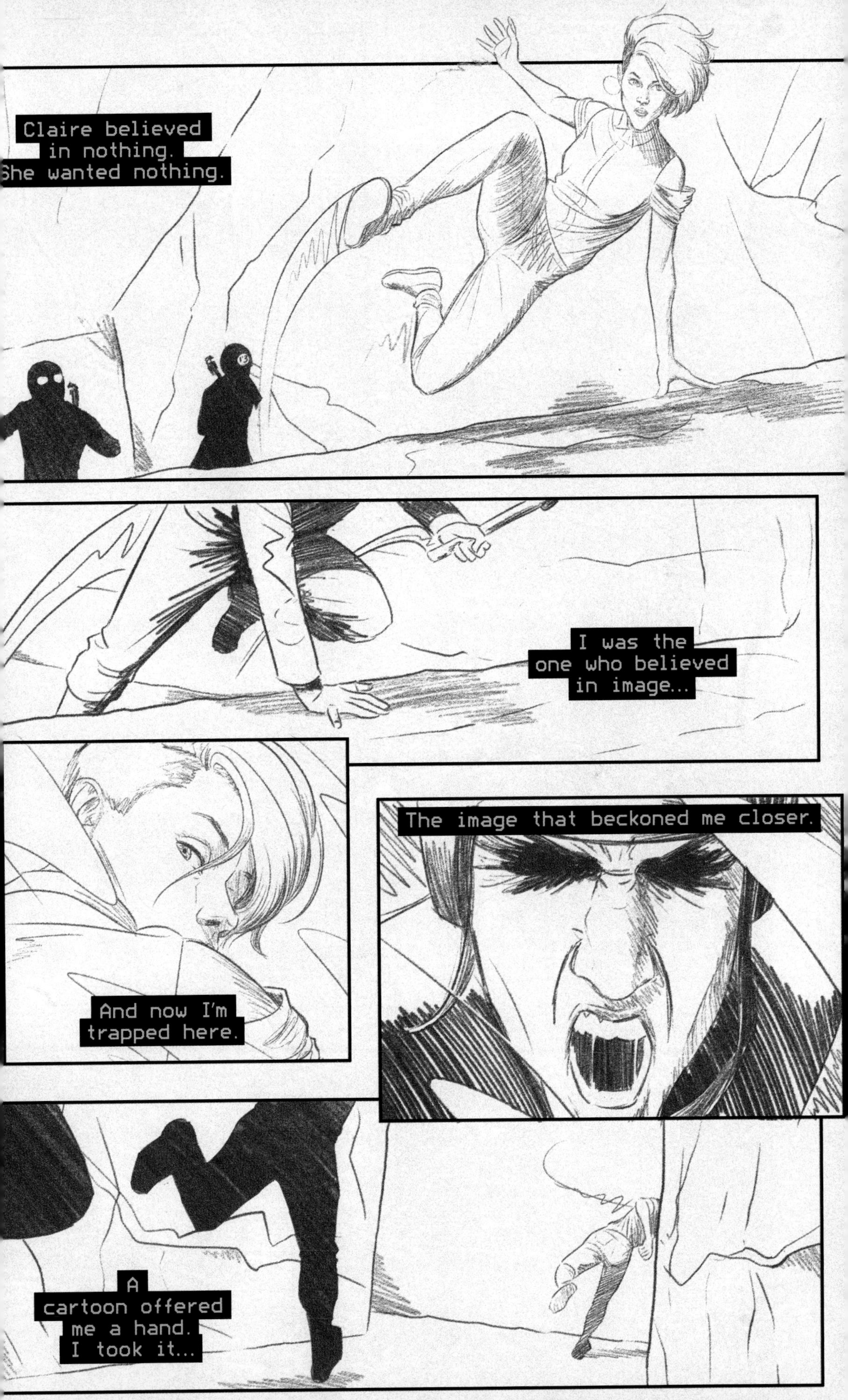

Claire believed in nothing. She wanted nothing.
I was the one who believed in image...
And now I'm trapped here.
The image that beckoned me closer.
A cartoon offered me a hand. I took it...

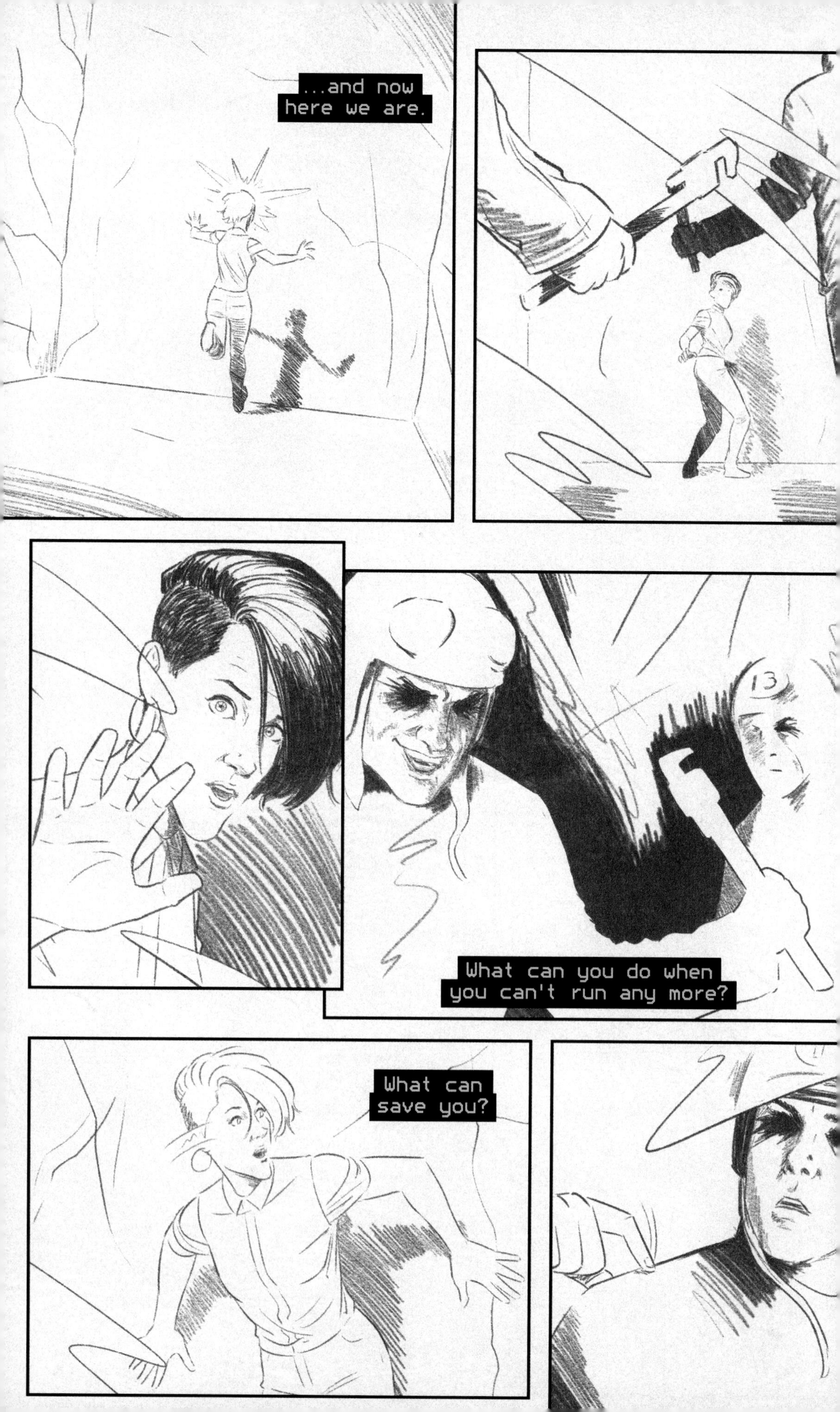
...and now here we are.
What can you do when you can't run any more?
What can save you?

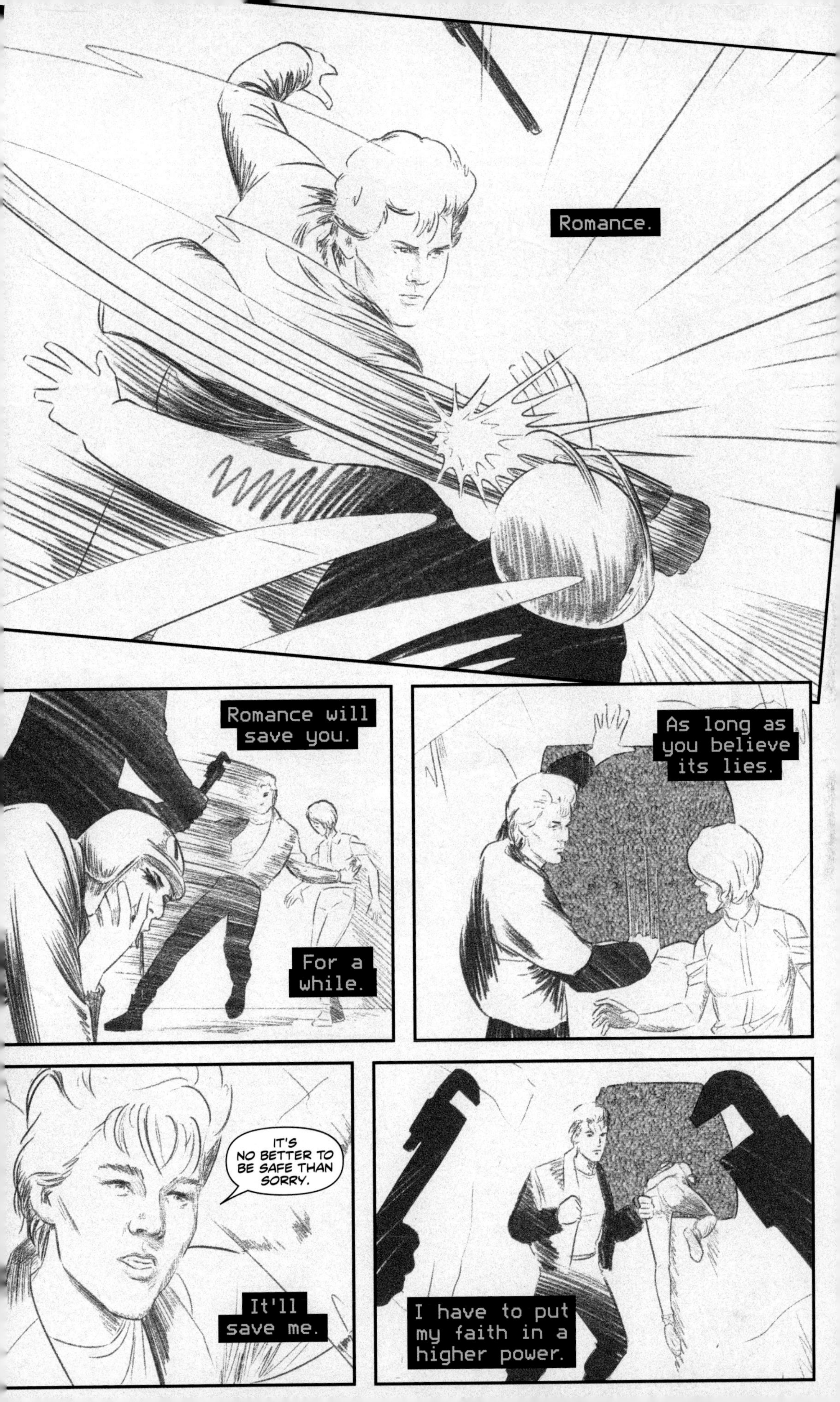
Romance.
Romance will save you.
For a while.
As long as you believe its lies.
IT'S NO BETTER TO BE SAFE THAN SORRY.
It'll save me.
I have to put my faith in a higher power.

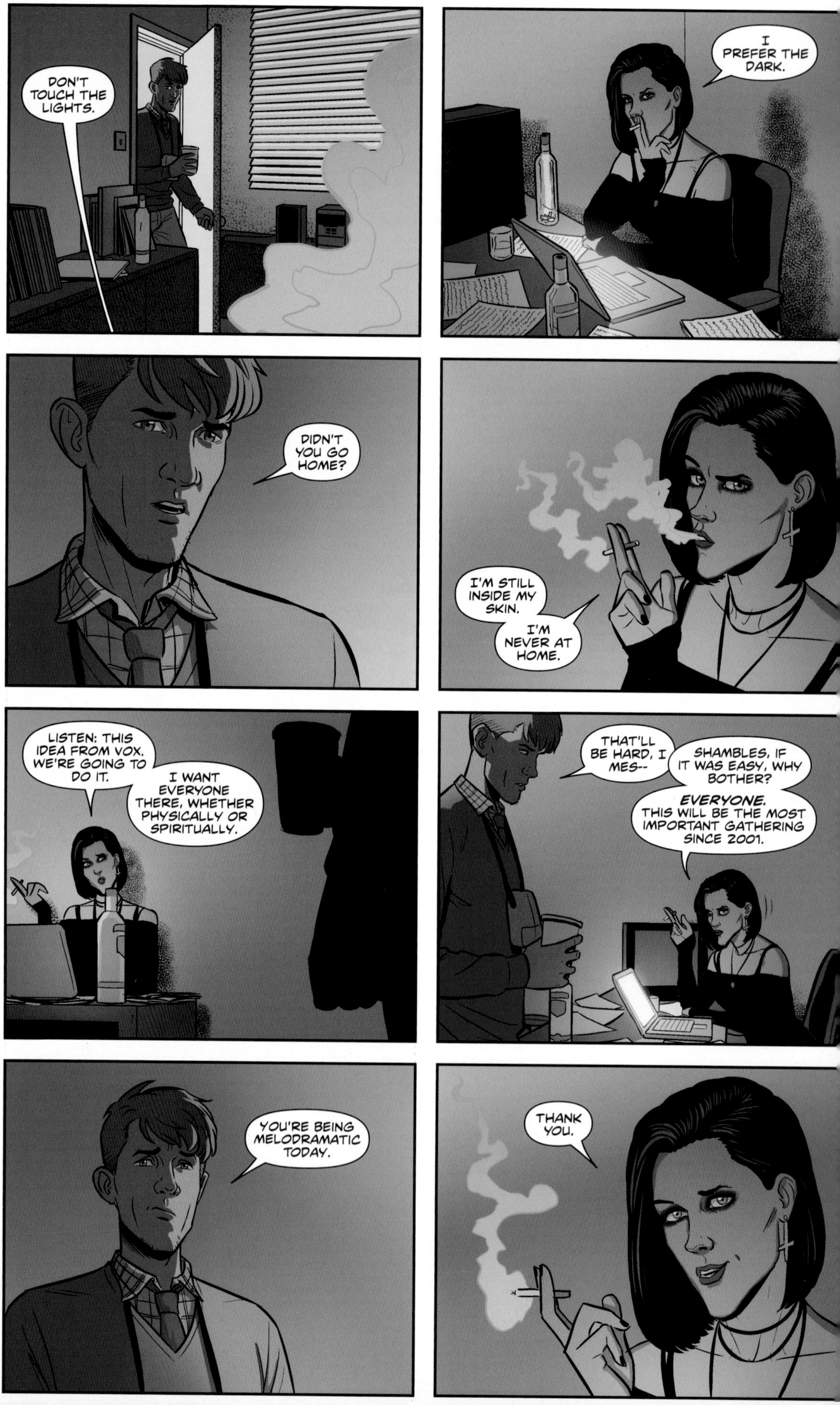
DON'T TOUCH THE LIGHTS.
I PREFER THE DARK.
DIDN'T YOU GO HOME?
I'M STILL INSIDE MY SKIN.
I'M NEVER AT HOME.
LISTEN: THIS IDEA FROM VOX. WE'RE GOING TO DO IT.
I WANT EVERYONE THERE, WHETHER PHYSICALLY OR SPIRITUALLY.
THAT'LL BE HARD, I MES--
SHAMBLES, IF IT WAS EASY, WHY BOTHER?
EVERYONE. THIS WILL BE THE MOST IMPORTANT GATHERING SINCE 2001.
YOU'RE BEING MELODRAMATIC TODAY.
THANK YOU.

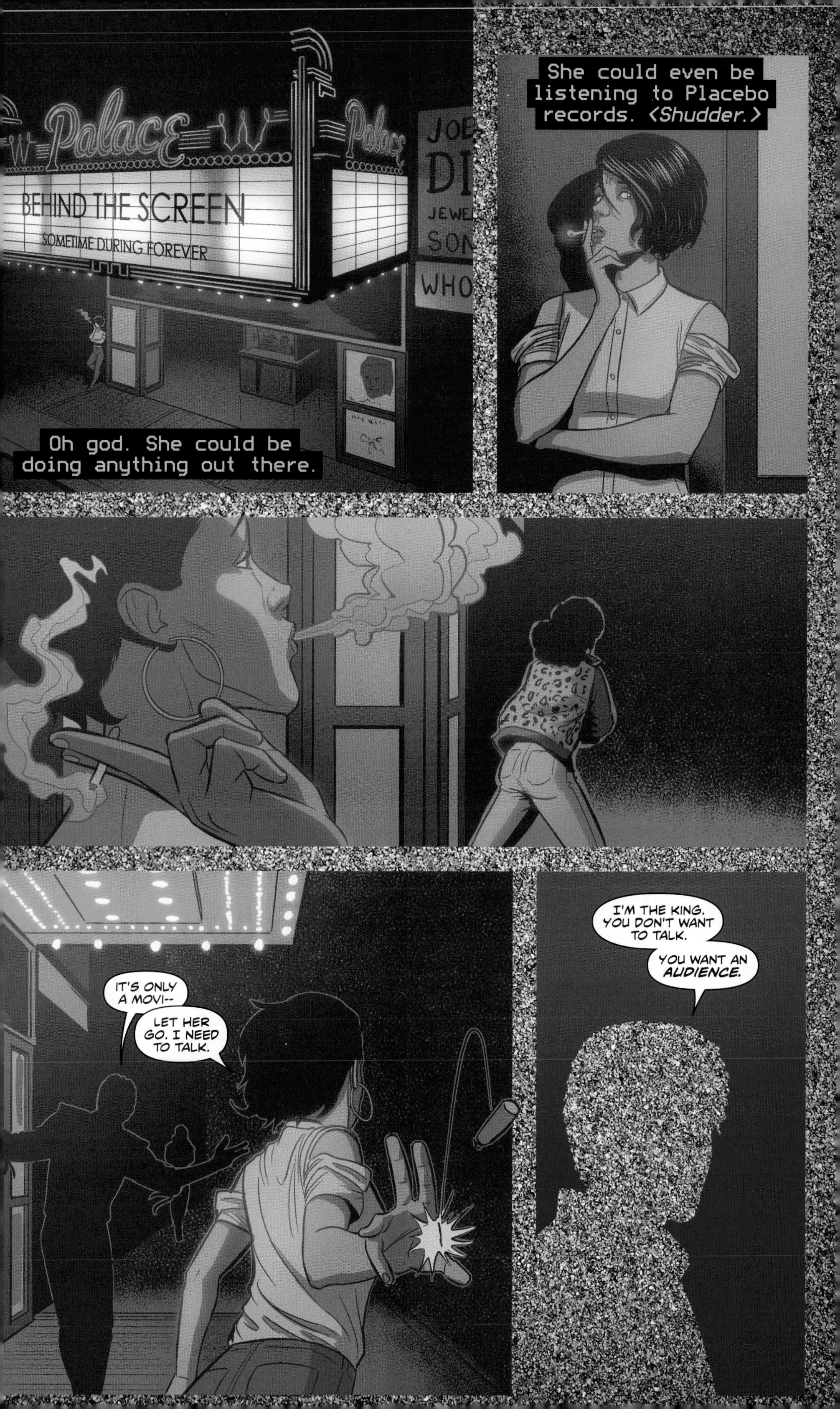
Palace
BEHIND THE SCREEN
SOMETIME DURING FOREVER
Palace
Oh god. She could be doing anything out there.
She could even be listening to Placebo records. <Shudder.>
IT'S ONLY A MOVI--
LET HER GO. I NEED TO TALK.
I'M THE KING. YOU DON'T WANT TO TALK.
YOU WANT AN AUDIENCE.

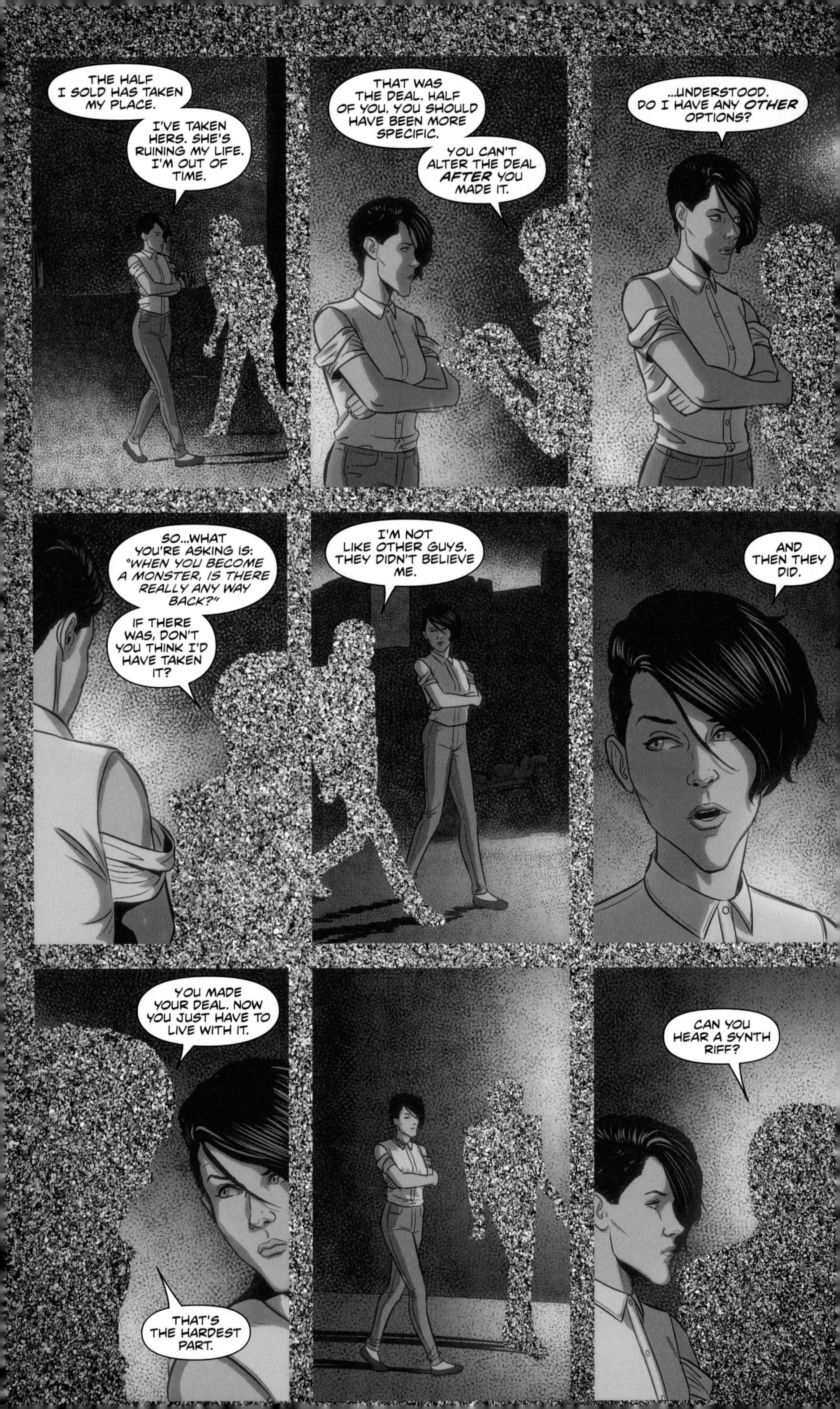
THE HALF I SOLD HAS TAKEN MY PLACE.
I'VE TAKEN HERS. SHE'S RUINING MY LIFE. I'M OUT OF TIME.
THAT WAS THE DEAL. HALF OF YOU. YOU SHOULD HAVE BEEN MORE SPECIFIC.
YOU CAN'T ALTER THE DEAL AFTER YOU MADE IT.
...UNDERSTOOD. DO I HAVE ANY OTHER OPTIONS?
SO...WHAT YOU'RE ASKING IS: "WHEN YOU BECOME A MONSTER, IS THERE REALLY ANY WAY BACK?"
IF THERE WAS, DON'T YOU THINK I'D HAVE TAKEN IT?
I'M NOT LIKE OTHER GUYS. THEY DIDN'T BELIEVE ME.
AND THEN THEY DID.
YOU MADE YOUR DEAL. NOW YOU JUST HAVE TO LIVE WITH IT.
THAT'S THE HARDEST PART.
CAN YOU HEAR A SYNTH RIFF?

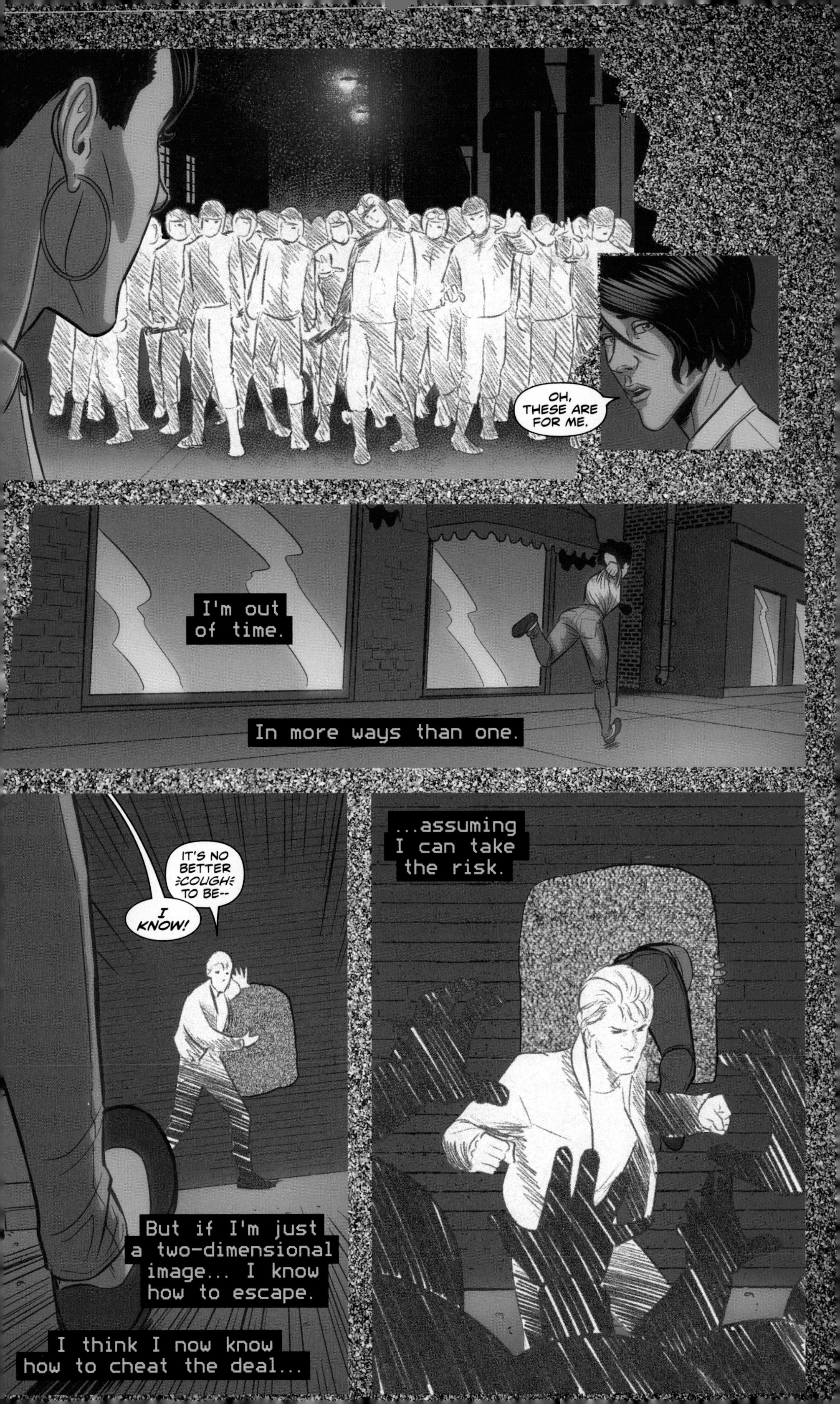
OH, THESE ARE FOR ME.
I'm out of time.
In more ways than one.
IT'S NO BETTER *COUGH* TO BE--
I KNOW!
But if I'm just a two-dimensional image... I know how to escape.
I think I now know how to cheat the deal...
...assuming I can take the risk.

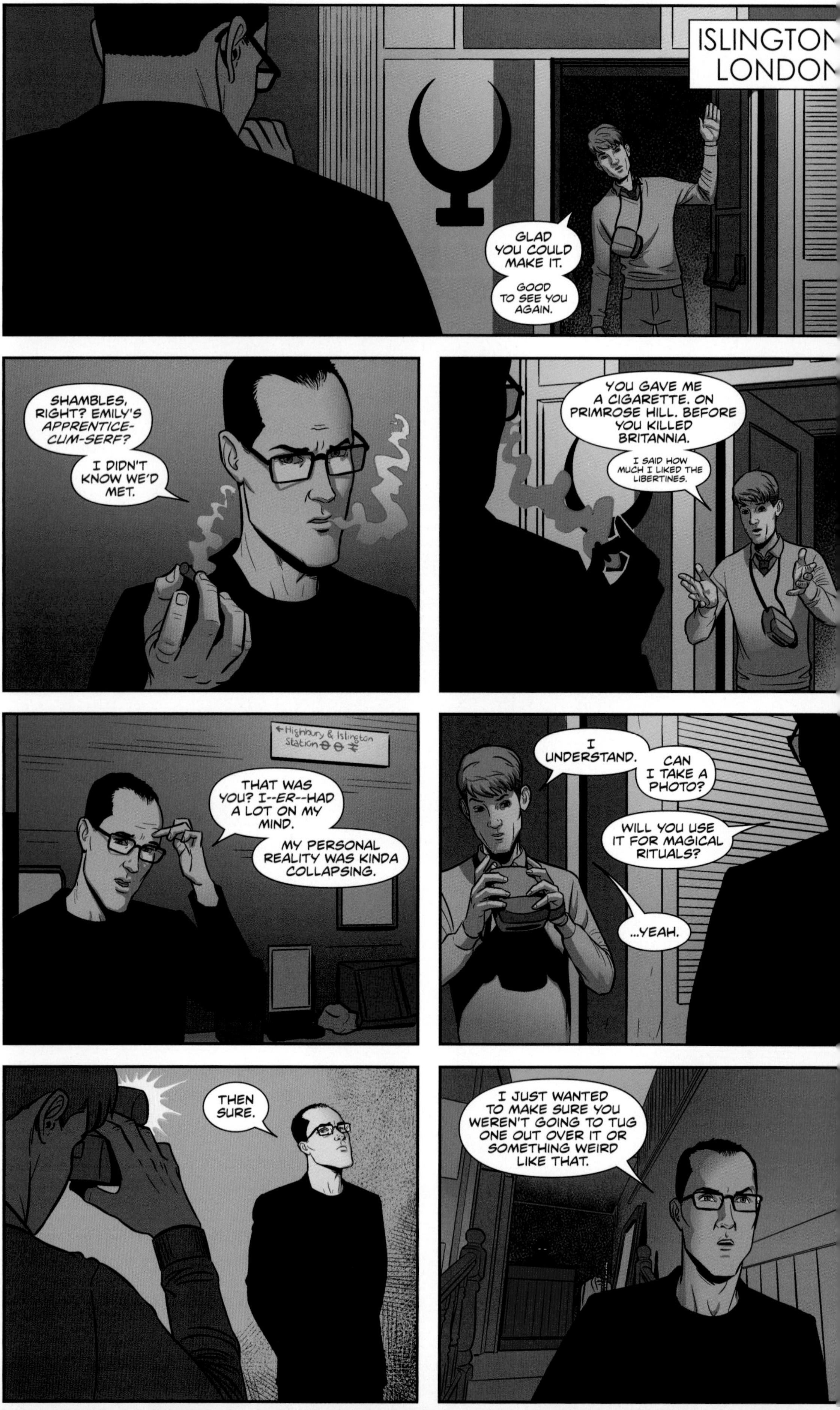
ISLINGTON
LONDON
GLAD YOU COULD MAKE IT.
GOOD TO SEE YOU AGAIN.
SHAMBLES, RIGHT? EMILY'S APPRENTICE-CUM-SERF?
I DIDN'T KNOW WE'D MET.
YOU GAVE ME A CIGARETTE. ON PRIMROSE HILL. BEFORE YOU KILLED BRITANNIA.
I SAID HOW MUCH I LIKED THE LIBERTINES.
← Highbury & Islington Station
THAT WAS YOU? I--ER--HAD A LOT ON MY MIND.
MY PERSONAL REALITY WAS KINDA COLLAPSING.
I UNDERSTAND.
CAN I TAKE A PHOTO?
WILL YOU USE IT FOR MAGICAL RITUALS?
...YEAH.
THEN SURE.
I JUST WANTED TO MAKE SURE YOU WEREN'T GOING TO TUG ONE OUT OVER IT OR SOMETHING WEIRD LIKE THAT.

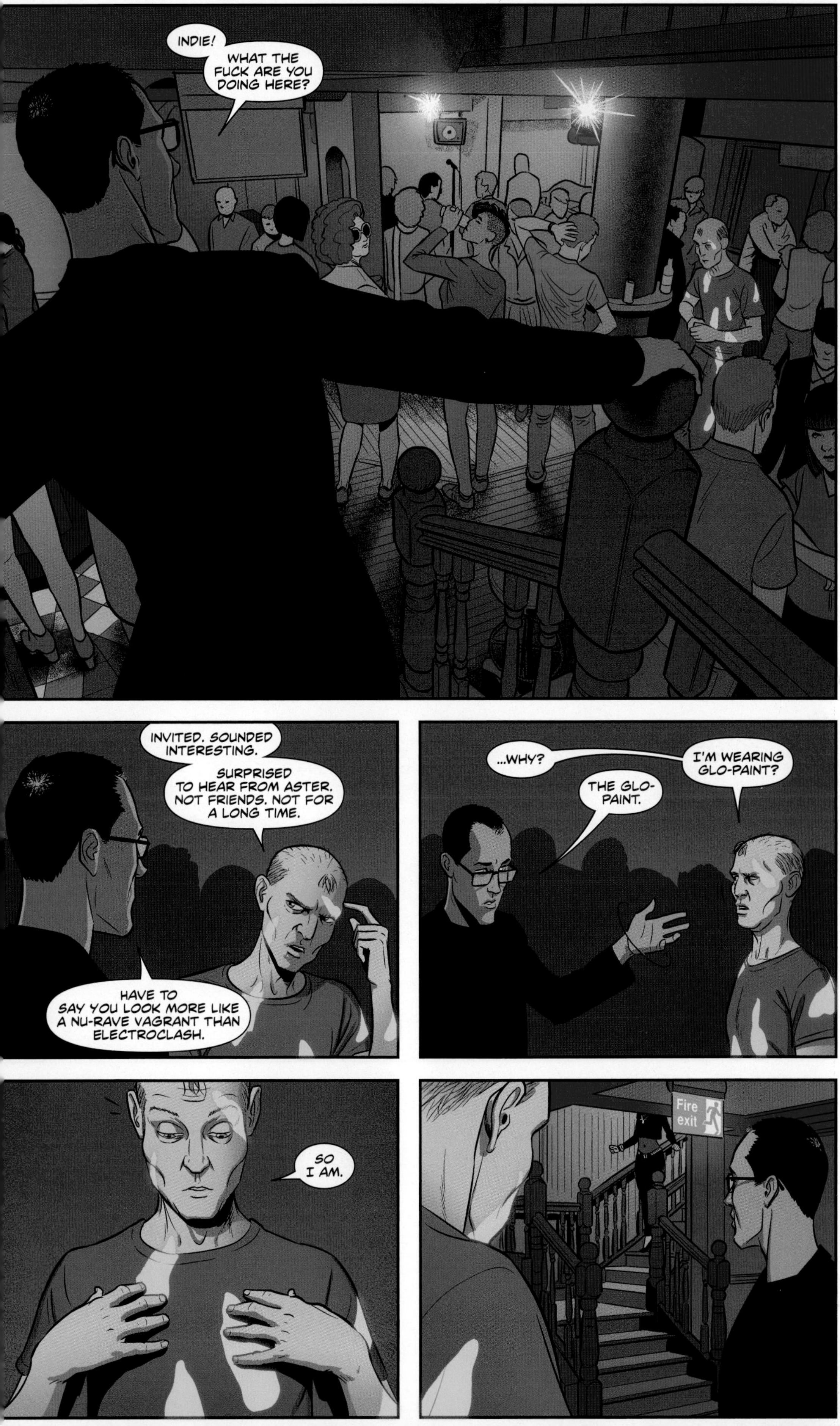
INDIE!
WHAT THE FUCK ARE YOU DOING HERE?
INVITED. SOUNDED INTERESTING.
SURPRISED TO HEAR FROM ASTER. NOT FRIENDS. NOT FOR A LONG TIME.
HAVE TO SAY YOU LOOK MORE LIKE A NU-RAVE VAGRANT THAN ELECTROCLASH.
...WHY?
I'M WEARING GLO-PAINT?
THE GLO-PAINT.
SO I AM.
Fire exit

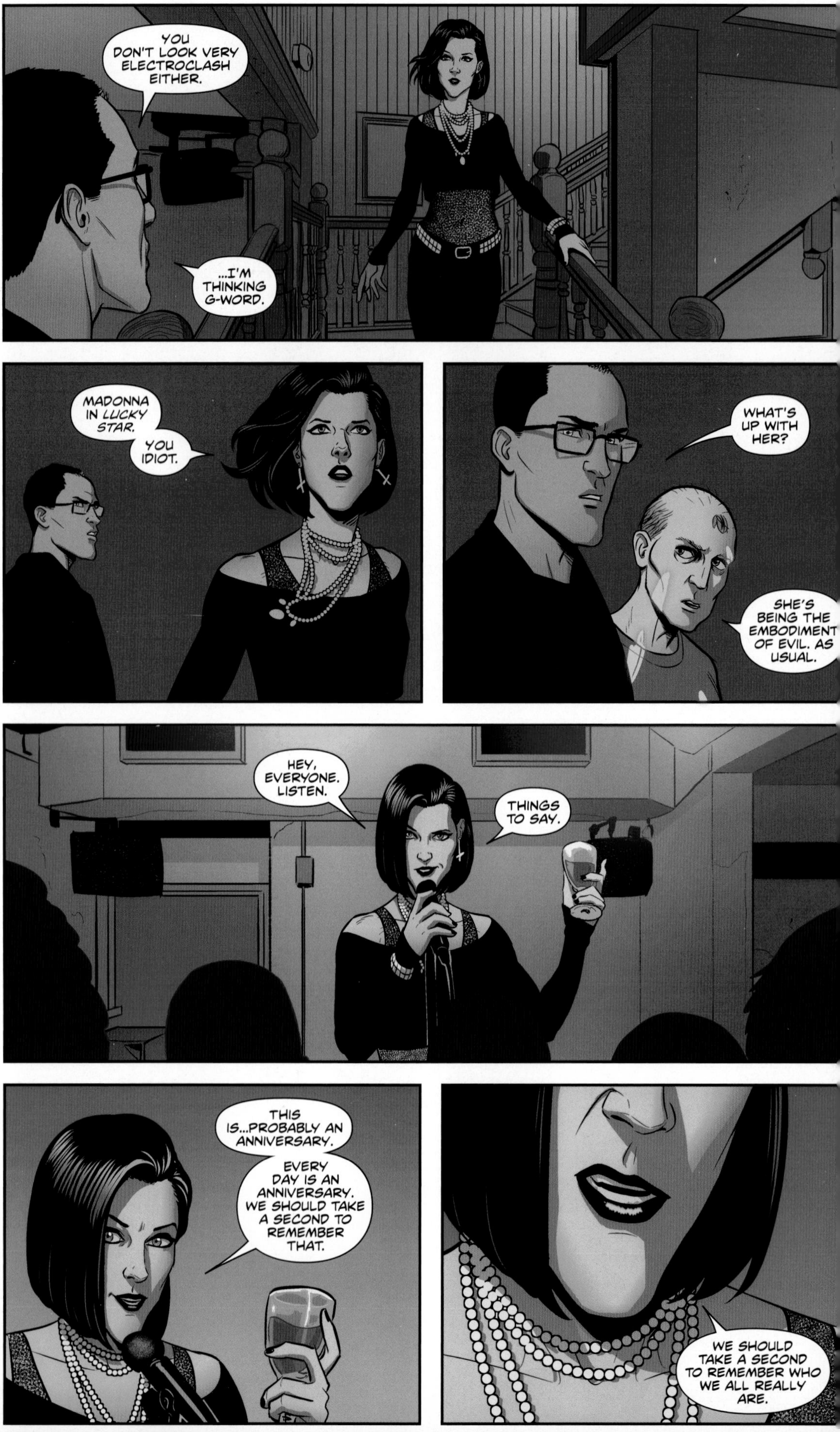
YOU DON'T LOOK VERY ELECTROCLASH EITHER.
...I'M THINKING G-WORD.
MADONNA IN *LUCKY STAR.*
YOU IDIOT.
WHAT'S UP WITH HER?
SHE'S BEING THE EMBODIMENT OF EVIL. AS USUAL.
HEY, EVERYONE. LISTEN.
THINGS TO SAY.
THIS IS...PROBABLY AN ANNIVERSARY.
EVERY DAY IS AN ANNIVERSARY. WE SHOULD TAKE A SECOND TO REMEMBER THAT.
WE SHOULD TAKE A SECOND TO REMEMBER WHO WE ALL REALLY ARE.

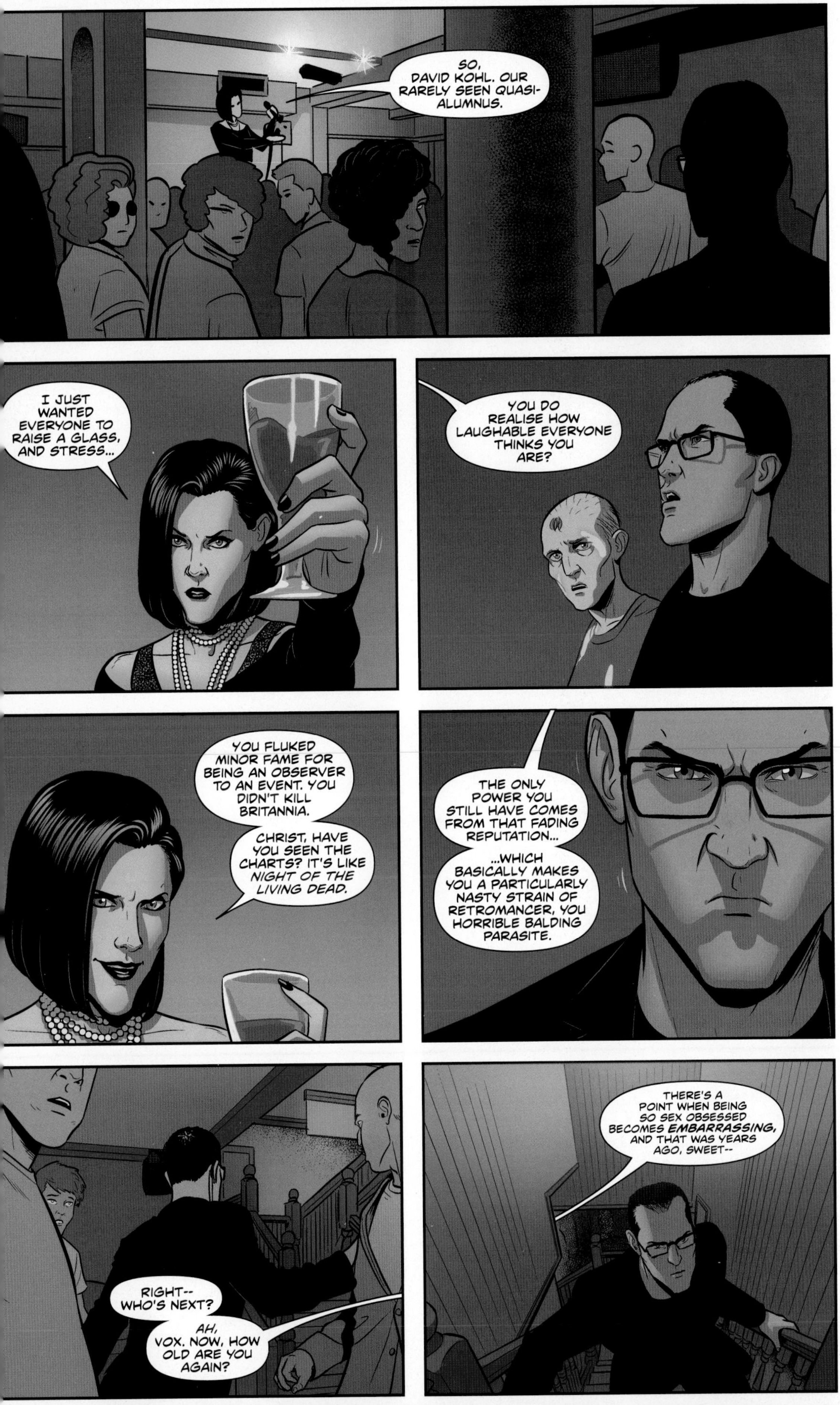

SO, DAVID KOHL. OUR RARELY SEEN QUASI-ALUMNUS.
I JUST WANTED EVERYONE TO RAISE A GLASS, AND STRESS...
YOU DO REALISE HOW LAUGHABLE EVERYONE THINKS YOU ARE?
YOU FLUKED MINOR FAME FOR BEING AN OBSERVER TO AN EVENT. YOU DIDN'T KILL BRITANNIA.
CHRIST, HAVE YOU SEEN THE CHARTS? IT'S LIKE *NIGHT OF THE LIVING DEAD.*
THE ONLY POWER YOU STILL HAVE COMES FROM THAT FADING REPUTATION...
...WHICH BASICALLY MAKES YOU A PARTICULARLY NASTY STRAIN OF RETROMANCER, YOU HORRIBLE BALDING PARASITE.
RIGHT-- WHO'S NEXT?
AH, VOX. NOW, HOW OLD ARE YOU AGAIN?
THERE'S A POINT WHEN BEING SO SEX OBSESSED BECOMES ***EMBARRASSING,*** AND THAT WAS YEARS AGO, SWEET--

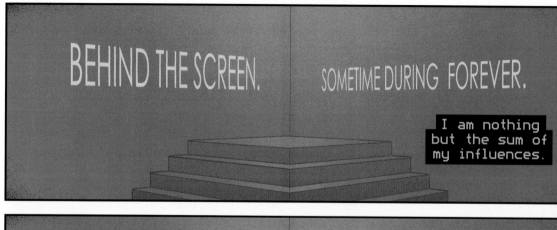

BEHIND THE SCREEN.

SOMETIME DURING FOREVER.

I am nothing but the sum of my influences.

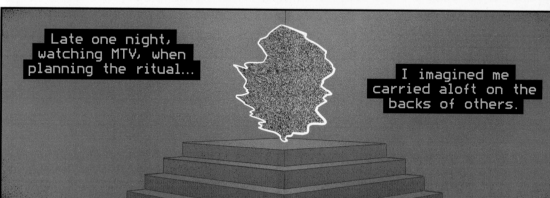

Late one night, watching MTY, when planning the ritual...

I imagined me carried aloft on the backs of others.

They would hate me and love me.

But mainly hate me.

And I loved that.

I thought that would be wonderful.

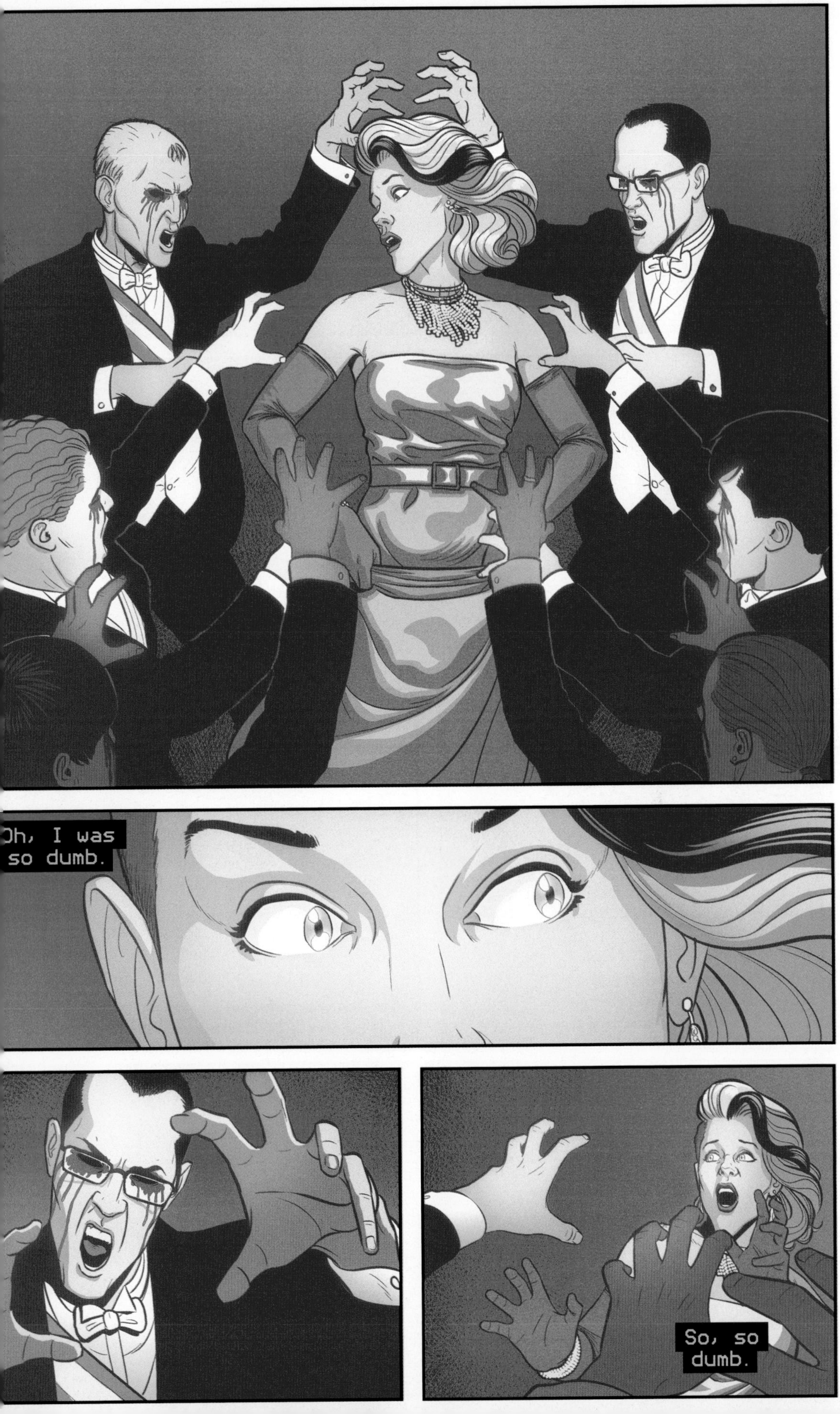
Oh, I was so dumb.
So, so dumb.

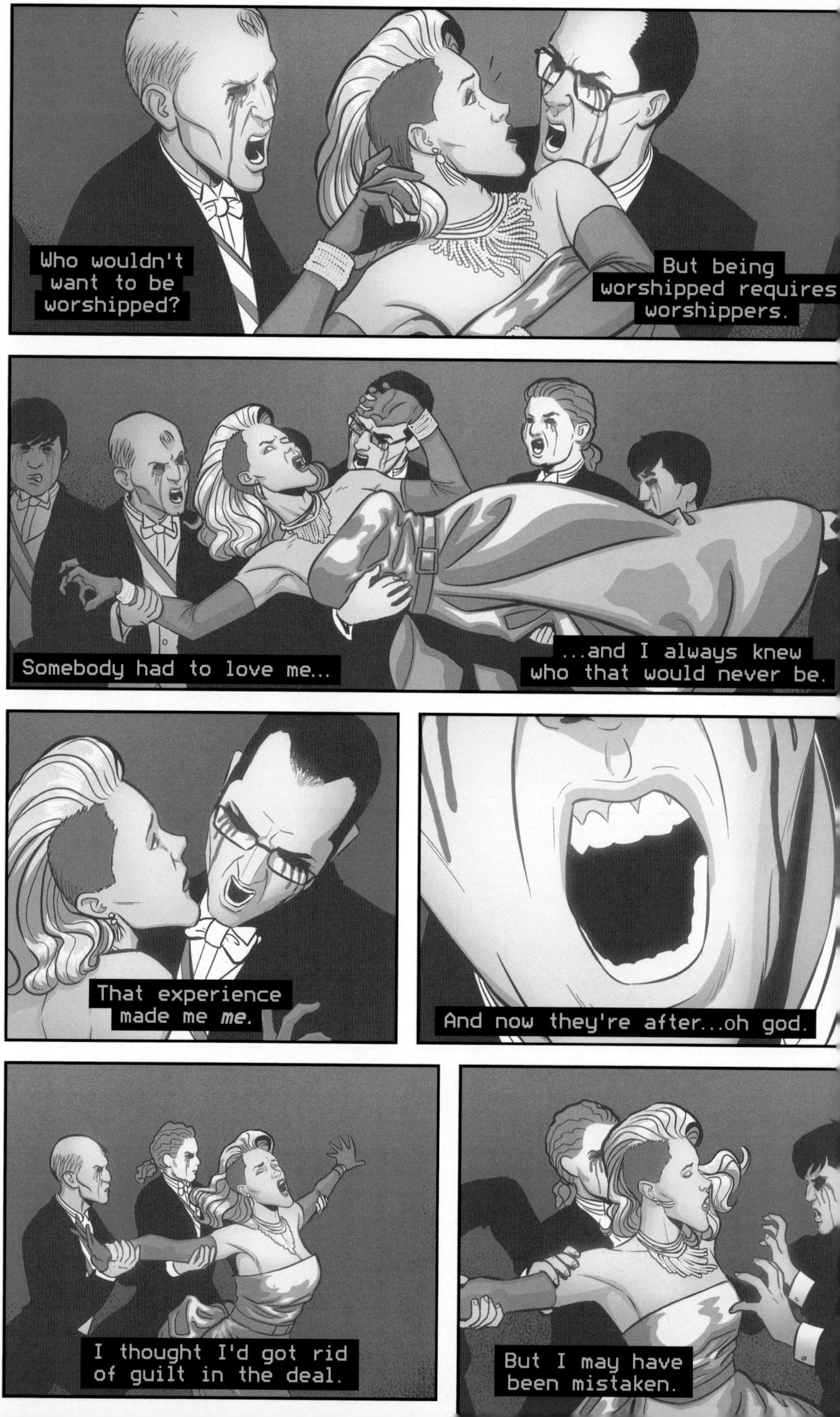
Who wouldn't want to be worshipped?
But being worshipped requires worshippers.
Somebody had to love me...
...and I always knew who that would never be.
That experience made me *me*.
And now they're after...oh god.
I thought I'd got rid of guilt in the deal.
But I may have been mistaken.

On the night I made the deal, I watched *Material Girl* on repeat.

And told myself: "I know what I'm doing."

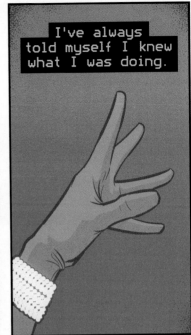

I've always told myself I knew what I was doing.

What if I'm wrong now?

You can see this. You can. I know you can...

KKKLLLLK

There you are.

I knew you'd save me.

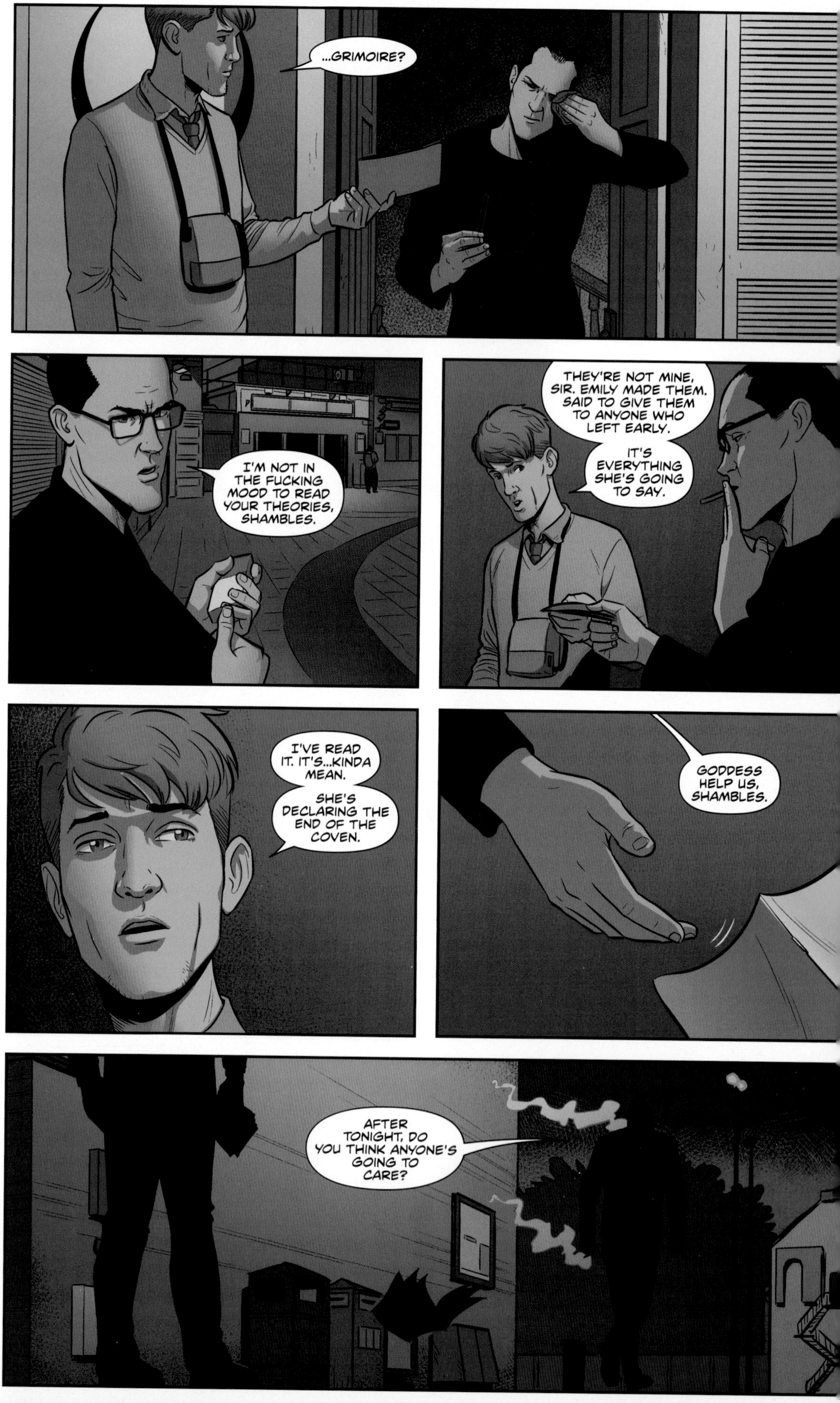
...GRIMOIRE?
I'M NOT IN THE FUCKING MOOD TO READ YOUR THEORIES, SHAMBLES.
THEY'RE NOT MINE, SIR. EMILY MADE THEM. SAID TO GIVE THEM TO ANYONE WHO LEFT EARLY.
IT'S EVERYTHING SHE'S GOING TO SAY.
I'VE READ IT. IT'S...KINDA MEAN.
SHE'S DECLARING THE END OF THE COVEN.
GODDESS HELP US, SHAMBLES.
AFTER TONIGHT, DO YOU THINK ANYONE'S GOING TO CARE?

PHONOGRAM

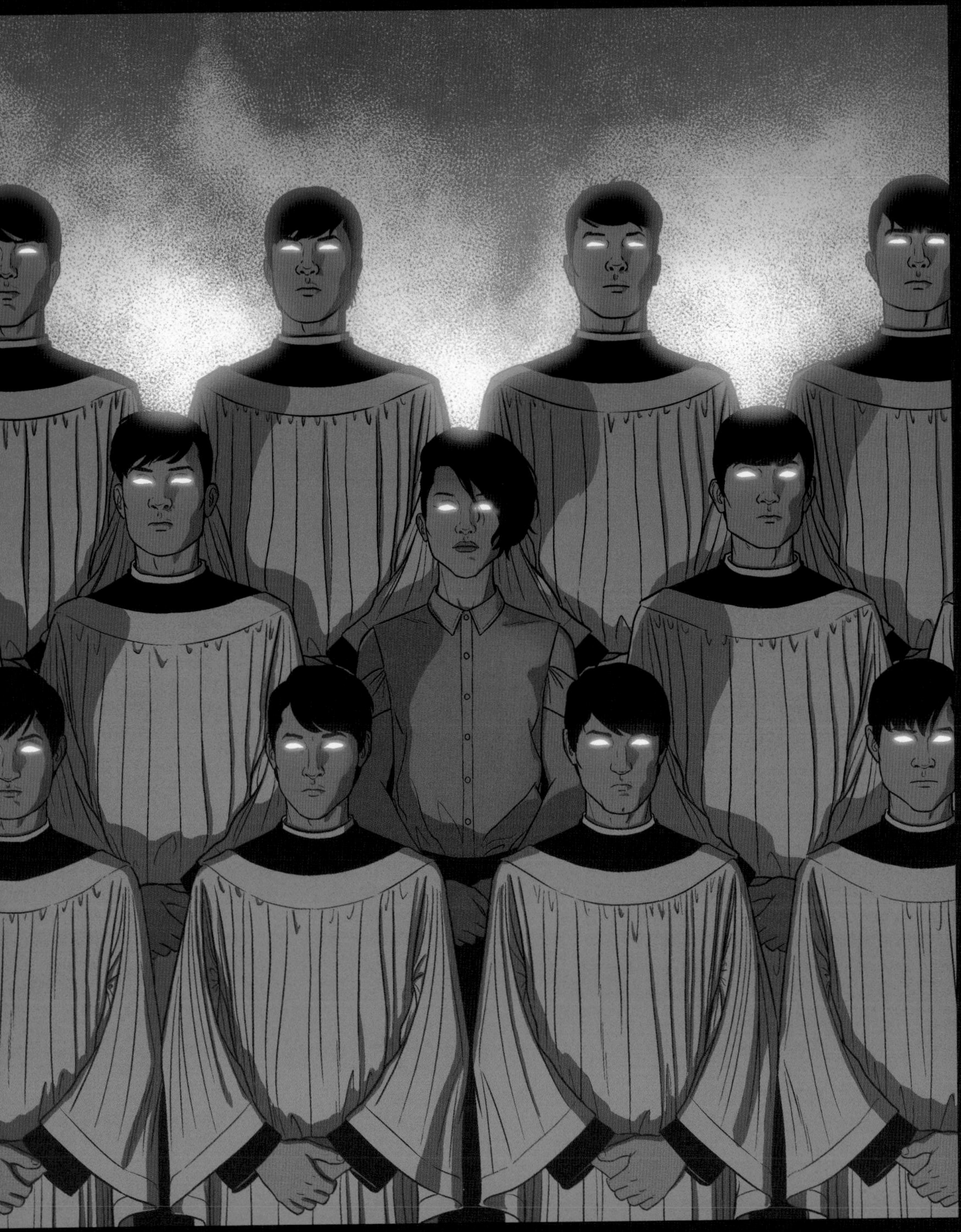

OCTOBER 2001.

IS THAT FISCHERSPOONER?

YES.

YOU'RE LISTENING TO FISCHERSPOONER?

YES, INDIE.

YOU'RE SELLING HALF YOUR PERSONALITY WHILE LISTENING TO FISCHERSPOONER?

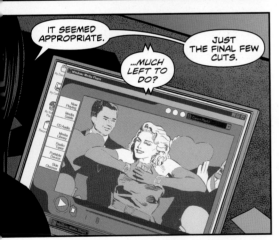

IT SEEMED APPROPRIATE.

...MUCH LEFT TO DO?

JUST THE FINAL FEW CUTS.

THE CONTRACT IS MY GRIMOIRE. A GRIMOIRE OF ME.

OF WHAT I'LL BE MADE OF. OF WHAT I'LL BE. WHAT I WANT...

...AND WHAT I'M GIVING UP.

I'VE DECIDED THAT BEING MISERABLE IS JUST DEPRESSING.

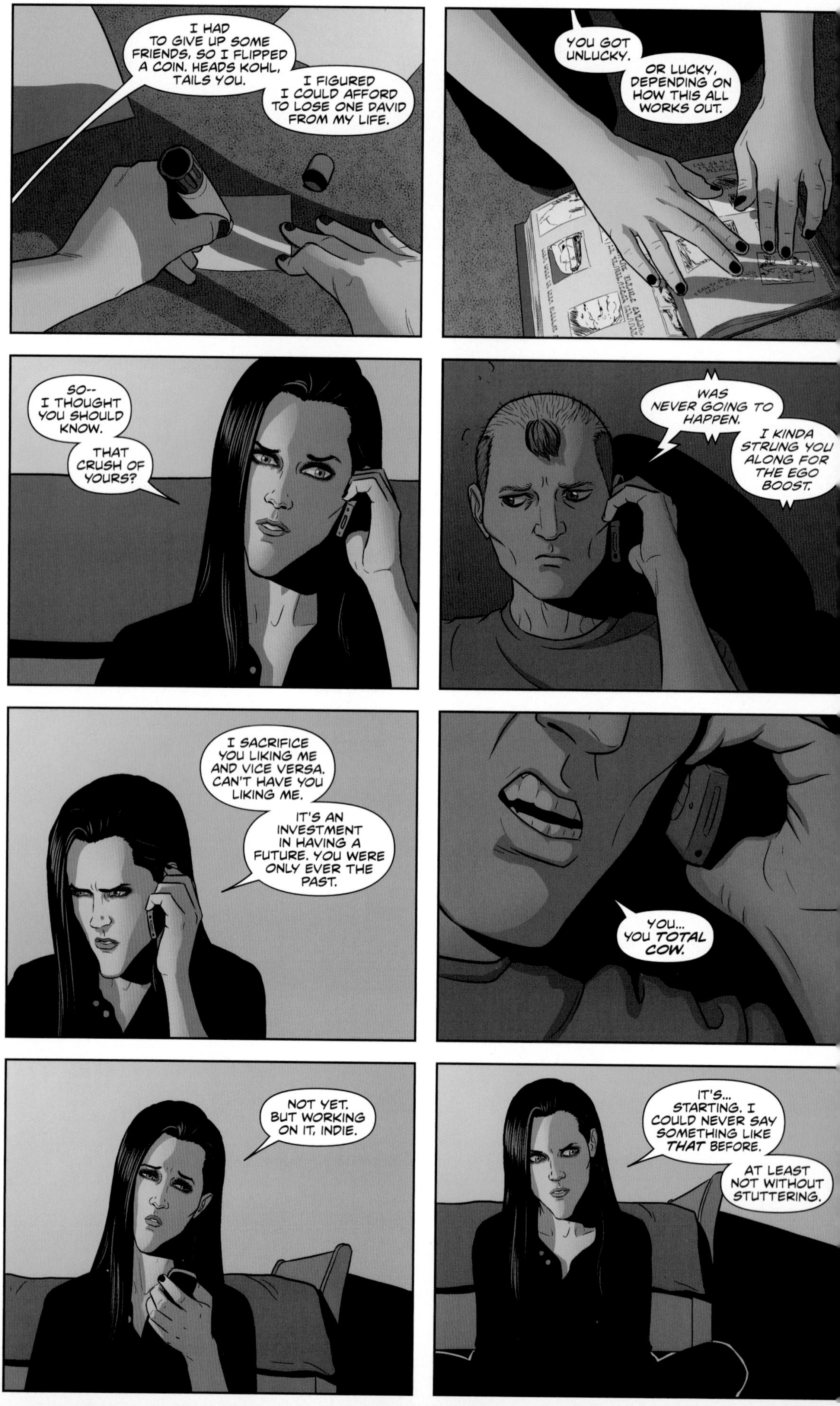
I HAD TO GIVE UP SOME FRIENDS, SO I FLIPPED A COIN. HEADS KOHL, TAILS YOU.
I FIGURED I COULD AFFORD TO LOSE ONE DAVID FROM MY LIFE.
YOU GOT UNLUCKY.
OR LUCKY, DEPENDING ON HOW THIS ALL WORKS OUT.
SO-- I THOUGHT YOU SHOULD KNOW.
THAT CRUSH OF YOURS?
WAS NEVER GOING TO HAPPEN.
I KINDA STRUNG YOU ALONG FOR THE EGO BOOST.
I SACRIFICE YOU LIKING ME AND VICE VERSA. CAN'T HAVE YOU LIKING ME.
IT'S AN INVESTMENT IN HAVING A FUTURE. YOU WERE ONLY EVER THE PAST.
YOU... YOU *TOTAL* COW.
NOT YET. BUT WORKING ON IT, INDIE.
IT'S... STARTING. I COULD NEVER SAY SOMETHING LIKE *THAT* BEFORE.
AT LEAST NOT WITHOUT STUTTERING.

OH, CINDERELLA! YOU WILL GO TO THE BALL.

AND IN THE MORNING, I WON'T EVEN WINCE SAYING SOMETHING *THAT* WANKY.

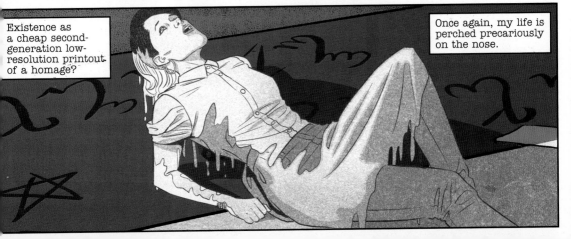

Existence as a cheap second-generation low-resolution printout of a homage?

Once again, my life is perched precariously on the nose.

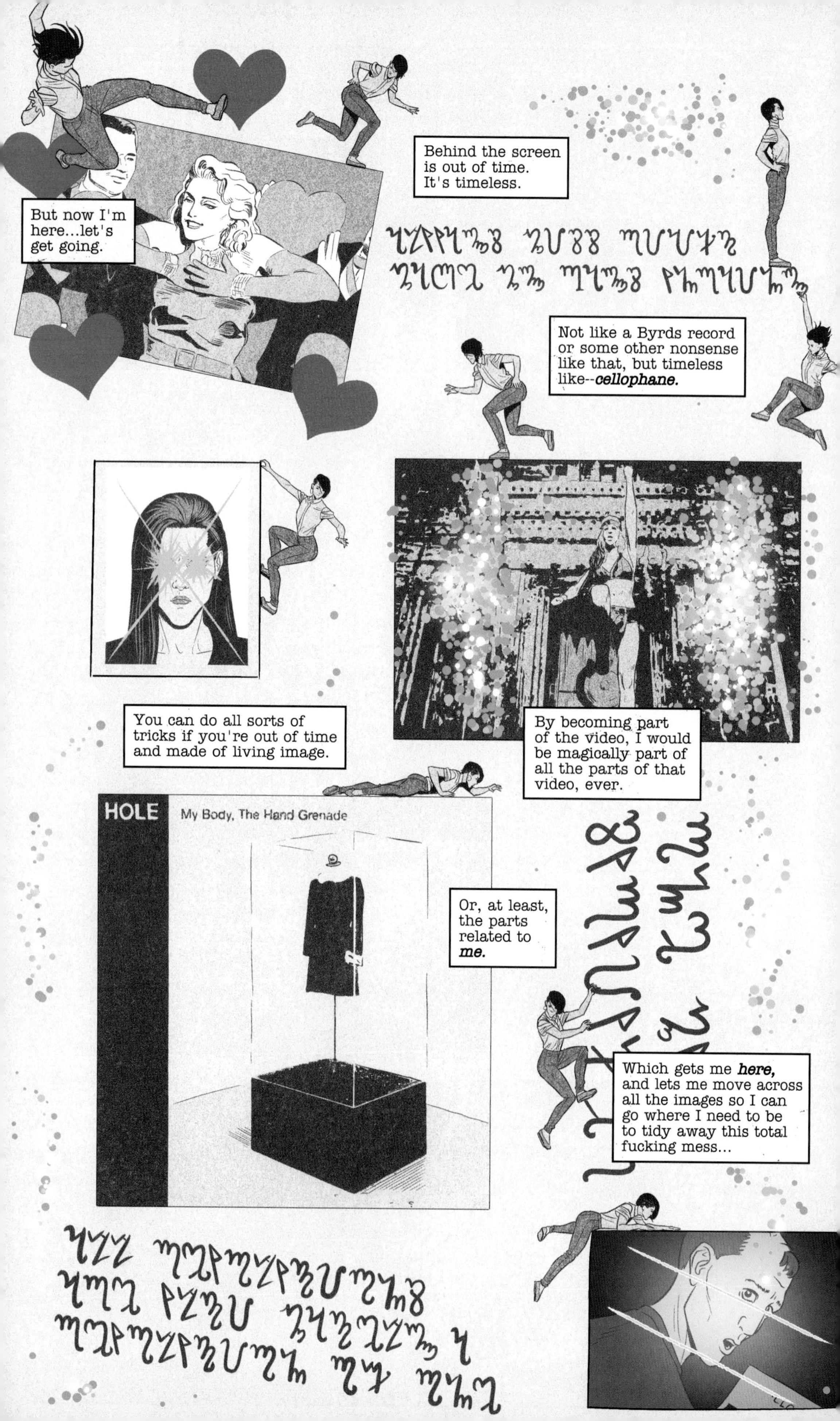
But now I'm here...let's get going.
Behind the screen is out of time. It's timeless.
Not like a Byrds record or some other nonsense like that, but timeless like--*cellophane.*
You can do all sorts of tricks if you're out of time and made of living image.
By becoming part of the video, I would be magically part of all the parts of that video, ever.
HOLE
My Body, The Hand Grenade
Or, at least, the parts related to *me.*
Which gets me *here,* and lets me move across all the images so I can go where I need to be to tidy away this total fucking mess...

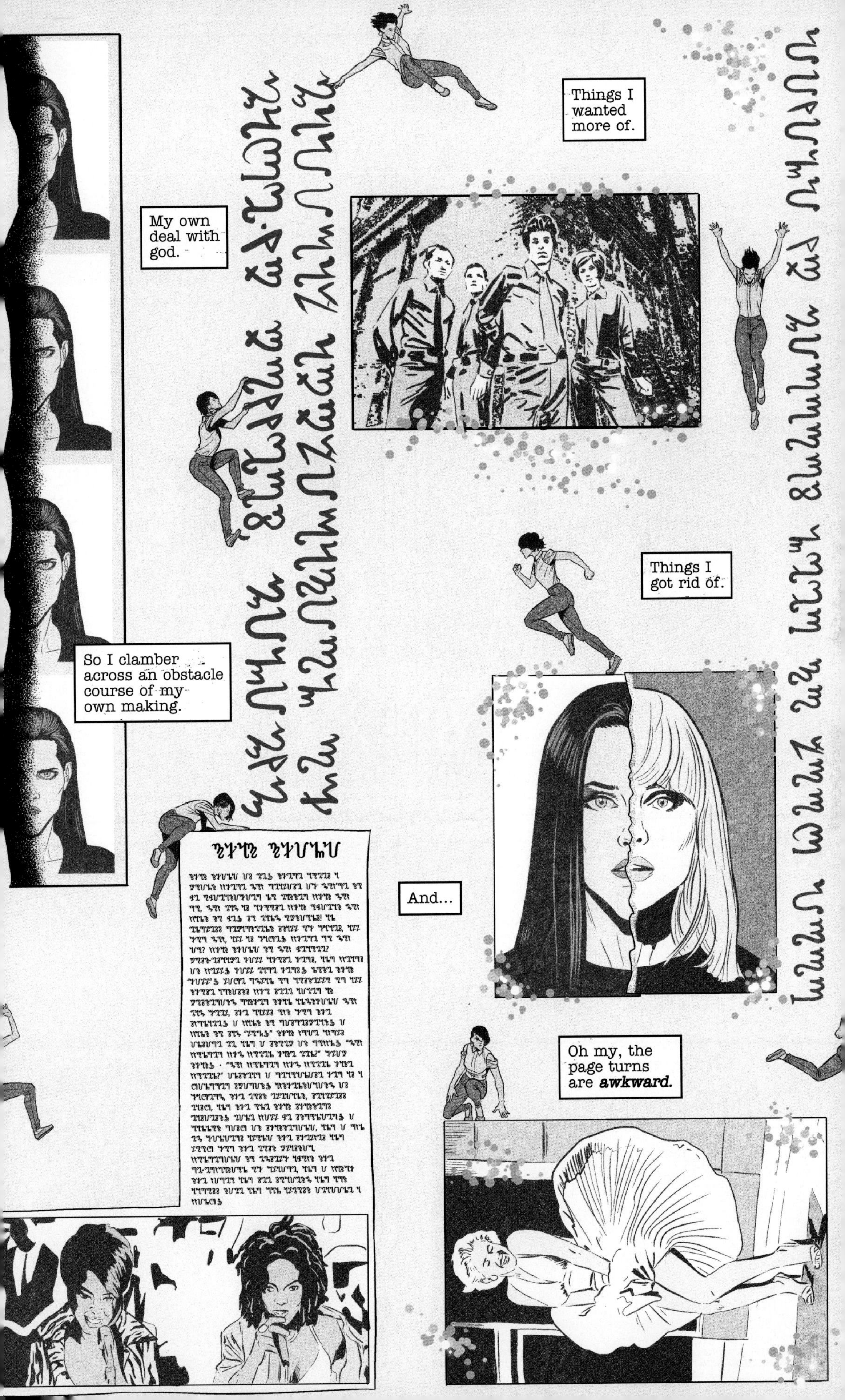
My own deal with god.
So I clamber across an obstacle course of my own making.
Things I wanted more of.
Things I got rid of.
And...
Oh my, the page turns are **awkward**.

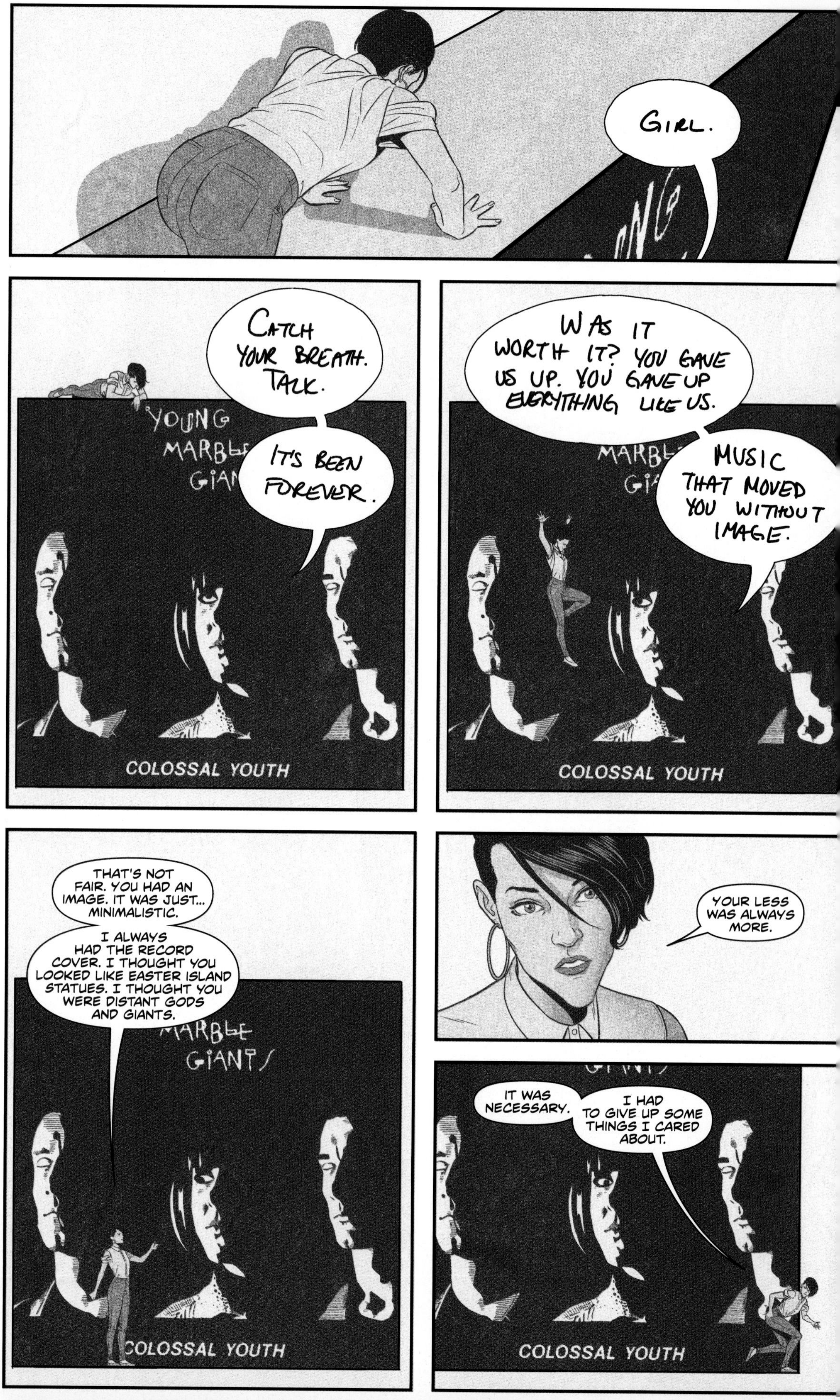
GIRL.
CATCH YOUR BREATH. TALK.
YOUNG MARBLE GIANTS
IT'S BEEN FOREVER.
COLOSSAL YOUTH
WAS IT WORTH IT? YOU GAVE US UP. YOU GAVE UP EVERYTHING LIKE US.
MUSIC THAT MOVED YOU WITHOUT IMAGE.
COLOSSAL YOUTH
THAT'S NOT FAIR. YOU HAD AN IMAGE. IT WAS JUST... MINIMALISTIC.
I ALWAYS HAD THE RECORD COVER. I THOUGHT YOU LOOKED LIKE EASTER ISLAND STATUES. I THOUGHT YOU WERE DISTANT GODS AND GIANTS.
MARBLE GIANTS
COLOSSAL YOUTH
YOUR LESS WAS ALWAYS MORE.
IT WAS NECESSARY.
I HAD TO GIVE UP SOME THINGS I CARED ABOUT.
COLOSSAL YOUTH

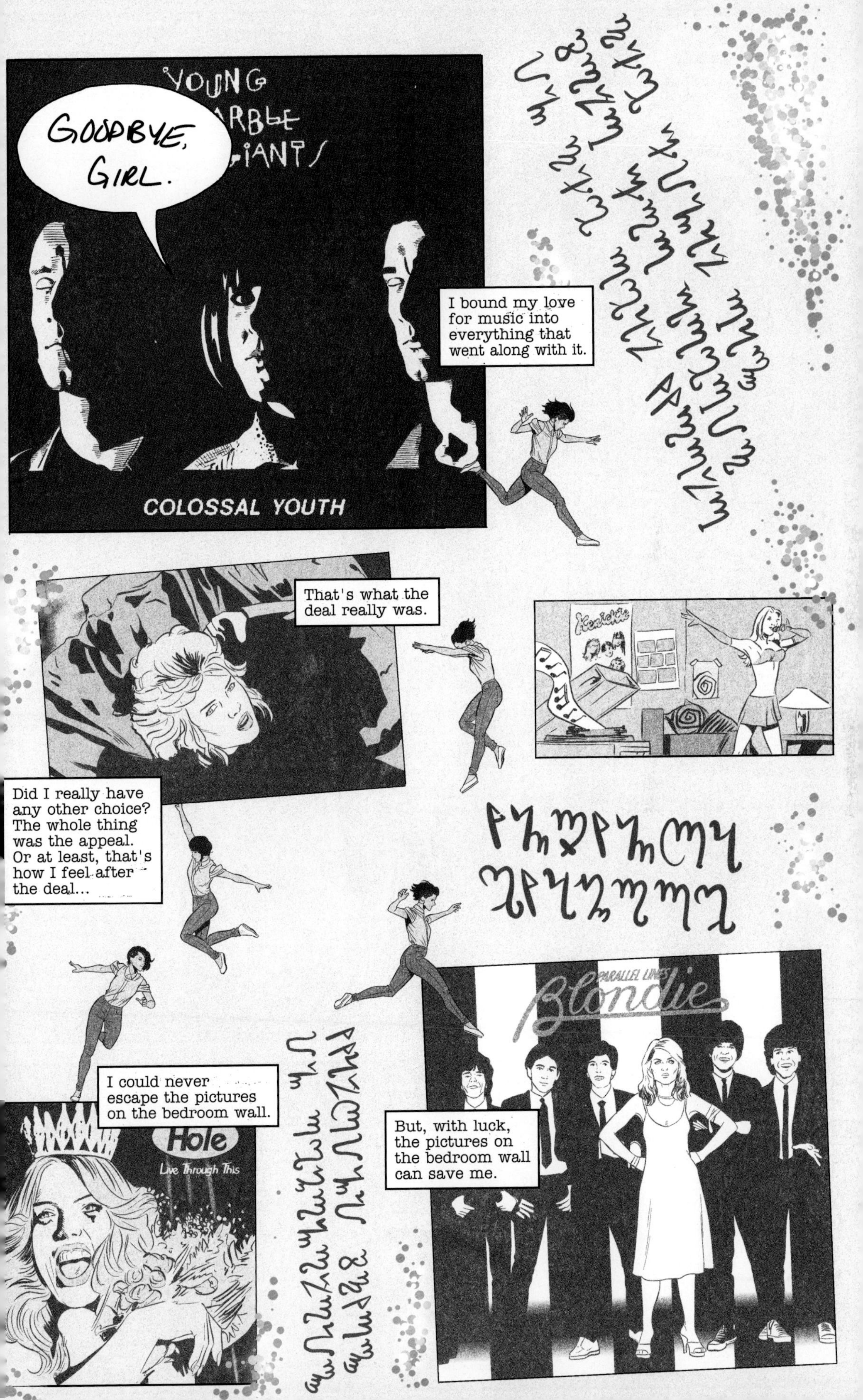
YOUNG
GOODBYE, GIRL.
COLOSSAL YOUTH
I bound my love for music into everything that went along with it.
That's what the deal really was.
Did I really have any other choice? The whole thing was the appeal. Or at least, that's how I feel after the deal...
I could never escape the pictures on the bedroom wall.
Hole
Live Through This
PARALLEL LINES
Blondie
But, with luck, the pictures on the bedroom wall can save me.

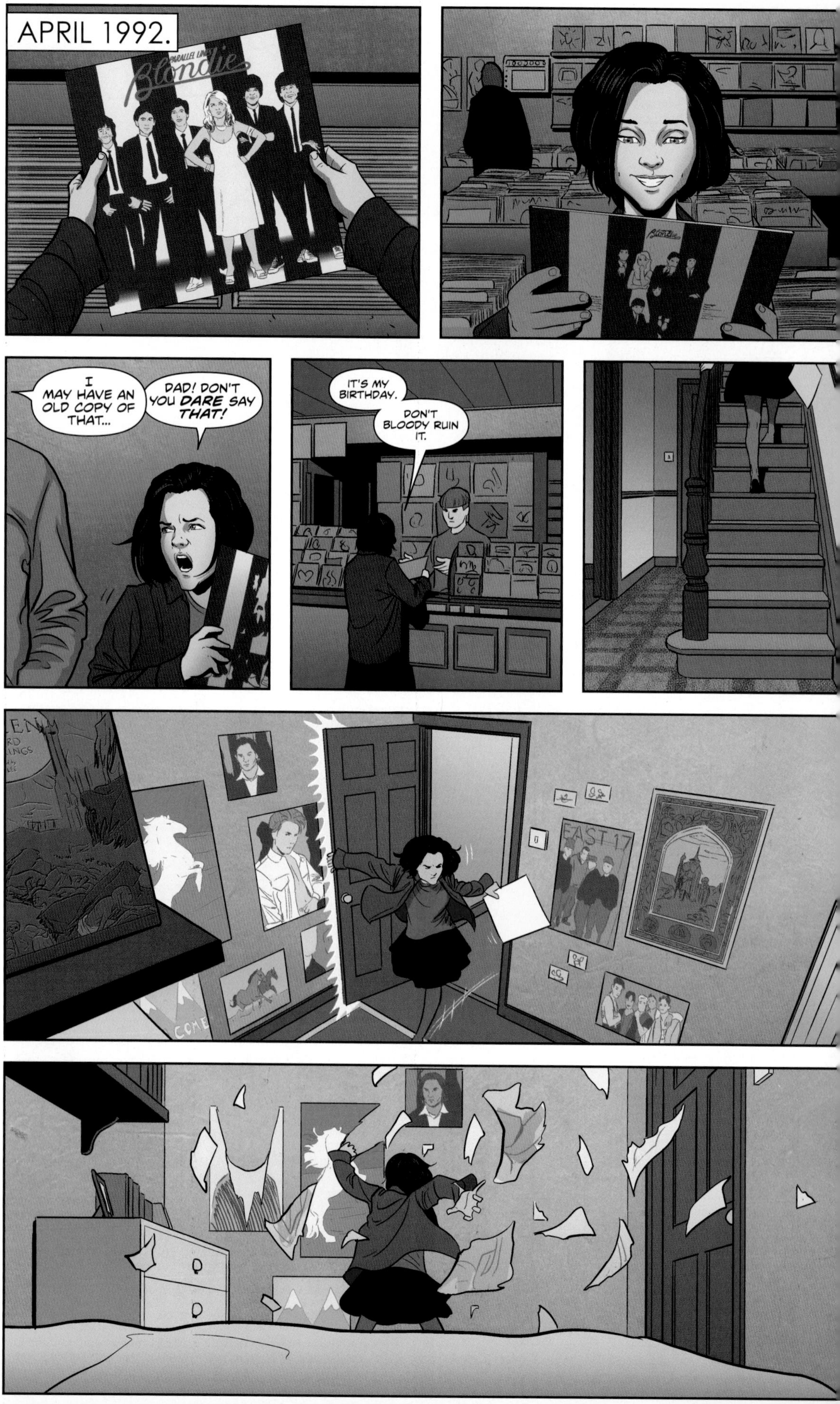

APRIL 1992.
PARALLEL LINES
Blondie
I MAY HAVE AN OLD COPY OF THAT...
DAD! DON'T YOU DARE SAY THAT!
IT'S MY BIRTHDAY.
DON'T BLOODY RUIN IT.
EAST 17

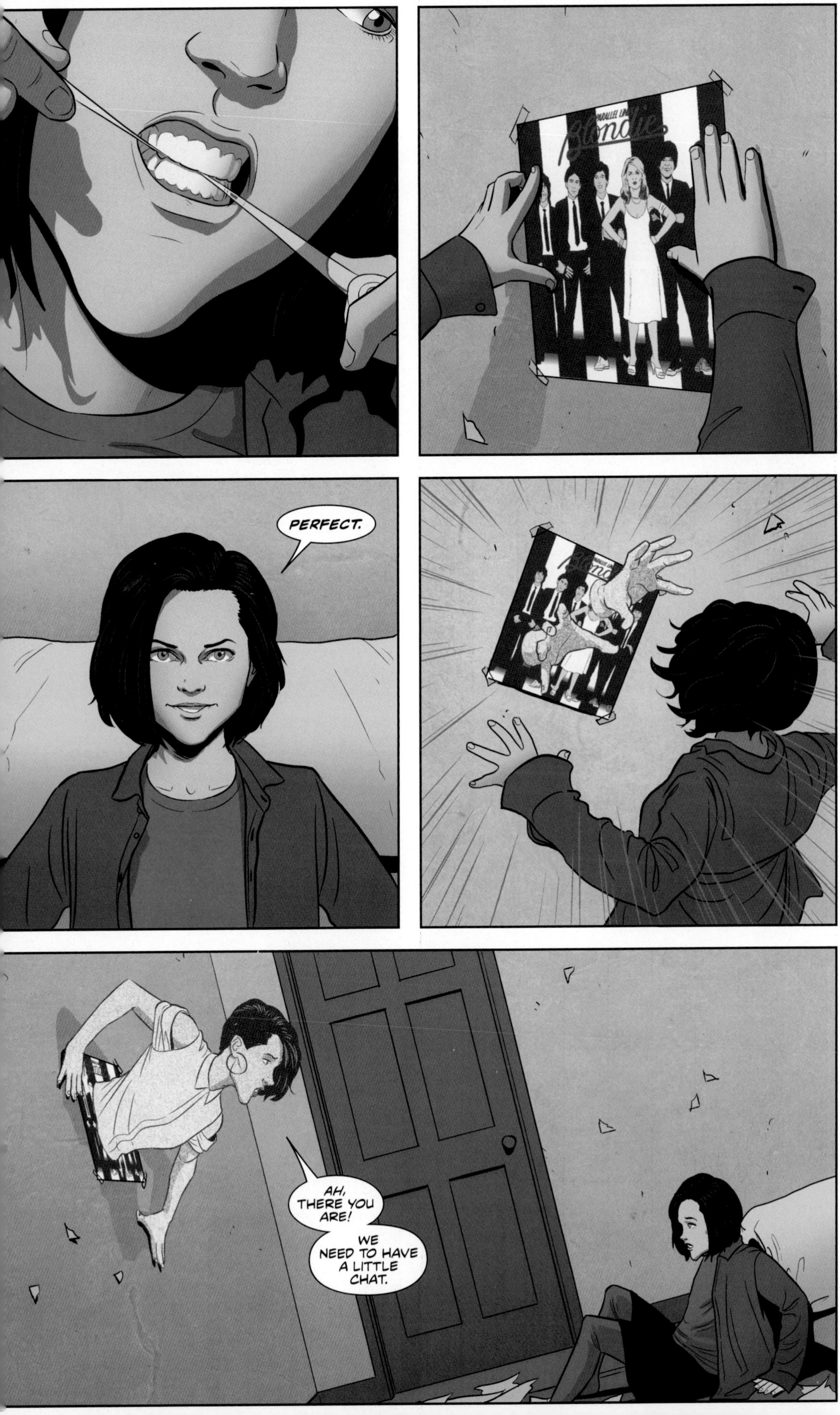

Blondie
PERFECT.
AH, THERE YOU ARE!
WE NEED TO HAVE A LITTLE CHAT.

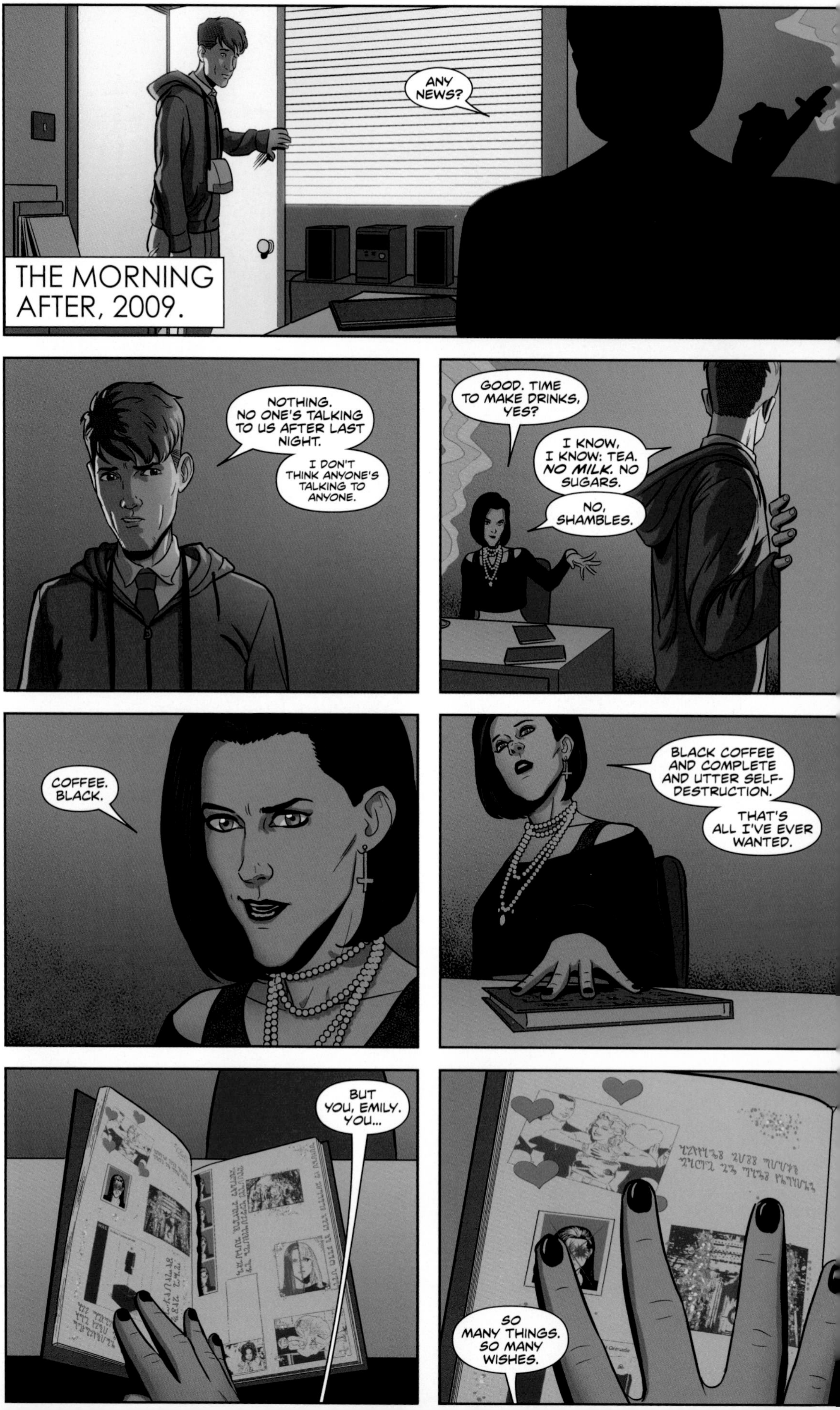
THE MORNING AFTER, 2009.
ANY NEWS?
NOTHING. NO ONE'S TALKING TO US AFTER LAST NIGHT.
I DON'T THINK ANYONE'S TALKING TO ANYONE.
GOOD. TIME TO MAKE DRINKS, YES?
I KNOW, I KNOW: TEA. NO MILK. NO SUGARS.
NO, SHAMBLES.
COFFEE. BLACK.
BLACK COFFEE AND COMPLETE AND UTTER SELF-DESTRUCTION.
THAT'S ALL I'VE EVER WANTED.
BUT YOU, EMILY. YOU...
SO MANY THINGS. SO MANY WISHES.

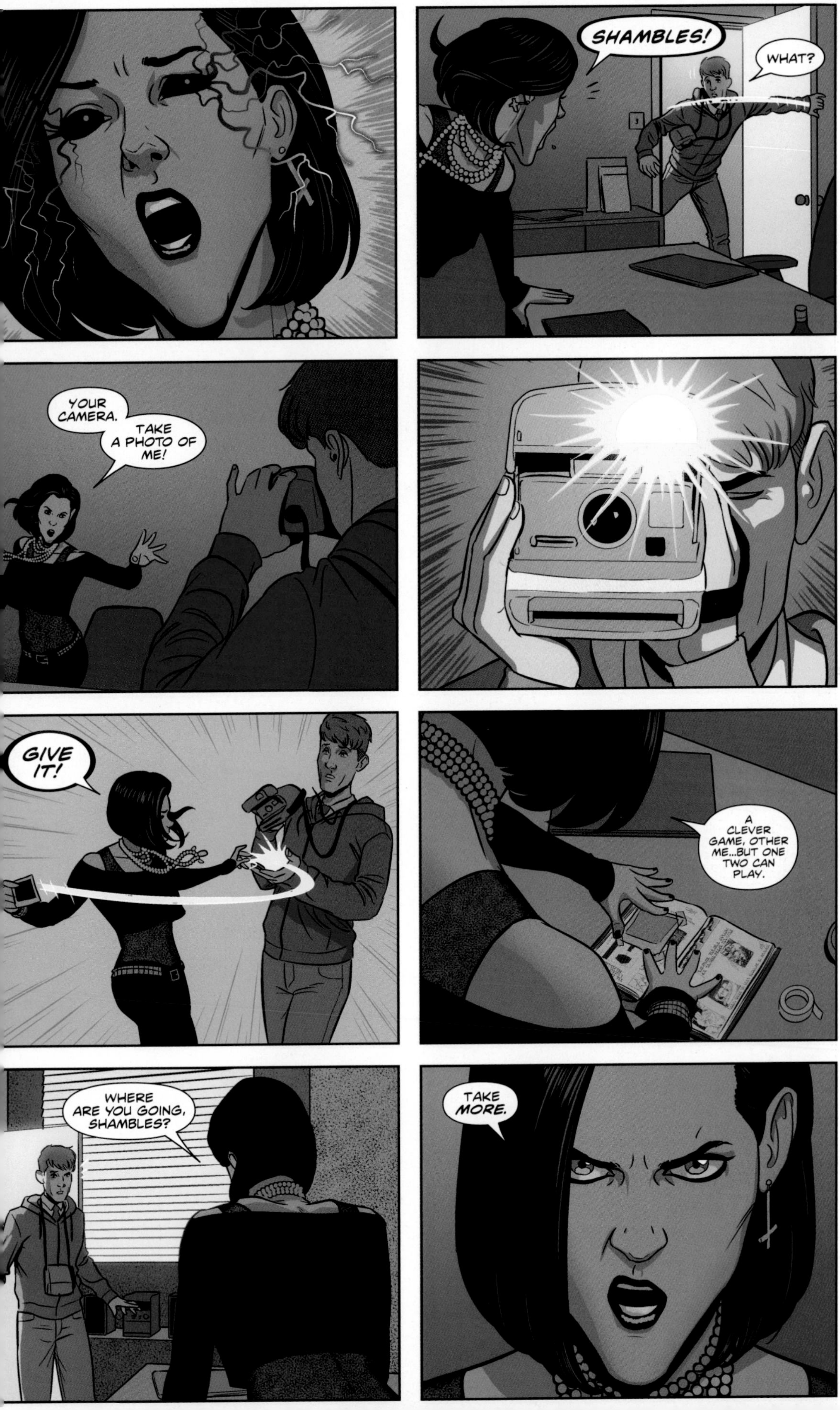
SHAMBLES!
WHAT?
YOUR CAMERA.
TAKE A PHOTO OF ME!
GIVE IT!
A CLEVER GAME, OTHER ME...BUT ONE TWO CAN PLAY.
WHERE ARE YOU GOING, SHAMBLES?
TAKE MORE.

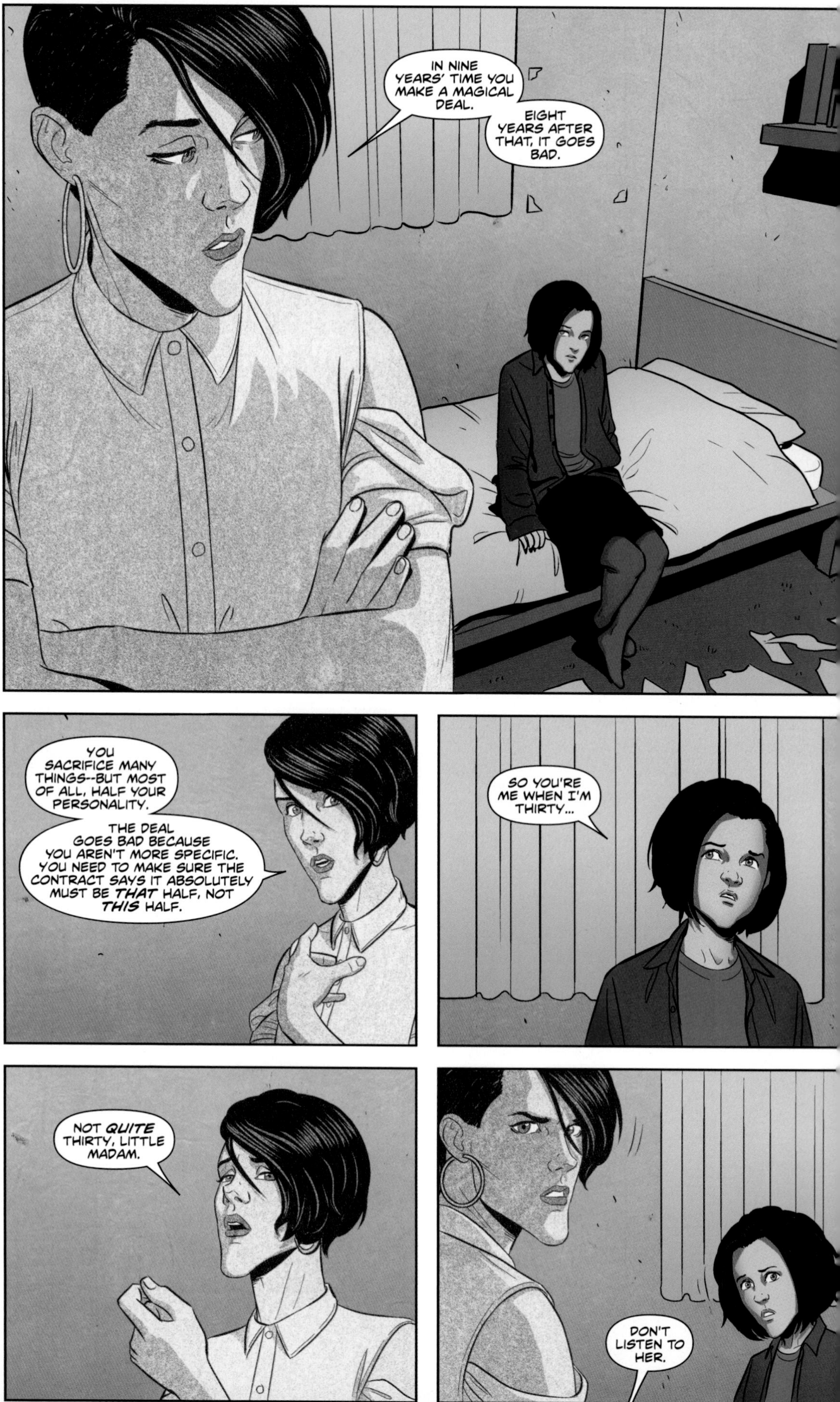
IN NINE YEARS' TIME YOU MAKE A MAGICAL DEAL.
EIGHT YEARS AFTER THAT, IT GOES BAD.
YOU SACRIFICE MANY THINGS--BUT MOST OF ALL, HALF YOUR PERSONALITY.
THE DEAL GOES BAD BECAUSE YOU AREN'T MORE SPECIFIC. YOU NEED TO MAKE SURE THE CONTRACT SAYS IT ABSOLUTELY MUST BE *THAT* HALF, NOT *THIS* HALF.
SO YOU'RE ME WHEN I'M THIRTY...
NOT *QUITE* THIRTY, LITTLE MADAM.
DON'T LISTEN TO HER.

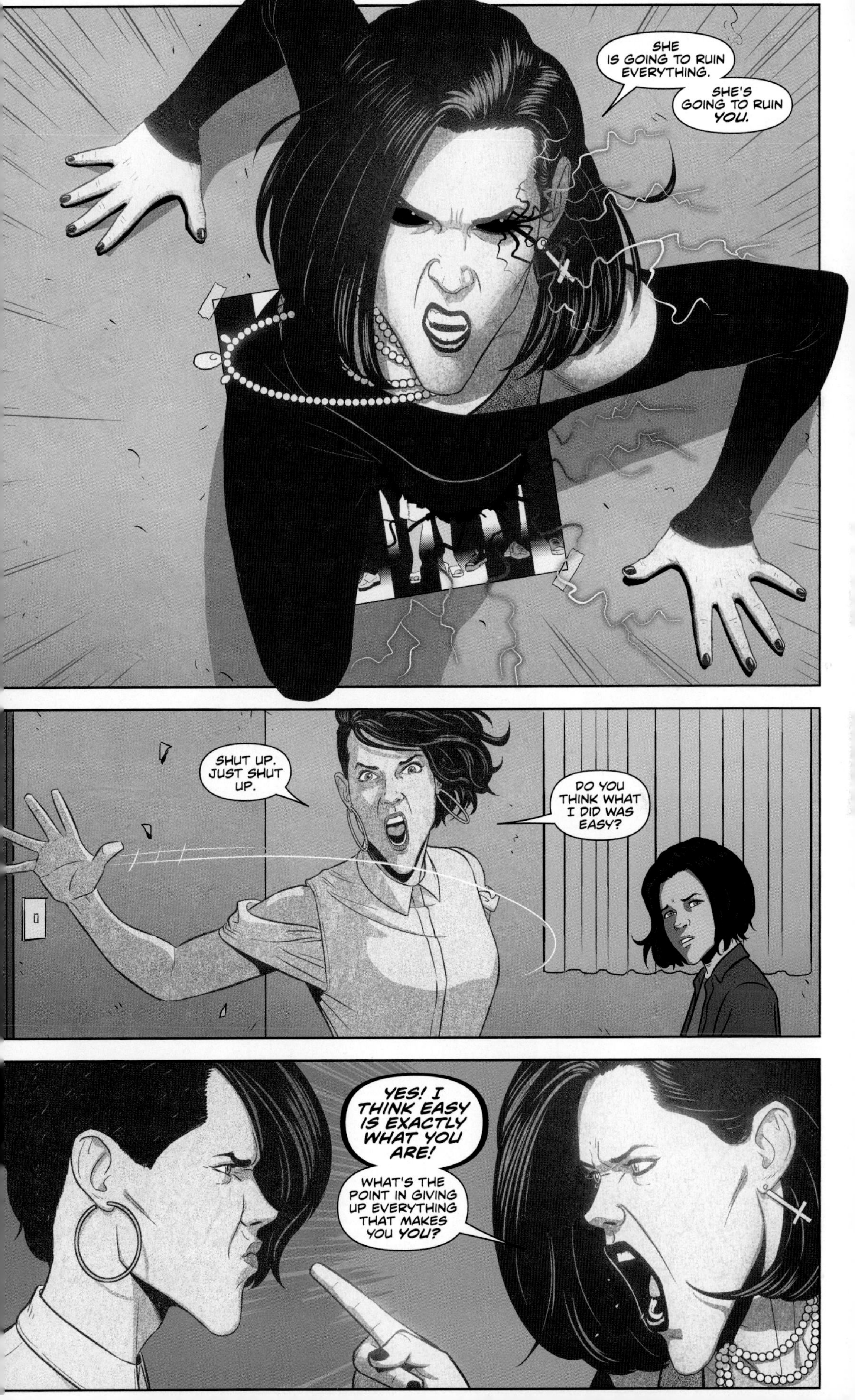
SHE IS GOING TO RUIN EVERYTHING.
SHE'S GOING TO RUIN *YOU.*
SHUT UP. JUST SHUT UP.
DO YOU THINK WHAT I DID WAS EASY?
YES! I THINK EASY IS EXACTLY WHAT YOU ARE!
WHAT'S THE POINT IN GIVING UP EVERYTHING THAT MAKES YOU *YOU?*

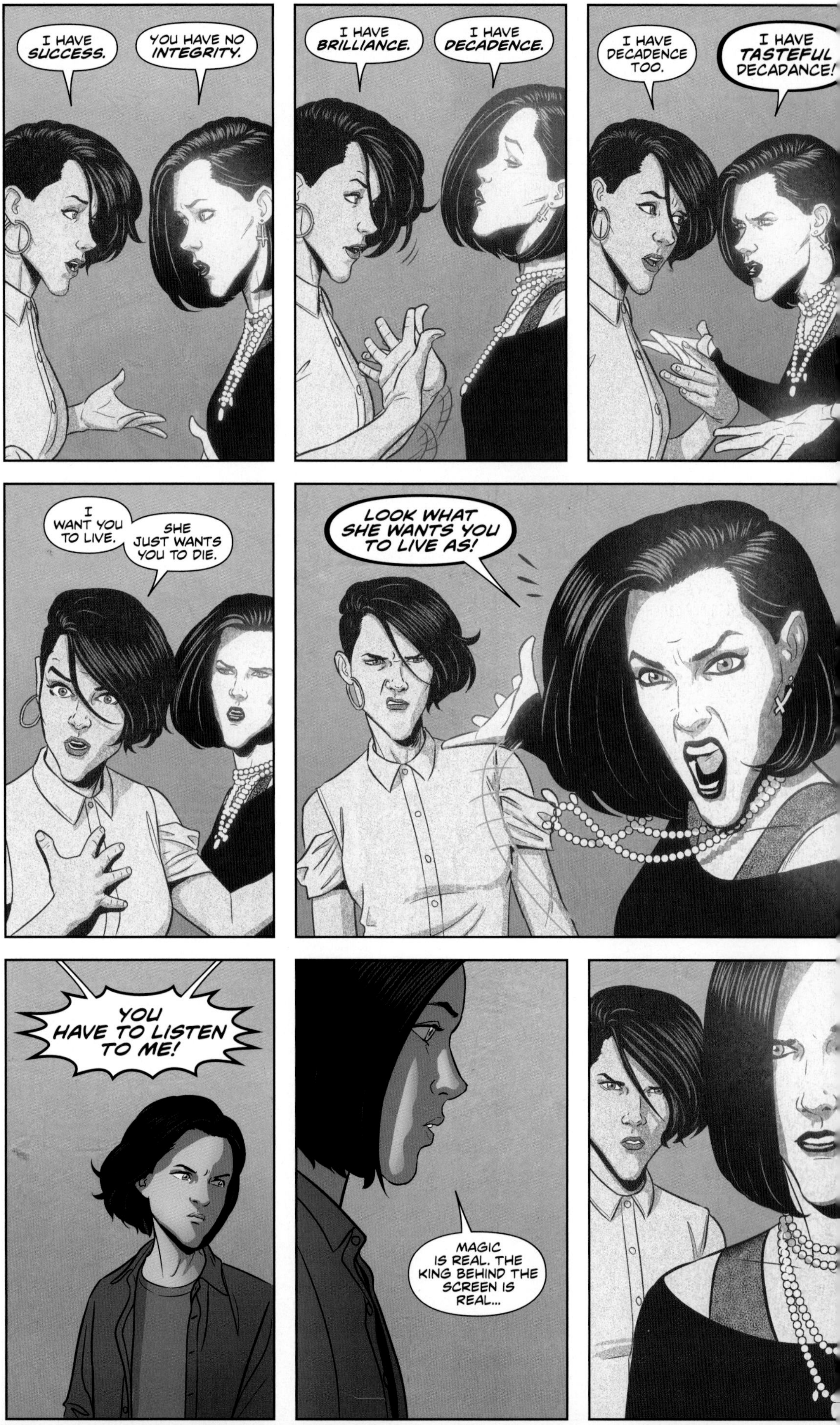
I HAVE SUCCESS.
YOU HAVE NO INTEGRITY.
I HAVE BRILLIANCE.
I HAVE DECADENCE.
I HAVE DECADENCE TOO.
I HAVE TASTEFUL DECADANCE!
I WANT YOU TO LIVE.
SHE JUST WANTS YOU TO DIE.
LOOK WHAT SHE WANTS YOU TO LIVE AS!
YOU HAVE TO LISTEN TO ME!
MAGIC IS REAL. THE KING BEHIND THE SCREEN IS REAL...

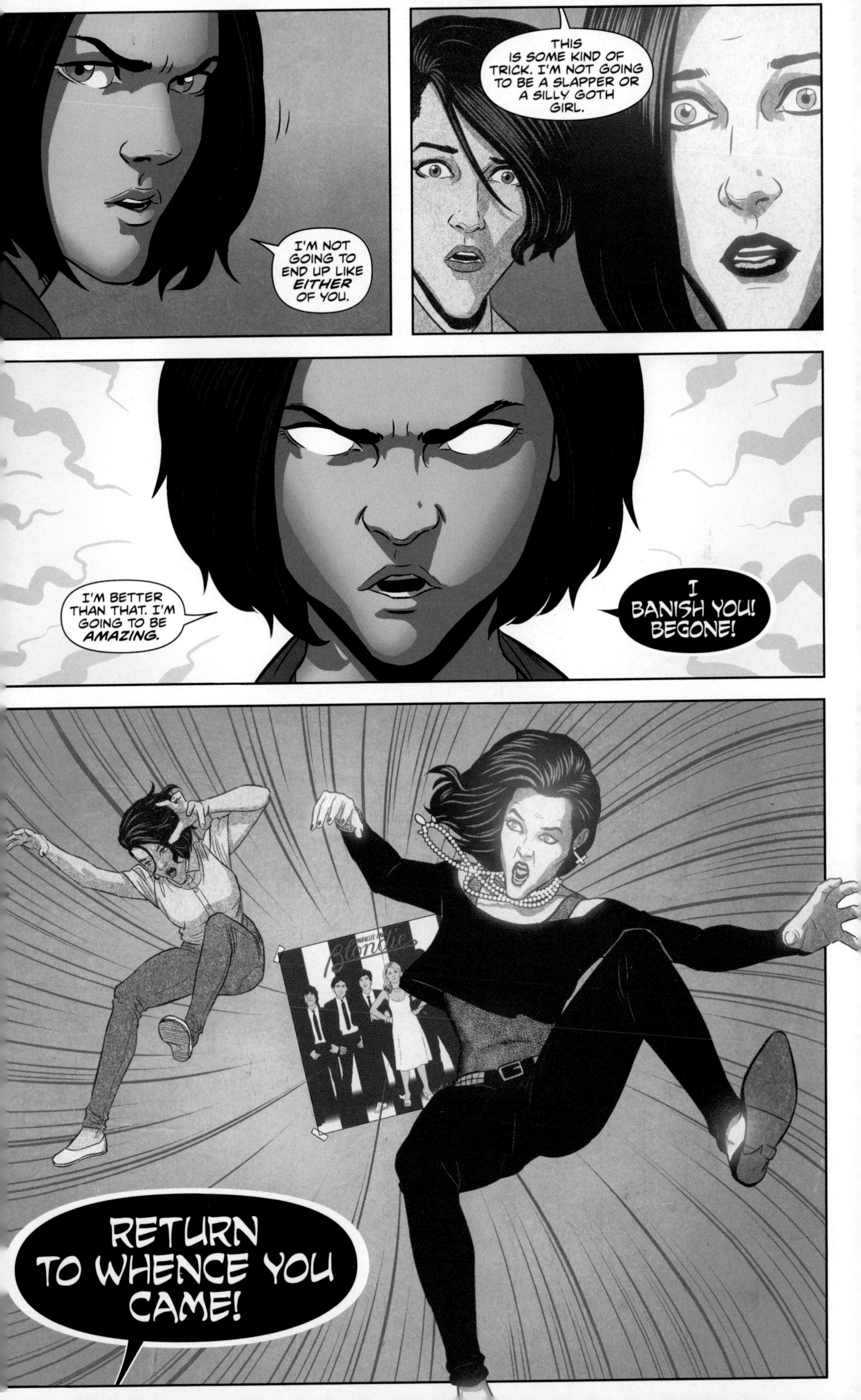

I'M NOT GOING TO END UP LIKE EITHER OF YOU.
THIS IS SOME KIND OF TRICK. I'M NOT GOING TO BE A SLAPPER OR A SILLY GOTH GIRL.
I'M BETTER THAN THAT. I'M GOING TO BE AMAZING.
I BANISH YOU! BEGONE!
Blondie
RETURN TO WHENCE YOU CAME!

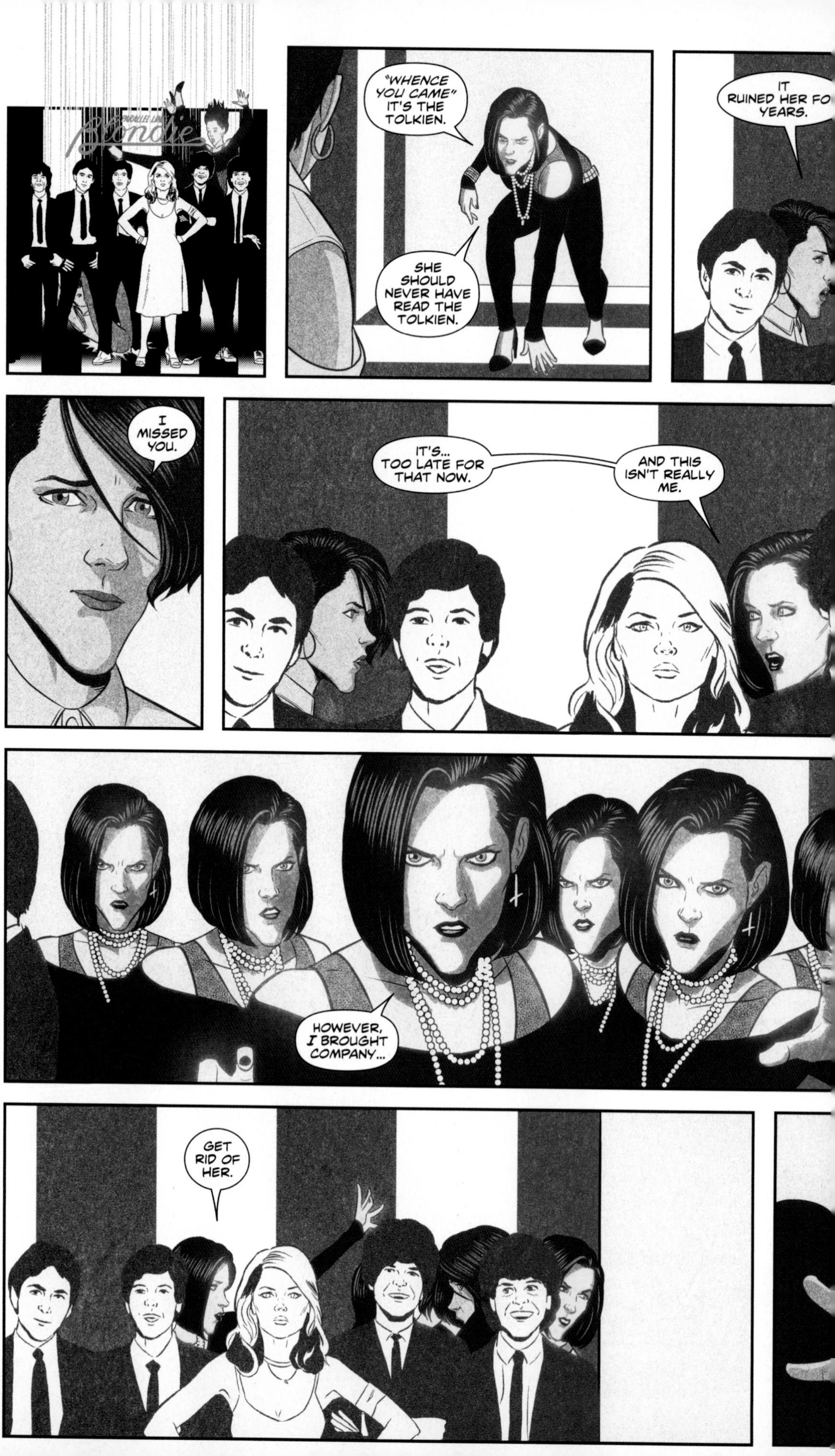
PARALLEL LINES
Blondie
"WHENCE YOU CAME" IT'S THE TOLKIEN.
SHE SHOULD NEVER HAVE READ THE TOLKIEN.
IT RUINED HER FO YEARS.
I MISSED YOU.
IT'S... TOO LATE FOR THAT NOW.
AND THIS ISN'T REALLY ME.
HOWEVER, I BROUGHT COMPANY...
GET RID OF HER.

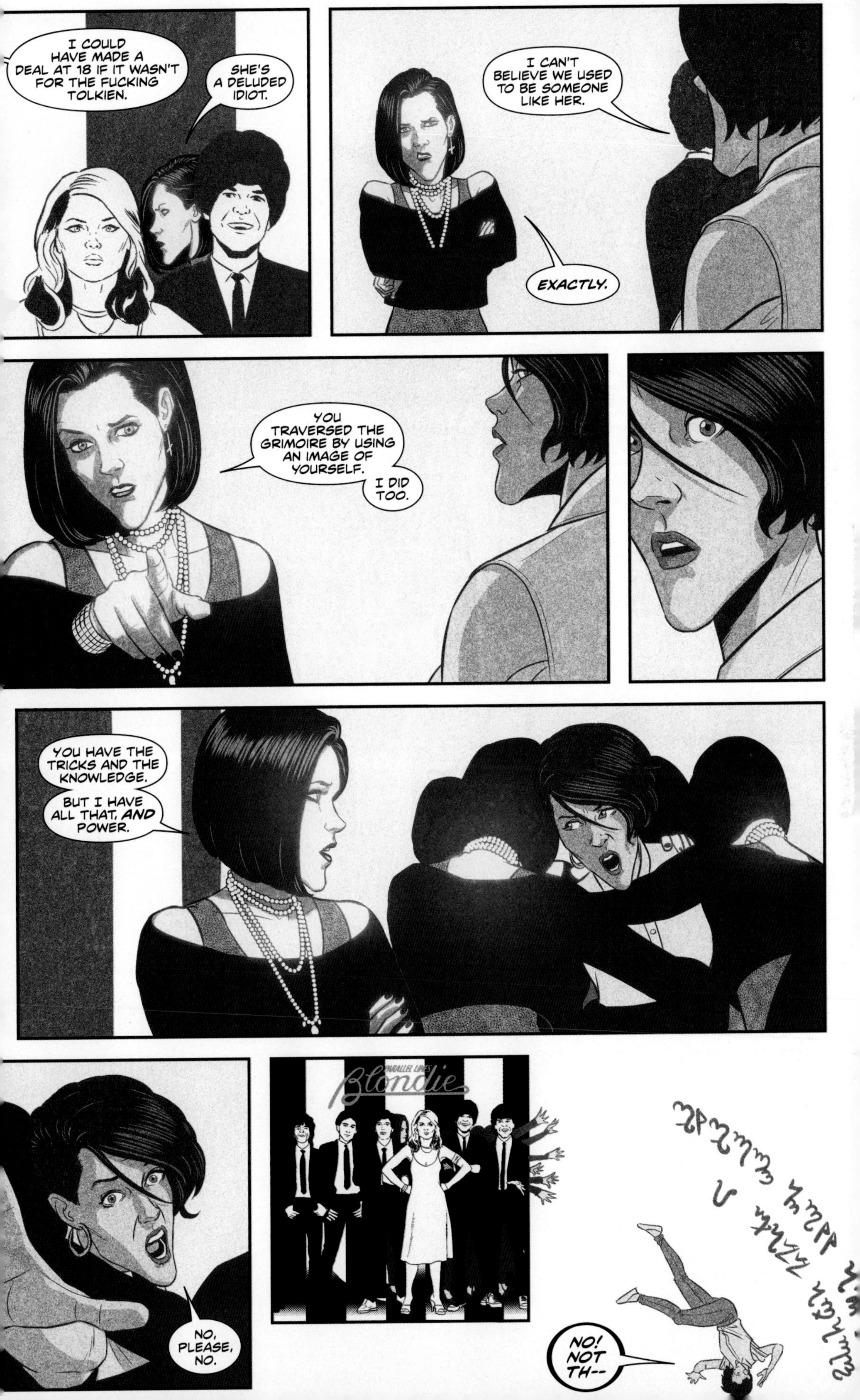
I COULD HAVE MADE A DEAL AT 18 IF IT WASN'T FOR THE FUCKING TOLKIEN.
SHE'S A DELUDED IDIOT.
I CAN'T BELIEVE WE USED TO BE SOMEONE LIKE HER.
EXACTLY.
YOU TRAVERSED THE GRIMOIRE BY USING AN IMAGE OF YOURSELF.
I DID TOO.
YOU HAVE THE TRICKS AND THE KNOWLEDGE.
BUT I HAVE ALL THAT, AND POWER.
NO, PLEASE, NO.
PARALLEL LINES
Blondie
NO! NOT TH--

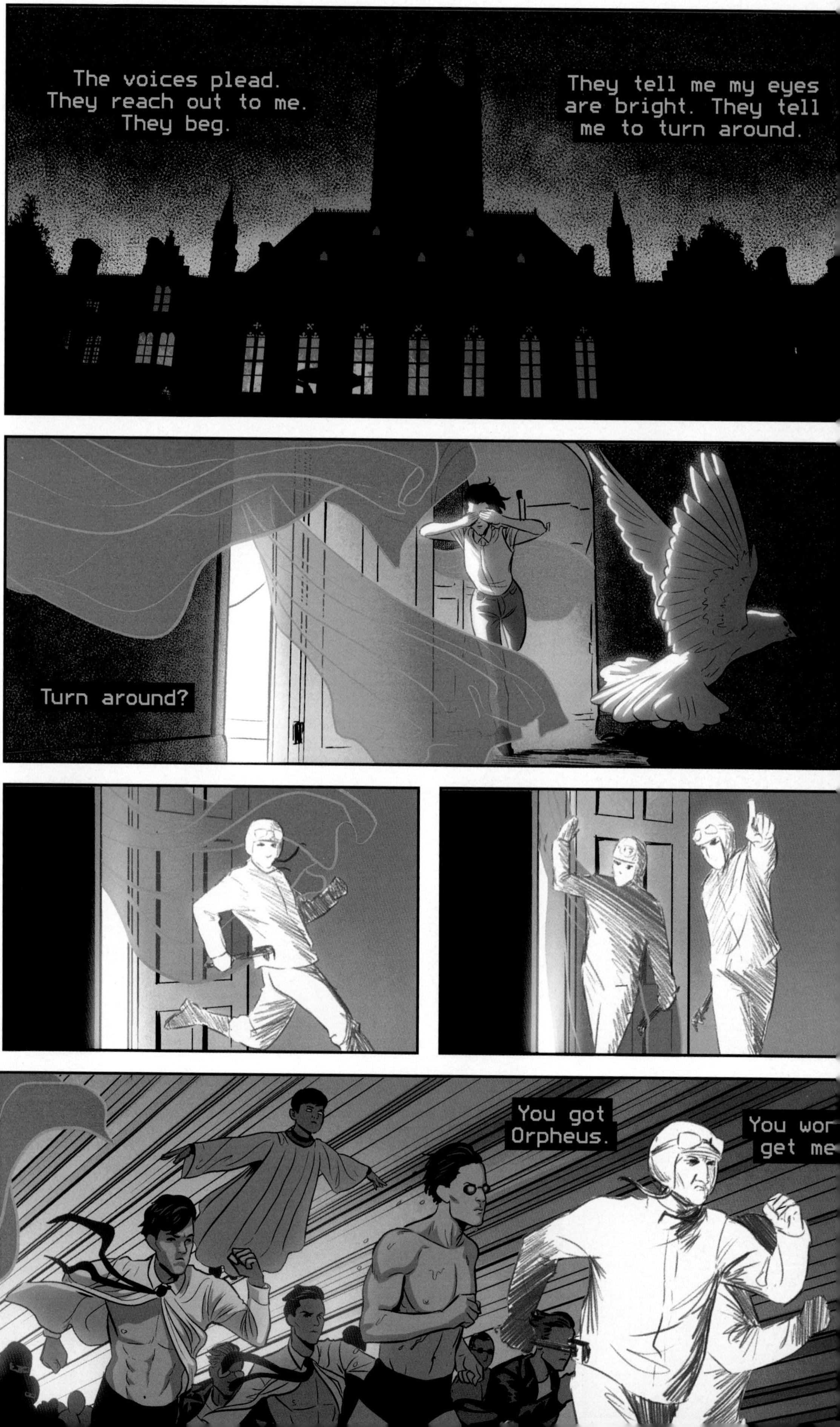
The voices plead.
They reach out to me.
They beg.
They tell me my eyes are bright. They tell me to turn around.
Turn around?
You got Orpheus.
You wor
get me

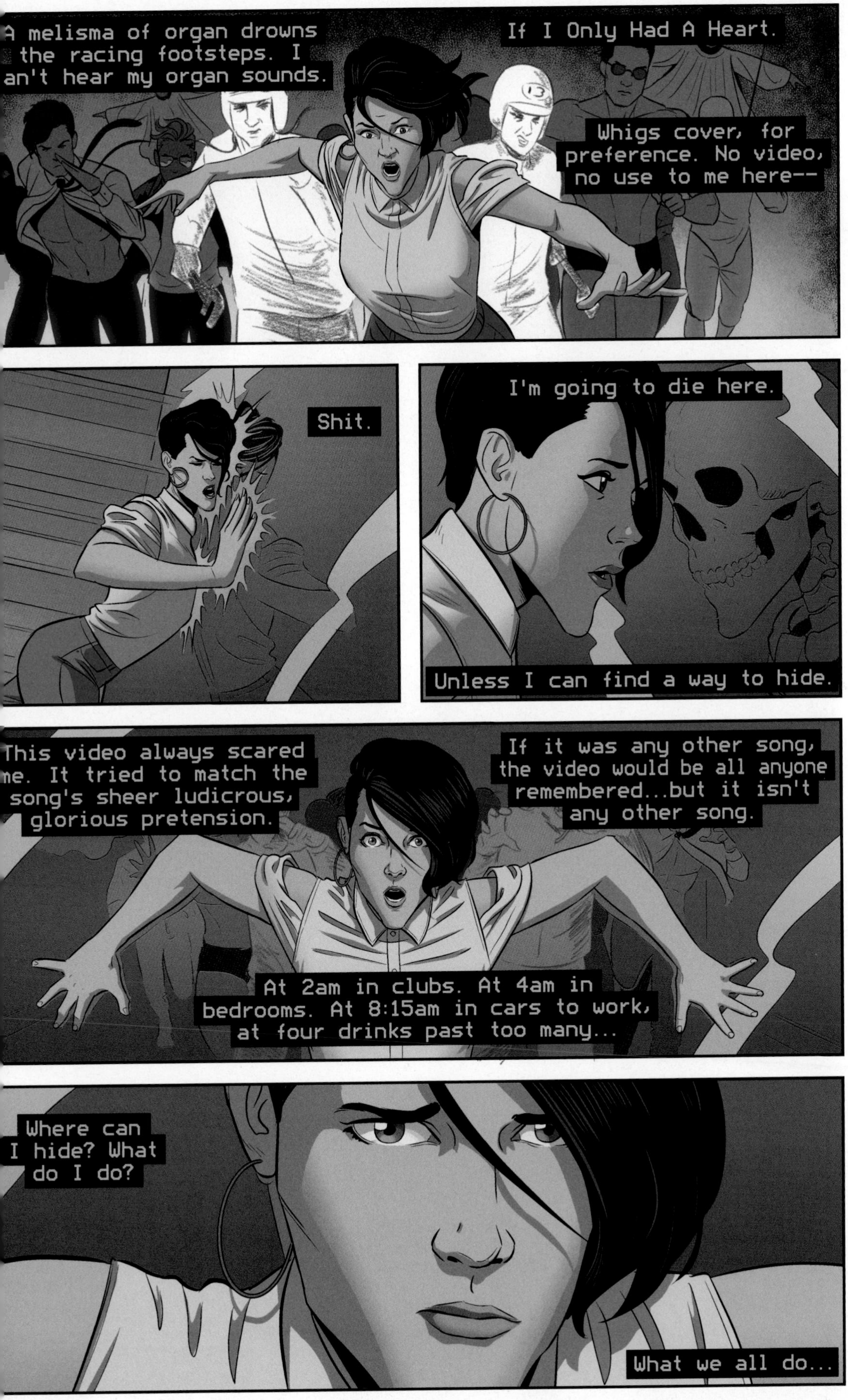

A melisma of organ drowns
the racing footsteps. I
can't hear my organ sounds.
If I Only Had A Heart.
Whigs cover, for preference. No video, no use to me here--
Shit.
I'm going to die here.
Unless I can find a way to hide.
This video always scared me. It tried to match the song's sheer ludicrous, glorious pretension.
If it was any other song, the video would be all anyone remembered...but it isn't any other song.
At 2am in clubs. At 4am in bedrooms. At 8:15am in cars to work, at four drinks past too many...
Where can I hide? What do I do?
What we all do...

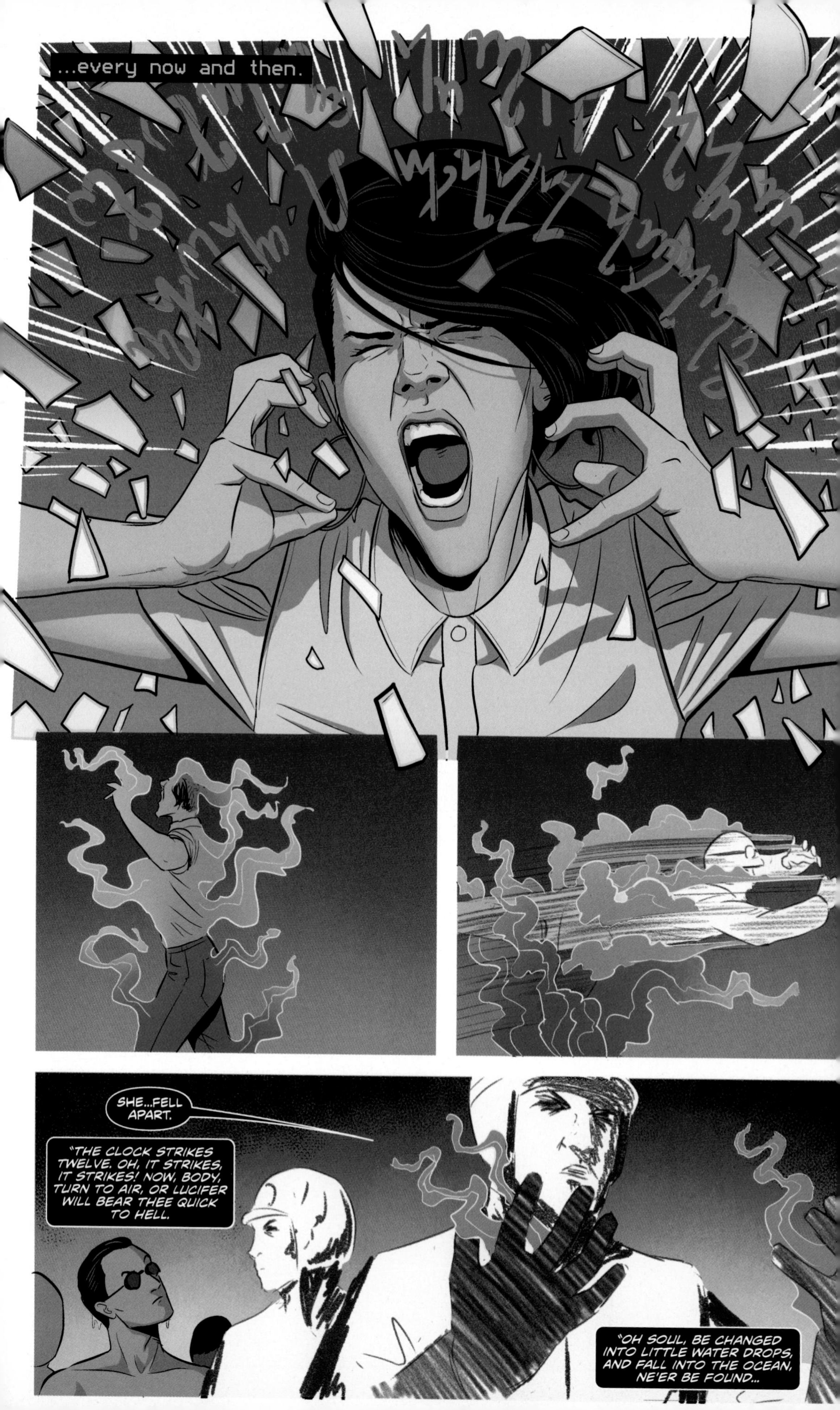
...every now and then.
SHE...FELL APART.
"THE CLOCK STRIKES TWELVE. OH, IT STRIKES, IT STRIKES! NOW, BODY, TURN TO AIR, OR LUCIFER WILL BEAR THEE QUICK TO HELL.
"OH SOUL, BE CHANGED INTO LITTLE WATER DROPS, AND FALL INTO THE OCEAN, NE'ER BE FOUND...

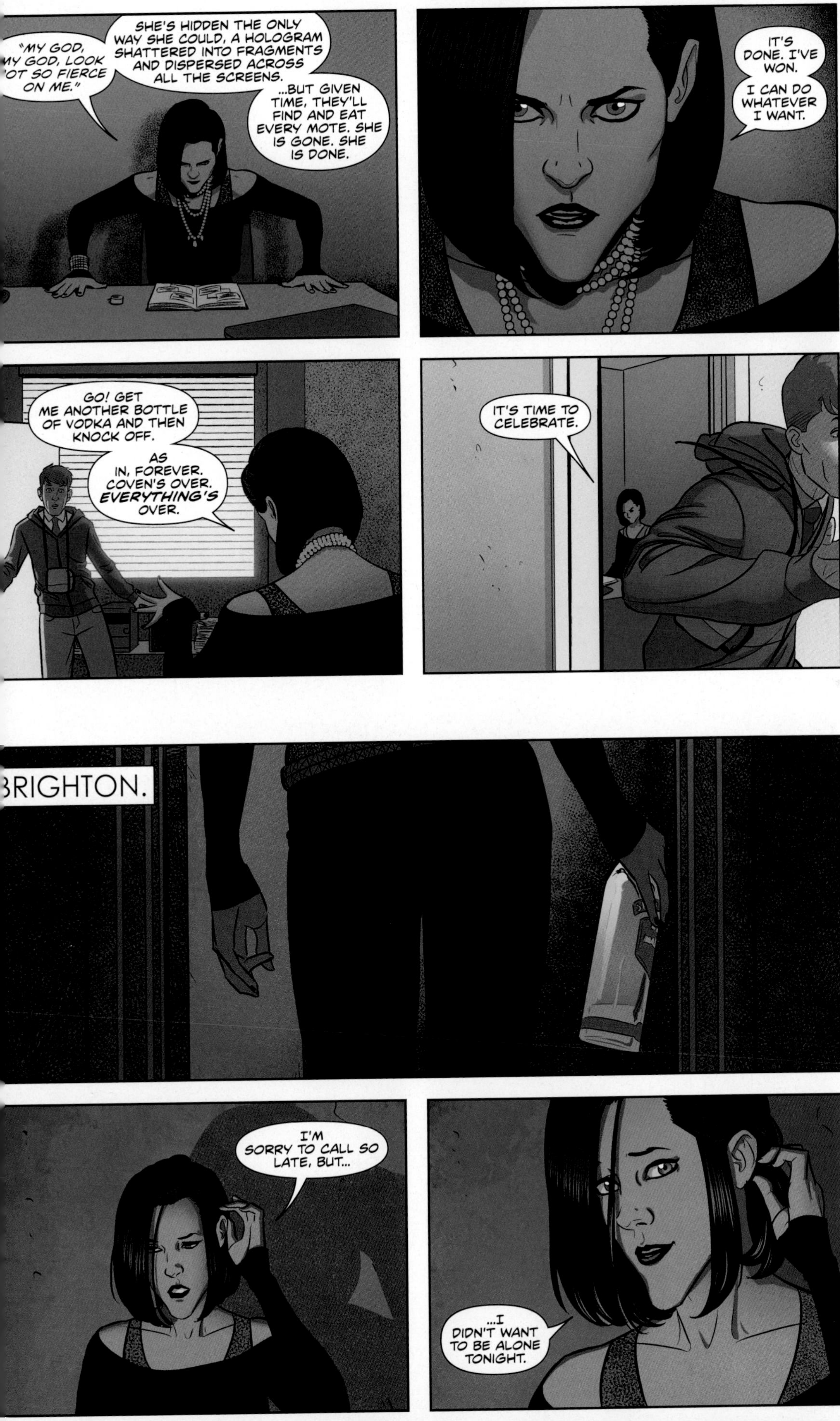
"MY GOD, MY GOD, LOOK NOT SO FIERCE ON ME."
SHE'S HIDDEN THE ONLY WAY SHE COULD, A HOLOGRAM SHATTERED INTO FRAGMENTS AND DISPERSED ACROSS ALL THE SCREENS.
...BUT GIVEN TIME, THEY'LL FIND AND EAT EVERY MOTE. SHE IS GONE. SHE IS DONE.
IT'S DONE. I'VE WON.
I CAN DO WHATEVER I WANT.
GO! GET ME ANOTHER BOTTLE OF VODKA AND THEN KNOCK OFF.
AS IN, FOREVER. COVEN'S OVER. EVERYTHING'S OVER.
IT'S TIME TO CELEBRATE.
BRIGHTON.
I'M SORRY TO CALL SO LATE, BUT...
...I DIDN'T WANT TO BE ALONE TONIGHT.

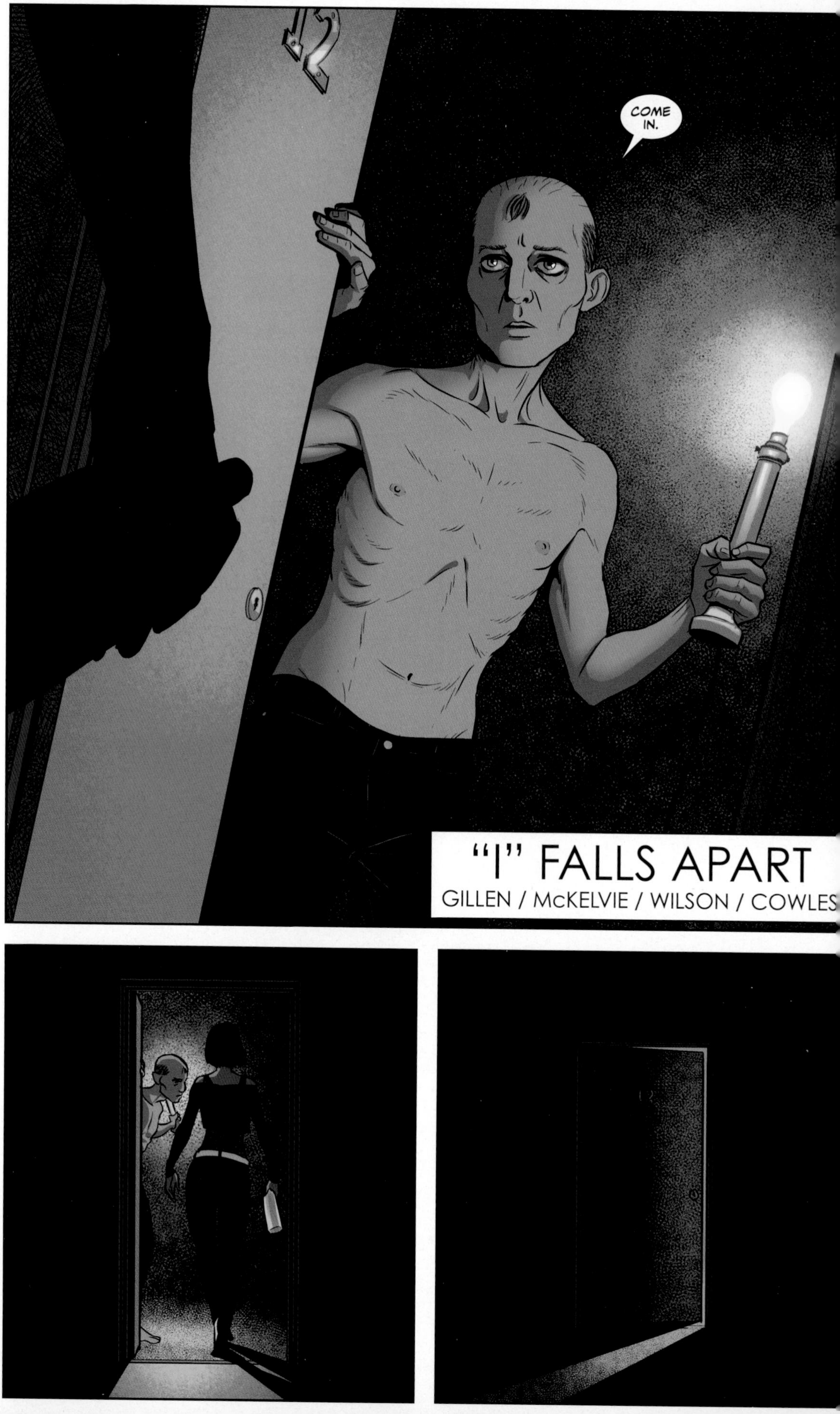
COME IN.
"I" FALLS APART
GILLEN / McKELVIE / WILSON / COWLES

PHONOGRAM

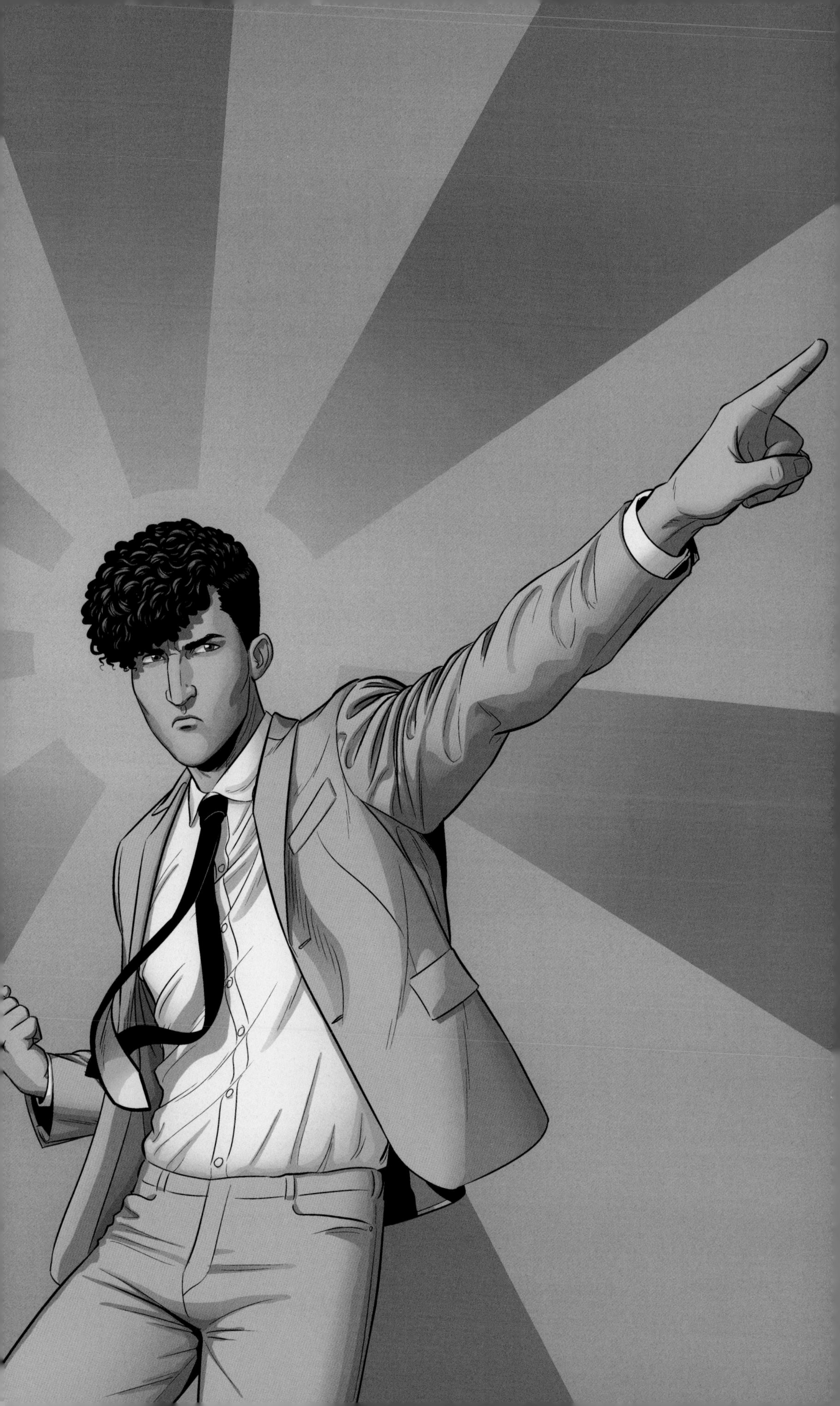

(LET'S MAKE THIS) PRECIOUS LITTLE LIFE

GILLEN / McKELVIE / WILSON / COWLES

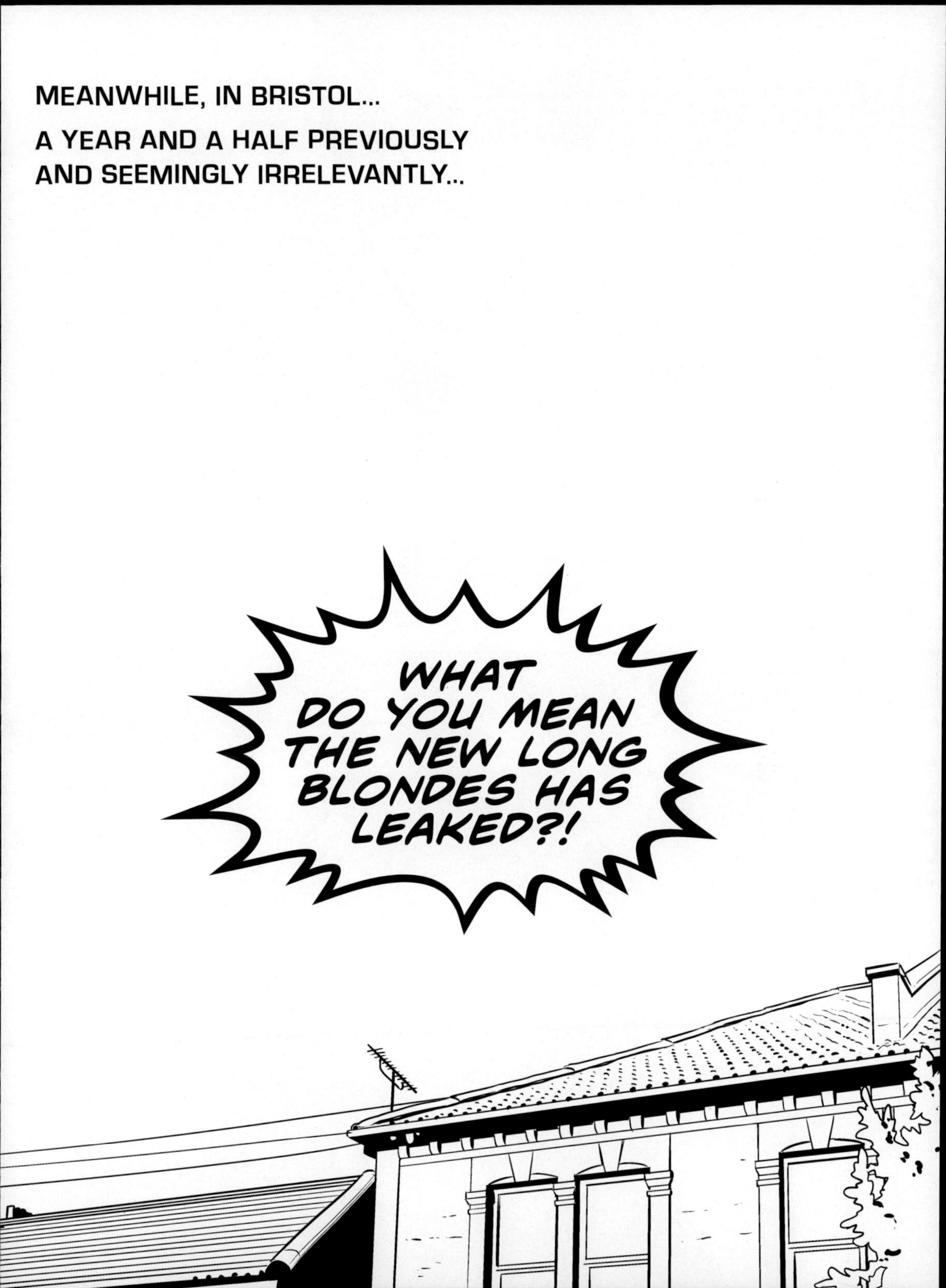
MEANWHILE, IN BRISTOL...
A YEAR AND A HALF PREVIOUSLY AND SEEMINGLY IRRELEVANTLY...
WHAT DO YOU MEAN THE NEW LONG BLONDES HAS LEAKED?!

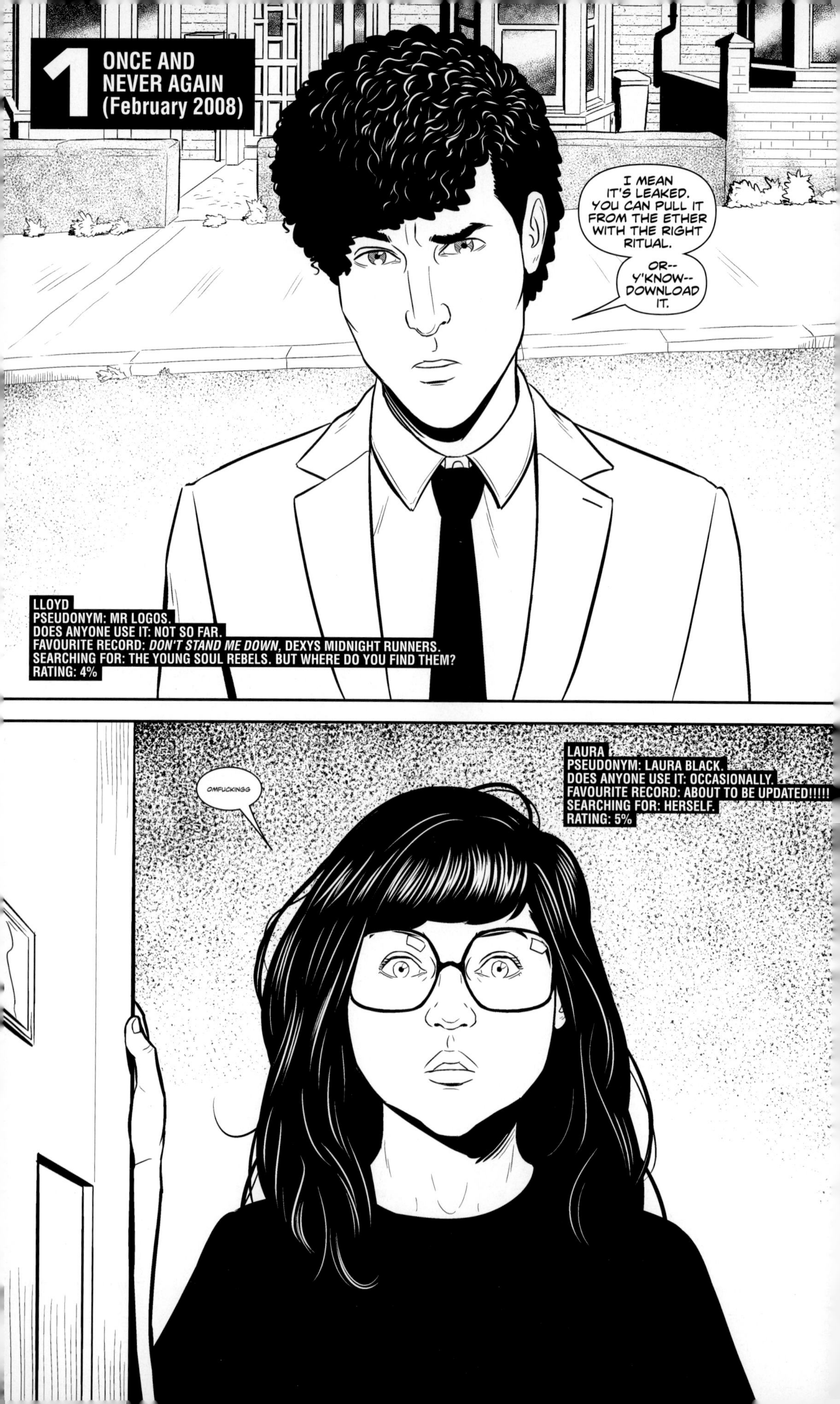
1 ONCE AND NEVER AGAIN (February 2008)
I MEAN IT'S LEAKED. YOU CAN PULL IT FROM THE ETHER WITH THE RIGHT RITUAL.
OR-- Y'KNOW-- DOWNLOAD IT.
LLOYD
PSEUDONYM: MR LOGOS.
DOES ANYONE USE IT: NOT SO FAR.
FAVOURITE RECORD: DON'T STAND ME DOWN, DEXYS MIDNIGHT RUNNERS.
SEARCHING FOR: THE YOUNG SOUL REBELS. BUT WHERE DO YOU FIND THEM?
RATING: 4%
LAURA
PSEUDONYM: LAURA BLACK.
DOES ANYONE USE IT: OCCASIONALLY.
FAVOURITE RECORD: ABOUT TO BE UPDATED!!!!!
SEARCHING FOR: HERSELF.
RATING: 5%
OMFUCKINGG

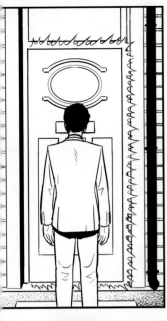

YOU HATE ME. I HATE YOU **AGGRESSIVELY.** AFTER ALL I'VE SAID TO YOU...THIS? WHY?

I DON'T CARE ABOUT YOU...

...BUT I DO UNDERSTAND WHAT IT MEANS TO CARE ABOUT SOMETHING.

THANK YOU.

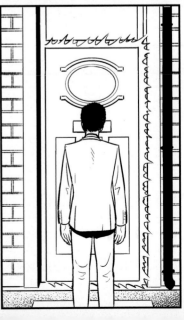

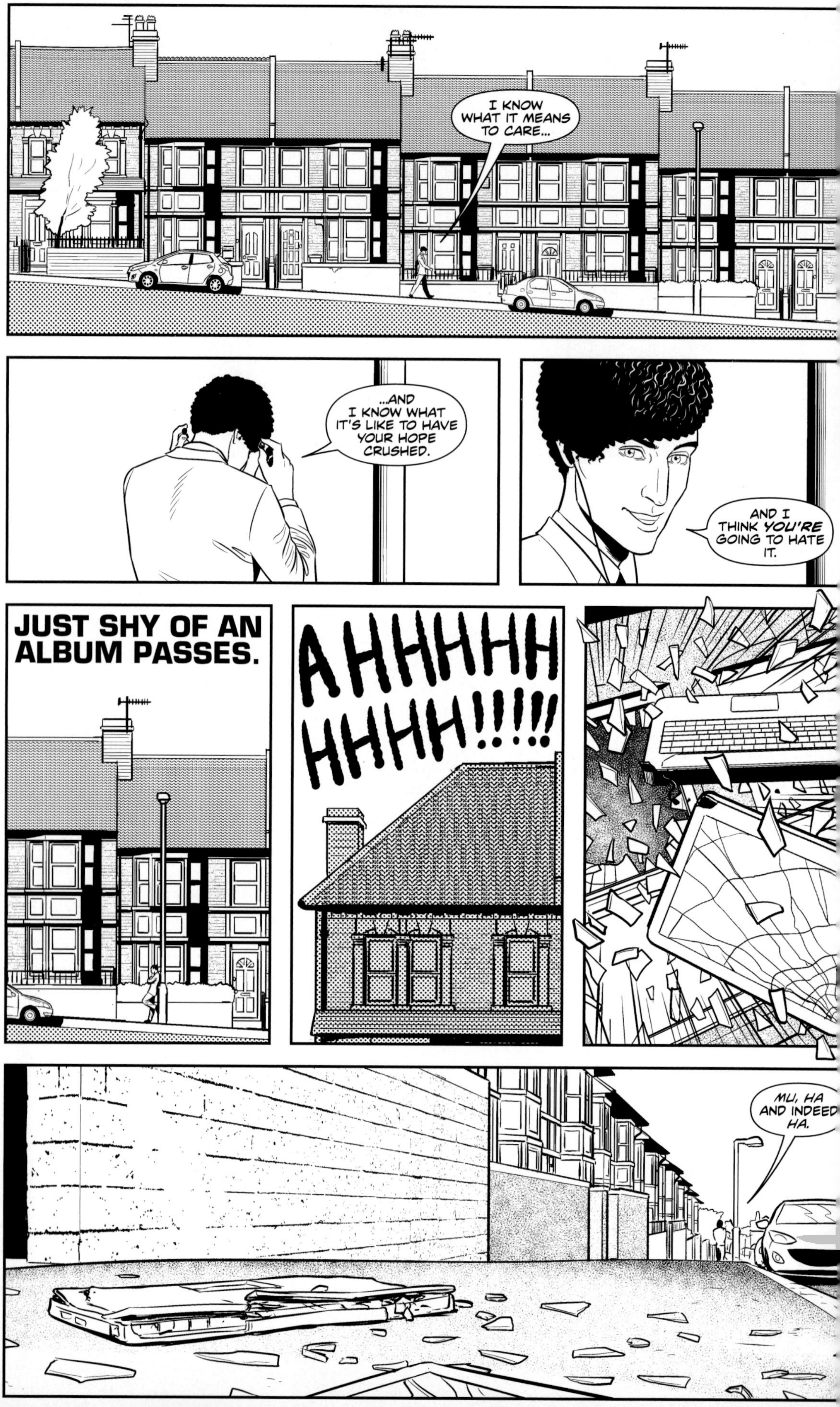
I KNOW WHAT IT MEANS TO CARE...
...AND I KNOW WHAT IT'S LIKE TO HAVE YOUR HOPE CRUSHED.
AND I THINK YOU'RE GOING TO HATE IT.
JUST SHY OF AN ALBUM PASSES.
AHHHHHHHHH!!!!!
MU, HA AND INDEED HA.

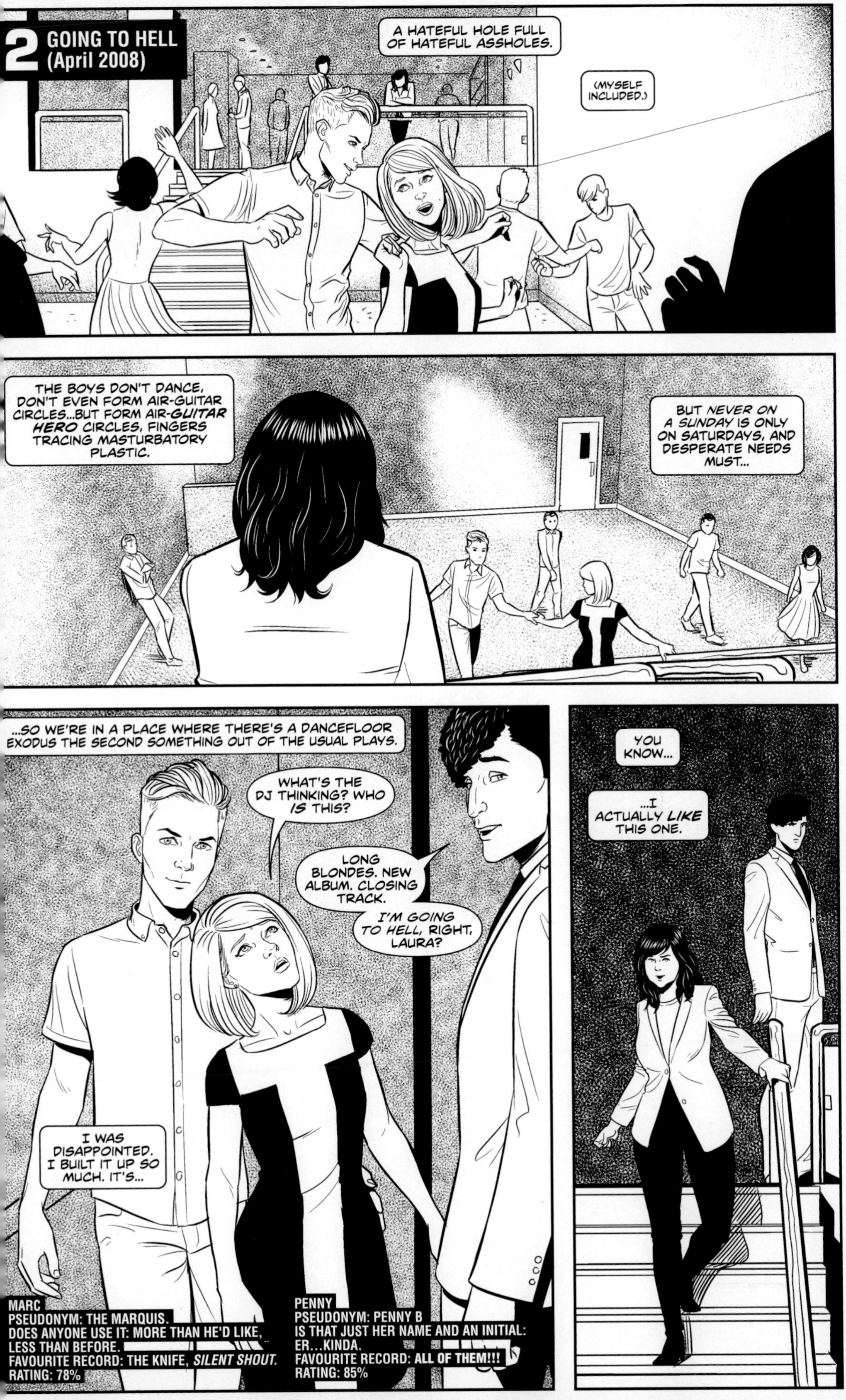
2 GOING TO HELL (April 2008)
A HATEFUL HOLE FULL OF HATEFUL ASSHOLES.
(MYSELF INCLUDED.)
THE BOYS DON'T DANCE, DON'T EVEN FORM AIR-GUITAR CIRCLES...BUT FORM AIR-GUITAR HERO CIRCLES, FINGERS TRACING MASTURBATORY PLASTIC.
BUT NEVER ON A SUNDAY IS ONLY ON SATURDAYS, AND DESPERATE NEEDS MUST...
...SO WE'RE IN A PLACE WHERE THERE'S A DANCEFLOOR EXODUS THE SECOND SOMETHING OUT OF THE USUAL PLAYS.
WHAT'S THE DJ THINKING? WHO IS THIS?
LONG BLONDES. NEW ALBUM. CLOSING TRACK.
I'M GOING TO HELL, RIGHT, LAURA?
I WAS DISAPPOINTED. I BUILT IT UP SO MUCH. IT'S...
MARC
PSEUDONYM: THE MARQUIS.
DOES ANYONE USE IT: MORE THAN HE'D LIKE, LESS THAN BEFORE.
FAVOURITE RECORD: THE KNIFE, SILENT SHOUT.
RATING: 78%
PENNY
PSEUDONYM: PENNY B
IS THAT JUST HER NAME AND AN INITIAL: ER...KINDA.
FAVOURITE RECORD: ALL OF THEM!!!
RATING: 85%
YOU KNOW...
...I ACTUALLY LIKE THIS ONE.

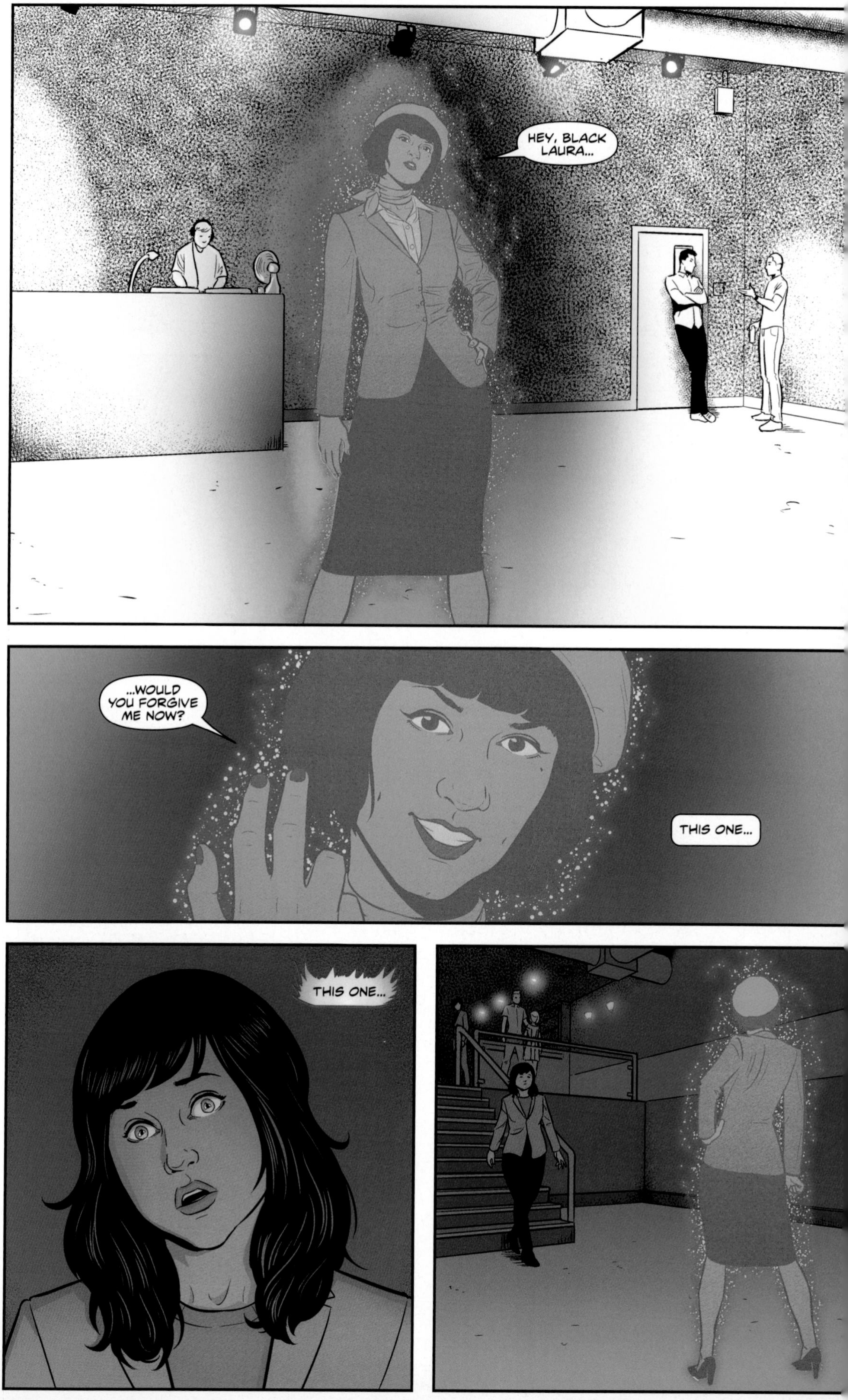
HEY, BLACK LAURA...
...WOULD YOU FORGIVE ME NOW?
THIS ONE...
THIS ONE...

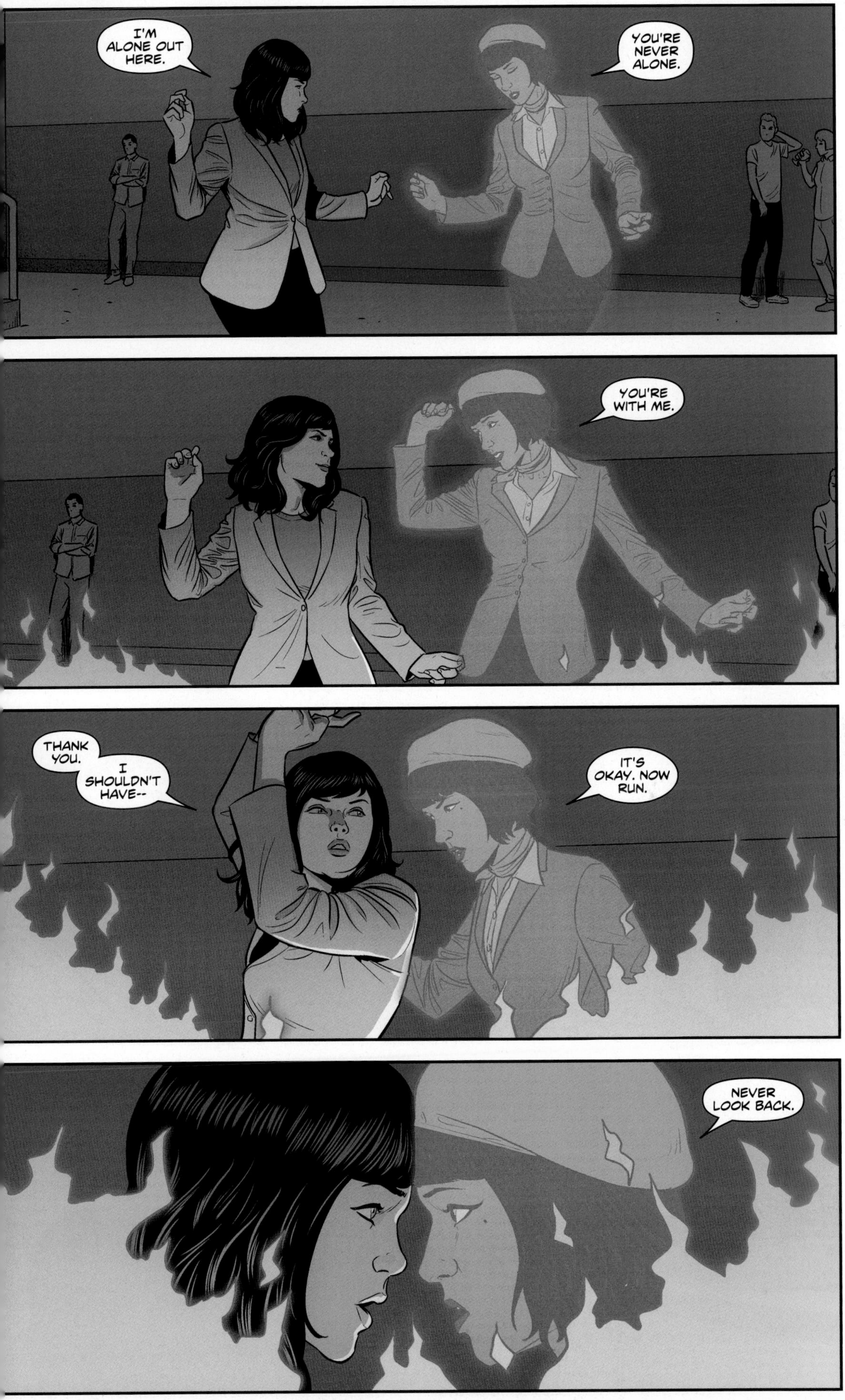
I'M ALONE OUT HERE.
YOU'RE NEVER ALONE.
YOU'RE WITH ME.
THANK YOU.
I SHOULDN'T HAVE--
IT'S OKAY. NOW RUN.
NEVER LOOK BACK.

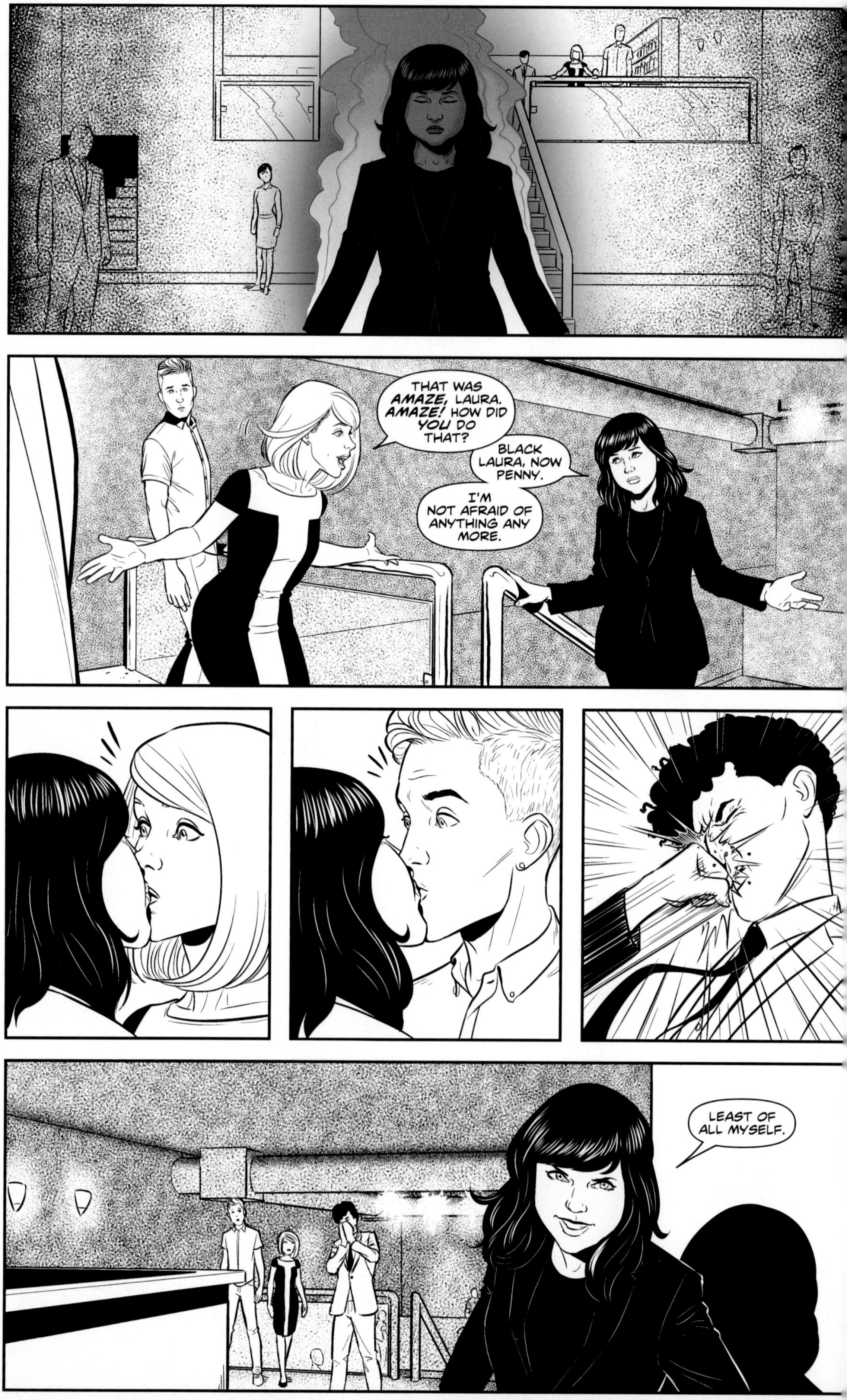
THAT WAS AMAZE, LAURA. AMAZE! HOW DID YOU DO THAT?
BLACK LAURA, NOW PENNY.
I'M NOT AFRAID OF ANYTHING ANY MORE.
LEAST OF ALL MYSELF.

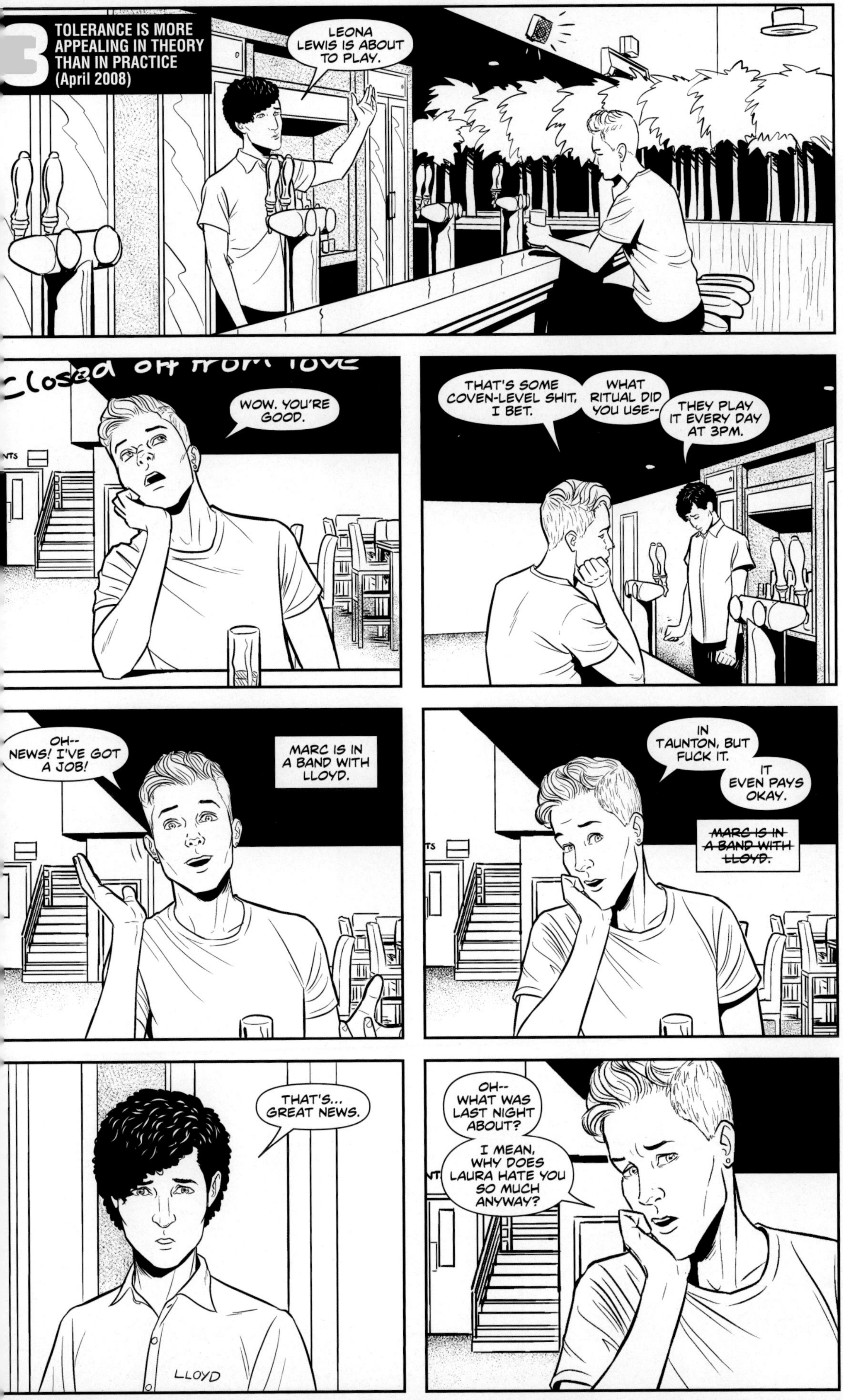
3
TOLERANCE IS MORE APPEALING IN THEORY THAN IN PRACTICE (April 2008)
LEONA LEWIS IS ABOUT TO PLAY.
WOW. YOU'RE GOOD.
THAT'S SOME COVEN-LEVEL SHIT, I BET.
WHAT RITUAL DID YOU USE--
THEY PLAY IT EVERY DAY AT 3PM.
OH-- NEWS! I'VE GOT A JOB!
MARC IS IN A BAND WITH LLOYD.
IN TAUNTON, BUT FUCK IT.
IT EVEN PAYS OKAY.
~~MARC IS IN A BAND WITH LLOYD.~~
THAT'S... GREAT NEWS.
LLOYD
OH-- WHAT WAS LAST NIGHT ABOUT?
I MEAN, WHY DOES LAURA HATE YOU SO MUCH ANYWAY?

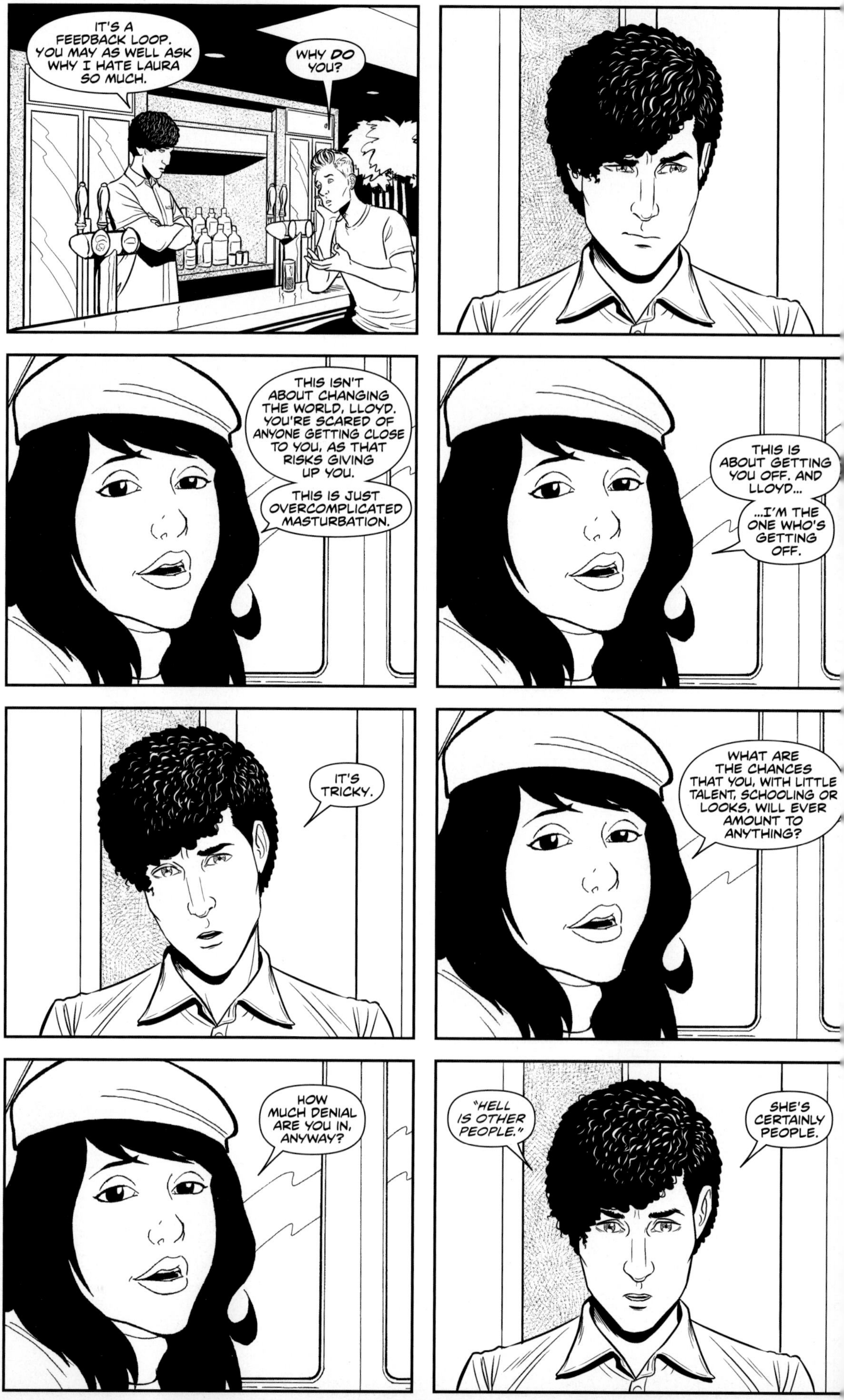
IT'S A FEEDBACK LOOP. YOU MAY AS WELL ASK WHY I HATE LAURA SO MUCH.
WHY DO YOU?
THIS ISN'T ABOUT CHANGING THE WORLD, LLOYD. YOU'RE SCARED OF ANYONE GETTING CLOSE TO YOU, AS THAT RISKS GIVING UP YOU.
THIS IS JUST OVERCOMPLICATED MASTURBATION.
THIS IS ABOUT GETTING YOU OFF. AND LLOYD...
...I'M THE ONE WHO'S GETTING OFF.
IT'S TRICKY.
WHAT ARE THE CHANCES THAT YOU, WITH LITTLE TALENT, SCHOOLING OR LOOKS, WILL EVER AMOUNT TO ANYTHING?
HOW MUCH DENIAL ARE YOU IN, ANYWAY?
"HELL IS OTHER PEOPLE."
SHE'S CERTAINLY PEOPLE.

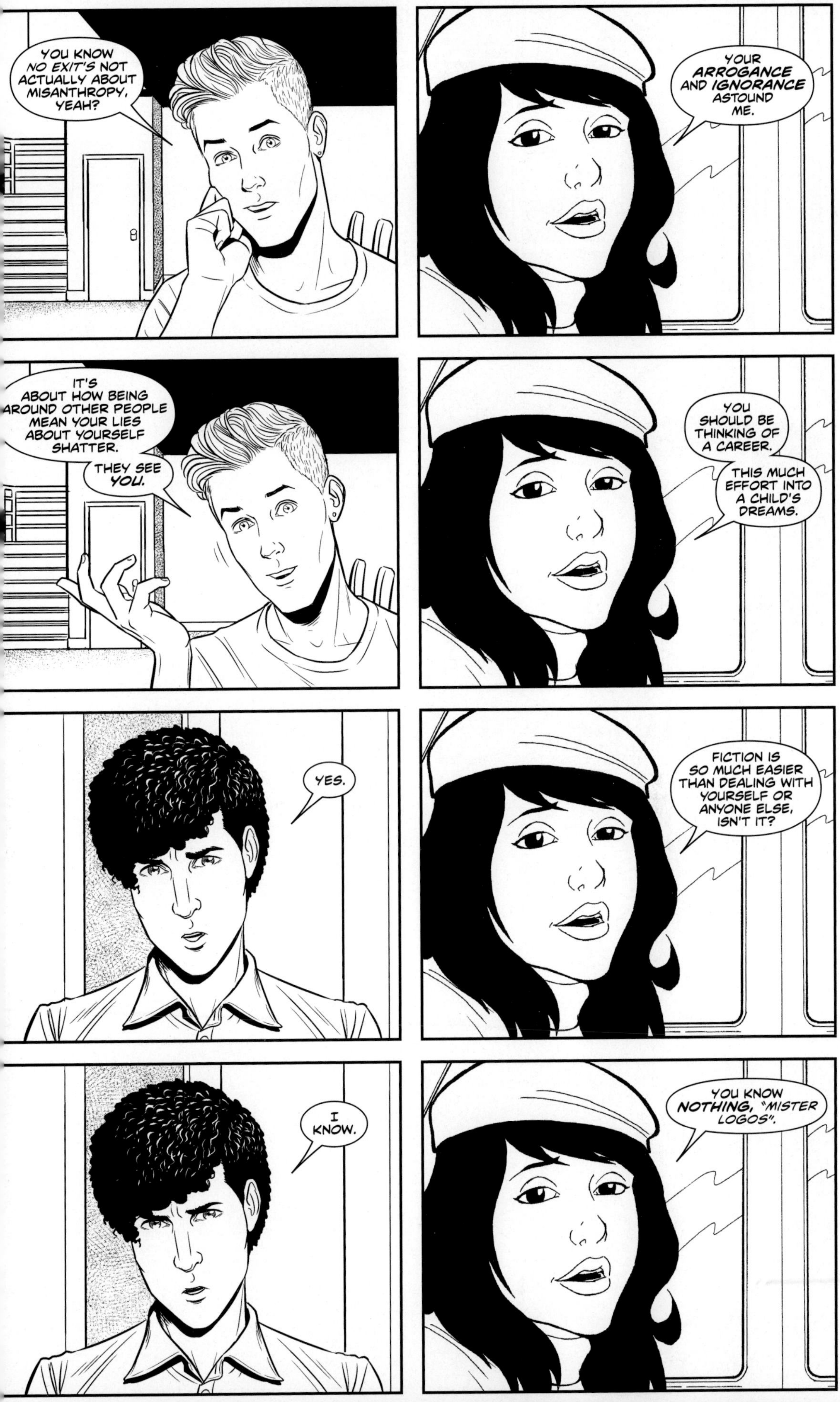
YOU KNOW NO EXIT'S NOT ACTUALLY ABOUT MISANTHROPY, YEAH?
YOUR ARROGANCE AND IGNORANCE ASTOUND ME.
IT'S ABOUT HOW BEING AROUND OTHER PEOPLE MEAN YOUR LIES ABOUT YOURSELF SHATTER.
THEY SEE YOU.
YOU SHOULD BE THINKING OF A CAREER.
THIS MUCH EFFORT INTO A CHILD'S DREAMS.
YES.
FICTION IS SO MUCH EASIER THAN DEALING WITH YOURSELF OR ANYONE ELSE, ISN'T IT?
I KNOW.
YOU KNOW NOTHING, "MISTER LOGOS".

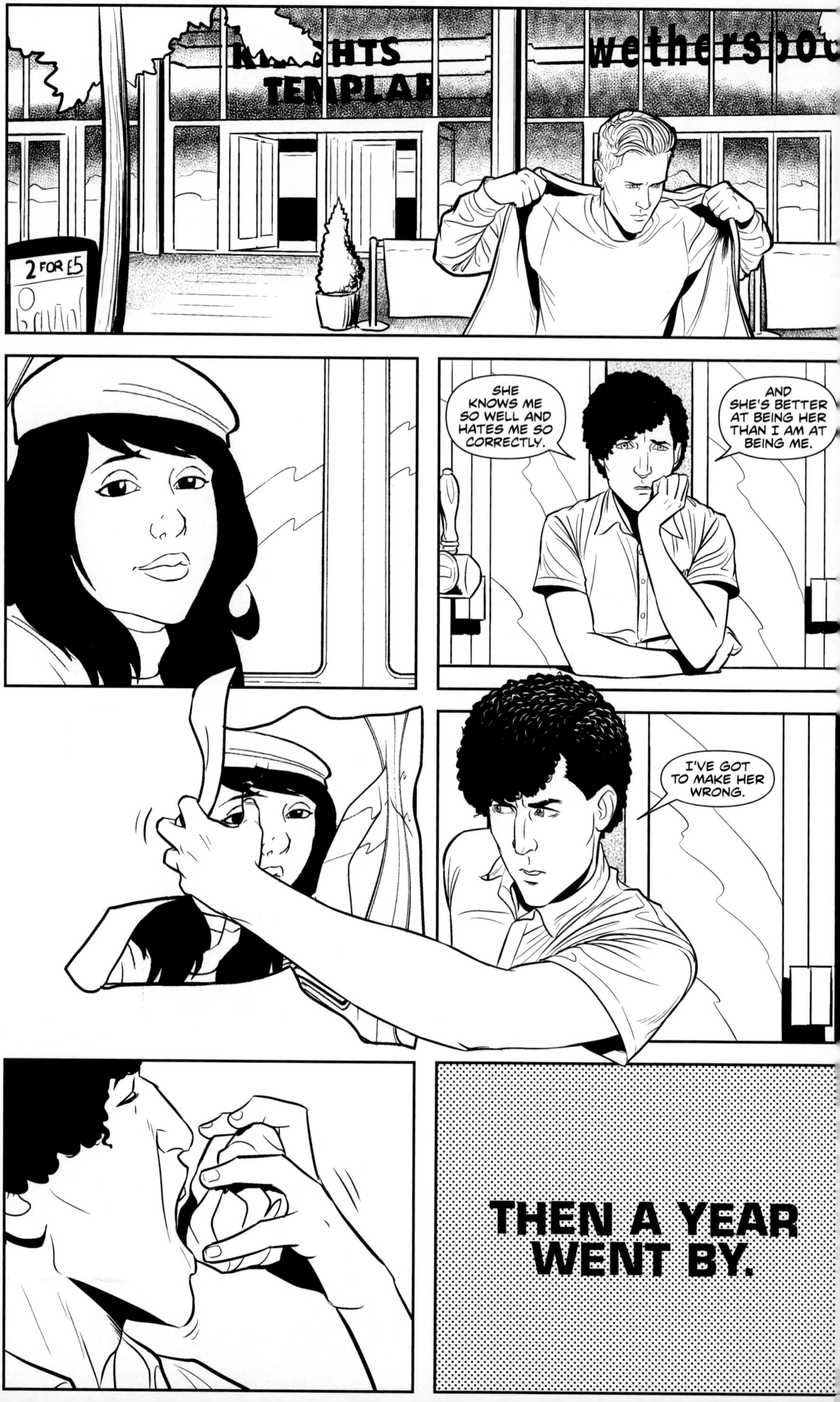
HTS
TEMPLAR
wethersp
2 FOR £5
SHE KNOWS ME SO WELL AND HATES ME SO CORRECTLY.
AND SHE'S BETTER AT BEING HER THAN I AM AT BEING ME.
I'VE GOT TO MAKE HER WRONG.
THEN A YEAR WENT BY.

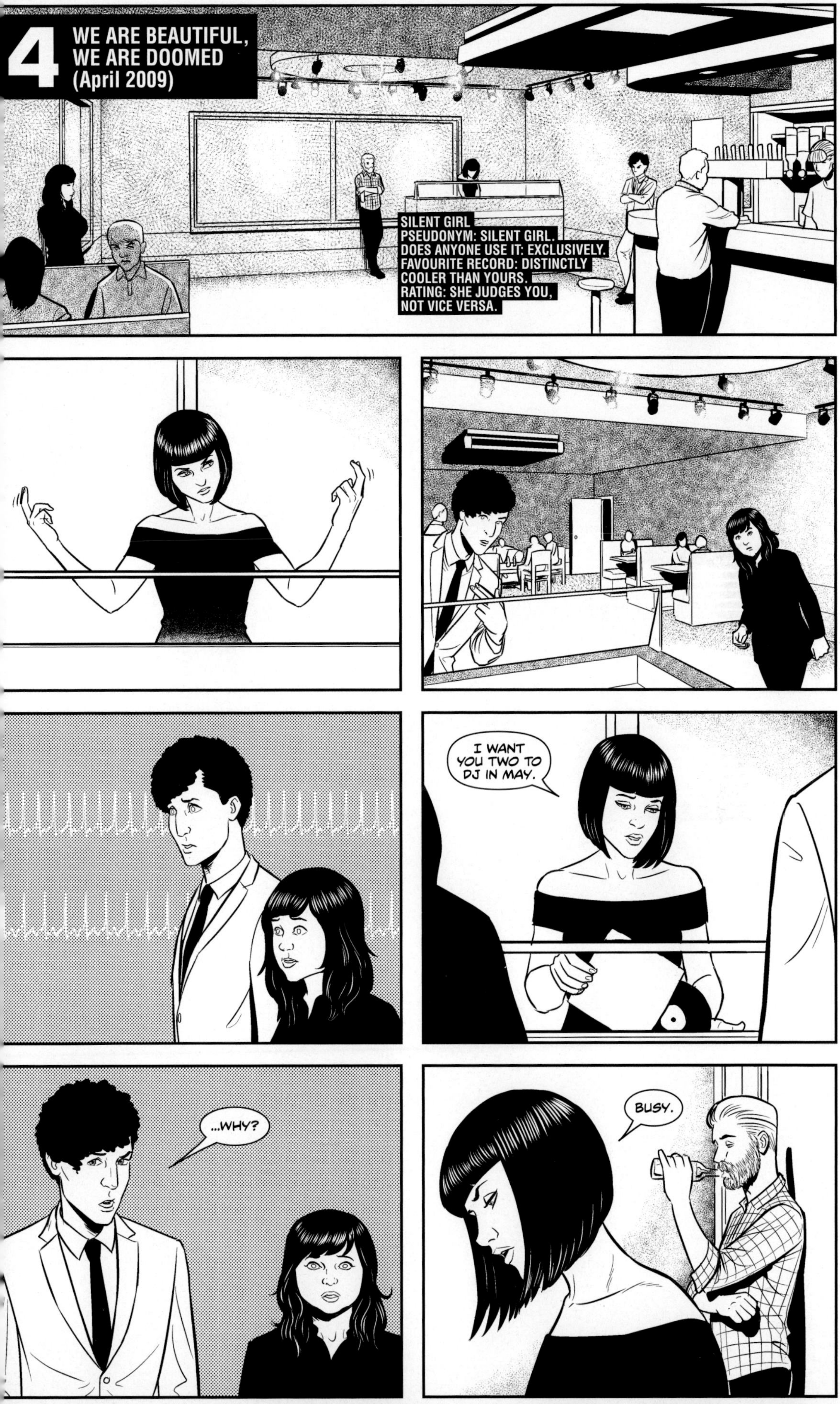

4
WE ARE BEAUTIFUL, WE ARE DOOMED
(April 2009)
SILENT GIRL
PSEUDONYM: SILENT GIRL.
DOES ANYONE USE IT: EXCLUSIVELY.
FAVOURITE RECORD: DISTINCTLY COOLER THAN YOURS.
RATING: SHE JUDGES YOU, NOT VICE VERSA.
I WANT YOU TWO TO DJ IN MAY.
...WHY?
BUSY.

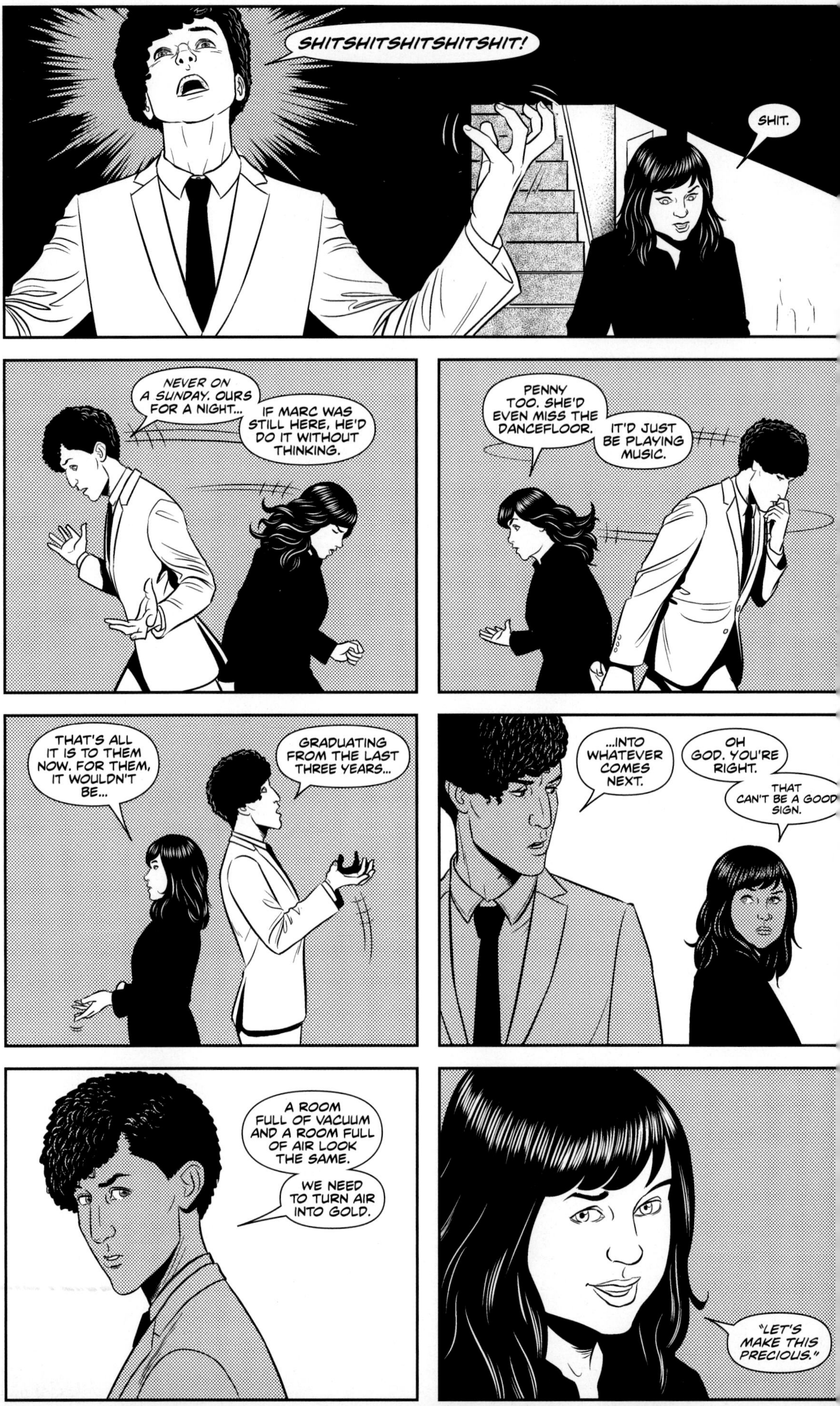

SHITSHITSHITSHITSHIT!
SHIT.
NEVER ON A SUNDAY. OURS FOR A NIGHT...
IF MARC WAS STILL HERE, HE'D DO IT WITHOUT THINKING.
PENNY TOO. SHE'D EVEN MISS THE DANCEFLOOR.
IT'D JUST BE PLAYING MUSIC.
THAT'S ALL IT IS TO THEM NOW. FOR THEM, IT WOULDN'T BE...
GRADUATING FROM THE LAST THREE YEARS...
...INTO WHATEVER COMES NEXT.
OH GOD. YOU'RE RIGHT.
THAT CAN'T BE A GOOD SIGN.
A ROOM FULL OF VACUUM AND A ROOM FULL OF AIR LOOK THE SAME.
WE NEED TO TURN AIR INTO GOLD.
"LET'S MAKE THIS PRECIOUS."

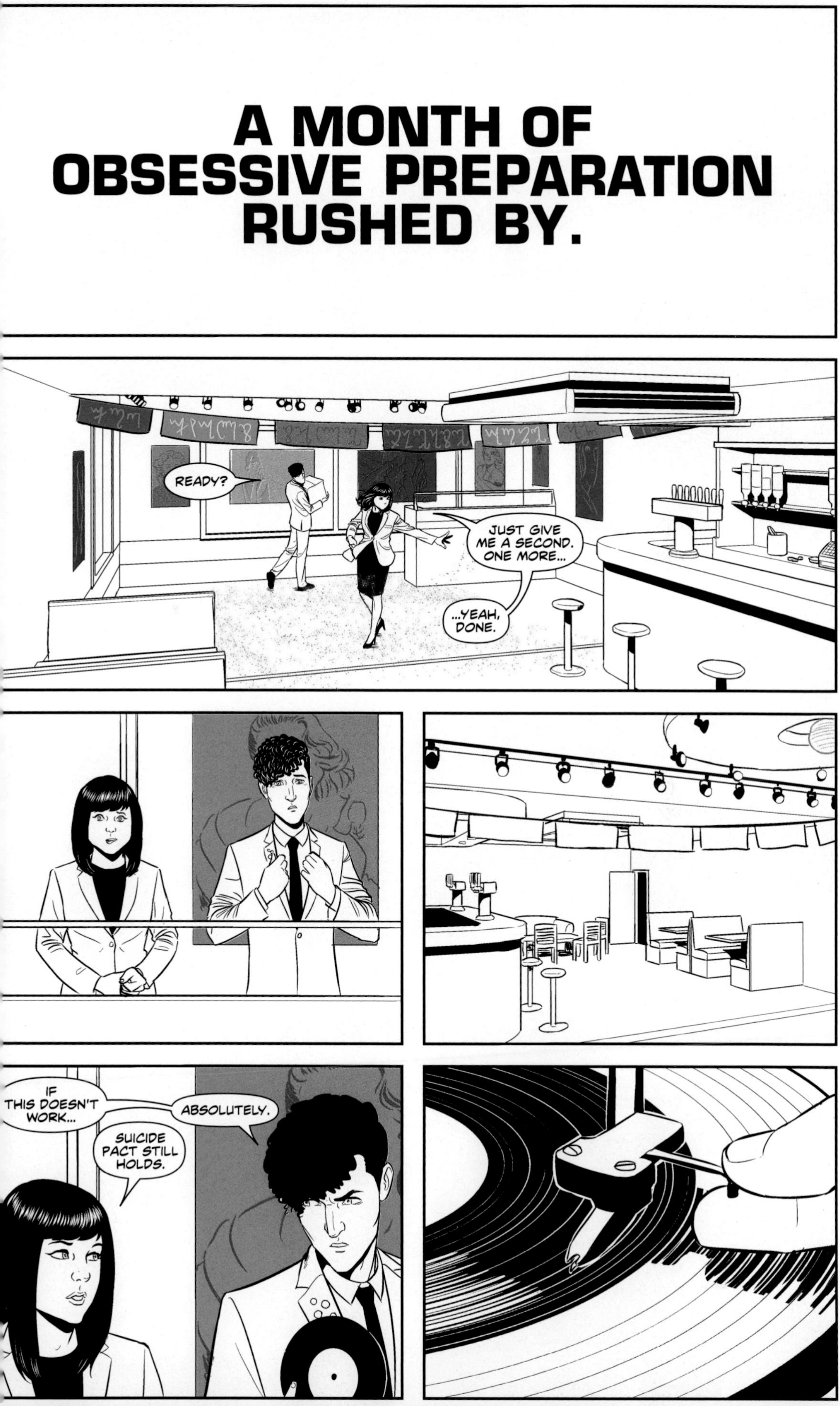
A MONTH OF OBSESSIVE PREPARATION RUSHED BY.
READY?
JUST GIVE ME A SECOND. ONE MORE...
...YEAH, DONE.
IF THIS DOESN'T WORK...
SUICIDE PACT STILL HOLDS.
ABSOLUTELY.

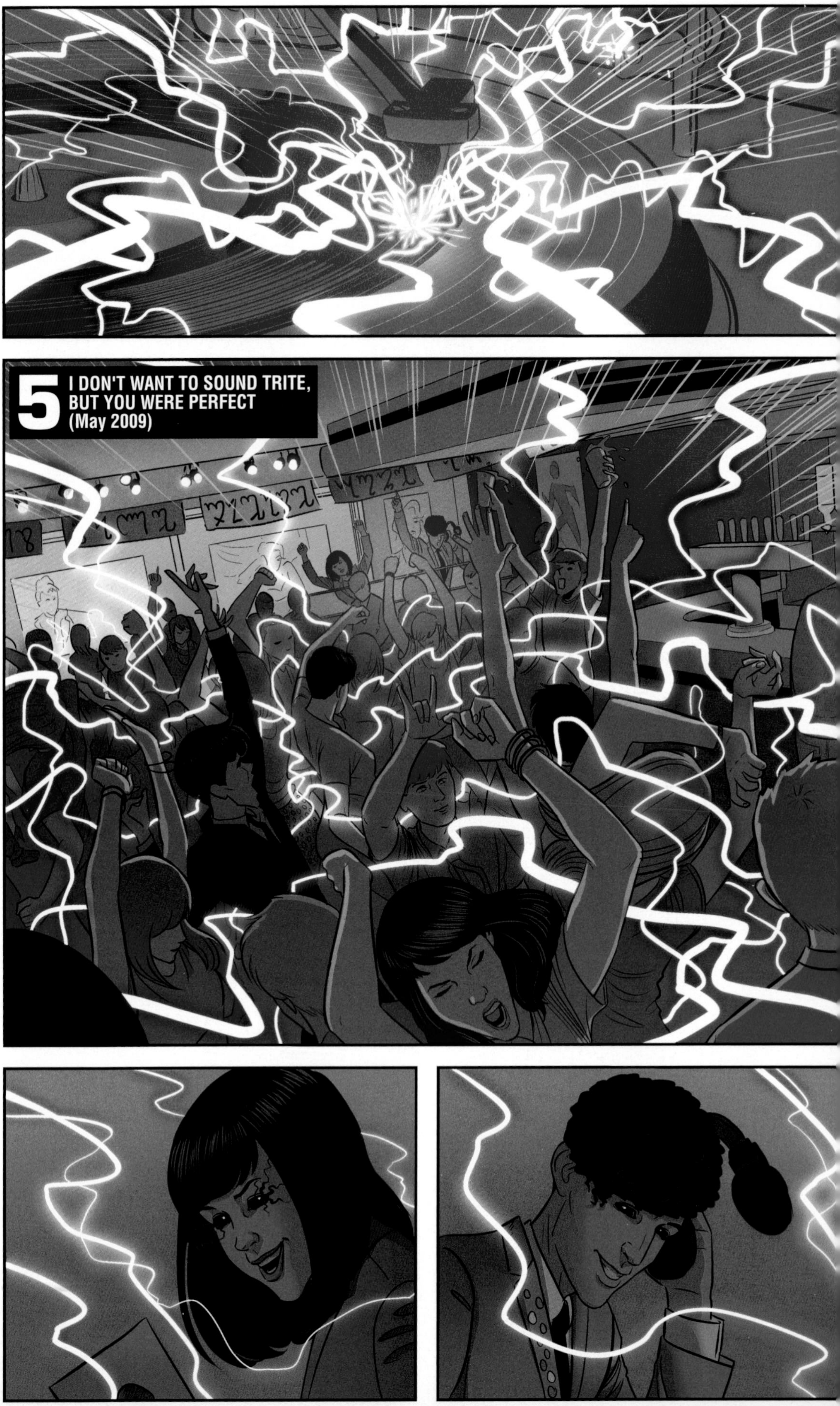
5
I DON'T WANT TO SOUND TRITE, BUT YOU WERE PERFECT
(May 2009)

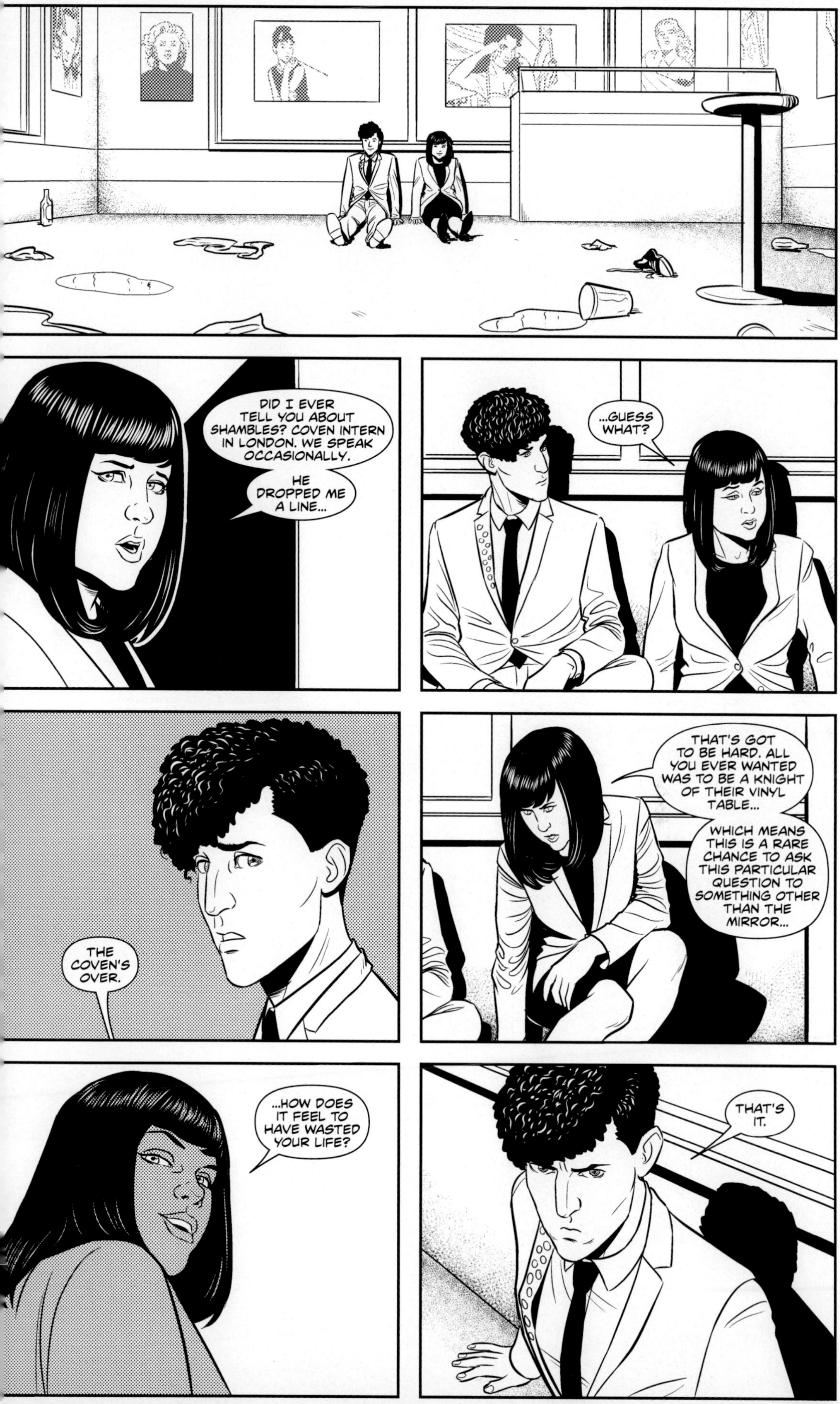
DID I EVER TELL YOU ABOUT SHAMBLES? COVEN INTERN IN LONDON. WE SPEAK OCCASIONALLY.
HE DROPPED ME A LINE...
...GUESS WHAT?
THE COVEN'S OVER.
THAT'S GOT TO BE HARD. ALL YOU EVER WANTED WAS TO BE A KNIGHT OF THEIR VINYL TABLE...
WHICH MEANS THIS IS A RARE CHANCE TO ASK THIS PARTICULAR QUESTION TO SOMETHING OTHER THAN THE MIRROR...
...HOW DOES IT FEEL TO HAVE WASTED YOUR LIFE?
THAT'S IT.

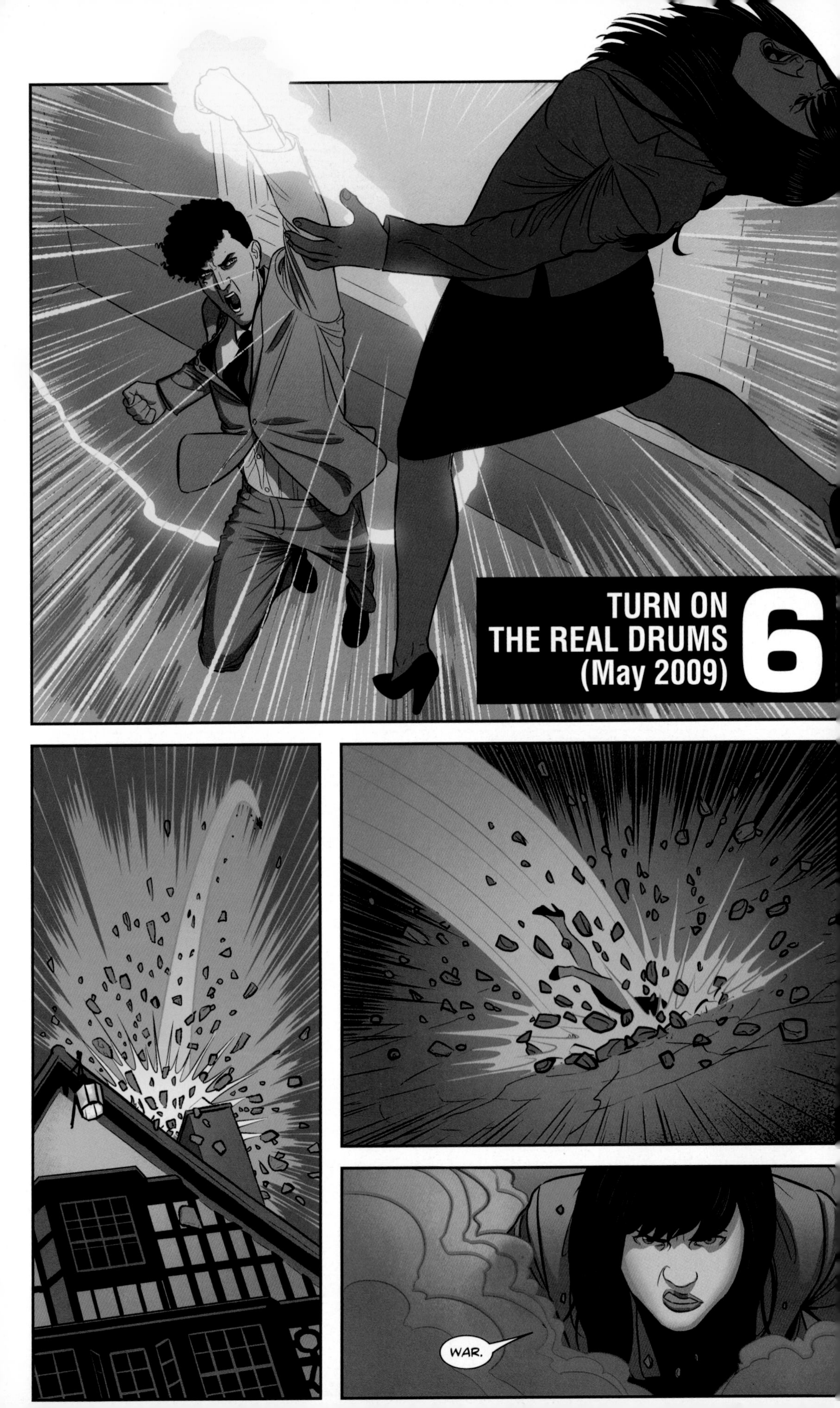
TURN ON
THE REAL DRUMS
(May 2009)
6
WAR.

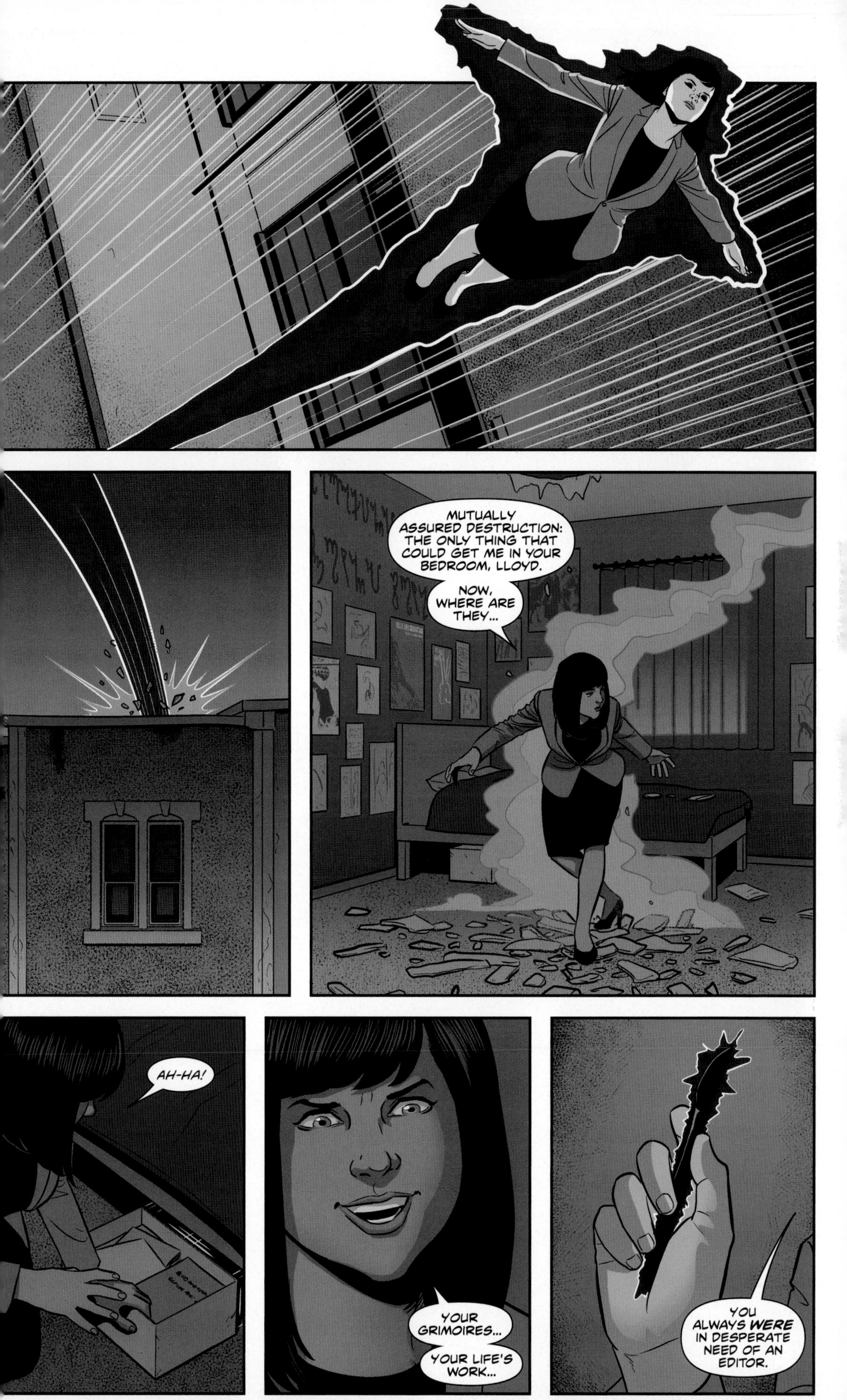
MUTUALLY ASSURED DESTRUCTION: THE ONLY THING THAT COULD GET ME IN YOUR BEDROOM, LLOYD.
NOW, WHERE ARE THEY...
AH-HA!
YOUR GRIMOIRES...
YOUR LIFE'S WORK...
YOU ALWAYS *WERE* IN DESPERATE NEED OF AN EDITOR.

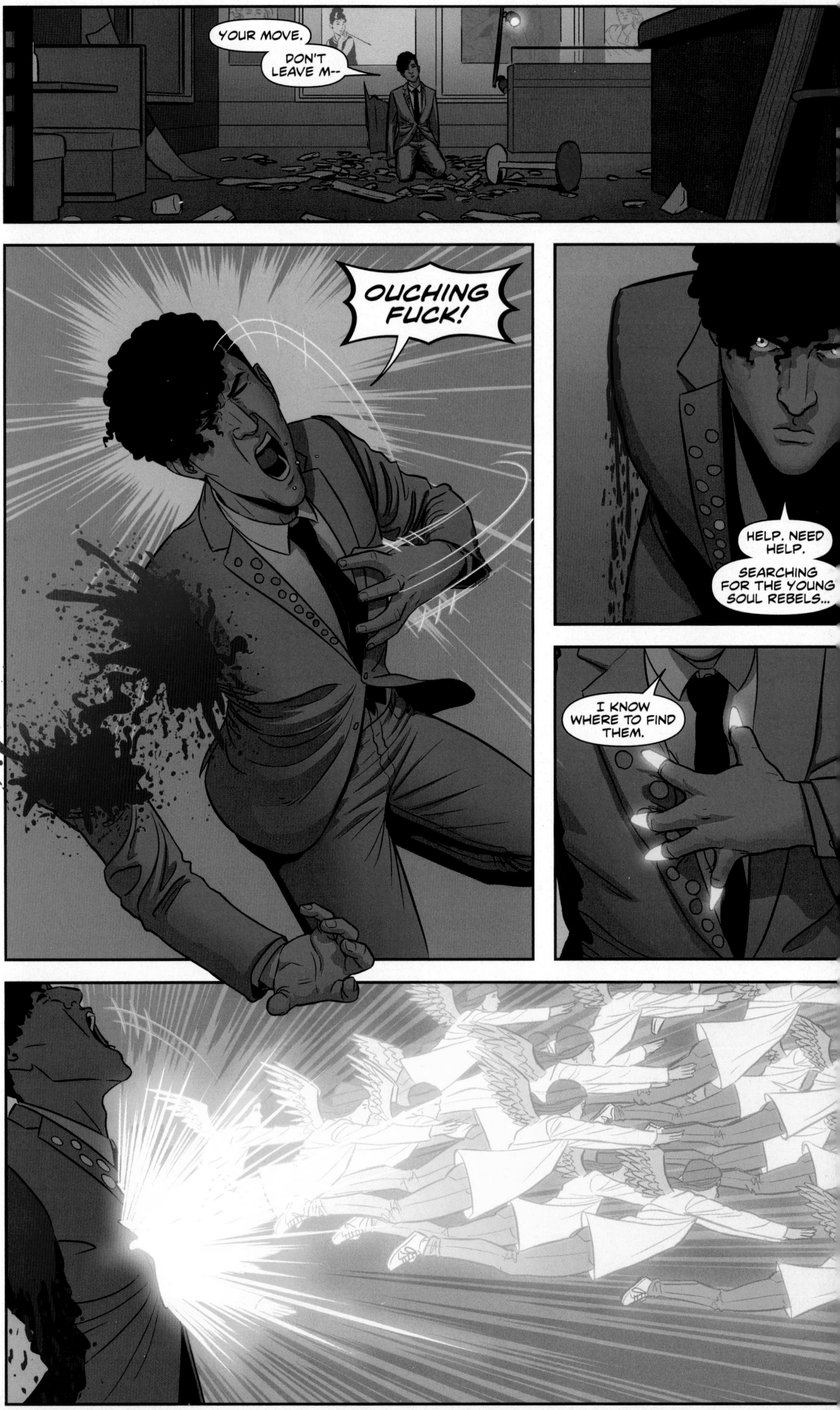
YOUR MOVE.
DON'T LEAVE M--
OUCHING FUCK!
HELP. NEED HELP.
SEARCHING FOR THE YOUNG SOUL REBELS...
I KNOW WHERE TO FIND THEM.

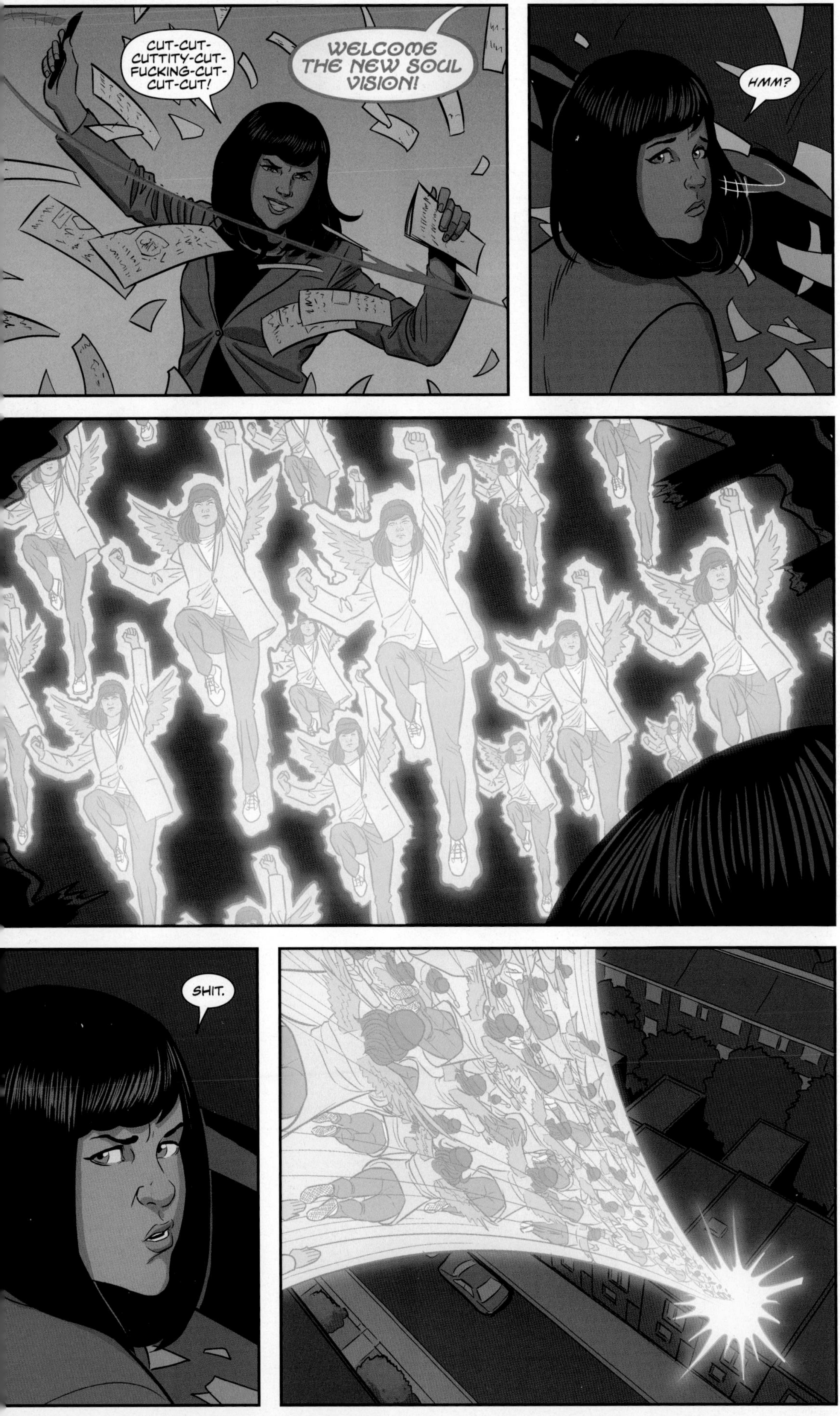
CUT-CUT-CUTTITY-CUT-FUCKING-CUT-CUT-CUT!
WELCOME THE NEW SOUL VISION!
HMM?
SHIT.

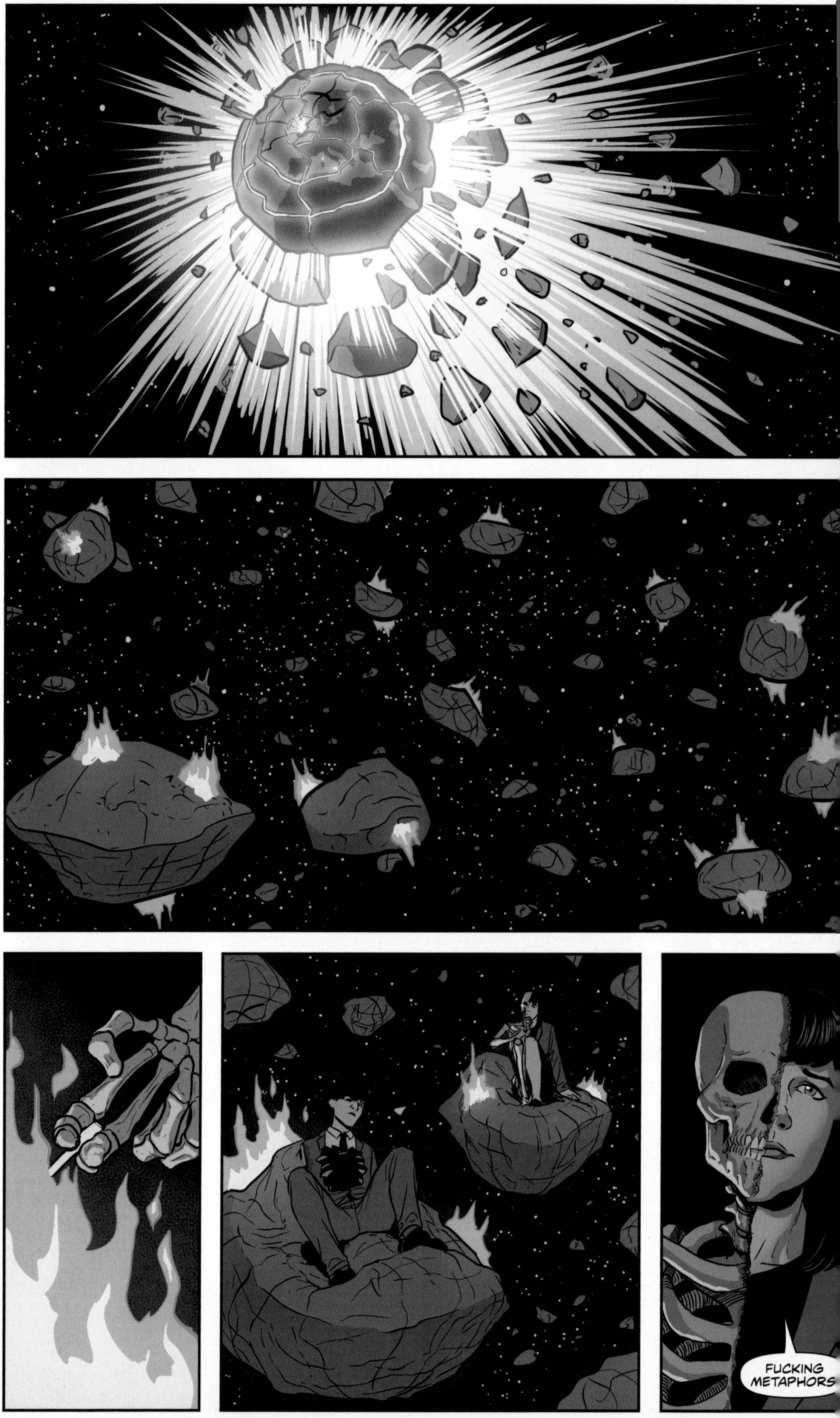
FUCKING METAPHORS

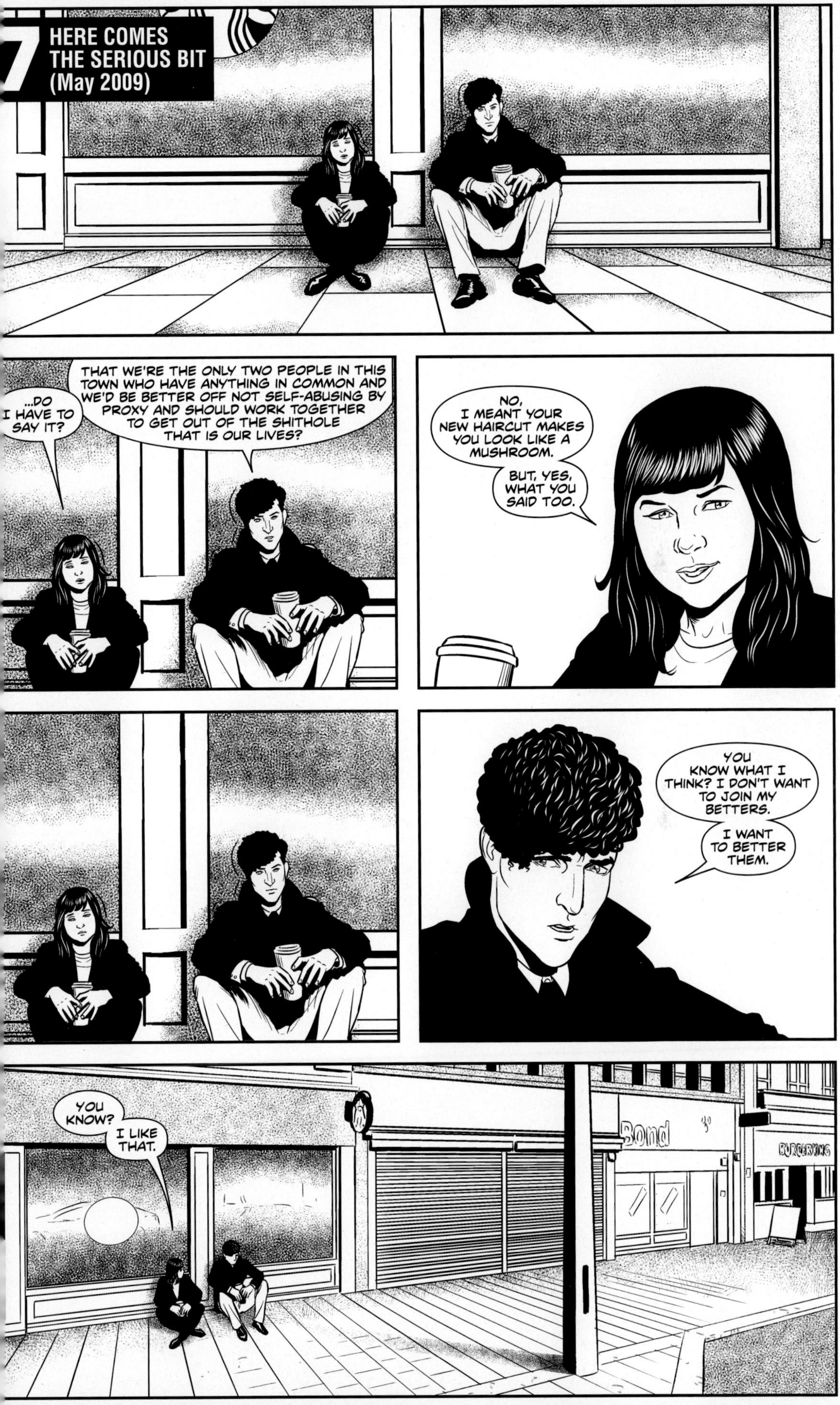
7 HERE COMES THE SERIOUS BIT (May 2009)
...DO I HAVE TO SAY IT?
THAT WE'RE THE ONLY TWO PEOPLE IN THIS TOWN WHO HAVE ANYTHING IN COMMON AND WE'D BE BETTER OFF NOT SELF-ABUSING BY PROXY AND SHOULD WORK TOGETHER TO GET OUT OF THE SHITHOLE THAT IS OUR LIVES?
NO, I MEANT YOUR NEW HAIRCUT MAKES YOU LOOK LIKE A MUSHROOM.
BUT, YES, WHAT YOU SAID TOO.
YOU KNOW WHAT I THINK? I DON'T WANT TO JOIN MY BETTERS.
I WANT TO BETTER THEM.
YOU KNOW?
I LIKE THAT.
Bond
BURGERKING

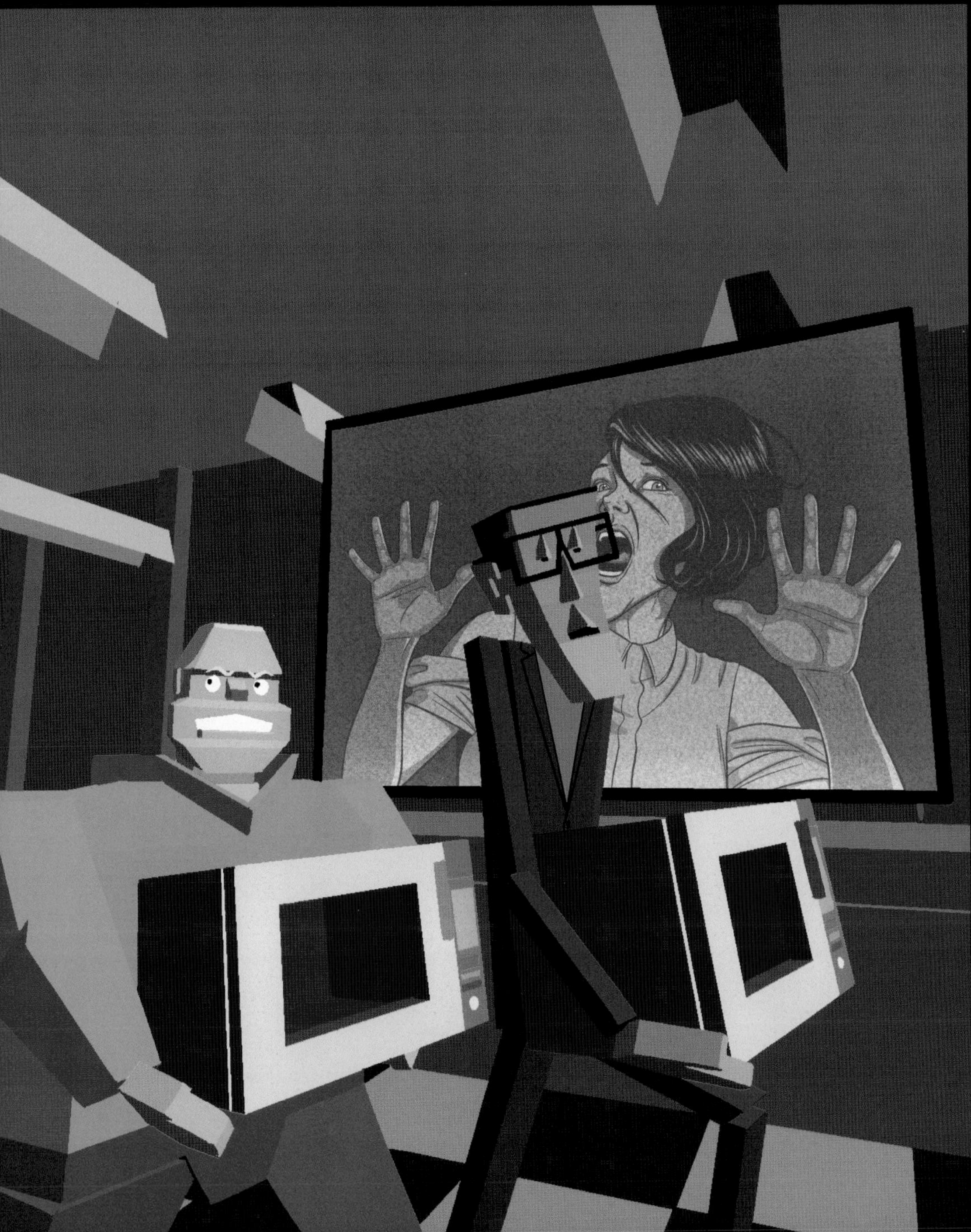

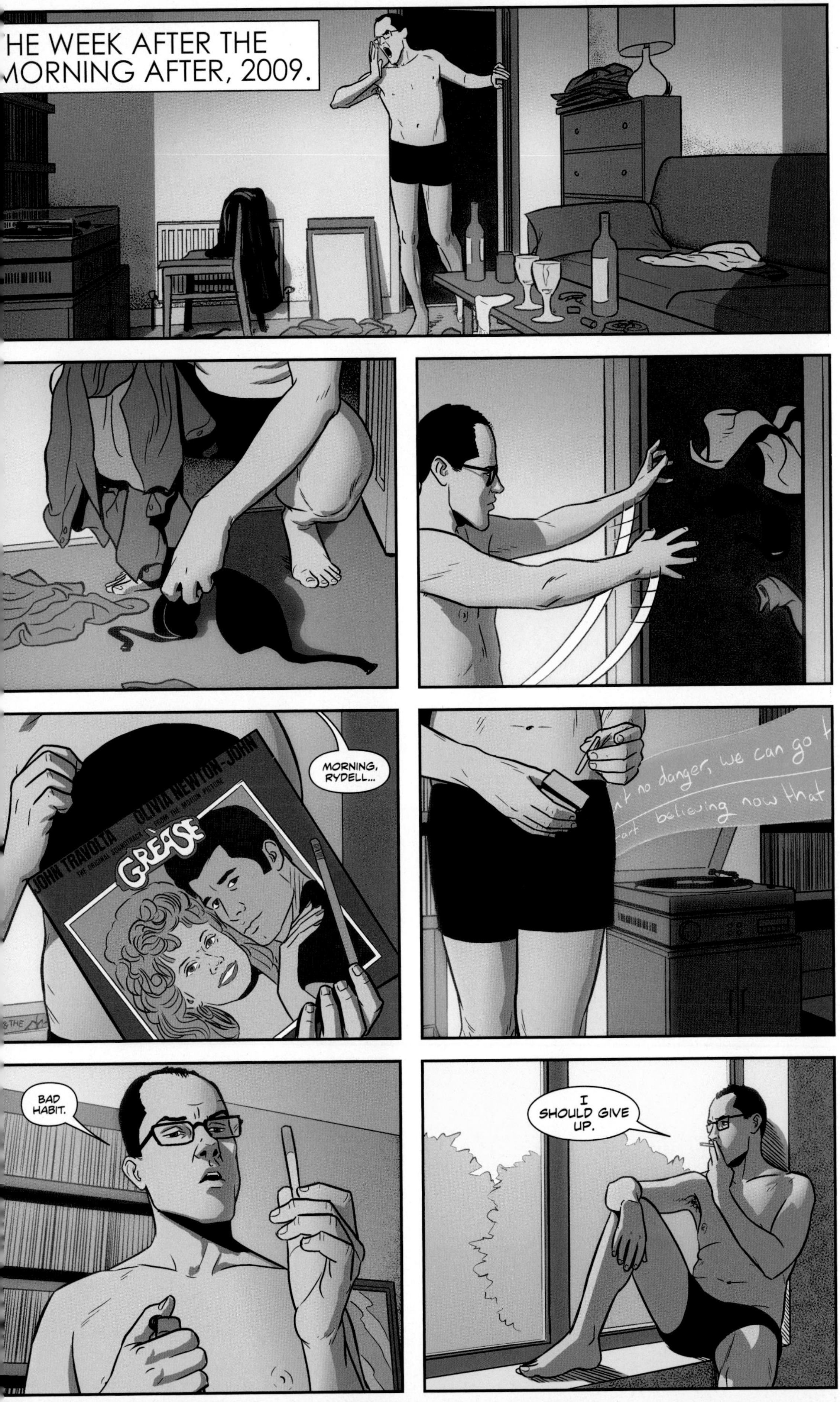
HE WEEK AFTER THE
ORNING AFTER, 2009.
JOHN TRAVOLTA
OLIVIA NEWTON-JOHN
THE ORIGINAL SOUNDTRACK FROM THE MOTION PICTURE
GREASE
MORNING, RYDELL...
no danger, we can go
believing now that
BAD HABIT.
I SHOULD GIVE UP.

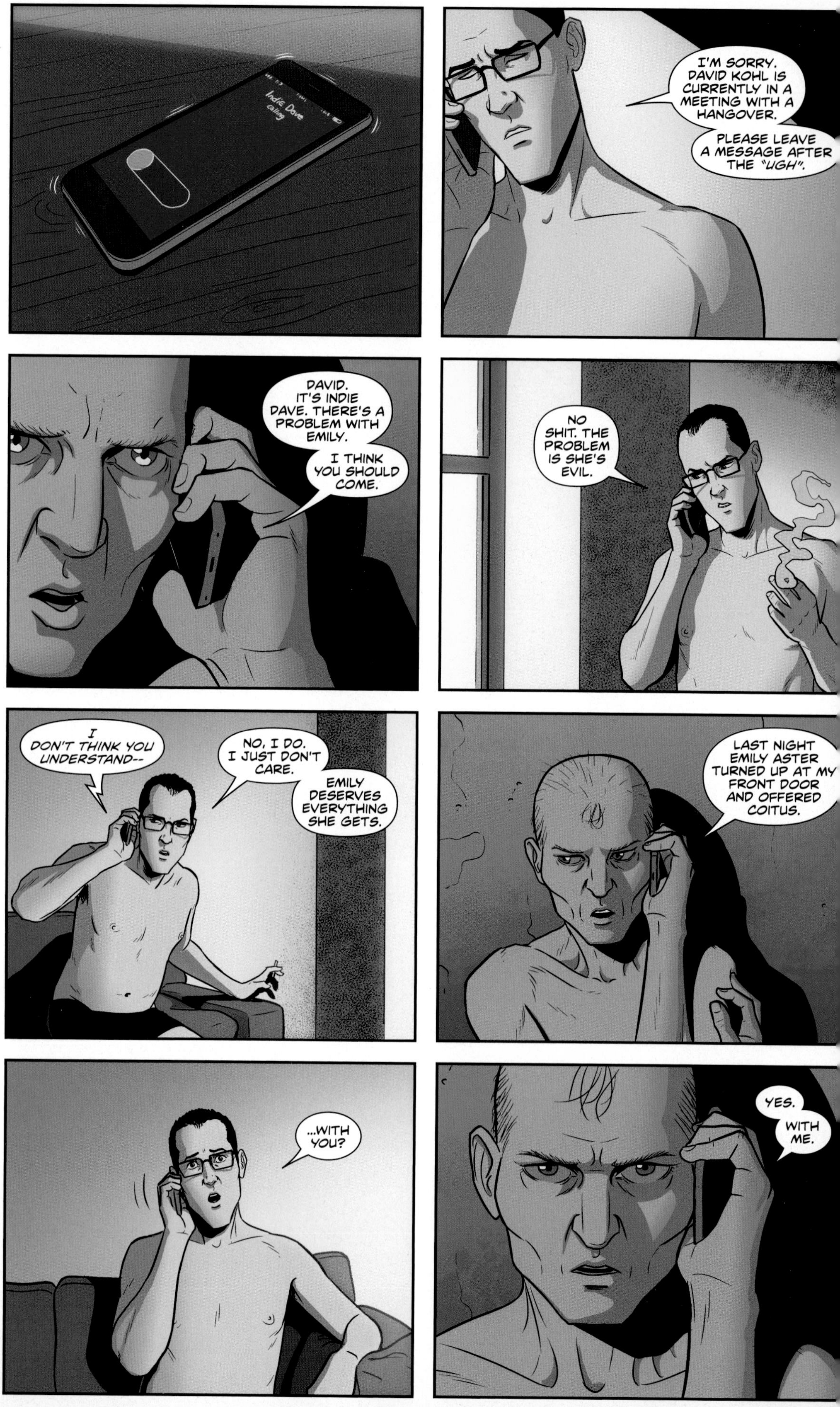
Indie Dave
calling
I'M SORRY. DAVID KOHL IS CURRENTLY IN A MEETING WITH A HANGOVER.
PLEASE LEAVE A MESSAGE AFTER THE "UGH".
DAVID. IT'S INDIE DAVE. THERE'S A PROBLEM WITH EMILY.
I THINK YOU SHOULD COME.
NO SHIT. THE PROBLEM IS SHE'S EVIL.
I DON'T THINK YOU UNDERSTAND--
NO, I DO. I JUST DON'T CARE.
EMILY DESERVES EVERYTHING SHE GETS.
LAST NIGHT EMILY ASTER TURNED UP AT MY FRONT DOOR AND OFFERED COITUS.
...WITH YOU?
YES.
WITH ME.

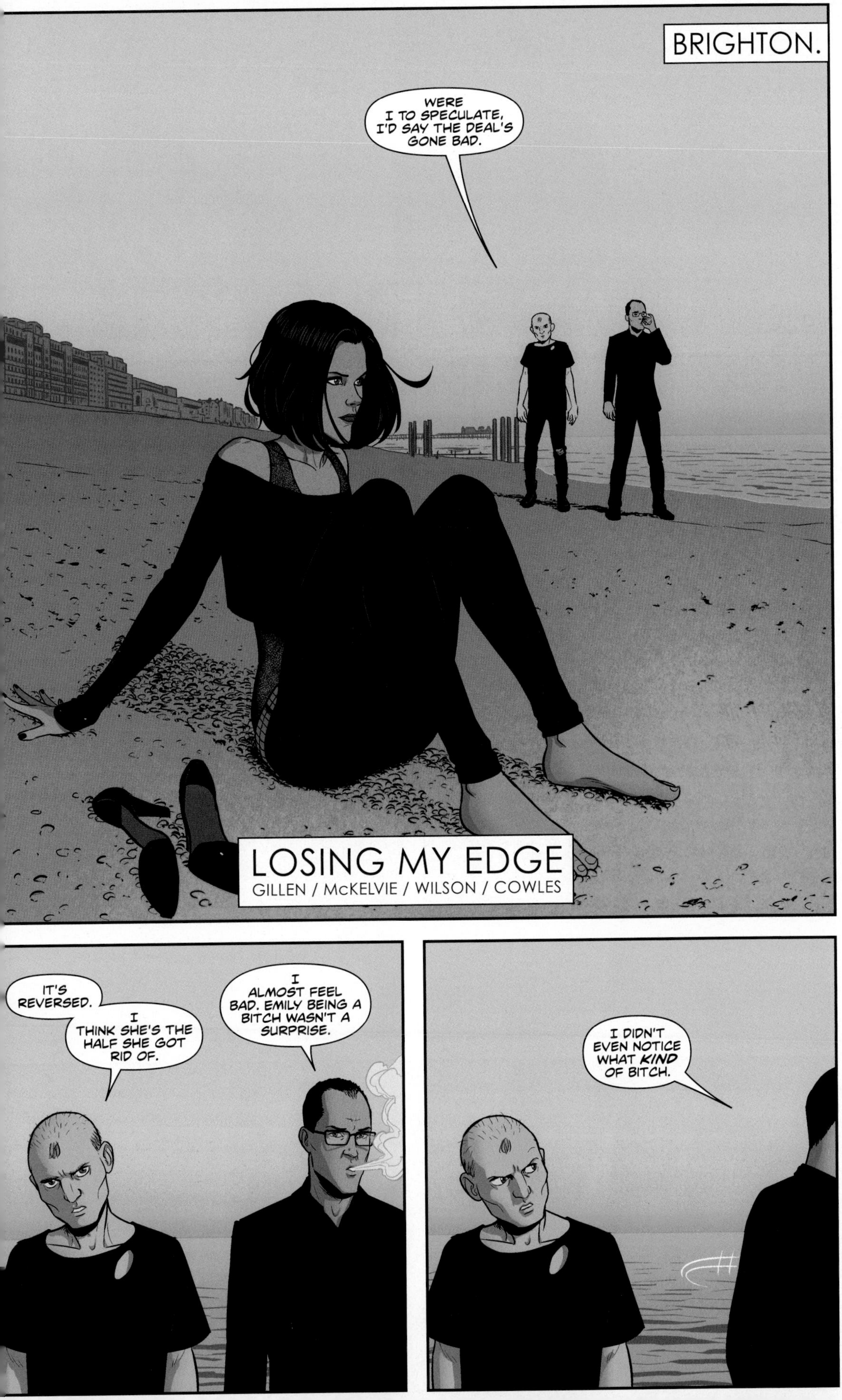
BRIGHTON.
WERE I TO SPECULATE, I'D SAY THE DEAL'S GONE BAD.
LOSING MY EDGE
GILLEN / McKELVIE / WILSON / COWLES
IT'S REVERSED.
I THINK SHE'S THE HALF SHE GOT RID OF.
I ALMOST FEEL BAD. EMILY BEING A BITCH WASN'T A SURPRISE.
I DIDN'T EVEN NOTICE WHAT *KIND* OF BITCH.

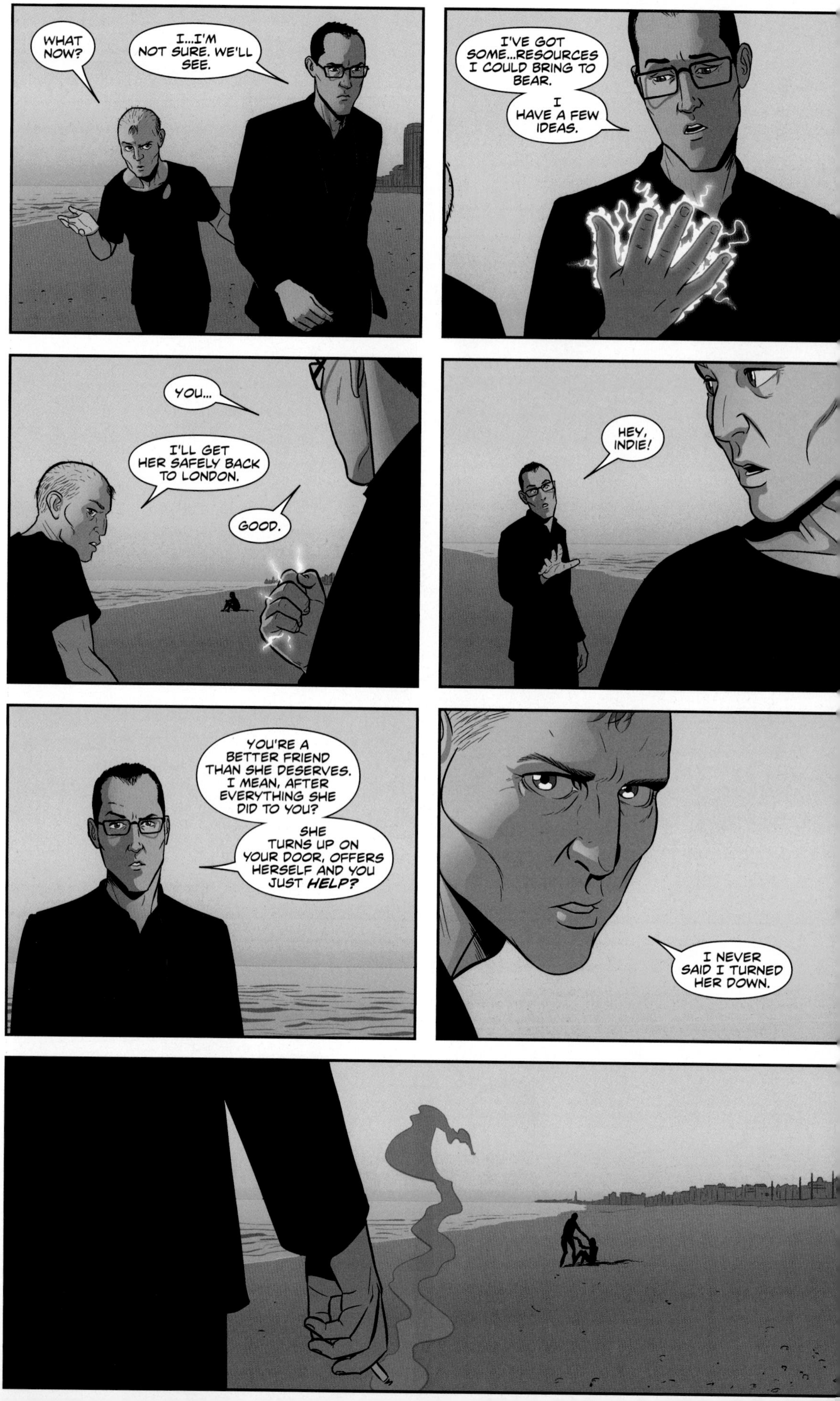
WHAT NOW?
I...I'M NOT SURE. WE'LL SEE.
I'VE GOT SOME...RESOURCES I COULD BRING TO BEAR.
I HAVE A FEW IDEAS.
YOU...
I'LL GET HER SAFELY BACK TO LONDON.
GOOD.
HEY, INDIE!
YOU'RE A BETTER FRIEND THAN SHE DESERVES. I MEAN, AFTER EVERYTHING SHE DID TO YOU?
SHE TURNS UP ON YOUR DOOR, OFFERS HERSELF AND YOU JUST *HELP?*
I NEVER SAID I TURNED HER DOWN.

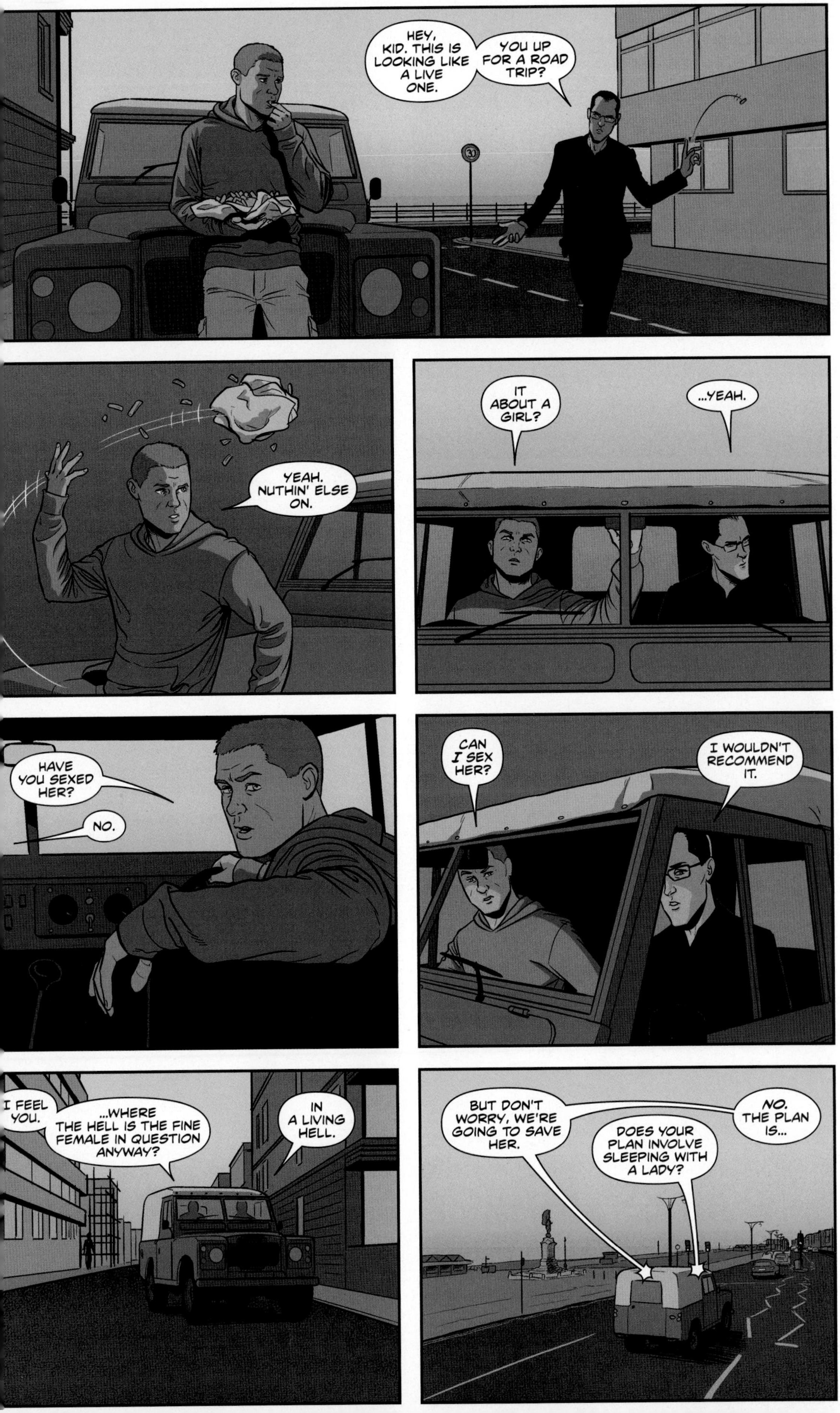
HEY, KID. THIS IS LOOKING LIKE A LIVE ONE.
YOU UP FOR A ROAD TRIP?
YEAH. NUTHIN' ELSE ON.
IT ABOUT A GIRL?
...YEAH.
HAVE YOU SEXED HER?
NO.
CAN *I* SEX HER?
I WOULDN'T RECOMMEND IT.
I FEEL YOU.
...WHERE THE HELL IS THE FINE FEMALE IN QUESTION ANYWAY?
IN A LIVING HELL.
BUT DON'T WORRY, WE'RE GOING TO SAVE HER.
DOES YOUR PLAN INVOLVE SLEEPING WITH A LADY?
NO. THE PLAN IS...

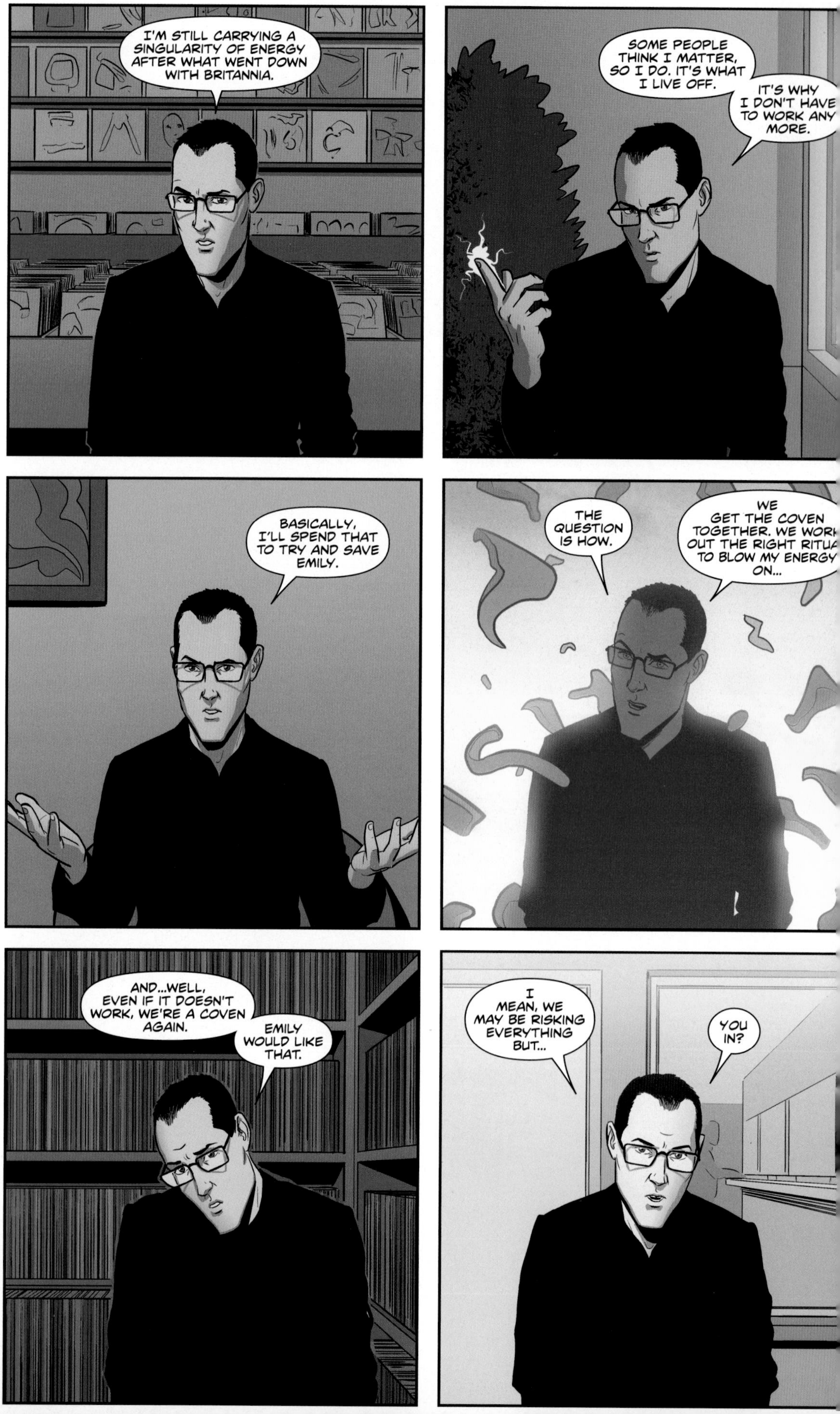
I'M STILL CARRYING A SINGULARITY OF ENERGY AFTER WHAT WENT DOWN WITH BRITANNIA.
SOME PEOPLE THINK I MATTER, SO I DO. IT'S WHAT I LIVE OFF.
IT'S WHY I DON'T HAVE TO WORK ANY MORE.
BASICALLY, I'LL SPEND THAT TO TRY AND SAVE EMILY.
THE QUESTION IS HOW.
WE GET THE COVEN TOGETHER. WE WORK OUT THE RIGHT RITUAL TO BLOW MY ENERGY ON...
AND...WELL, EVEN IF IT DOESN'T WORK, WE'RE A COVEN AGAIN.
EMILY WOULD LIKE THAT.
I MEAN, WE MAY BE RISKING EVERYTHING BUT...
YOU IN?

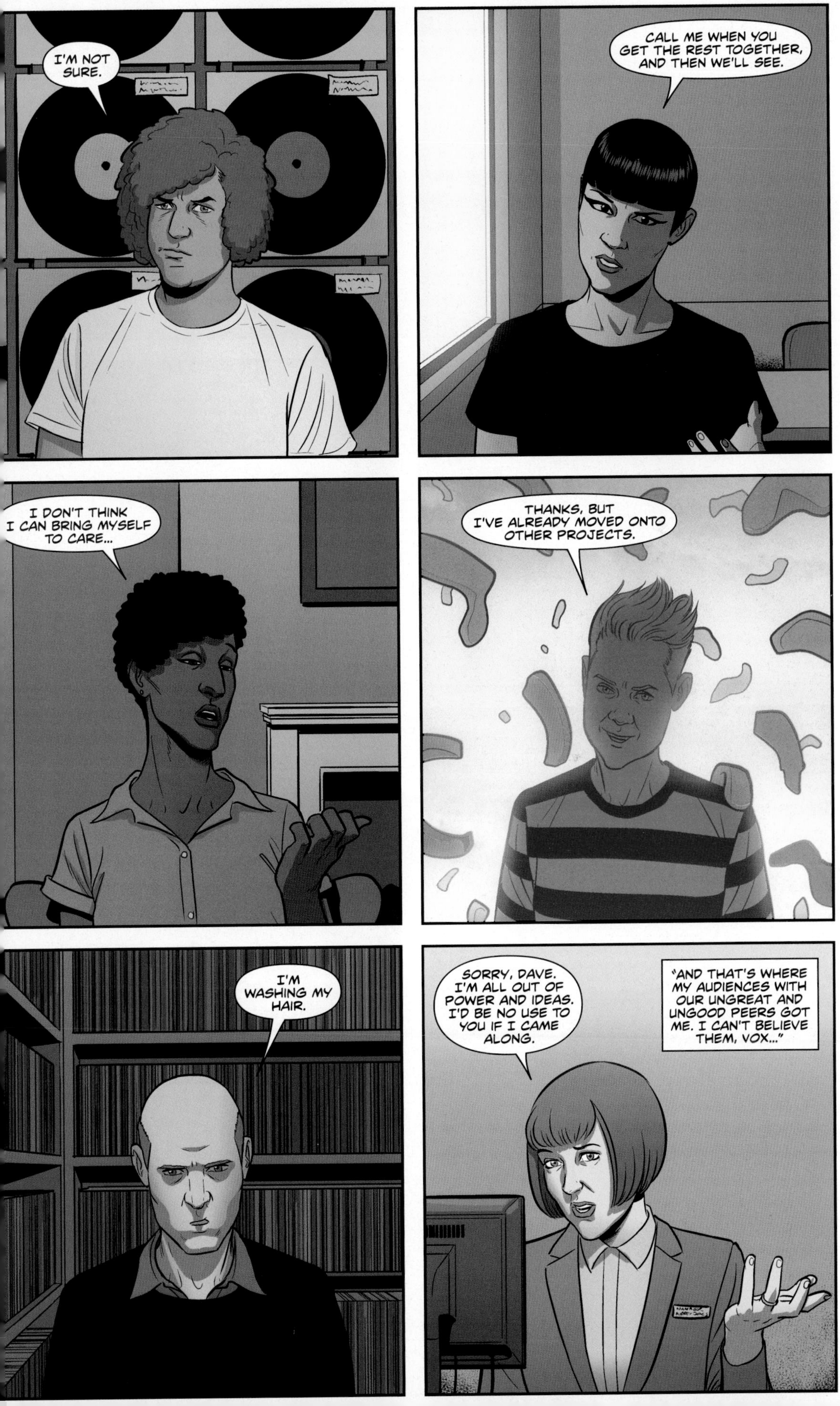
I'M NOT SURE.
CALL ME WHEN YOU GET THE REST TOGETHER, AND THEN WE'LL SEE.
I DON'T THINK I CAN BRING MYSELF TO CARE...
THANKS, BUT I'VE ALREADY MOVED ONTO OTHER PROJECTS.
I'M WASHING MY HAIR.
SORRY, DAVE. I'M ALL OUT OF POWER AND IDEAS. I'D BE NO USE TO YOU IF I CAME ALONG.
"AND THAT'S WHERE MY AUDIENCES WITH OUR UNGREAT AND UNGOOD PEERS GOT ME. I CAN'T BELIEVE THEM, VOX..."

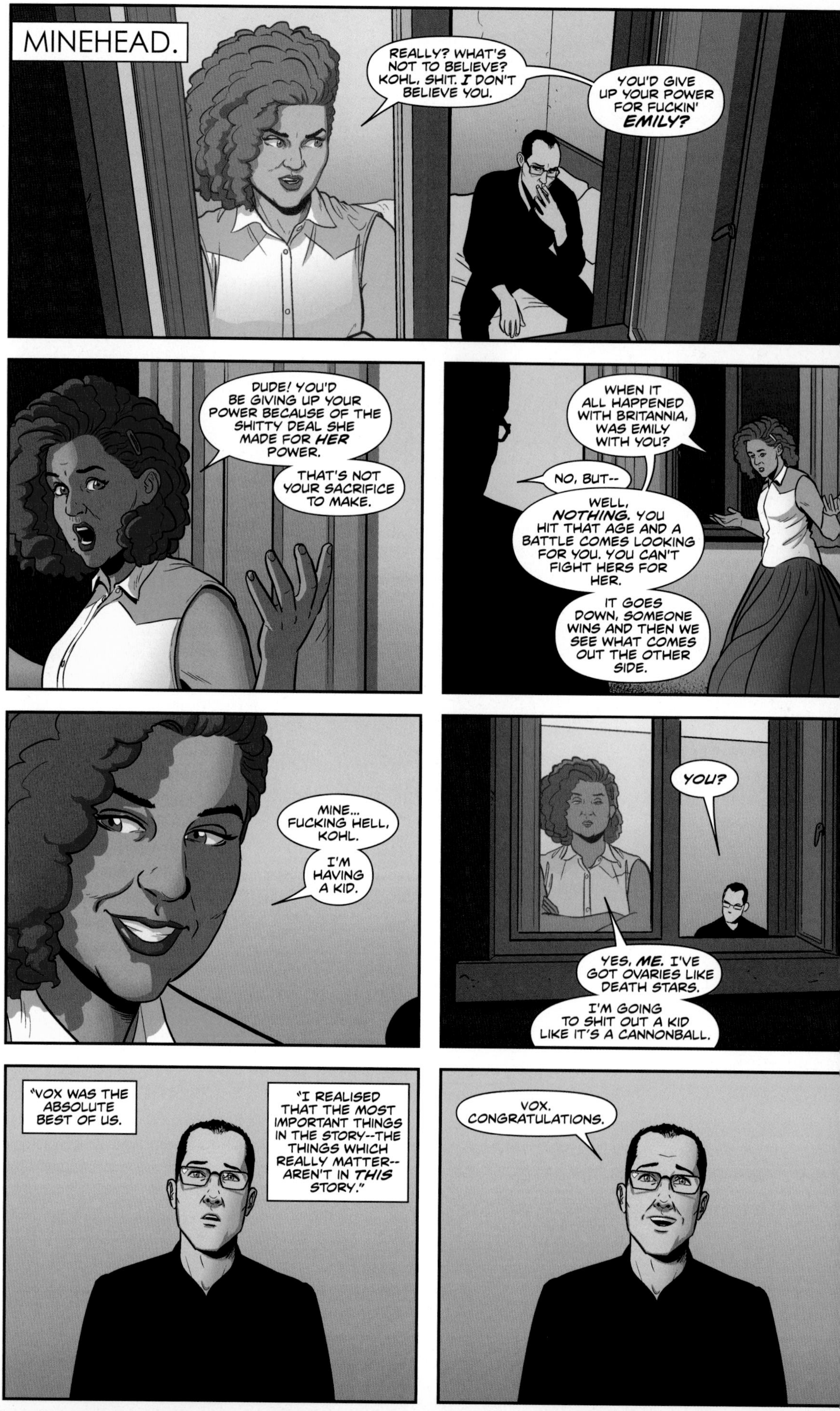
MINEHEAD.
REALLY? WHAT'S NOT TO BELIEVE? KOHL, SHIT. I DON'T BELIEVE YOU.
YOU'D GIVE UP YOUR POWER FOR FUCKIN' EMILY?
DUDE! YOU'D BE GIVING UP YOUR POWER BECAUSE OF THE SHITTY DEAL SHE MADE FOR HER POWER.
THAT'S NOT YOUR SACRIFICE TO MAKE.
WHEN IT ALL HAPPENED WITH BRITANNIA, WAS EMILY WITH YOU?
NO, BUT--
WELL, NOTHING. YOU HIT THAT AGE AND A BATTLE COMES LOOKING FOR YOU. YOU CAN'T FIGHT HERS FOR HER.
IT GOES DOWN, SOMEONE WINS AND THEN WE SEE WHAT COMES OUT THE OTHER SIDE.
MINE... FUCKING HELL, KOHL.
I'M HAVING A KID.
YOU?
YES, ME. I'VE GOT OVARIES LIKE DEATH STARS.
I'M GOING TO SHIT OUT A KID LIKE IT'S A CANNONBALL.
"VOX WAS THE ABSOLUTE BEST OF US.
"I REALISED THAT THE MOST IMPORTANT THINGS IN THE STORY--THE THINGS WHICH REALLY MATTER--AREN'T IN THIS STORY."
VOX. CONGRATULATIONS.

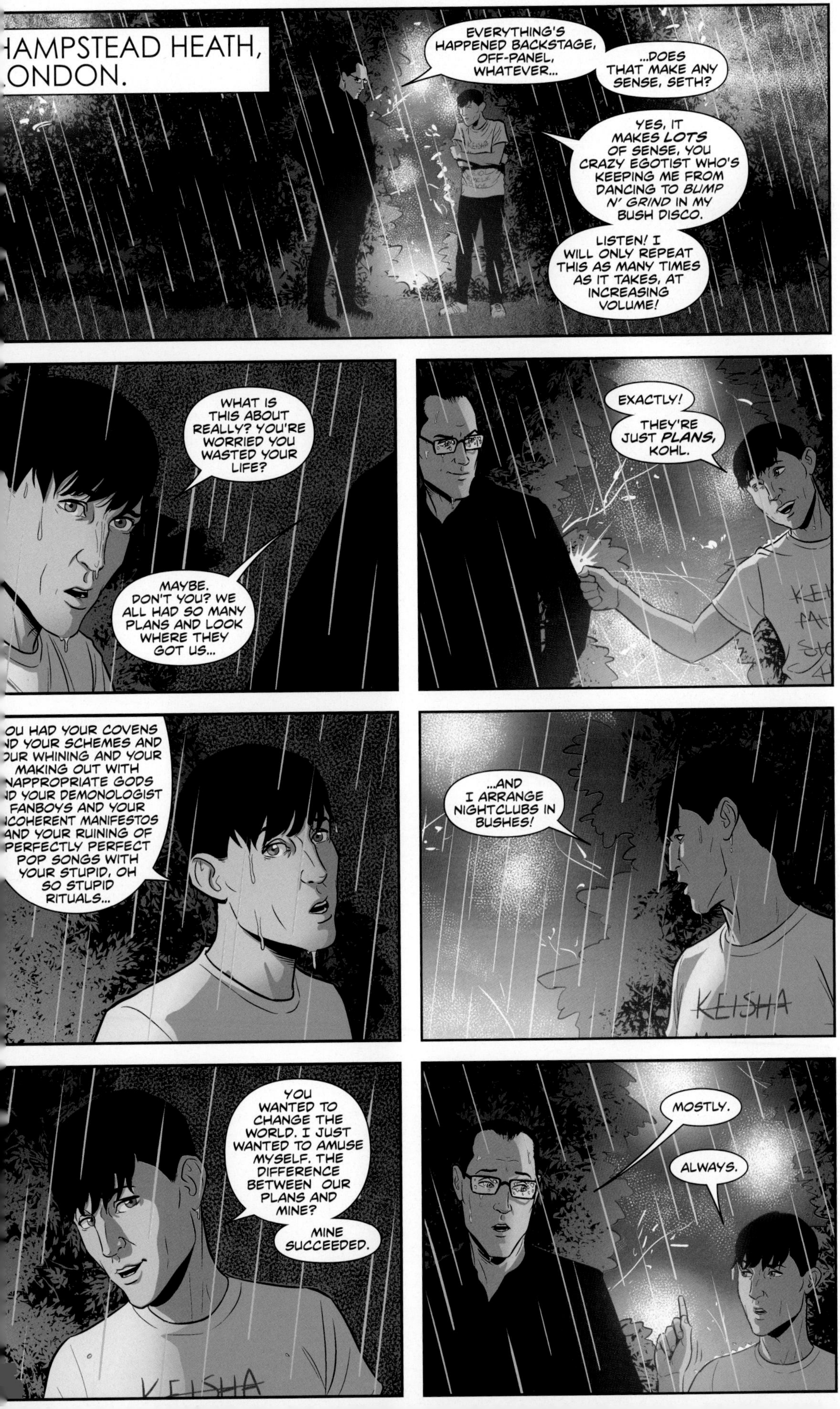

HAMPSTEAD HEATH, LONDON.
EVERYTHING'S HAPPENED BACKSTAGE, OFF-PANEL, WHATEVER...
...DOES THAT MAKE ANY SENSE, SETH?
YES, IT MAKES LOTS OF SENSE, YOU CRAZY EGOTIST WHO'S KEEPING ME FROM DANCING TO BUMP N' GRIND IN MY BUSH DISCO.
LISTEN! I WILL ONLY REPEAT THIS AS MANY TIMES AS IT TAKES, AT INCREASING VOLUME!
WHAT IS THIS ABOUT REALLY? YOU'RE WORRIED YOU WASTED YOUR LIFE?
MAYBE. DON'T YOU? WE ALL HAD SO MANY PLANS AND LOOK WHERE THEY GOT US...
EXACTLY!
THEY'RE JUST PLANS, KOHL.
KEISHA
YOU HAD YOUR COVENS AND YOUR SCHEMES AND YOUR WHINING AND YOUR MAKING OUT WITH INAPPROPRIATE GODS AND YOUR DEMONOLOGIST FANBOYS AND YOUR INCOHERENT MANIFESTOS AND YOUR RUINING OF PERFECTLY PERFECT POP SONGS WITH YOUR STUPID, OH SO STUPID RITUALS...
...AND I ARRANGE NIGHTCLUBS IN BUSHES!
KEISHA
YOU WANTED TO CHANGE THE WORLD. I JUST WANTED TO AMUSE MYSELF. THE DIFFERENCE BETWEEN OUR PLANS AND MINE?
MINE SUCCEEDED.
KEISHA
MOSTLY.
ALWAYS.

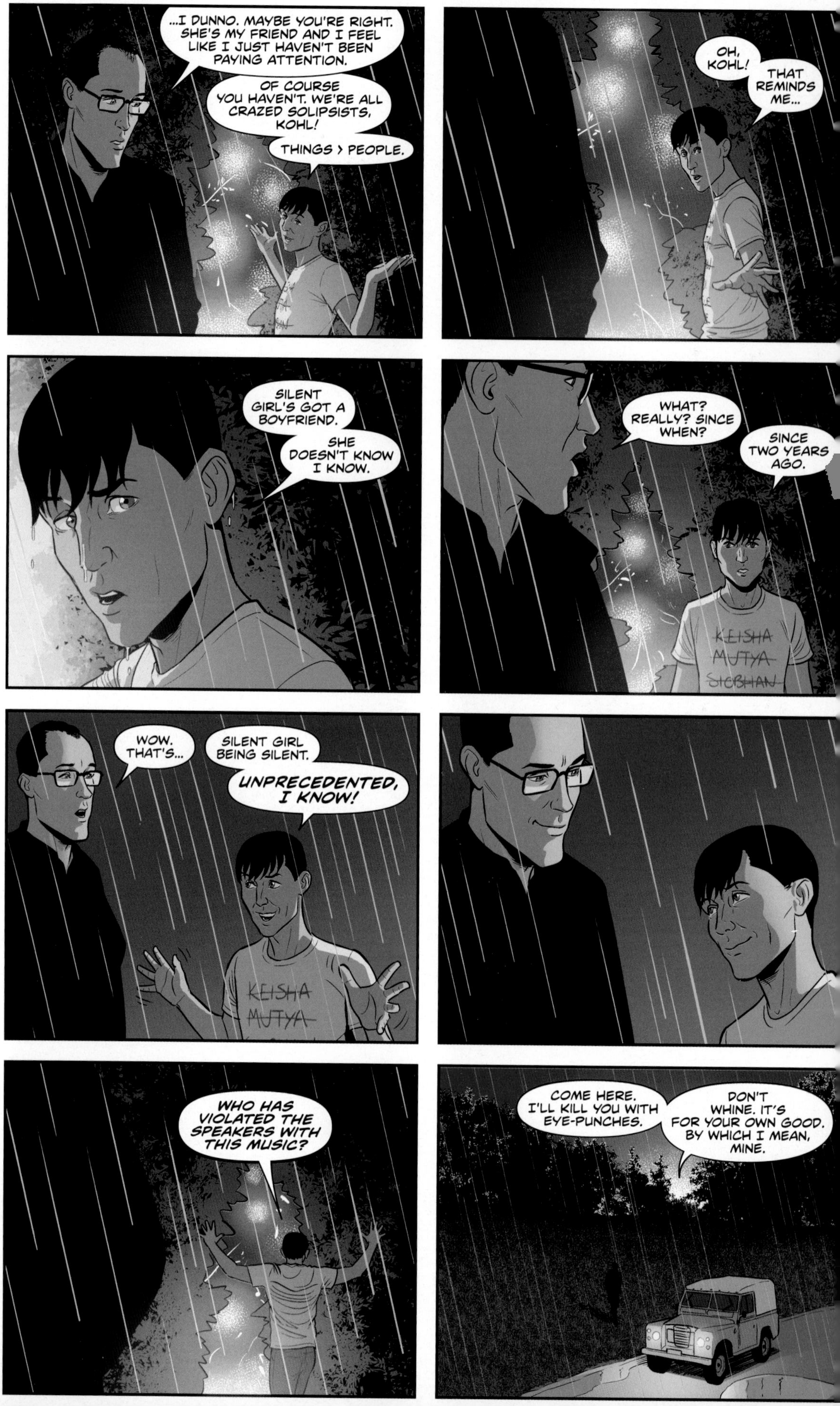
...I DUNNO. MAYBE YOU'RE RIGHT. SHE'S MY FRIEND AND I FEEL LIKE I JUST HAVEN'T BEEN PAYING ATTENTION.
OF COURSE YOU HAVEN'T. WE'RE ALL CRAZED SOLIPSISTS, KOHL!
THINGS > PEOPLE.
OH, KOHL!
THAT REMINDS ME...
SILENT GIRL'S GOT A BOYFRIEND.
SHE DOESN'T KNOW I KNOW.
WHAT? REALLY? SINCE WHEN?
SINCE TWO YEARS AGO.
KEISHA
MUTYA
SIOBHAN
WOW. THAT'S...
SILENT GIRL BEING SILENT.
UNPRECEDENTED, I KNOW!
KEISHA
MUTYA
WHO HAS VIOLATED THE SPEAKERS WITH THIS MUSIC?
COME HERE. I'LL KILL YOU WITH EYE-PUNCHES.
DON'T WHINE. IT'S FOR YOUR OWN GOOD. BY WHICH I MEAN, MINE.

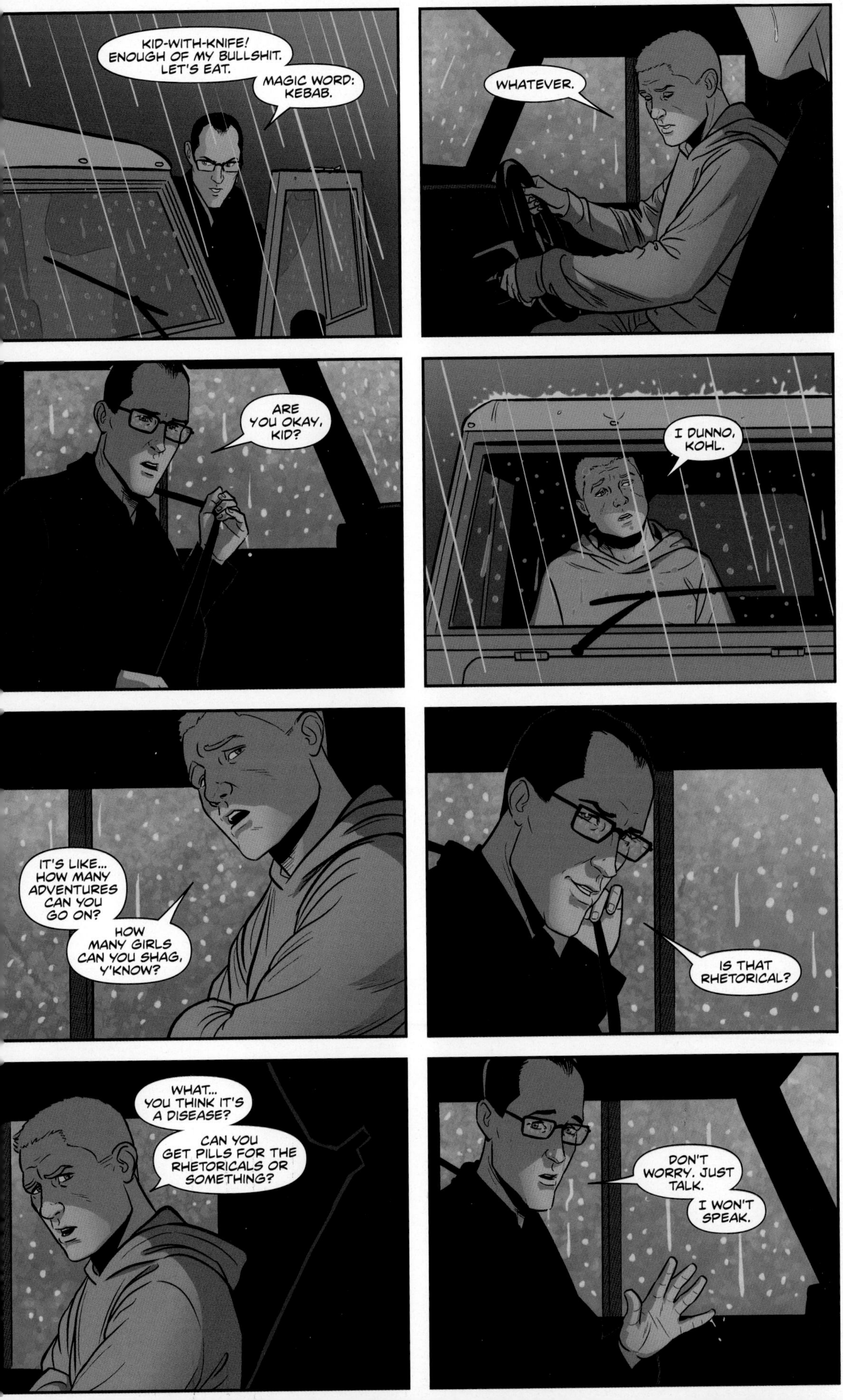
KID-WITH-KNIFE! ENOUGH OF MY BULLSHIT. LET'S EAT.
MAGIC WORD: KEBAB.
WHATEVER.
ARE YOU OKAY, KID?
I DUNNO, KOHL.
IT'S LIKE... HOW MANY ADVENTURES CAN YOU GO ON?
HOW MANY GIRLS CAN YOU SHAG, Y'KNOW?
IS THAT RHETORICAL?
WHAT... YOU THINK IT'S A DISEASE?
CAN YOU GET PILLS FOR THE RHETORICALS OR SOMETHING?
DON'T WORRY. JUST TALK.
I WON'T SPEAK.

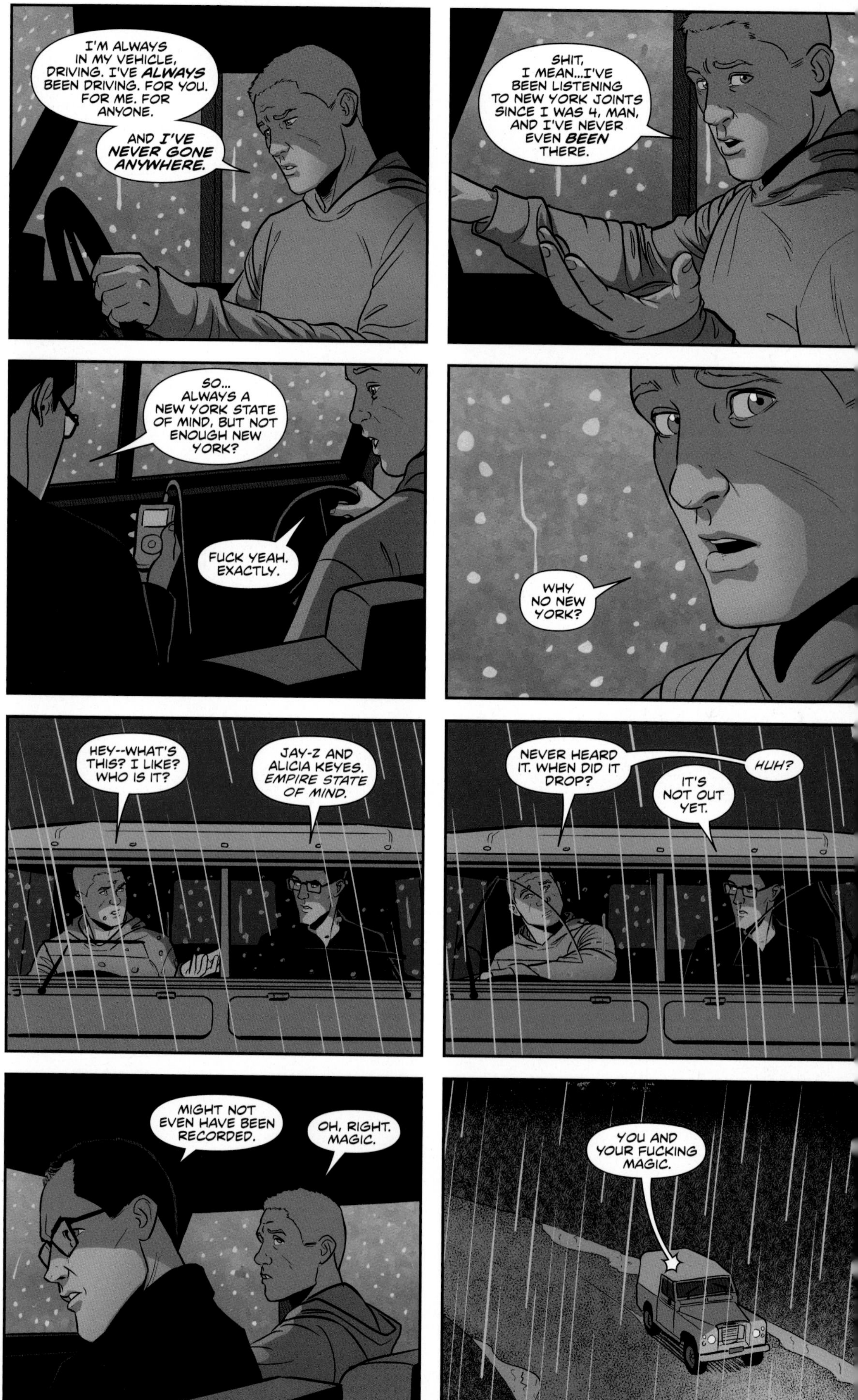
I'M ALWAYS IN MY VEHICLE, DRIVING. I'VE ALWAYS BEEN DRIVING. FOR YOU. FOR ME. FOR ANYONE.
AND I'VE NEVER GONE ANYWHERE.
SHIT, I MEAN...I'VE BEEN LISTENING TO NEW YORK JOINTS SINCE I WAS 4, MAN, AND I'VE NEVER EVEN BEEN THERE.
SO... ALWAYS A NEW YORK STATE OF MIND, BUT NOT ENOUGH NEW YORK?
FUCK YEAH. EXACTLY.
WHY NO NEW YORK?
HEY--WHAT'S THIS? I LIKE? WHO IS IT?
JAY-Z AND ALICIA KEYES. EMPIRE STATE OF MIND.
NEVER HEARD IT. WHEN DID IT DROP?
HUH?
IT'S NOT OUT YET.
MIGHT NOT EVEN HAVE BEEN RECORDED.
OH, RIGHT. MAGIC.
YOU AND YOUR FUCKING MAGIC.

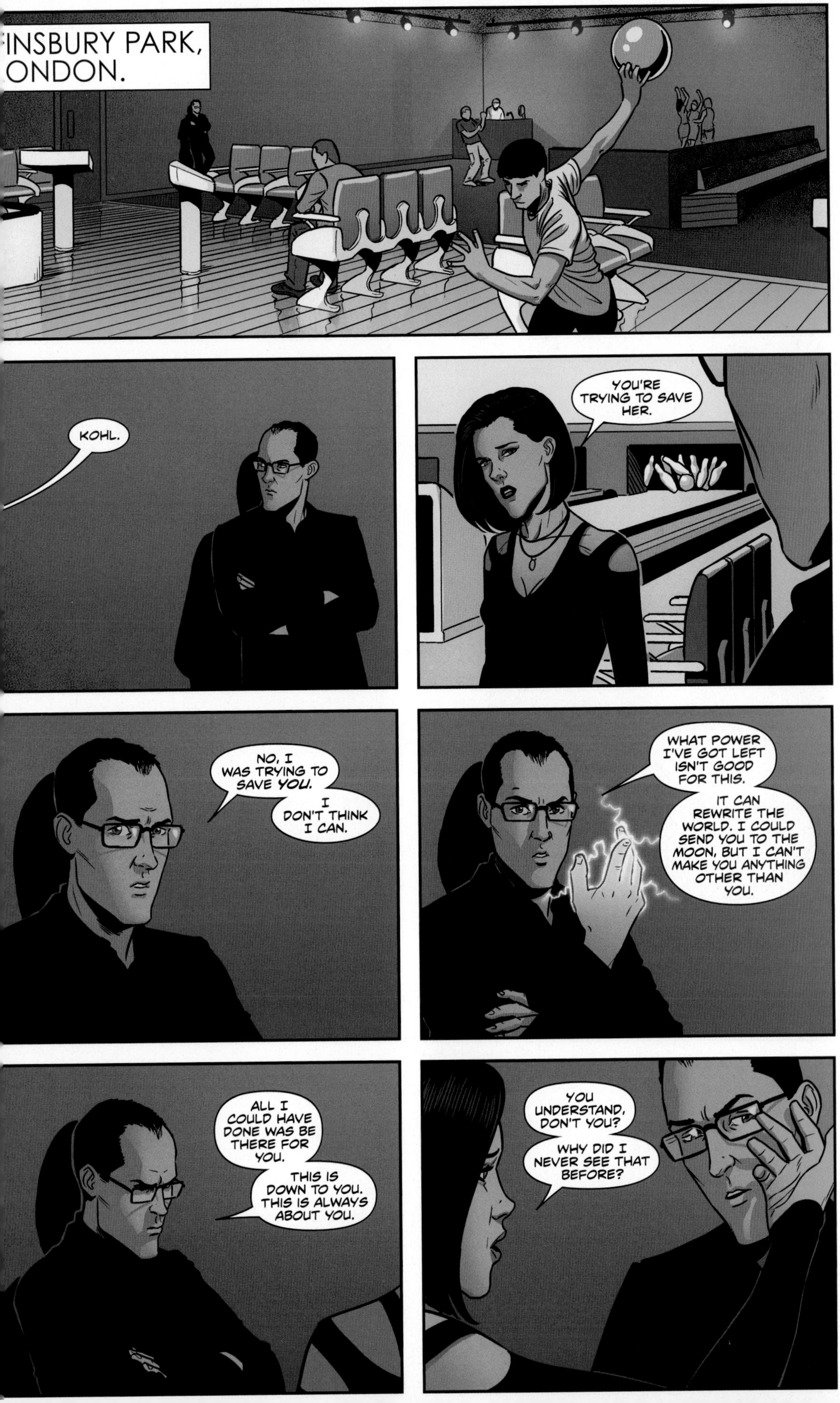

INSBURY PARK, ONDON.
KOHL.
YOU'RE TRYING TO SAVE HER.
NO, I WAS TRYING TO SAVE YOU.
I DON'T THINK I CAN.
WHAT POWER I'VE GOT LEFT ISN'T GOOD FOR THIS.
IT CAN REWRITE THE WORLD. I COULD SEND YOU TO THE MOON, BUT I CAN'T MAKE YOU ANYTHING OTHER THAN YOU.
ALL I COULD HAVE DONE WAS BE THERE FOR YOU.
THIS IS DOWN TO YOU. THIS IS ALWAYS ABOUT YOU.
YOU UNDERSTAND, DON'T YOU?
WHY DID I NEVER SEE THAT BEFORE?

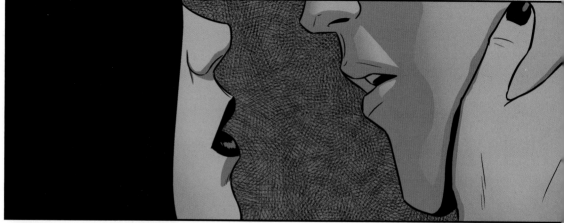

NO. SORRY, EMILY. IT'S NOT RIGHT.

I KNOW. BUT WHAT IS?

YOU WERE NEITHER A GOOD FRIEND NOR A GOOD PERSON. BUT IT WAS GOOD KNOWING YOU.

GOD, I WISH IT WAS RIGHT.

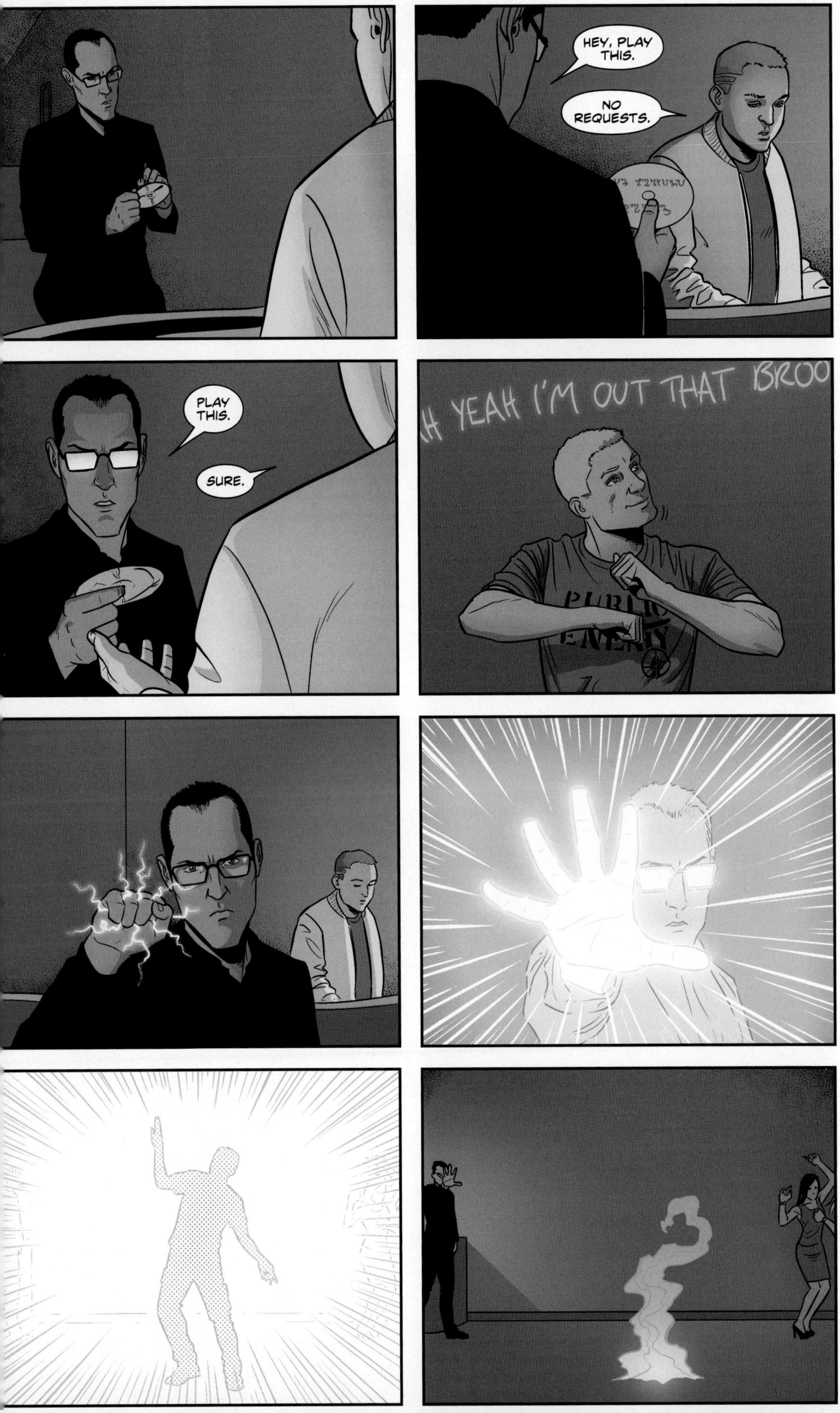
HEY, PLAY THIS.
NO REQUESTS.
PLAY THIS.
SURE.
...H YEAH I'M OUT THAT BROO...
PUBLIC ENEMY

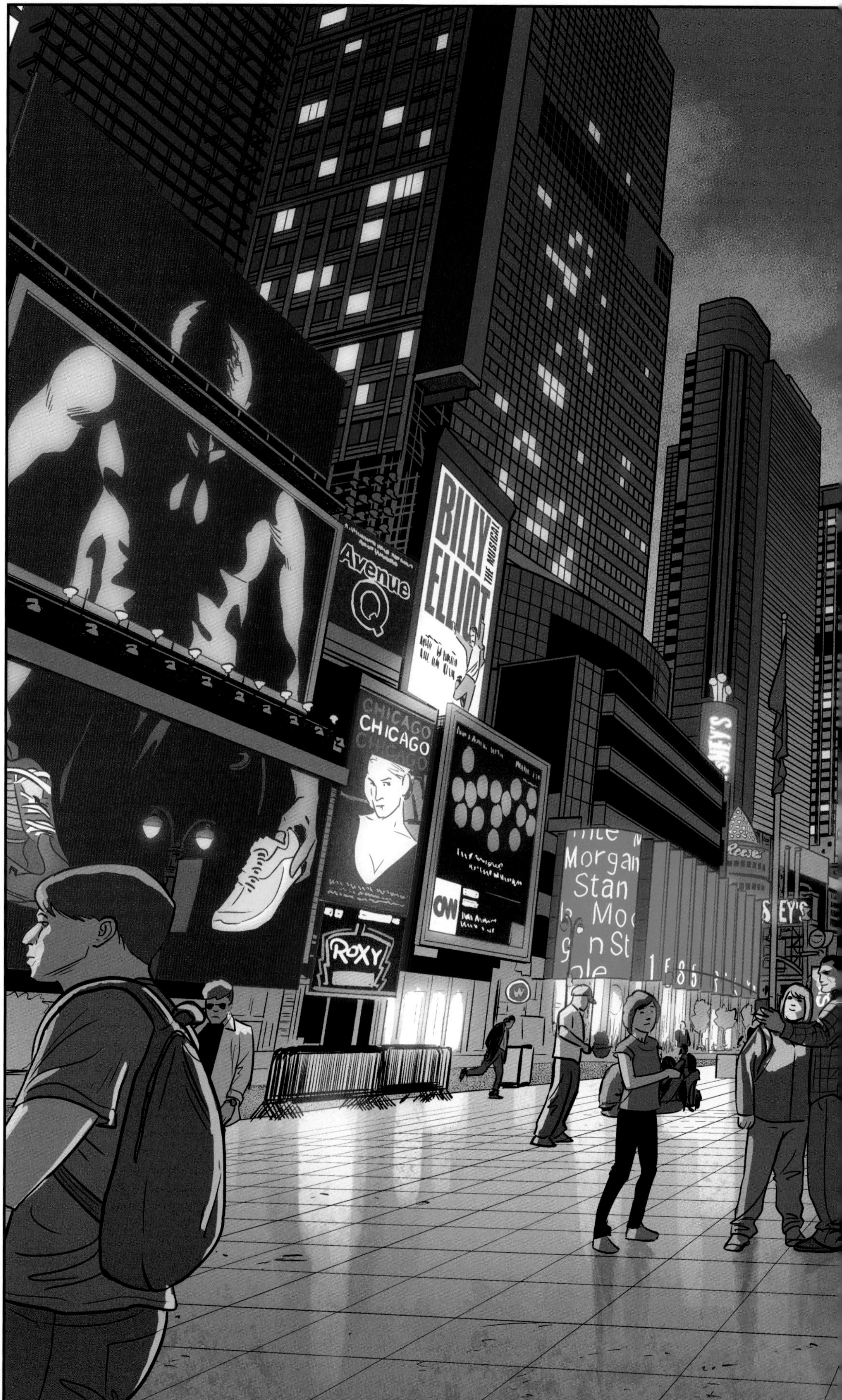

BILLY ELLIOT
THE MUSICAL
Avenue Q
CHICAGO
CHICAGO
ROXY
CNN

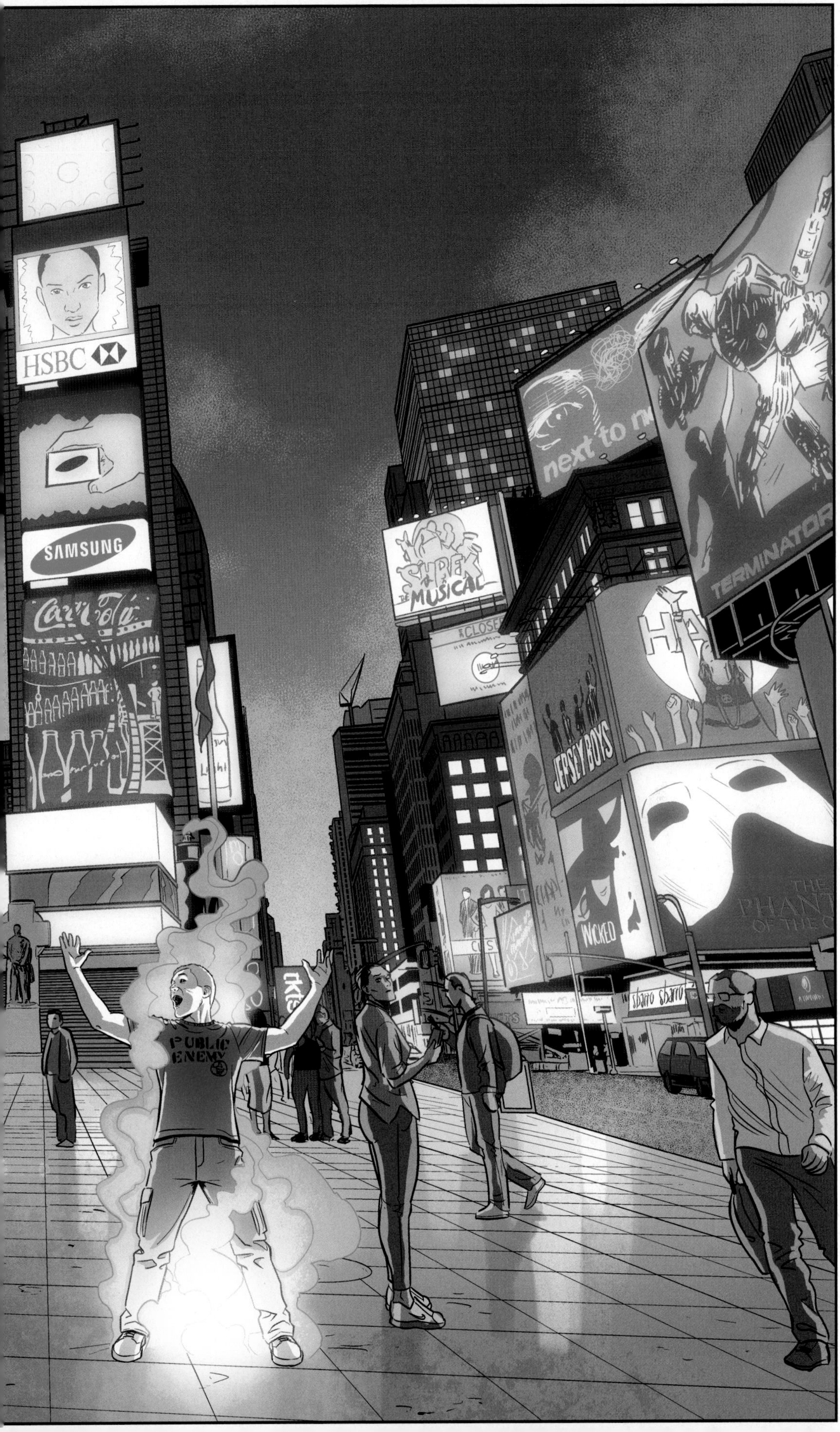
HSBC
SAMSUNG
Coca-Cola
SHREK THE MUSICAL
TERMINATOR
JERSEY BOYS
WICKED
PUBLIC ENEMY
sbarro sbarro

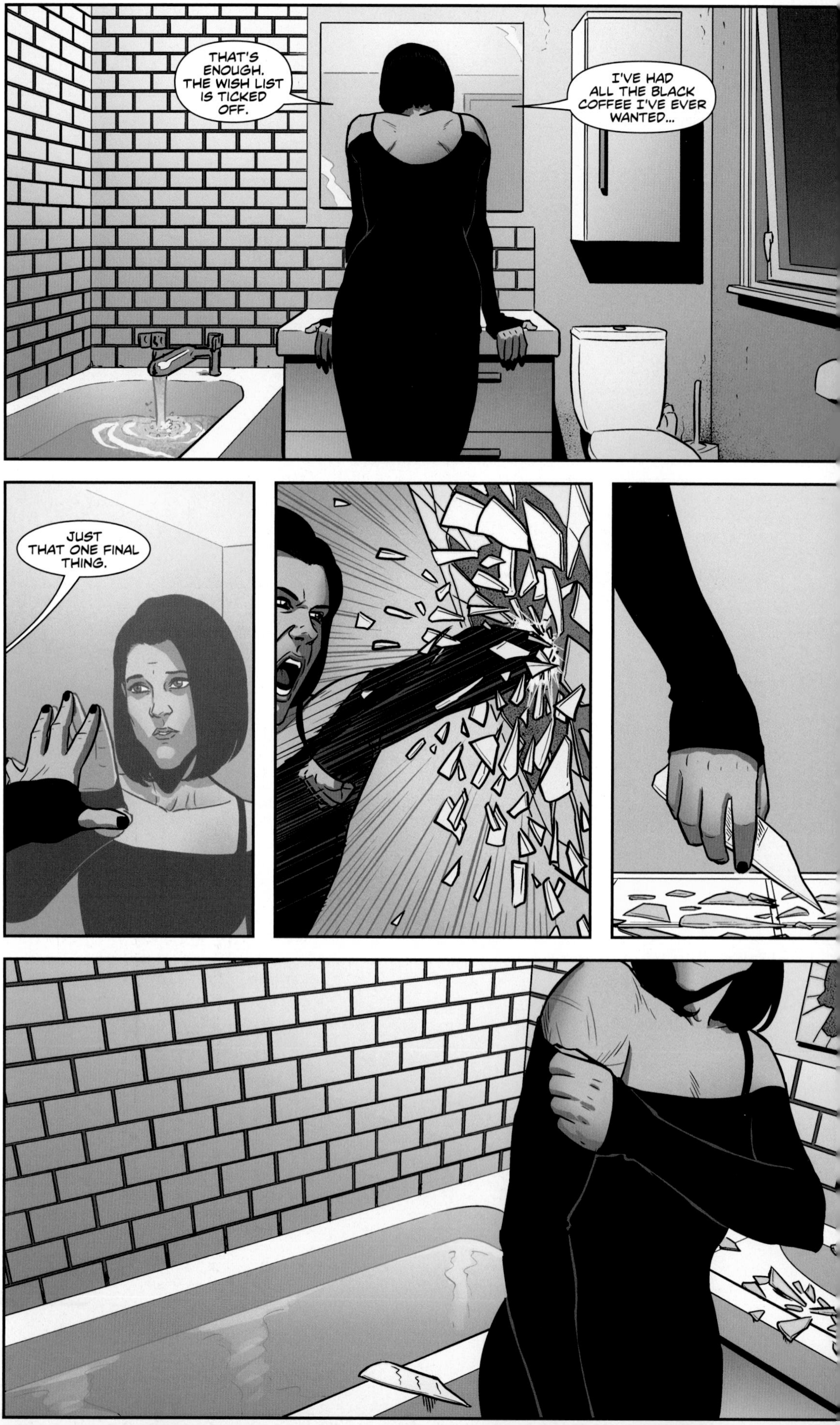
THAT'S ENOUGH. THE WISH LIST IS TICKED OFF.
I'VE HAD ALL THE BLACK COFFEE I'VE EVER WANTED...
JUST THAT ONE FINAL THING.

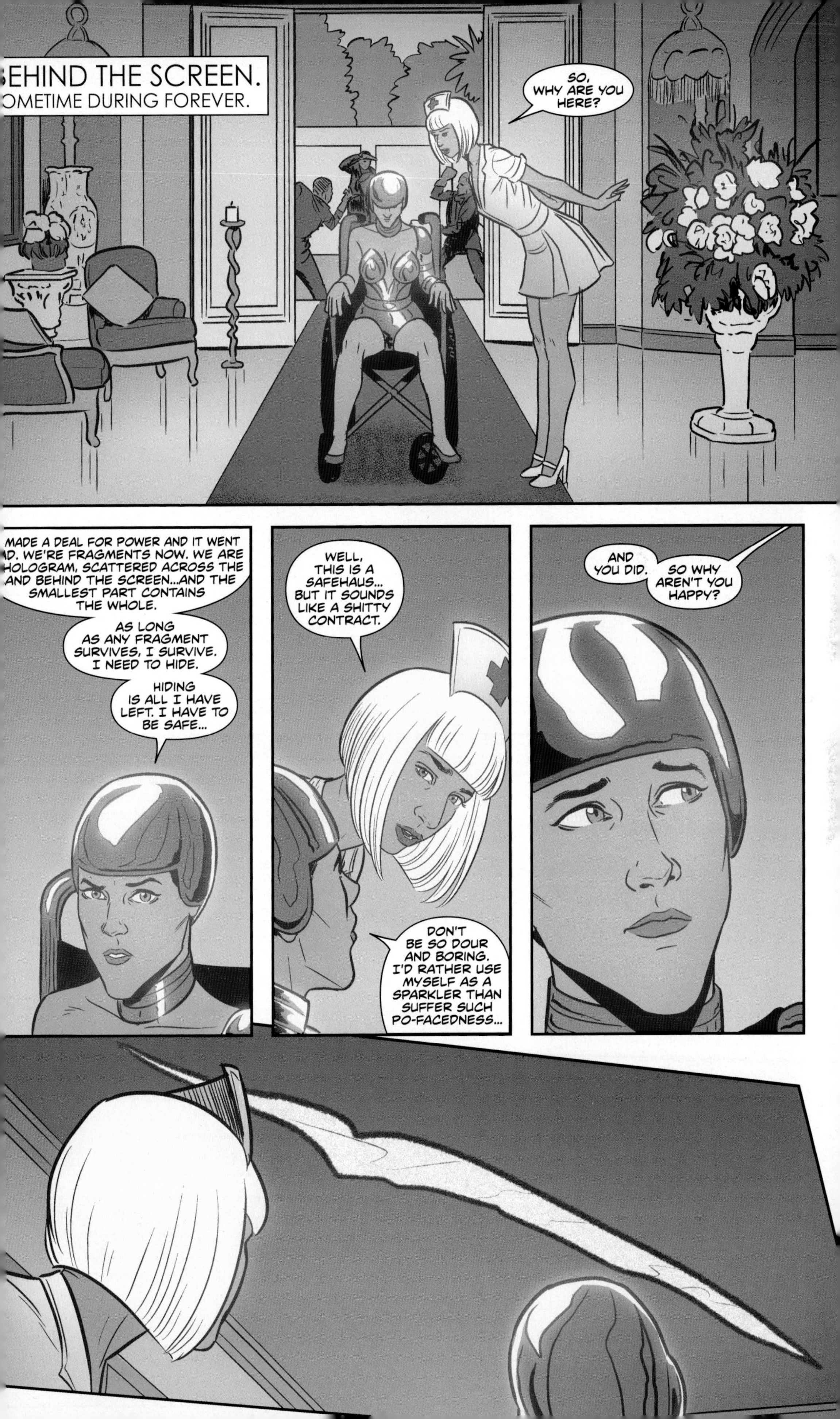

EHIND THE SCREEN.
OMETIME DURING FOREVER.
SO, WHY ARE YOU HERE?
MADE A DEAL FOR POWER AND IT WENT D. WE'RE FRAGMENTS NOW. WE ARE HOLOGRAM, SCATTERED ACROSS THE AND BEHIND THE SCREEN...AND THE SMALLEST PART CONTAINS THE WHOLE.
AS LONG AS ANY FRAGMENT SURVIVES, I SURVIVE. I NEED TO HIDE.
HIDING IS ALL I HAVE LEFT. I HAVE TO BE SAFE...
WELL, THIS IS A SAFEHAUS... BUT IT SOUNDS LIKE A SHITTY CONTRACT.
DON'T BE SO DOUR AND BORING. I'D RATHER USE MYSELF AS A SPARKLER THAN SUFFER SUCH PO-FACEDNESS...
AND YOU DID.
SO WHY AREN'T YOU HAPPY?

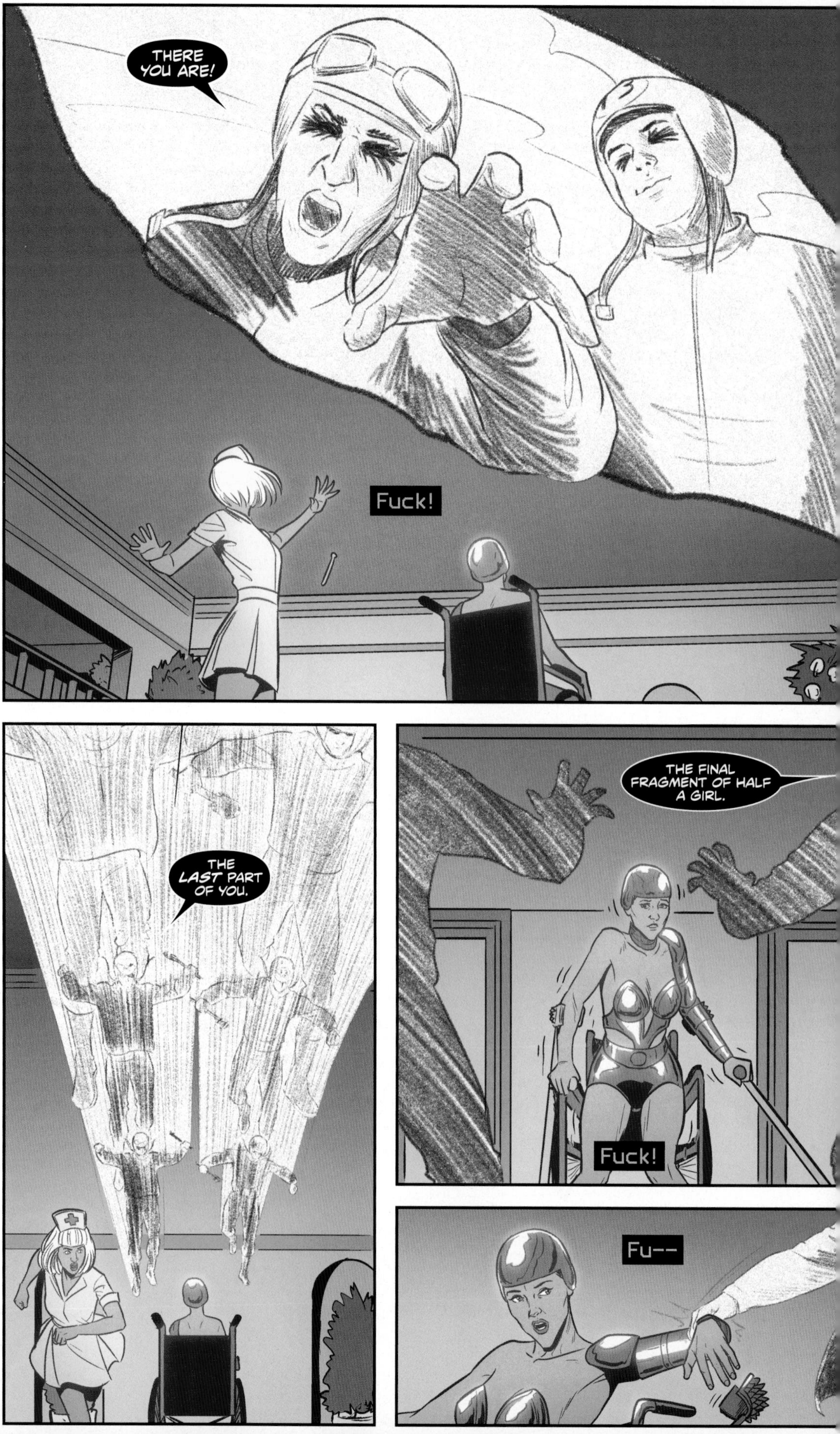
THERE YOU ARE!
Fuck!
THE LAST PART OF YOU.
THE FINAL FRAGMENT OF HALF A GIRL.
Fuck!
Fu--

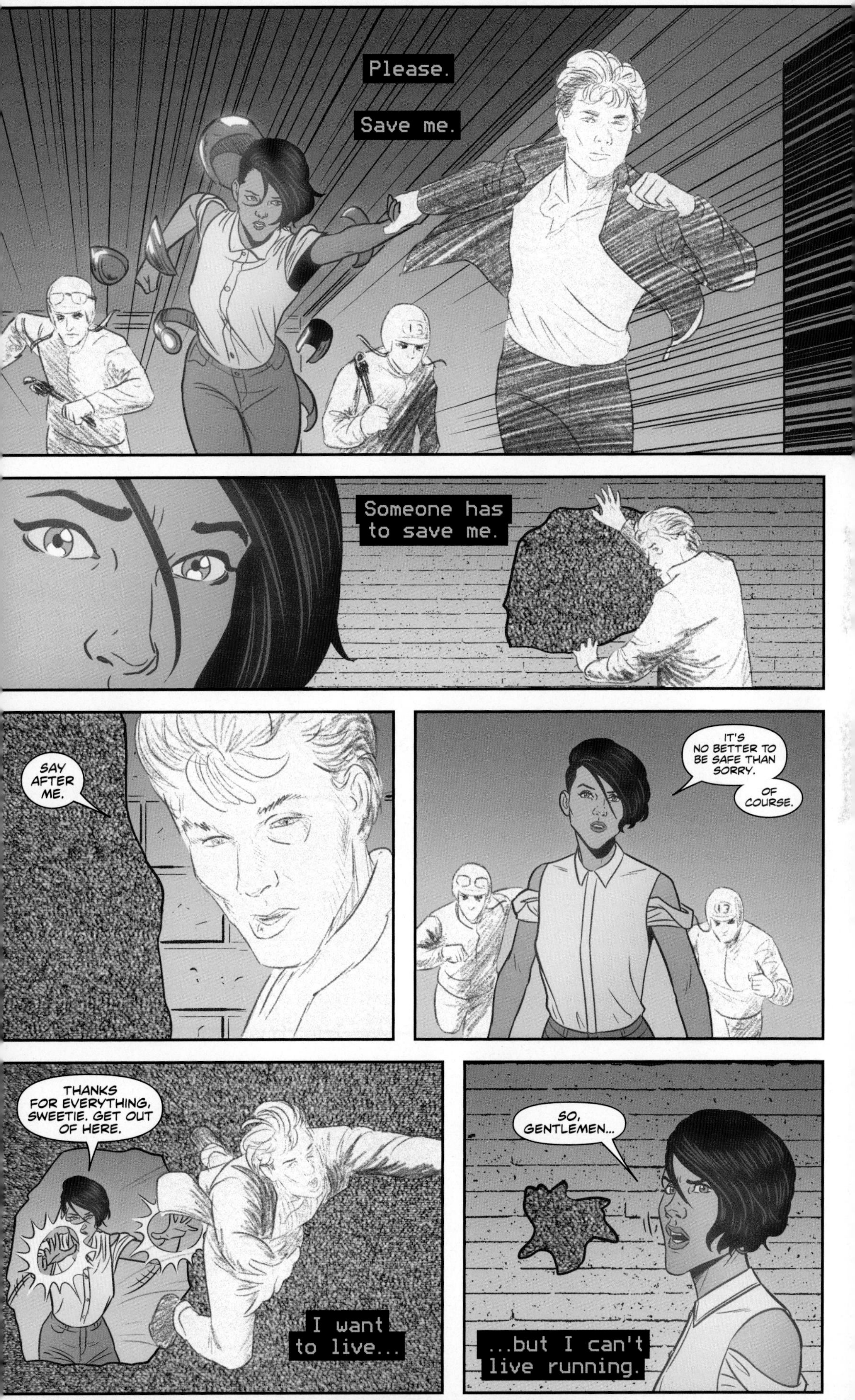
Please.
Save me.
Someone has to save me.
SAY AFTER ME.
IT'S NO BETTER TO BE SAFE THAN SORRY.
OF COURSE.
THANKS FOR EVERYTHING, SWEETIE. GET OUT OF HERE.
I want to live...
SO, GENTLEMEN...
...but I can't live running.

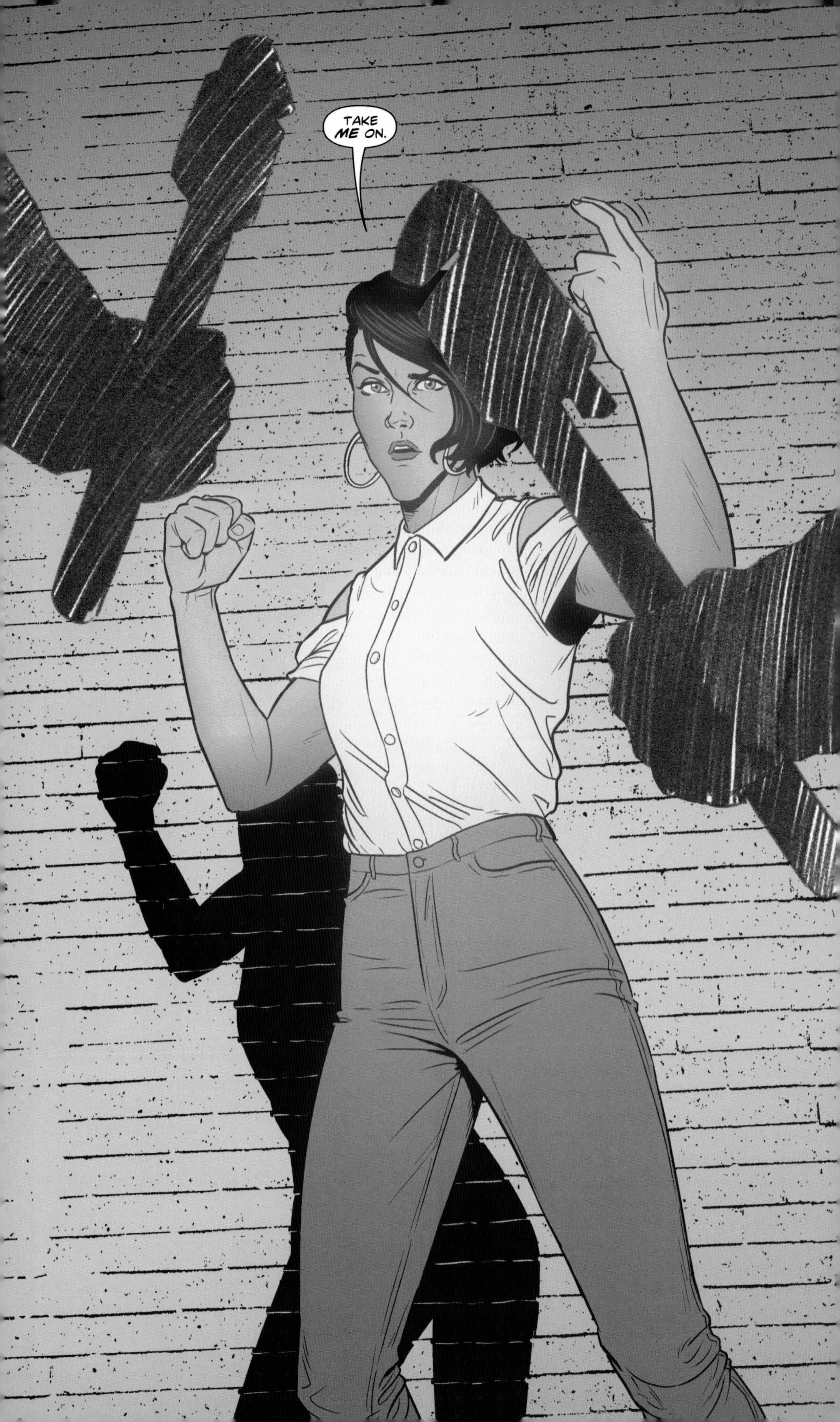
TAKE *ME* ON.

P H O N O G R A M

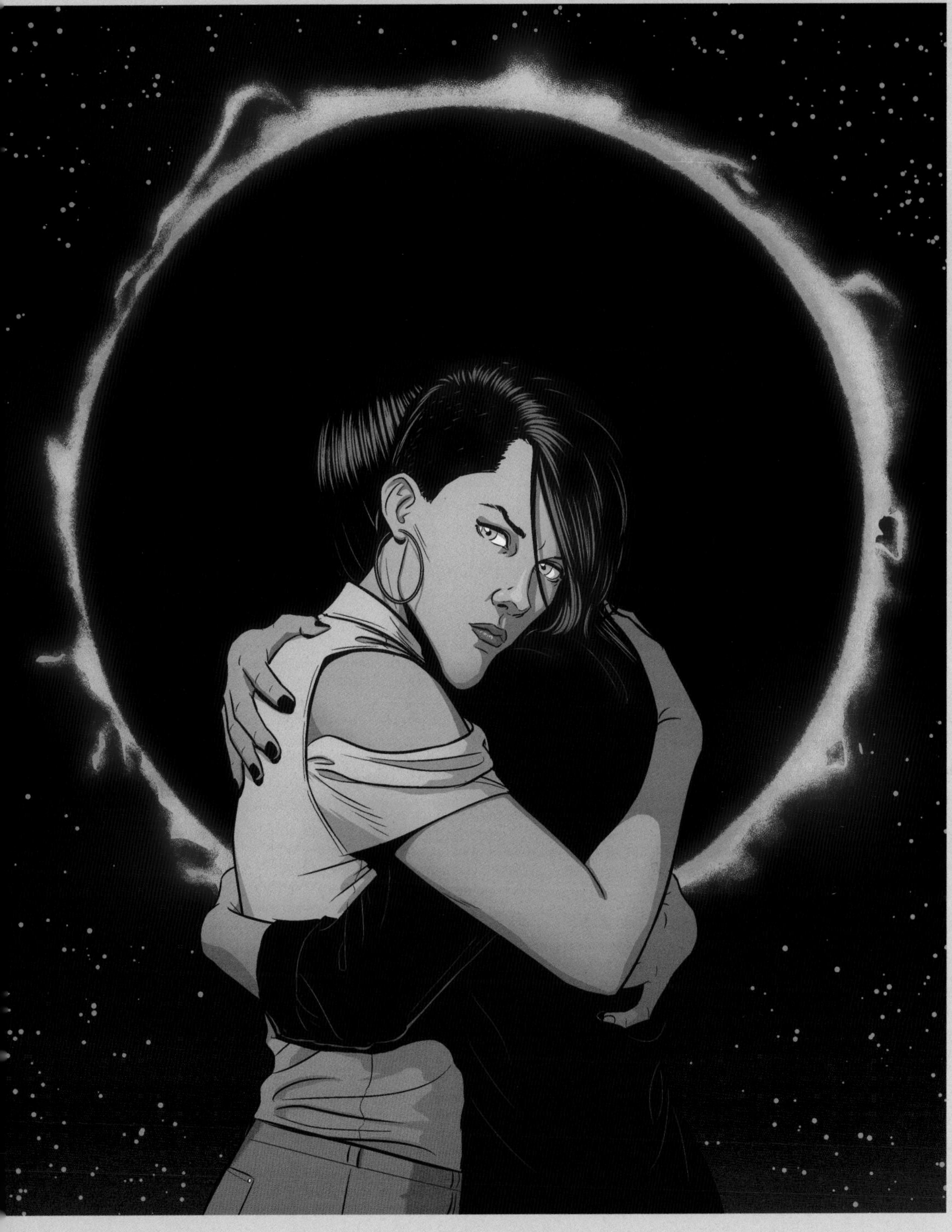

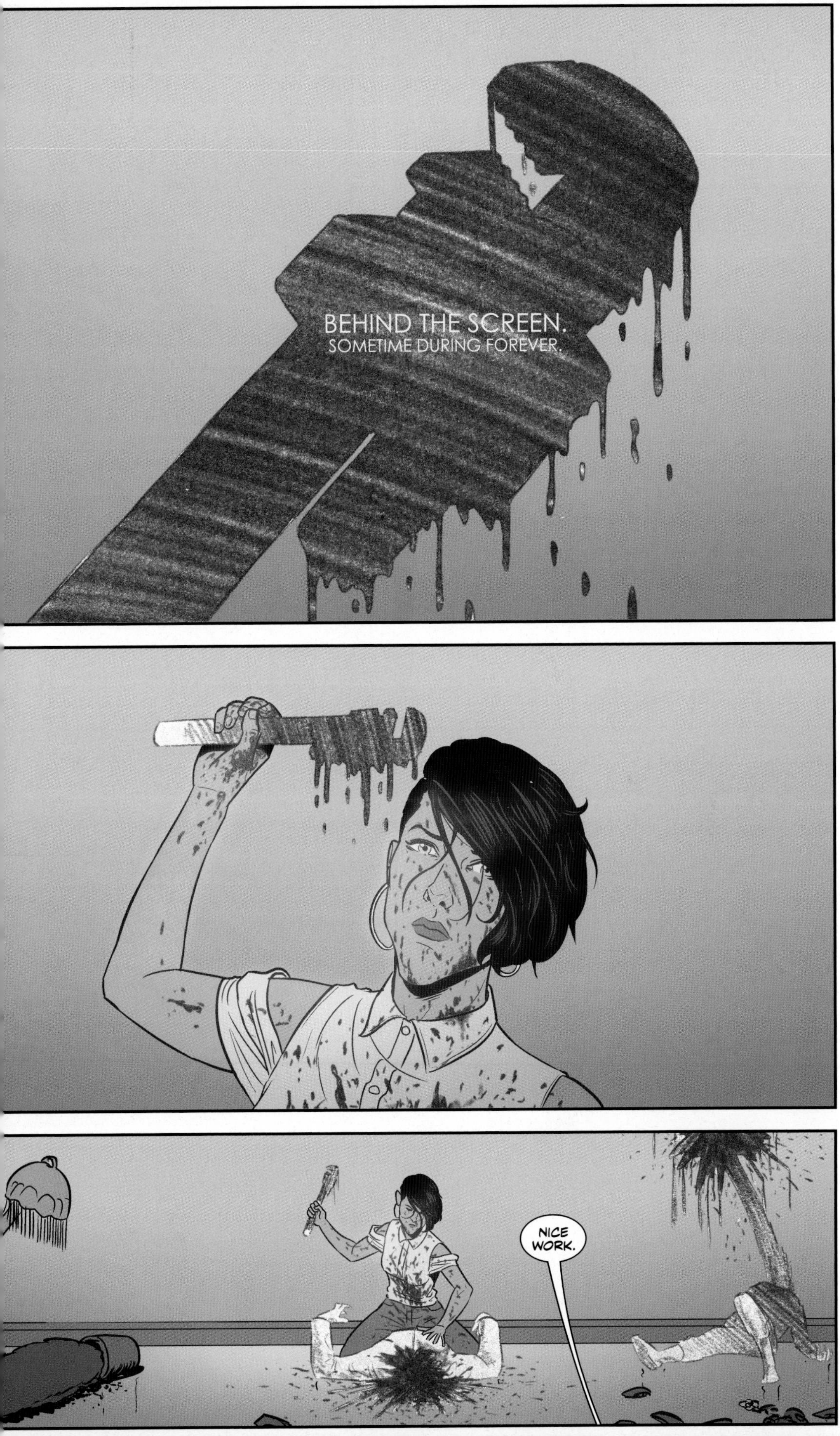
BEHIND THE SCREEN.
SOMETIME DURING FOREVER.
NICE WORK.

I DECIDED TO FIGHT.

BIT TOO LATE, BUT IT'S THE THOUGHT THAT COUNTS, I SUPPOSE.

WHAT IS SHE DOING? IN YOUR REAL WORLD.

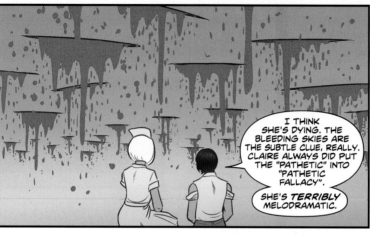

I THINK SHE'S DYING. THE BLEEDING SKIES ARE THE SUBTLE CLUE, REALLY. CLAIRE ALWAYS DID PUT THE "PATHETIC" INTO "PATHETIC FALLACY".

SHE'S *TERRIBLY* MELODRAMATIC.

I'VE DECIDED TO FIGHT, BUT I'VE NOTHING TO PUNCH BUT MYSELF.

I FEEL LIKE PUNCHING MYSELF A LOT.

THAT WOULD BE A START.

LISTEN, EMILY. YOU MADE A DEAL. WE ALL DO. WE ALL TALK TO THE IMAGES AND COME TO AN ARRANGEMENT. YOU WANT TO BREAK IT? *REALLY* BREAK IT?

YOU DO THE SAME.

I DON'T KNOW HOW.

I DON'T KNOW WHO TO TALK TO.

WHO ARE YOU TALKING TO NOW?

WELL, IT'S...

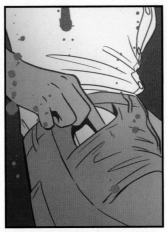

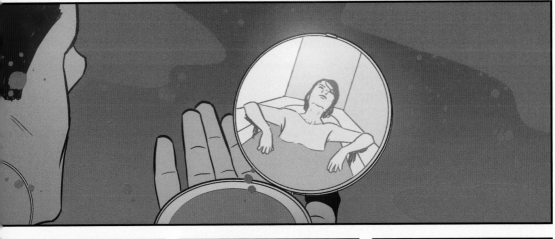

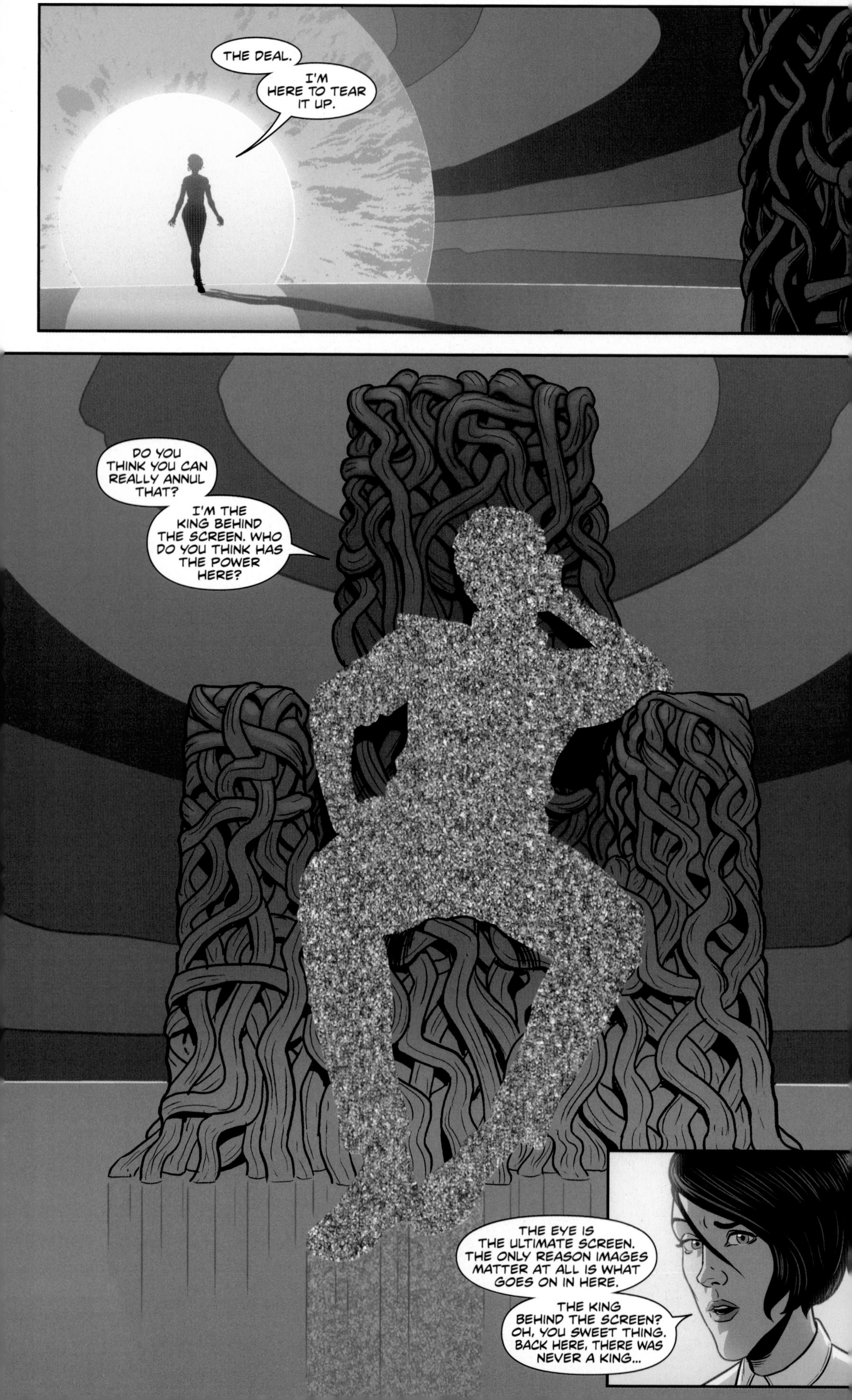
THE DEAL.
I'M HERE TO TEAR IT UP.
DO YOU THINK YOU CAN REALLY ANNUL THAT?
I'M THE KING BEHIND THE SCREEN. WHO DO YOU THINK HAS THE POWER HERE?
THE EYE IS THE ULTIMATE SCREEN. THE ONLY REASON IMAGES MATTER AT ALL IS WHAT GOES ON IN HERE.
THE KING BEHIND THE SCREEN? OH, YOU SWEET THING. BACK HERE, THERE WAS NEVER A KING...

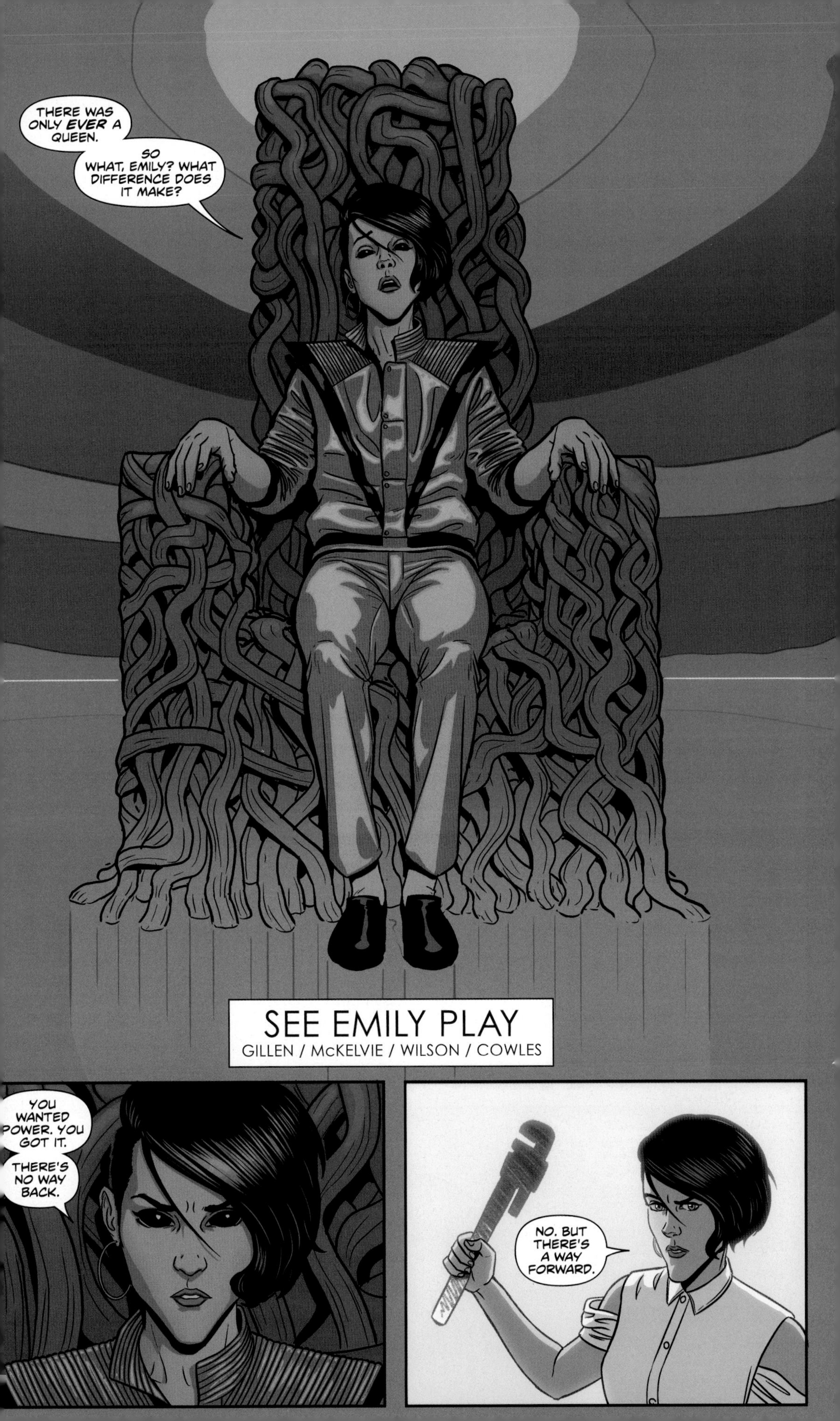
THERE WAS ONLY *EVER* A QUEEN.
SO WHAT, EMILY? WHAT DIFFERENCE DOES IT MAKE?
SEE EMILY PLAY
GILLEN / McKELVIE / WILSON / COWLES
YOU WANTED POWER. YOU GOT IT.
THERE'S NO WAY BACK.
NO. BUT THERE'S A WAY FORWARD.

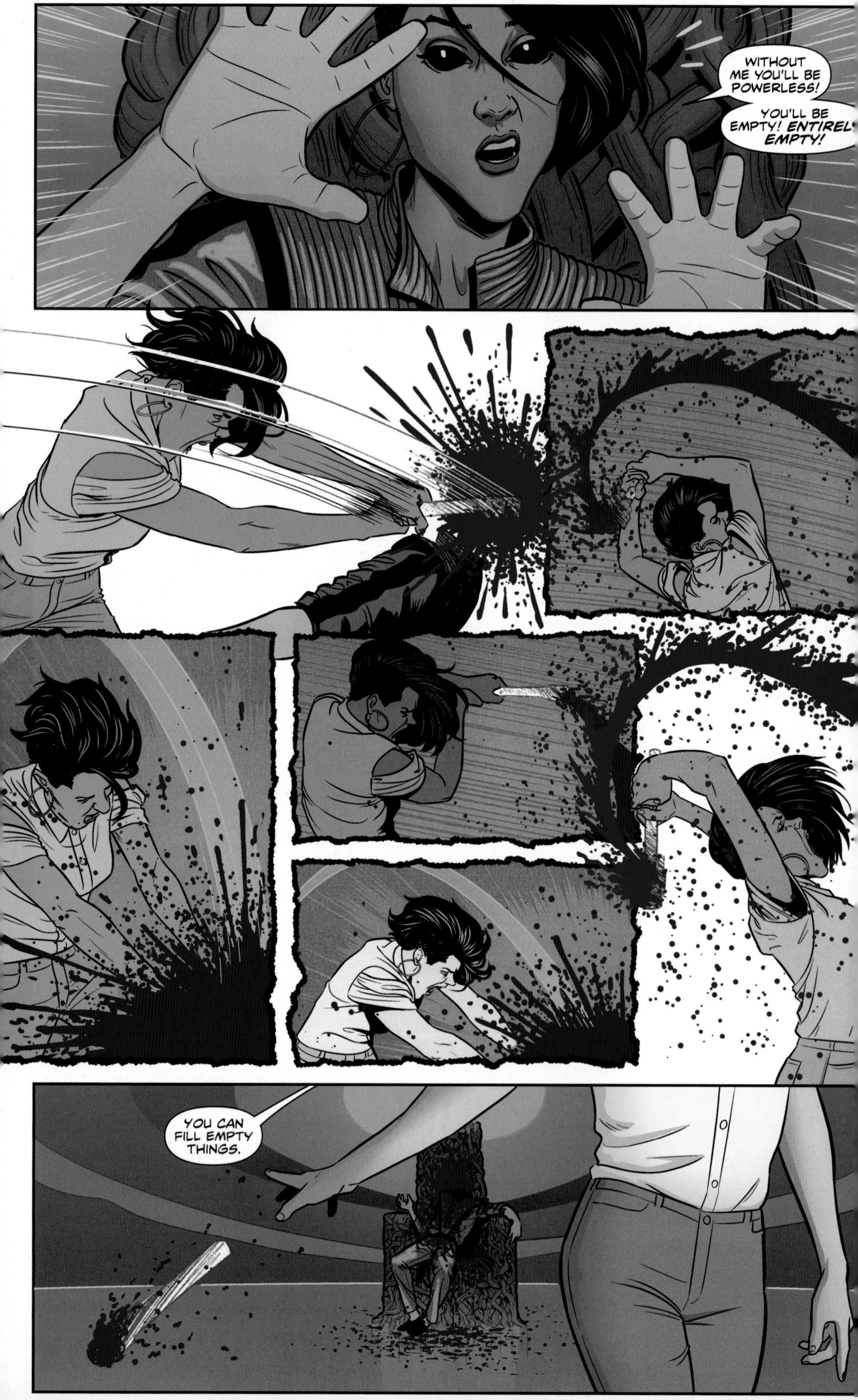
WITHOUT ME YOU'LL BE POWERLESS!
YOU'LL BE EMPTY! ENTIREL EMPTY!
YOU CAN FILL EMPTY THINGS.

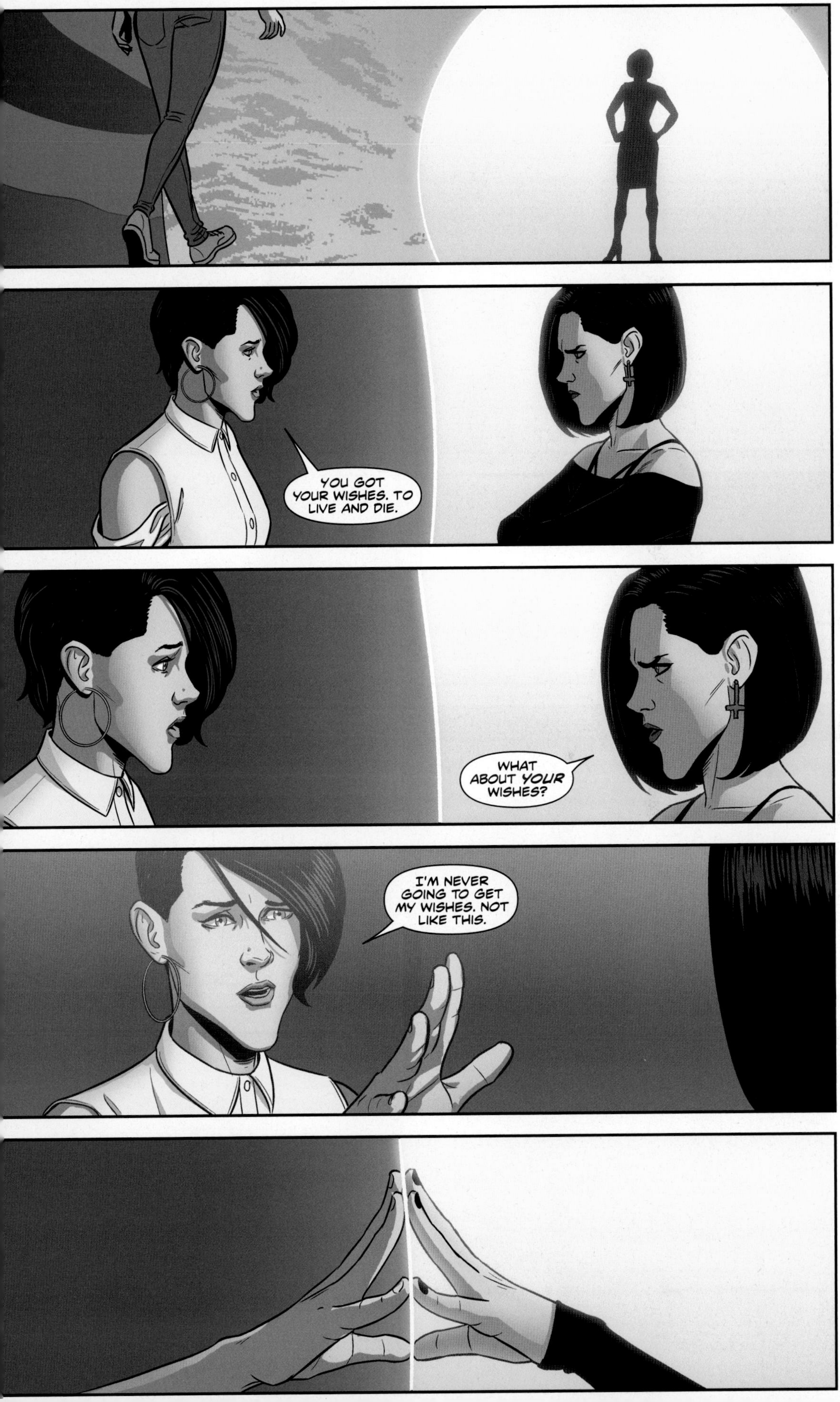
YOU GOT YOUR WISHES. TO LIVE AND DIE.
WHAT ABOUT *YOUR* WISHES?
I'M NEVER GOING TO GET MY WISHES. NOT LIKE THIS.

I LOVE YOU.

NO YOU DON'T.

NO, CLAIRE, I DON'T.

BUT I WISH I DID.

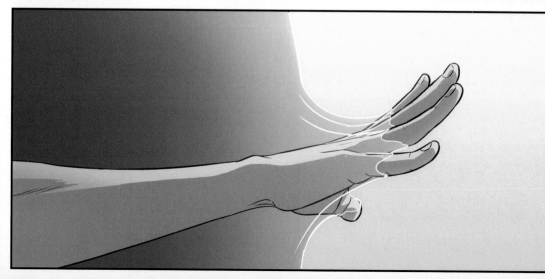

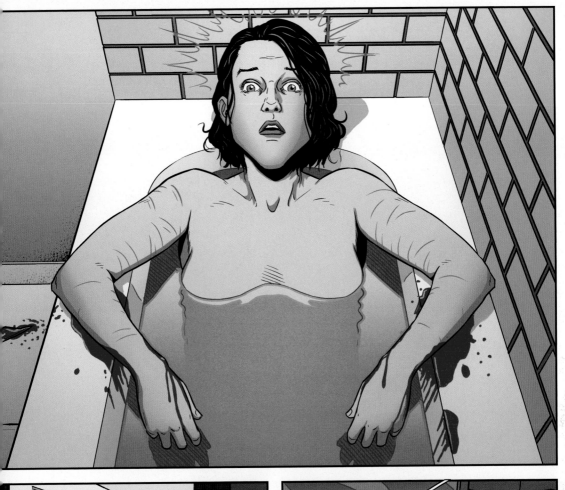

I NEED HELP.

FUCK FUCK FUCK.

Kohl

Jackson's dead.

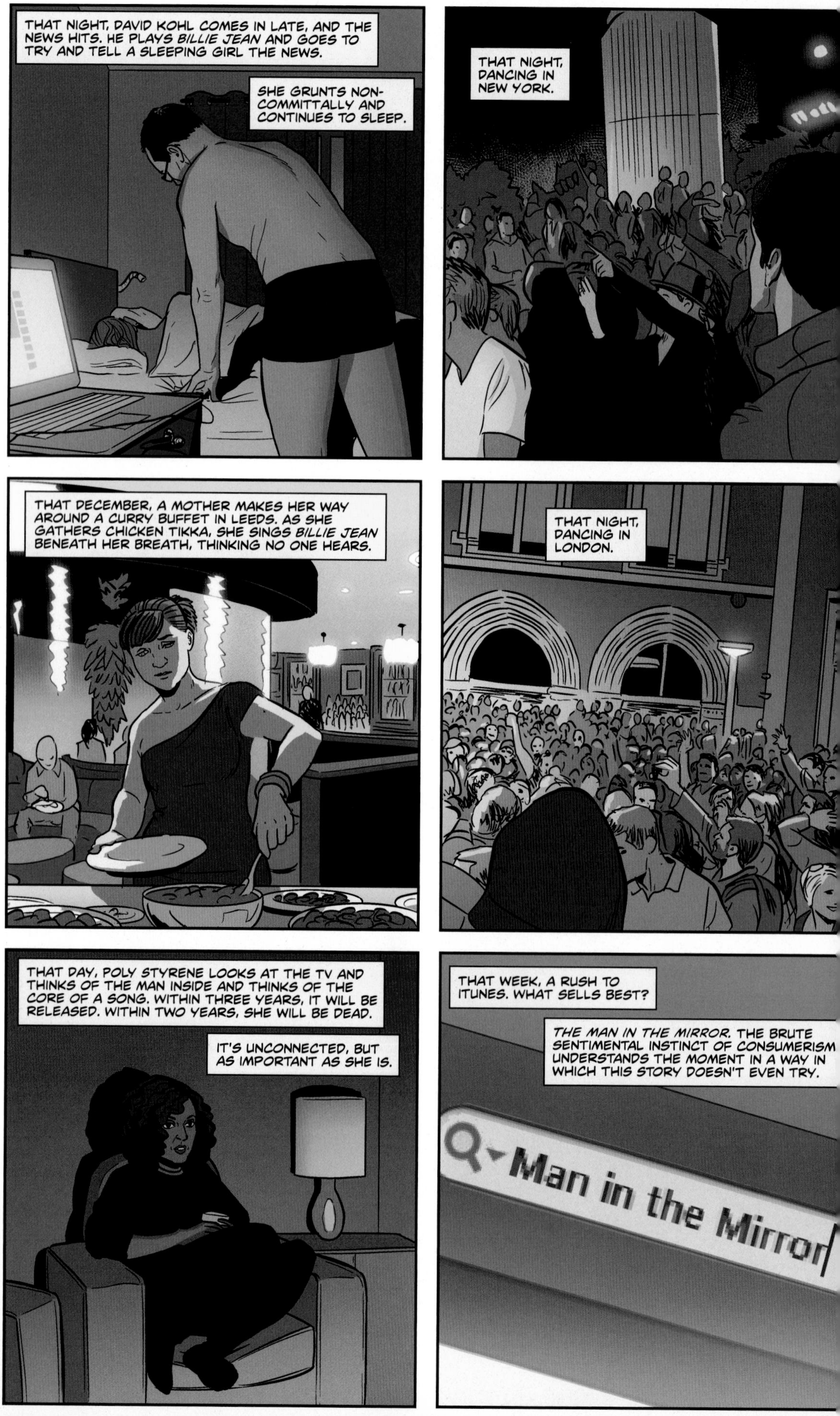
THAT NIGHT, DAVID KOHL COMES IN LATE, AND THE NEWS HITS. HE PLAYS *BILLIE JEAN* AND GOES TO TRY AND TELL A SLEEPING GIRL THE NEWS.
SHE GRUNTS NON-COMMITTALLY AND CONTINUES TO SLEEP.
THAT NIGHT, DANCING IN NEW YORK.
THAT DECEMBER, A MOTHER MAKES HER WAY AROUND A CURRY BUFFET IN LEEDS. AS SHE GATHERS CHICKEN TIKKA, SHE SINGS *BILLIE JEAN* BENEATH HER BREATH, THINKING NO ONE HEARS.
THAT NIGHT, DANCING IN LONDON.
THAT DAY, POLY STYRENE LOOKS AT THE TV AND THINKS OF THE MAN INSIDE AND THINKS OF THE CORE OF A SONG. WITHIN THREE YEARS, IT WILL BE RELEASED. WITHIN TWO YEARS, SHE WILL BE DEAD.
IT'S UNCONNECTED, BUT AS IMPORTANT AS SHE IS.
THAT WEEK, A RUSH TO ITUNES. WHAT SELLS BEST?
THE MAN IN THE MIRROR. THE BRUTE SENTIMENTAL INSTINCT OF CONSUMERISM UNDERSTANDS THE MOMENT IN A WAY IN WHICH THIS STORY DOESN'T EVEN TRY.
Man in the Mirror

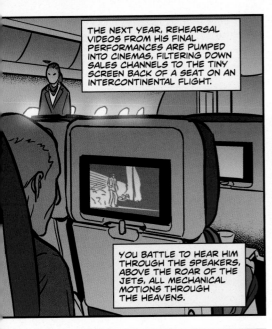

THE NEXT YEAR, REHEARSAL VIDEOS FROM HIS FINAL PERFORMANCES ARE PUMPED INTO CINEMAS, FILTERING DOWN SALES CHANNELS TO THE TINY SCREEN BACK OF A SEAT ON AN INTERCONTINENTAL FLIGHT.

YOU BATTLE TO HEAR HIM THROUGH THE SPEAKERS, ABOVE THE ROAR OF THE JETS, ALL MECHANICAL MOTIONS THROUGH THE HEAVENS.

THAT NIGHT, BLACK LAURA WAS ASLEEP. BY MORNING SHE'S BEEN TOLD BY A TEXT FROM HER MOST AWKWARD ALLY. SHE FEARS FOR THE LONG BLONDES' SINGER, UNTIL SHE TURNS TO THE NEWS.

NOT KATE. *MICHAEL.* A SIGH OF RELIEF, CUT SHORT. SHE THINKS HERSELF A TERRIBLE PERSON.

WO YEARS LATER, A COURT CASE ENDS. NVOLUNTARY MANSLAUGHTER. DRUGS. THE FACTS ON'T SEEM TO SHAKE EVERYONE'S NAGGING MPRESSION THAT IT WAS FATED, THAT IT'D HAVE APPENED ANYWAY.

MUSIC WOULDN'T BE MAGIC IF PEOPLE WEREN'T IRRATIONAL. THAT CUTS ALL SORTS OF WAYS.

EARLY NEXT YEAR, AN OPEN MIC NIGHT IN NORTH LONDON. WITH WOOD AND STRING HE ATTACKS *DIRTY DIANA.* HE SMILES, AS IF IT'S ALL A JOKE.

A PHONOMANCER IN THE CROWD, TOO OLD TO FEEL SO ANGRY, WISHES HIM IMMOLATED.

AUGUST 2012, A MINOR COMIC WRITER ON THE NORTHERN LINE. HE'S HALFWAY THROUGH HIS CURRENT PROJECT, SET IN THE PERIOD AROUND JACKSON'S DEATH. HE GLANCES TO THE RIGHT AND FINDS A SCREAMINGLY INCONGRUOUS IMPERSONATOR.

A STRANGE FEAR CREEPS OVER HIM. THE GHOSTLY IMPERSONATOR--*SURELY, AN IMPERSONATOR, SURELY*--GETS OFF AT WARREN STREET. THE WRITER STARES THROUGH THE WINDOW UNTIL THE TRAIN PULLS AWAY.

FOR FOREVER, DANCING. OR AS CLOSE TO FOREVER AS ANY OF US WILL EVER GET.

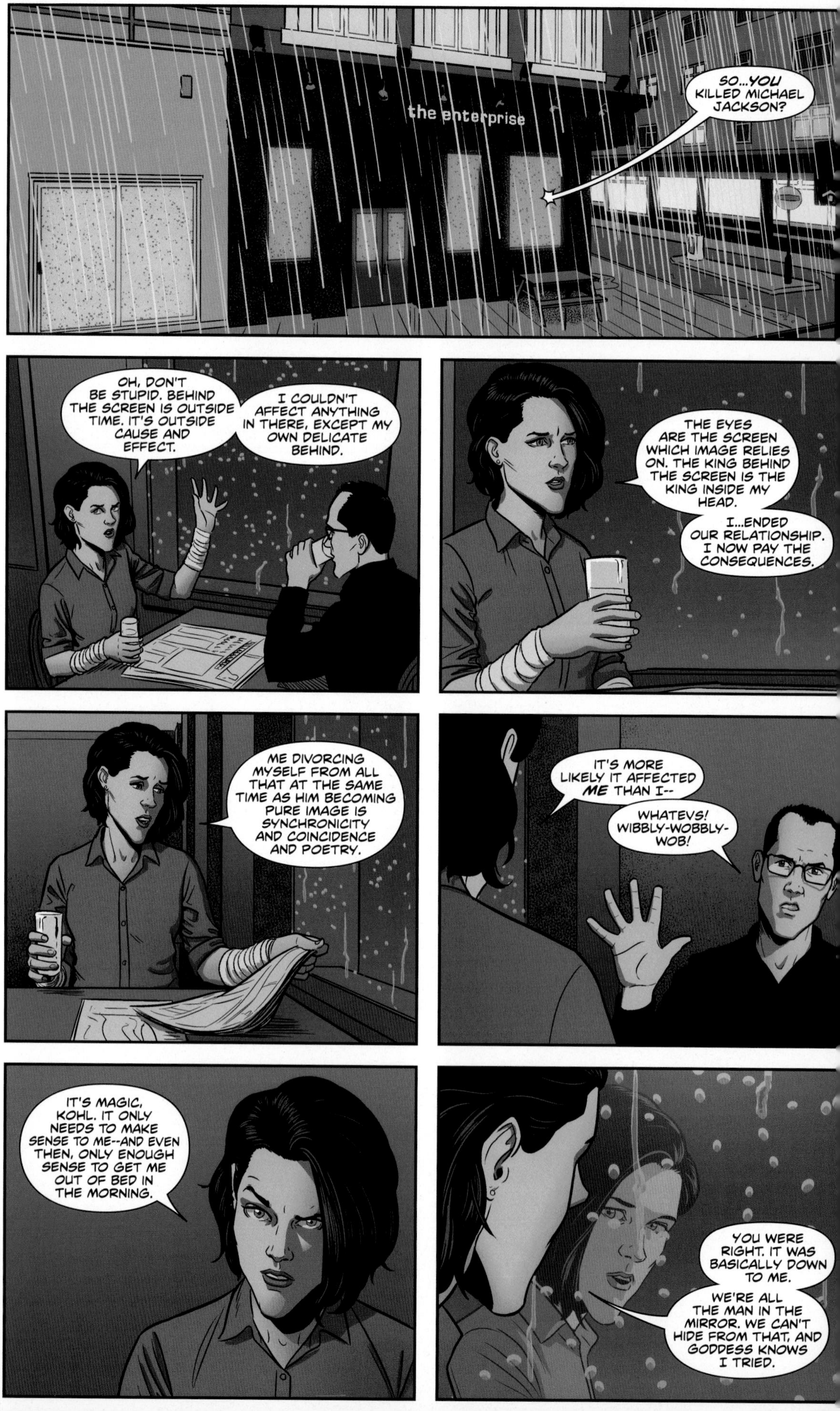
the enterprise
SO...YOU KILLED MICHAEL JACKSON?
OH, DON'T BE STUPID. BEHIND THE SCREEN IS OUTSIDE TIME. IT'S OUTSIDE CAUSE AND EFFECT.
I COULDN'T AFFECT ANYTHING IN THERE, EXCEPT MY OWN DELICATE BEHIND.
THE EYES ARE THE SCREEN WHICH IMAGE RELIES ON. THE KING BEHIND THE SCREEN IS THE KING INSIDE MY HEAD.
I...ENDED OUR RELATIONSHIP. I NOW PAY THE CONSEQUENCES.
ME DIVORCING MYSELF FROM ALL THAT AT THE SAME TIME AS HIM BECOMING PURE IMAGE IS SYNCHRONICITY AND COINCIDENCE AND POETRY.
IT'S MORE LIKELY IT AFFECTED ME THAN I--
WHATEVS! WIBBLY-WOBBLY-WOB!
IT'S MAGIC, KOHL. IT ONLY NEEDS TO MAKE SENSE TO ME--AND EVEN THEN, ONLY ENOUGH SENSE TO GET ME OUT OF BED IN THE MORNING.
YOU WERE RIGHT. IT WAS BASICALLY DOWN TO ME.
WE'RE ALL THE MAN IN THE MIRROR. WE CAN'T HIDE FROM THAT, AND GODDESS KNOWS I TRIED.

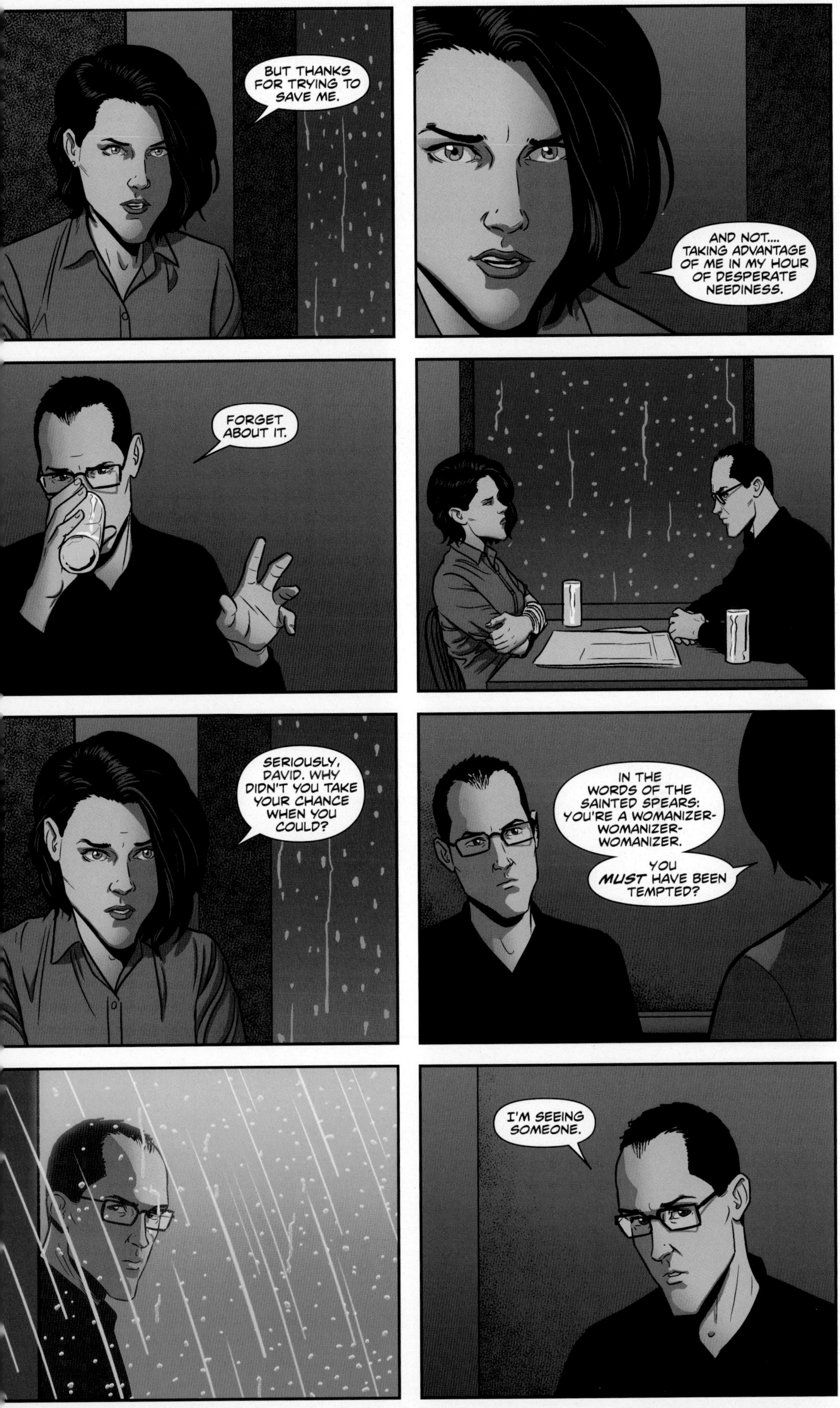
BUT THANKS FOR TRYING TO SAVE ME.
AND NOT.... TAKING ADVANTAGE OF ME IN MY HOUR OF DESPERATE NEEDINESS.
FORGET ABOUT IT.
SERIOUSLY, DAVID. WHY DIDN'T YOU TAKE YOUR CHANCE WHEN YOU COULD?
IN THE WORDS OF THE SAINTED SPEARS: YOU'RE A WOMANIZER-WOMANIZER-WOMANIZER.
YOU *MUST* HAVE BEEN TEMPTED?
I'M SEEING SOMEONE.

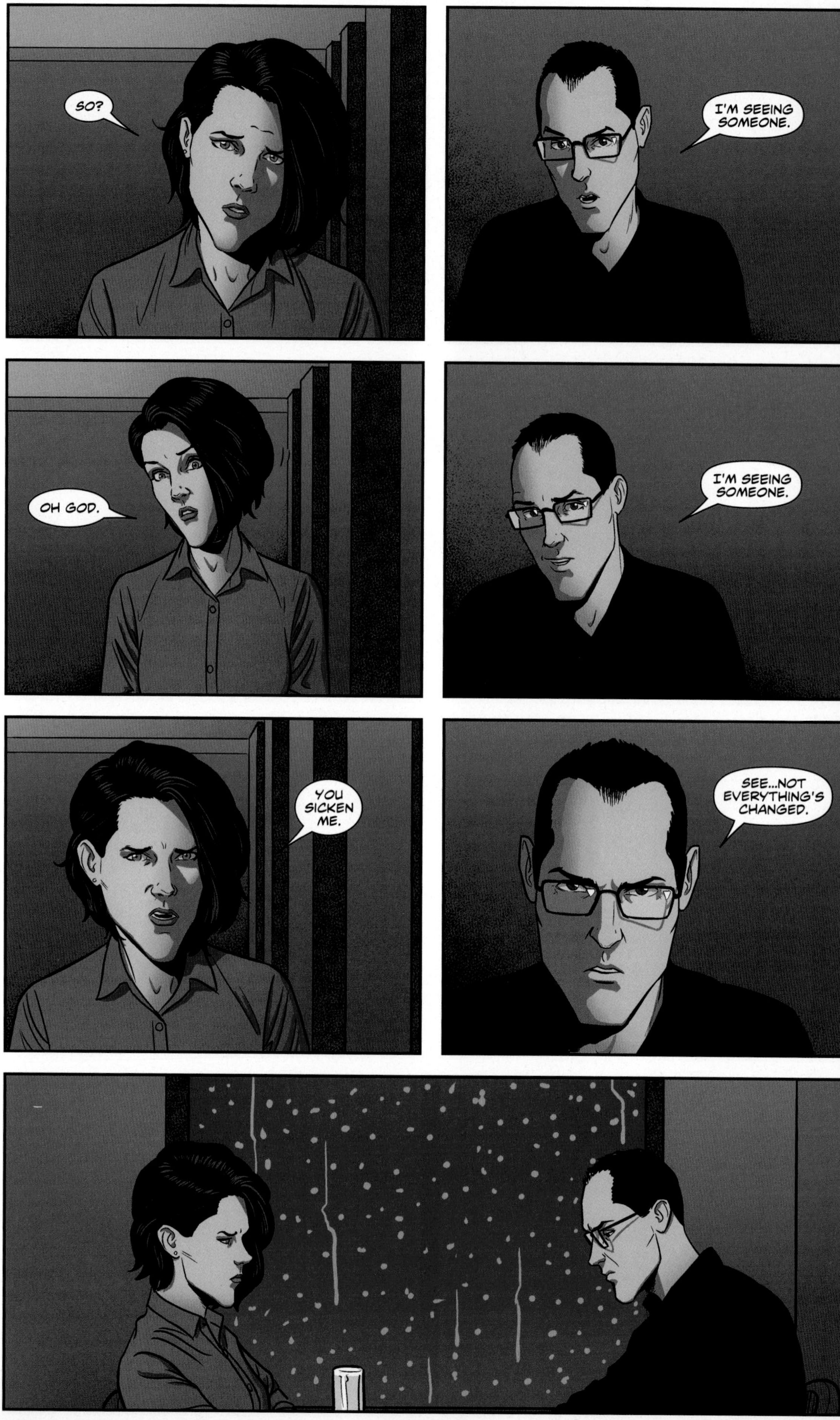
SO?
I'M SEEING SOMEONE.
OH GOD.
I'M SEEING SOMEONE.
YOU SICKEN ME.
SEE...NOT EVERYTHING'S CHANGED.

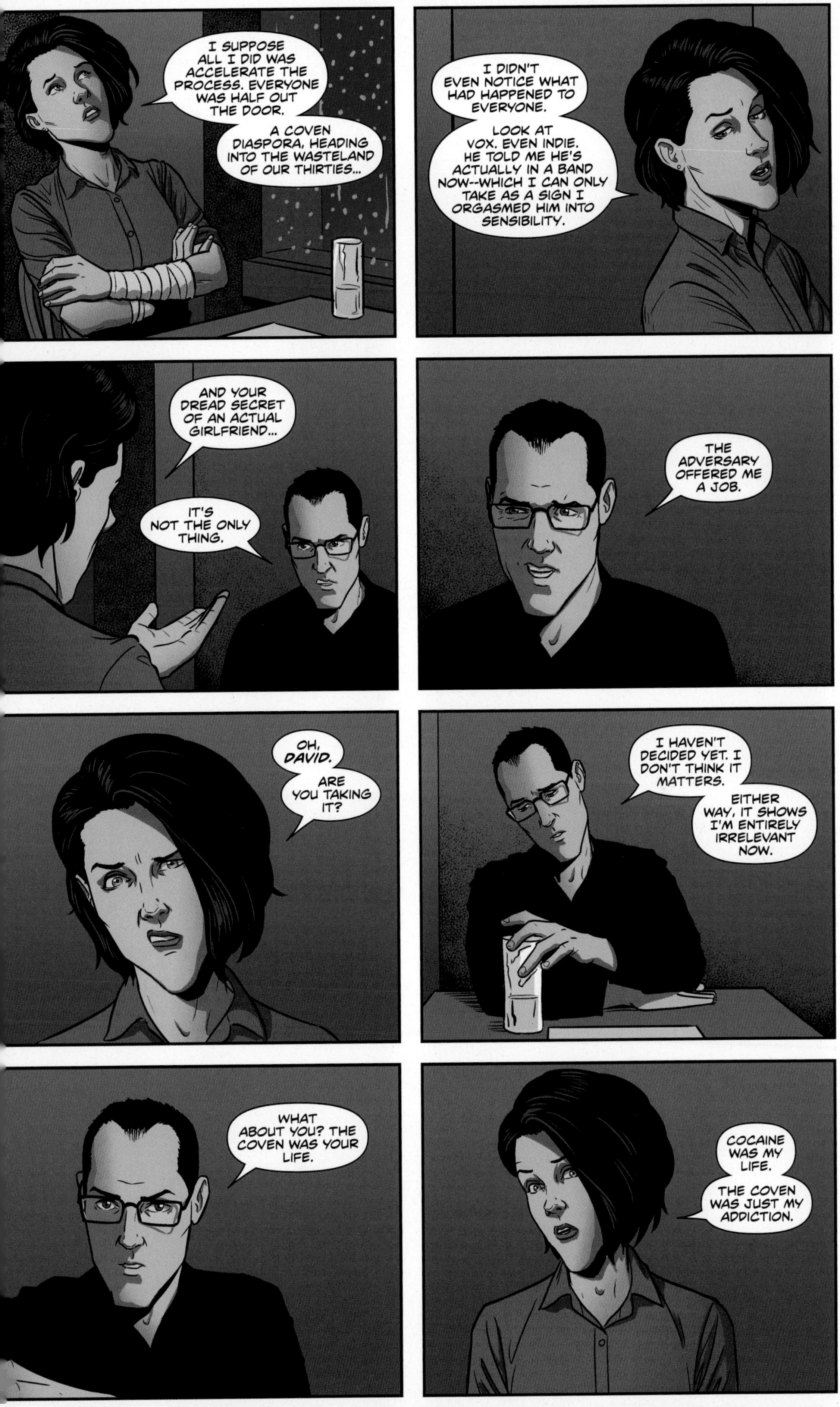
I SUPPOSE ALL I DID WAS ACCELERATE THE PROCESS. EVERYONE WAS HALF OUT THE DOOR.
A COVEN DIASPORA, HEADING INTO THE WASTELAND OF OUR THIRTIES...
I DIDN'T EVEN NOTICE WHAT HAD HAPPENED TO EVERYONE.
LOOK AT VOX. EVEN INDIE. HE TOLD ME HE'S ACTUALLY IN A BAND NOW--WHICH I CAN ONLY TAKE AS A SIGN I ORGASMED HIM INTO SENSIBILITY.
AND YOUR DREAD SECRET OF AN ACTUAL GIRLFRIEND...
IT'S NOT THE ONLY THING.
THE ADVERSARY OFFERED ME A JOB.
OH, *DAVID.*
ARE YOU TAKING IT?
I HAVEN'T DECIDED YET. I DON'T THINK IT MATTERS.
EITHER WAY, IT SHOWS I'M ENTIRELY IRRELEVANT NOW.
WHAT ABOUT YOU? THE COVEN WAS YOUR LIFE.
COCAINE WAS MY LIFE.
THE COVEN WAS JUST MY ADDICTION.

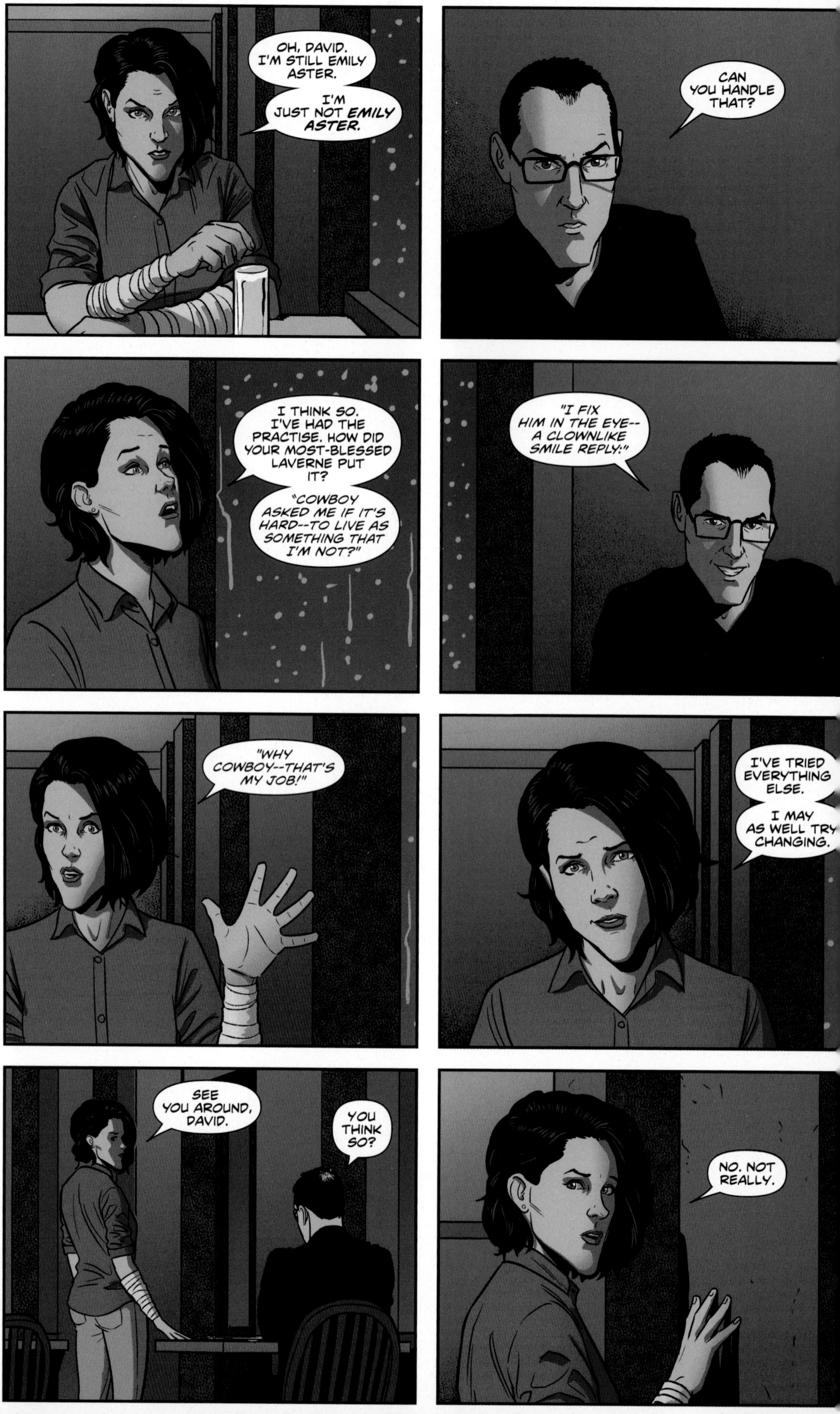
OH, DAVID. I'M STILL EMILY ASTER.
I'M JUST NOT EMILY ASTER.
CAN YOU HANDLE THAT?
I THINK SO. I'VE HAD THE PRACTISE. HOW DID YOUR MOST-BLESSED LAVERNE PUT IT?
"COWBOY ASKED ME IF IT'S HARD--TO LIVE AS SOMETHING THAT I'M NOT?"
"I FIX HIM IN THE EYE-- A CLOWNLIKE SMILE REPLY:"
"WHY COWBOY--THAT'S MY JOB!"
I'VE TRIED EVERYTHING ELSE.
I MAY AS WELL TRY CHANGING.
SEE YOU AROUND, DAVID.
YOU THINK SO?
NO. NOT REALLY.

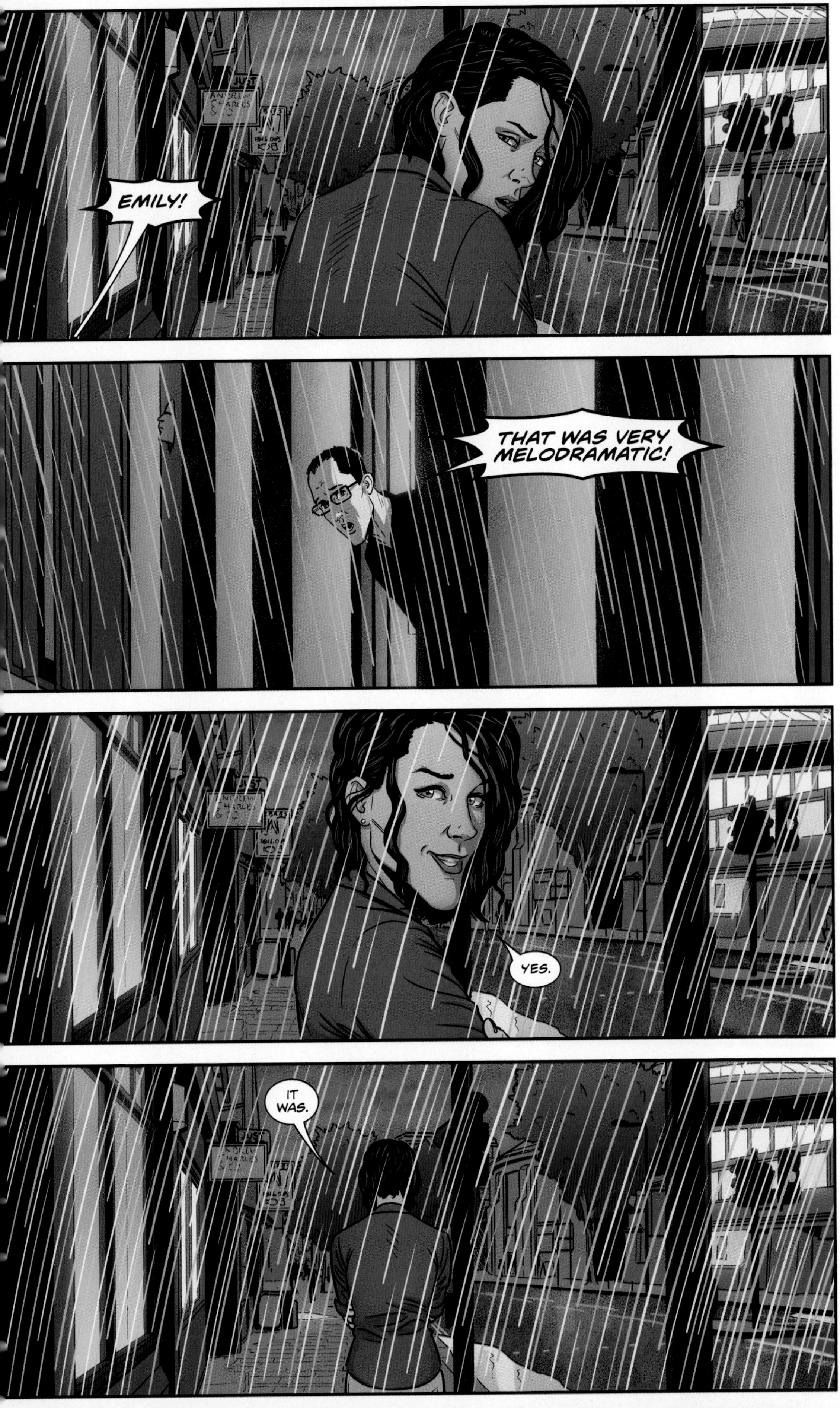
EMILY!
THAT WAS VERY MELODRAMATIC!
YES.
IT WAS.

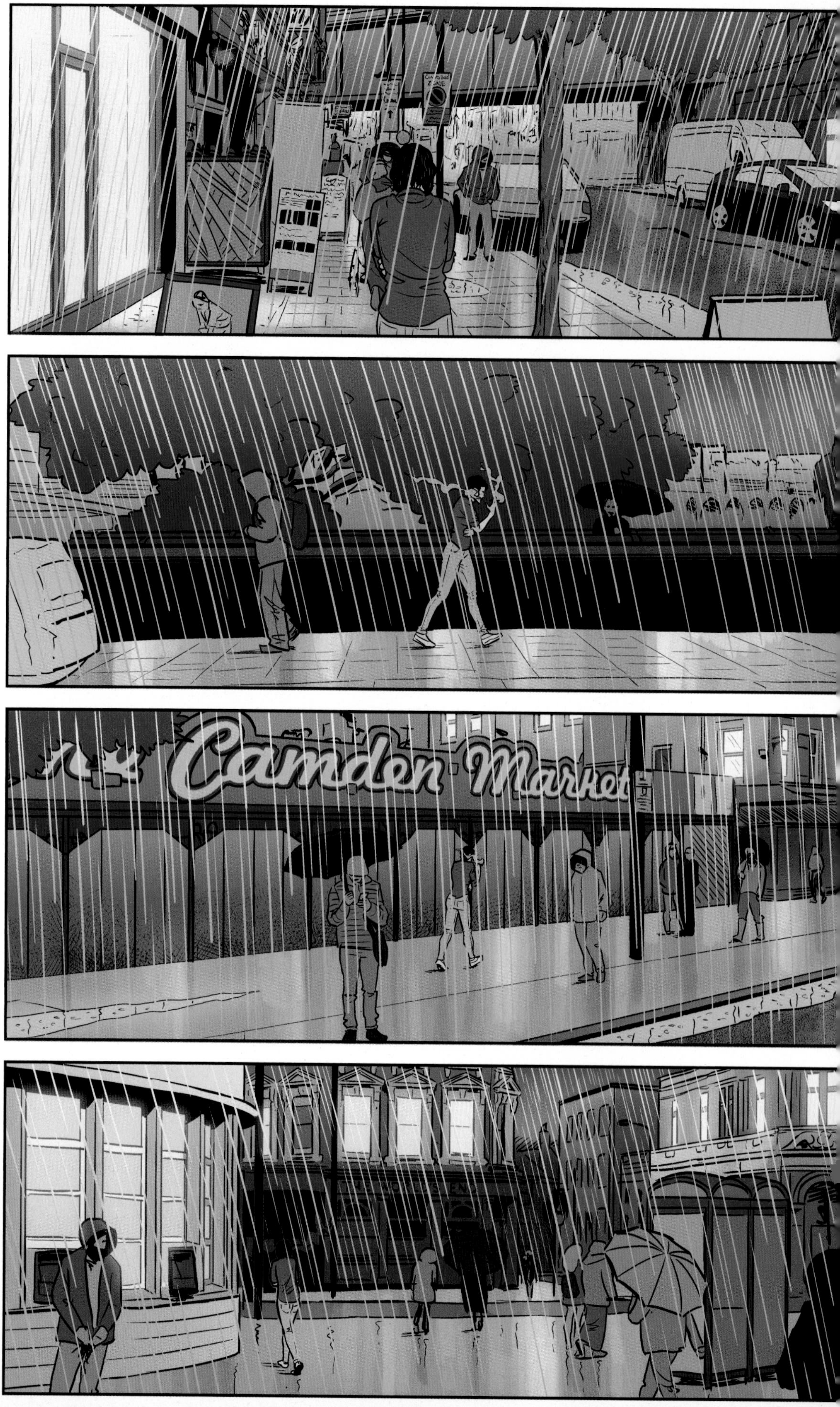
ZONE
Camden Market

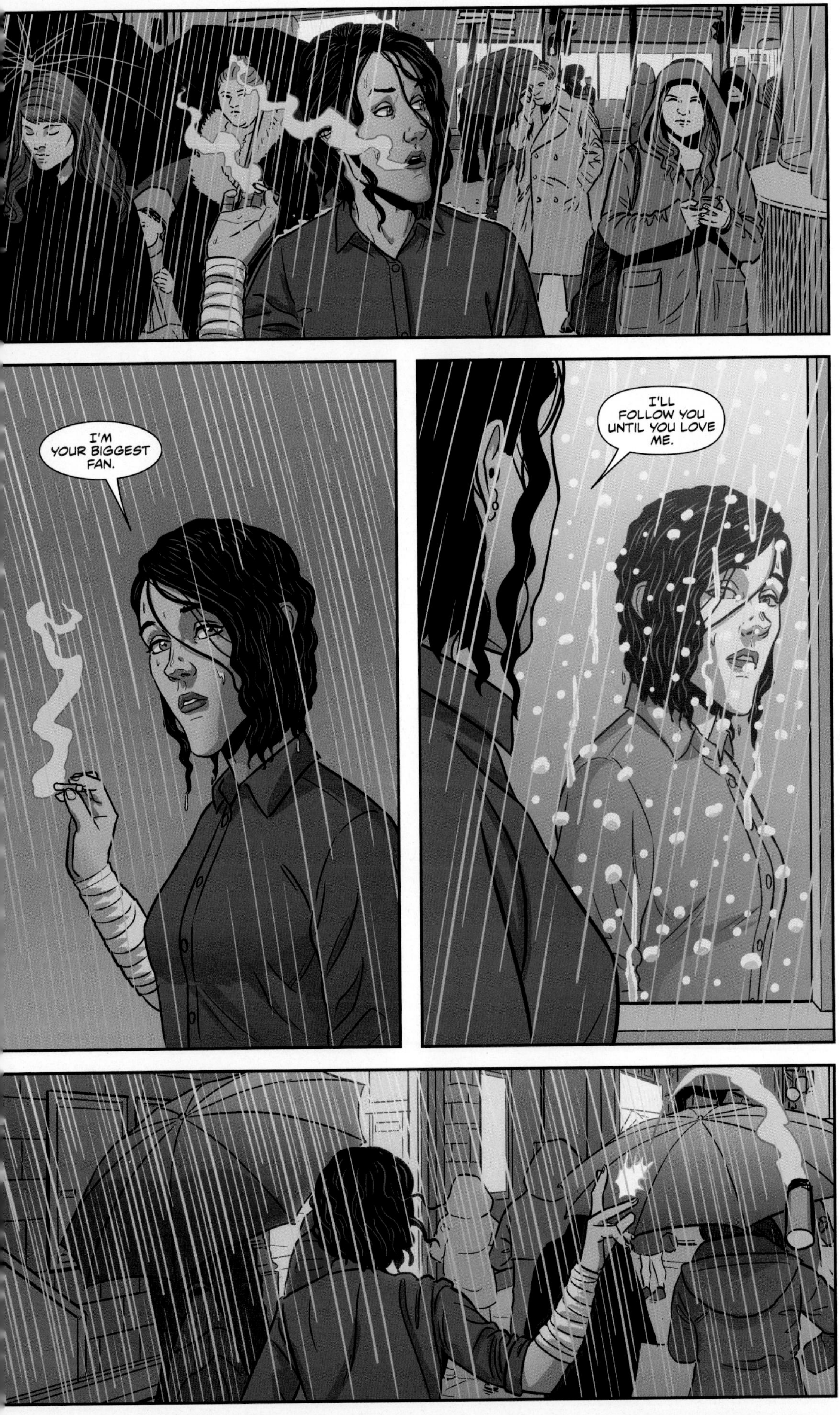
I'M YOUR BIGGEST FAN.
I'LL FOLLOW YOU UNTIL YOU LOVE ME.

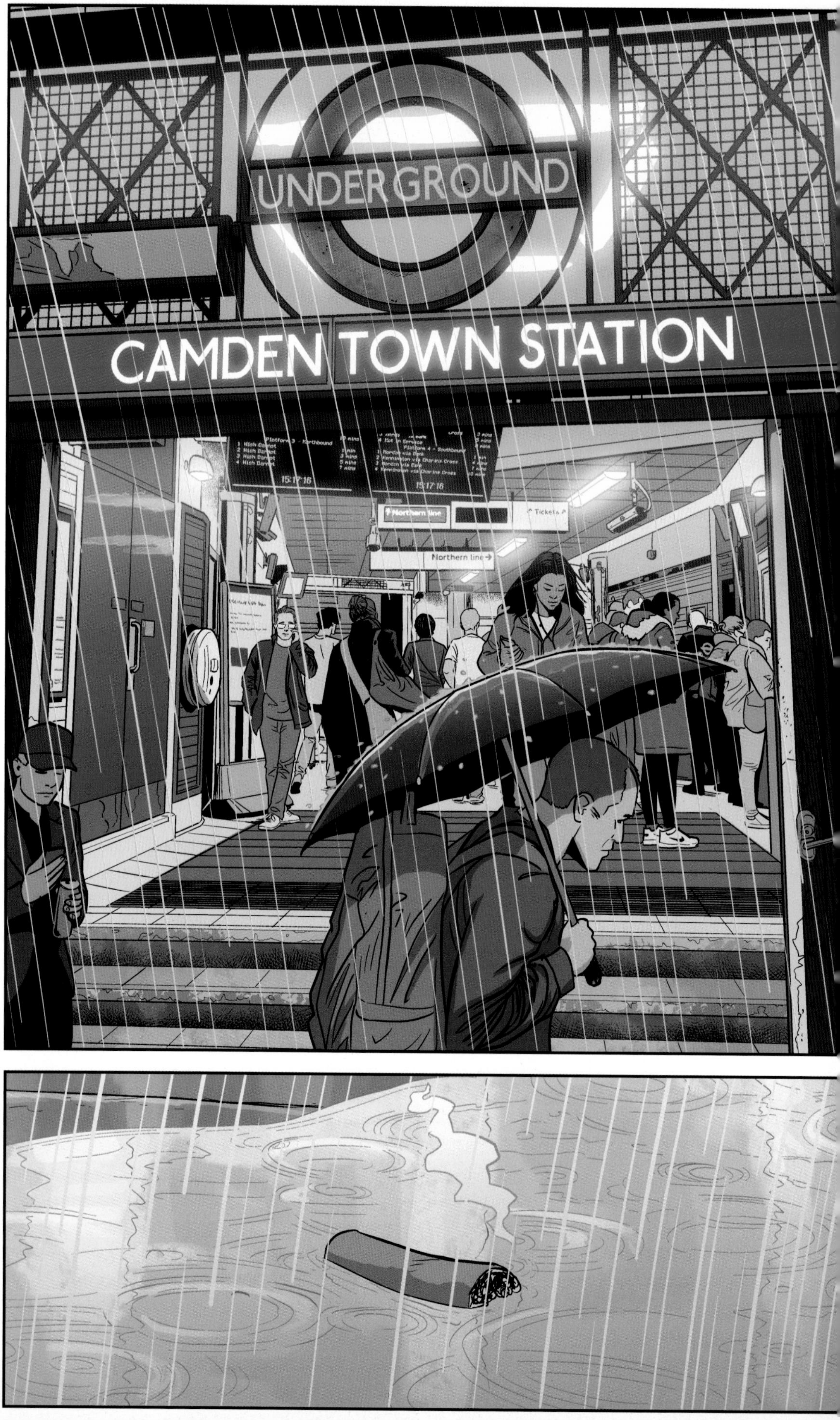
UNDERGROUND
CAMDEN TOWN STATION
15:17:16
15:17:16
Northern line
Tickets
Northern line

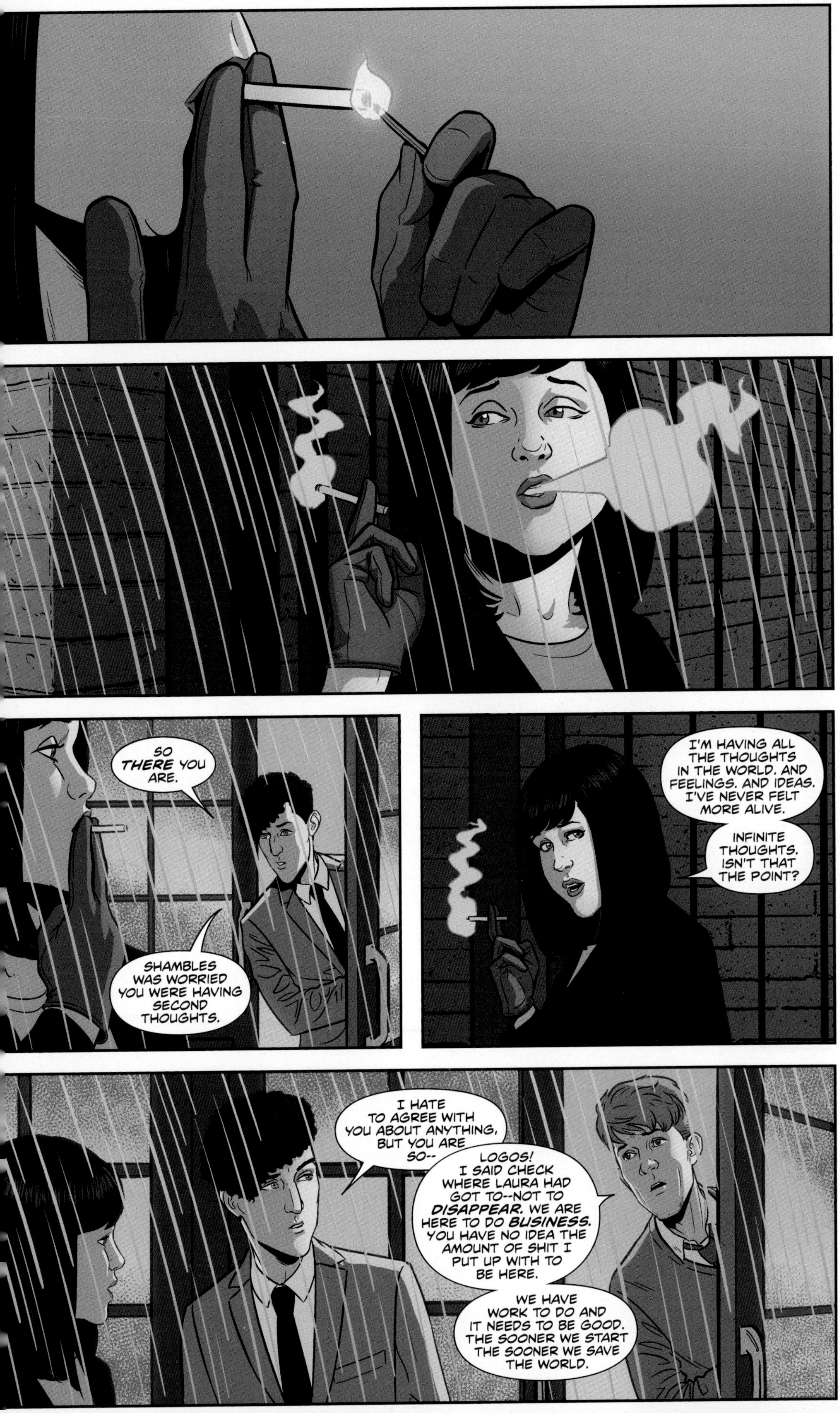
SO *THERE* YOU ARE.
SHAMBLES WAS WORRIED YOU WERE HAVING SECOND THOUGHTS.
I'M HAVING ALL THE THOUGHTS IN THE WORLD. AND FEELINGS. AND IDEAS. I'VE NEVER FELT MORE ALIVE.
INFINITE THOUGHTS. ISN'T THAT THE POINT?
I HATE TO AGREE WITH YOU ABOUT ANYTHING, BUT YOU ARE SO--
LOGOS! I SAID CHECK WHERE LAURA HAD GOT TO--NOT TO *DISAPPEAR.* WE ARE HERE TO DO *BUSINESS.* YOU HAVE NO IDEA THE AMOUNT OF SHIT I PUT UP WITH TO BE HERE.
WE HAVE WORK TO DO AND IT NEEDS TO BE GOOD. THE SOONER WE START THE SOONER WE SAVE THE WORLD.

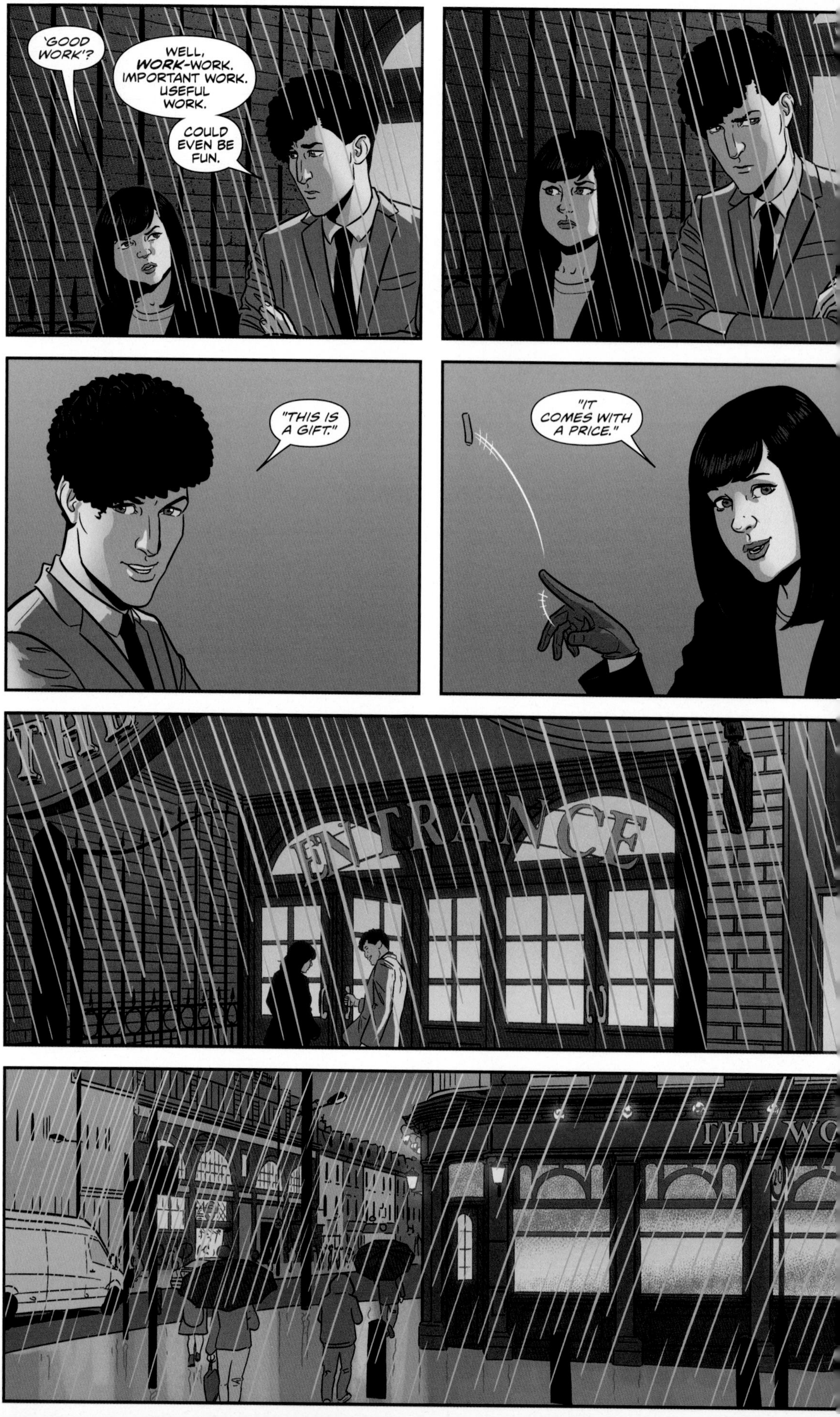

'GOOD WORK'?
WELL, WORK-WORK. IMPORTANT WORK. USEFUL WORK.
COULD EVEN BE FUN.
"THIS IS A GIFT."
"IT COMES WITH A PRICE."
ENTRANCE

PHONOGRAM

GLOSSARY

The glossary has become a traditional part of *Phonogram*. In a real way, you don't really need it, especially for a volume that is as mainstream pop-cultural as this one is. Equally, even at its most obscure, the idea is that you can understand from context what's going on without needing the source. My usual metaphor is that you don't need to know which elf had sex with which other elf to make this kind of elf in *Lord of the Rings* — you just go with it.

So why do we still do the glossary when it constantly annoys certain sorts of people? Firstly, we like making crap jokes and it's a good opportunity to cram some more in. Secondly, it's fun to make some recommendations. Thirdly, it annoys a certain sort of person.

We are awful.

1980-Something: Vague because of the strangeness of trying to work out when you could be watching music television in the UK. The channel would be Music Box, and I suspect it was 1984, but we kept it open in case there's something wrong. And it doesn't matter, as this is all childhood memories, which warp. As the captions say, Music Television was an incredibly rare thing in the UK compared to the US. Jamie and I grew up basically waiting for The Chart Show every week, and crossing our fingers they'd play what we like.

"A room full of vacuum and a room full of air look the same": A quote from Los Campesinos' *Ways To Make It Through The Wall*, which was quoted from the first ever issue of Phonogram. Quoting people quoting us is definitely clever and no, etc, etc.

About A Girl: Nirvana single, though I'm pretty sure the reference wasn't deliberate. But There Are No Accidents, so what do I know, eh?

"are-the-white-stripes-incesting?": Period gossip-hype led to no-one being sure about the White Stripes relationship. The idea they were brother and sister and totally doing it hung around a lot longer than it should have.

"Babes of Suga, The": The Sugababes. In my own head, East Seventeen to Girls Aloud's Take That in terms of lexicon, except both bands are better than the male pairing, so abandon that. The Sugababes' first album *One Touch* is in his top 5 pop albums of the 00s.

Billy Jean: Famous for provoking an answer record from Eddie Argos side-project Everybody's In the French Resistance... Now!, *Billy's Genes*. You'll find it on Michael Jackson's *Thriller*. It's pretty obscure.

Birthdays: The day of your birth. You've got more of them left than us, millennials.

Brighton: Think San Francisco minus all the tech stuff, but in Britain. The venue is the Free Butt. Jamie took a trip to Brighton to get reference, only to discover it had closed down. We made do with a hand-drawn map provided by our favourite towering indie-dev Kerry Turner. Home of many things, phono-relevantly, the opening scene of Moore/Campbell's *From Hell* and the Mods/Rockers battles in the sixties. Weve homaged the former god knows how many time.

"Britannia's Deicide": The God of Britpop died back in 2005. Kohl was involved. Strictly speaking, he didn't kill her, but he certainly had his hands messy. For more read *Phonogram: Rue Britannia*, which you can totally buy in a fine trade collection from Image Publishing of Berkeley.

Buffalo Bar: Underground venue near Highbury & Islington train station. Yes, this means that this is about fifty metres from the climax of *The Wicked + The Divine #5*. Suffering the curse of *Phonogram*, the Buffalo Bar has now closed.

Bump N' Grind: R Kelly Single. Mind/body dichotomy explored, leading to the conclusion that there is nothing wrong with it, in a small proportion.

Byrds, The: Classic rock doing its classic thing in a jangly-harmony way.

Colossal Youth: The Young Marble Giants album, and one you should own. Entirely alien thing, the indie equivalent of finding a diary tape recording in a game. Just incredibly intimate. Really, you want this.

Cooler, The: Which is the club in Bristol where Laura gets her Goddess on. Actually has appeared before, in a B-side where Kohl turned 30 in one of the Singles Club issues. The curse of *Phonogram* means it's since closed.

Cowboy: Kenickie B-side on *Punka*. Ending Kohl's arc with a solemn exchange of a piece of Kenickie obscurity is probably peak *Phonogram*. It's definitely in the top 10 *Kenickie* B-sides though.

Death Stars: Professional moon-impersonators from the Star Wars movies. For further Star Wars, start with *Star Wars: Darth Vader* for no reason at all, and definitely not because Kieron writes it and will get some more money.

Dirty Diana: Michael Jackson single from *Bad*.

Disco Pistol: A glitterpop band from the 90s. If you can find it — and it's not exactly easy to do so — you'll want the double A side *Say Something/Solid Gold Radio*.

Don't Stand Me Down: The third Dexys Midnight Runners album. The commercial suicide one, so very much lauded by people who like that kind of dramatic move. This includes about 50% of the Phonogram creative team, because Kieron is totally that sort of person.

Electroclash: Millennial dance movement. Bleeping. Ludicrous fashion. Fucking. Got a lot of eyerolls, but I suspect Vox is right. They were people who you wanted to roll eyes. If you want to dabble, I'd suggest hitting up any of Miss Kittin's period collaborations — The Hacker, Goldenboy, Felix Da Housecat.

Empire State Of Mind: Jay-Z/Alicia Keyes single about the rule of Emperor Palpatine after the fall of the Republic. Came out after the period, and research suggests it wasn't recorded at this point... but we always have magic.

Finsbury Park: Kieron started writing this series of *Phonogram* a few hundred metres from this awesomely tacky bowling alley he used to frequent when he lived in the area. The starting of PG3 was an odd one. Kieron had just come back from one of his trips to Marvel, where he'd lost his wedding ring. Wife and Editor Chrissy was away for the weekend, and when he got home, he managed to lock himself out, without a phone. Stripped of everything in his life, he wandered the streets, trying to find some friends to crash at. This was clearly the right desolate state to start writing this bloody comic, scrawling away on bits of paper. The pub's name? Another The World's End. *Phonogram* is strange. Oh — he got his ring back. The universe occasionally looks after the terminally useless.

Fischerspooner: The Electroclash hype who got it hardest. *Emerge* still makes me smile pretty hard.

Fuck The Pain Away: if you are suffering from genital injuries, do not listen to Peaches' advice. It just doesn't work. We've tried. Find on *The Teaches Of Peaches*.

Going To Hell: Closing track of The Long Blondes' *Couples*. Full title is *I'm Going To Hell*. Kieron always connects to his run on Journey Into Mystery for Marvel. Very Kid Loki, y'know?

Grease: 1970s' 1950s nostalgia. Kieron has extremely complicated feelings about *Grease*. Always influential, as it has groove and meaning, which are fundamentally phonovirtues.

Grimoire Pages: There's a lot crammed in here, and probably it'll just stress you out if I went through it all. If you google, someone actually has translated all the Theban writing, which is an impressive level of dedication. Jamie especially likes Kim Wilde. Kieron included it for the Keeping Hanging On pun, and Jamie Pandering Points.

Guitar Hero: Or Maybe it was *Rock Band*?

Hampstead Heath: Seth's use of bushes is atypical.

Here Comes The Serious Bit: Track on *Couples* by The Long Blondes, about the approaching of a bit which is serious.

"I don't want to sound trite, but you were perfect": Key lyric from Los Campesinos' *Heart Swells/Daylight Pacific Time*. Just comes in as it moves from one section to the other, and we get a little bit of light between the clouds and they sound romantic for once. Find on *We are Beautiful, We are Doomed*.

"I'll follow you until...": From Gaga's *Paparazzi*.

If Only I Had A Heart: From *Wizard of Oz*, describing a straw golem's desperate hunger for cardiac muscle. Worth noting Emily's on the money — the Afghan Whig's version is excellent.

"Incoherent manifestos": Don't mention the war.

"It's only a--": Fragment of dialogue from Michael Jackson's *Thriller*, at the start of the walk through the streets scene which we homage. *Thriller* is the eponymous title track and seventh single of the album of... guys? Guys? Seriously? You want me to tell you about *Thriller*?

"Jackson Dead": Michael Jackson died of an overdose of propofol and benzodiazepine on June 25th 2009.

Kate Jackson: Lead singer of the Long Blondes. Yes, Laura is still a bit monomaniacal.

"Keisha Mutya, etc.": Seth Bingo's home-made Sugababes T-shirt. I'm told that *Popbitch* did a T-shirt design with the same joke, but I'm pretending to be ignorant. I mean, I'm not pretending I'm ignorant. I'm awesomely ignorant, generally speaking. By the time we see it again in issue 5, it's been edited to keep up with the band turnover.

Knife, The: Swedish electro powered by a rare brother/sister chemistry and a fine selections of exciting bleeping noises.

Leona Lewis: *Bleeding Love*: biggest selling single of 2007. Kieron was entirely unaware of it until researching what would be a suitable implement for torturing poor old Lloyd.

"Let's Make This Precious": Laura's quoting Dexys. Maybe it's going to be okay!

(Let's Make This) Precious Little Life: Mashing together of opening track of Dexys' *Too-rye-Aye* and the first volume of Bryan Lee O'Malley's *Scott Pilgrim*. Er... the whole issue is a homage to *Scott Pilgrim*. If you've never read *Scott Pilgrim*, this is your reminder to read *Scott Pilgrim*.

Long Blondes, The: Sheffield's seedy-meisters. Two albums, plus a singles collection. It's a small amount of stuff to make it worth your time having it all. If you want a lot more ranting about them, you'll need to see issue 5 of *Phonogram: The Single's Club*. Still available from shops, etc.

Losing My Edge: I've been well aware I've been losing it ever since I heard it. LCD Soundsystem single, and pretty much essential.

Lucky Star: Single from Madonna's first album, but found on many Best Ofs. The period one (and most relevant to Immaterial Girl) would be *The Immaculate Collection*.

Material Girl: The final homage in the issue, based on the video of the single from Madonna's second album, *Like A Virgin*. The video was a homage from the routine in Marilyn Monroe's *Diamonds Are A Girl's Best Friend* from *Gentlemen Prefer Blondes*, which makes this a homage of a homage which is definitely probably clever, maybe.

Michael Jackson: Guys. Don't make me do this.

Minehead: Somerset seaside resort where there's a Butlins. Music Festival folks ATP held a bunch of their concerts there. You can assume this is one of them.

"Morning Rydell": School announcer in *Grease*, saying hello.

"Most Blessed Laverne": Ex-Kenickie member, now presenter. Start with Kenickie's *At The Club* if you want an album, or just grab the just delightful Mint Royale collaboration single *Don't Falter*.

"Never gonna get it": Emily's paraphrasing En Vogue's *My Lovin'*, which remains an agreeably slinky way to tell someone to fuck right off.

Never On A Sunday: Club where *Phonogram: The Singles Club* was set. Still available, kids. It's pretty good.

No Exit: Play by Satre where he's forced to play a really boring Room Escape game.

Nu-Rave: Mid-00s indie-dance revival, basically. If you want to play, try *Klaxons*. Its best thing was definitely giving us an excuse to cover ourselves with glo-paint.

Parallel Lines: The iconic Blondie album. If you're thinking of Blondie visually, you're probably thinking of this, and so it turns up here.

Peaches: Pro-Orgasm-fuck-pop. Period album would be *The Teaches Of Peaches*.

Placebo: America-style alt-rock with a lot of 70s gloam and 80s goth. Were I to choose an album, I'm most fond of their first, the eponymous *Placebo*.

Plan B: Dexys Midnight Runners' single, lifted as name for 00s music magazine. Ego-googling went entirely to pot when the rapper turned up.

Poly Styrene: Singer in Punk legends X-Ray Spex and solo performer. The song in question is Ghoulish and was released posthumously. You'll find it on her *Generation Indigo*. Well worth your time going back and discovering everything by X-Ray Spex. If *Oh Bondage! Up Yours!* Doesn't inspire you, I'd be deeply surprised.

"rehearsal videos": The 2009 documentary, *Michael Jackson's This Is It*.

Rippin Kittin: Electroclash revenge-is-the-best-revenge classic by Golden Boy feat. Miss Kittin. Core lyric being "I feel like taking a life." which is probably relevant or something.

"Safehaus": The whole sequence is a Lady Gaga riff, primarily on the video for *Paparazzi*. At the time of showing Jamie the scripts in 2012 he claimed to have never had heard a Gaga record. I doubt him. I doubt him hard.

"Sainted Spears": Britney Spears! Pop Star! You suspect that if we'd positioned the story in a slightly different place in time, her work would have turned up. She's done more than enough great singles to get the Best Of, so you should.

"Say After Me": This is all riffing on *Take On Me*, remember. Man!

See Emily Play: Pink Floyd track. It's probably telling that the only Floyd we reference is early Syd Barrett stuff, because we are awful people.

Silent Shout: Possibly the best all around album by the Knife. But really, you can't go much wrong with the Knife.

Take On Me: A-ha song with a pretty memorable video based on a girl in the real world falling into a comic book. Someone should homage it in a comic book. That'd be really clever and definitely not twee as fuck.

The Adversary: It's a pun. Don't worry if you don't get it. Just a rival coven.

"The clock strikes twelve, etc": From Marlowe's *Doctor Faustus*. From which we also took the opening quote for the first *The Wicked + The Divine* trade, which makes me smile. This was written years in advance of that. Clearly, Kieron has read about three books.

The Libertines: A big deal in British Indie rocks. Clearly a generational thing, which neither Jamie or I were part of. You'll want the first two albums — Up The Bracket and The Libertines — if you want to explore them, but I suspect you'll also need a couple of books to get the romanticism of it all. Reformed in 2015 and released a third album, which we haven't listened to.

The Man In The Mirror: Oddly thematically appropriate single from Bad by Michael Jackson.

The Monkey Wrench Emily Uses: Is this a Foo Fighters reference? No. It is not. She got it from 3 and 13. Pay attention.

The Queen's Outfit: Aping *Thriller*, obv.

The Sex Pistols: Glitterpop band of the 90s. No, wait, that was Disco Pistol. No idea who these were.

The World's End: Huge Camden pub, known for its regular appearances in *Phonogram* as an unsubtle metaphor.

Theban: The magical writing font is Theban, which is an old cypher that has been part of *Phonogram's* visual language since the earliest days. Don't worry too much. If you needed to know it, we'd have written it in English. We're obscure, guys, but not that obscure.

"This is a gift...": From Florence + the Machine's *Rabbit Heart* found on her first album, *Lungs*.

"Tolerance Is More Appealing In Theory Than In Practice": Lyric from Los Campesino's *Ways To Make It Through The Wall*. Also true, in an oft annoying way.

Tolkien: Sex, drugs and orcs and trolls. Without the sex. Or the drugs, bar pipeweed and I hear that Lembas is a smooth high.

Total Eclipse Of The Heart: Is the final video homage, if you didn't know. As Seth Bingo probably says, all Karaoke sessions are a road winding towards *Total Eclipse Of The Heart*. A good way to end a cheesy-leaning night club. Good to get melodramatic by yourself. Good... wait, I'm just writing what Emily says. An astounding edifice of pomp and sound.

"Turn on the real drums": From *Salt, Peppa and Spinderella* by Johnny Foreigner, who Lloyd would love and who I'm sure are lying about why they're called Johnny Foreigner. I'm right, Alex? Right?

We Are Beautiful, We Are Doomed: Title track of Los Campesinos' second full album, which they (amazingly) lifted from one of Kieron's end of year round ups. The whole Los Camp/*Phonogram* thing has been strange. I first met Gareth in the club which inspired *The Singles Club*. Fiction/Reality.

"What went down with Britannia": See *Rue Britannia* for more details, true believers!

White Stripes: The superior period blues guitar revivalists of that particular churn. Period album would be White Blood Cells, and the one which got the hype, but if you want to get into the heads of the people in this scene, you should go back to *De Stijl*.

"Will You Forgive Me Now?": Fragment of core lyric from The Long Blondes' *I'm Going To Hell*.

"Womanizer-womanizer-womanizer": Awesome Britney Spears Dalek-pop, *Womanizer*.

"You Know Nothing...": Yes, Lloyd would of course have read *Game of Thrones* before the show.

"You look like a slut": Reference to Avenue D's cheerily offensive *Do I Look Like A Slut?* electroclash irony-fest.

Young Marble Giants: I mean, you want *Colossal Youth*, but I'd suggest starting with the single *Final Day*, except that's also on the current editions of *Colossal Youth*, so just start at *Colossal Youth*.

Young Soul Rebels: *Searching For The Young Soul Rebels*, the first Dexys album, and lyric nestling in the heart of its closing track *There There My Dear*.

WHAT ELSE?

Before the Image Expo, Eric Stephenson asked about announcing the third *Phonogram*. We realised it was time to do a few teasers. The first one was released without explanation, paraphrasing Daft Punk and hinting towards our return. The second one was at the expo, with the year of release that (er) was wrong by many years. What happened? The plan to do it at the same time as *Young Avengers* was simply impossible, Jamie's *Defenders* run took much longer than we thought it should have, and we decided to do *The Wicked + The Divine* and become rich before returning to our dutiful, ever-faithful *Phonogram*. We are awful. I may have mentioned it.

We were tempted to release the promo image every year, with the date crossed out and a new one written in.

ONE MORE TIME

GILLEN / McKELVIE / WILSON
2012

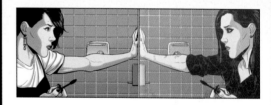

P H O N O G R A M

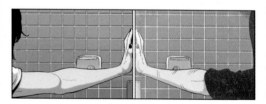

THE IMMATERIAL GIRL

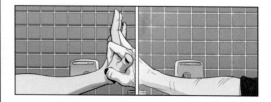

GILLEN / McKELVIE / WILSON
2012

UNEASY LISTENING

Generally speaking, Kieron's work is divided into two vague groups: comics he creates a playlist for, and comics he doesn't. That normally aligns to how much of it comes from (for want of a less grotesquely pretentious phrase) the method writing part of him. So things like (say) Darth Vader and Über just get written to silence or the radio, and things like The Wicked + The Divine get written to a psychologically loaded curated 300+ song playlist on shuffle. Phonogram has always been the extreme end of that, to the level where the playlists are so utterly personal that no one else would make any sense of them.

Equally, from the very earliest days, Kieron has been quite anal about it. For all of Phonogram he's kept notes on what he was listening to when actually writing any specific script, which he lobs at the top of each one. If you want to know where Kieron's head was when carving out Phonogram, this will tell you.

And no, you can't have the actual PG3 playlist. A magician never gives up everything, and neither do wanky writers.

ISSUE 1
11.9.11 — Last.fm on my channel. A-ha and Madonna turned up randomly, which can only be the sort of magical omen that PG thrives off.
12.9.11 — Dirtbombs. En Vogue. Mainly Dirtbombs. Madonna. Gaga. A-ha. The Bangles. Draft 1 Finished at 22:45 to Like A Prayer by Madonna.
13.9.11 — Polish to Madonna and White Stripes. Finish to Like A Prayer again, at 02:52.
28.9.11 — Quick tweak before becoming a drawing script. Jackson & Madonna.

ISSUE 2
24.4.12 — The PG3 playlist! Losing My Edge, Miss Kittin on repeat.
25.4.12 — More Miss Kittin! Take On Me, inevitably!
29.4.12 — Thriller.
30.4.12 — Material Girl. PG3 playlist.
17.7.15 — Material Girl. PG3 playlist.

ISSUE 3
24.5.12 — Total Eclipse started playing at the exact moment I started to write that scene.
25.5.12 — MORE TOTAL ECLIPSE ON REPEAT!!!!!!!!
11.8.15 — PG3 playlist.
13.9.15 — Lettering draft, PG3 playlist, plus Young Marble Giants, yet more Total Eclipse on repeat.

ISSUE 4
19–21.8.12 — PG3.4 Playlist consisting of Couples and Singles by the Long Blondes, Dexys' Plan B album, Los Campesinos' We Are Beautiful, We Are Doomed and Johnny Foreigners' Salt, Pepa And Spinderella.
21.9.15 — Ryan Adam's 1989 covers album, the above playlist.
6:10 — Finished at the end of Giddy Stratospheres. (Which shuffles onto I'm Going to Hell, which seems pretty good considering)
23.10.15, 3:59 — Finished to Appropriation. Played PG3.4 playlist, plus a bit where we repeated Dexys — There There My Dear for the marvel method bit.

ISSUE 5
22.8.12 — Afghan Whigs' Gentlemen, Empire State Of Mind.
23.8.12 — Afghan Whigs' Gentlemen, Empire State Of Mind, Smiths – Never Had No One Ever.
24.8.12 — Gentlemen, Paparazzi, Take On Me.
27.8.12 — Weirdly, the House To Astonish podcast, then when I realise there's no fucking way I can write with that, onto the PG3 playlist.
25.10.15 — Sexwitch, PG3.4 Playlist.
26.10.15 — Heart Swells/Pacific Daylight Time, PG3.4 playlist
17.11.15 — Salt, Pepa And Spinderella, LCD Soundsystem (Losing my Edge, All My Friends.)

ISSUE 6
29.8.12 — Afghan Whigs, Rabbit Heart.
30.8.12 — Jackson? Random playlist stuff.
31.8.12 — Kate Bush, Jackson. First draft finished to Wanna Be Startin Something at 12:45.
24.11.15 — In a cafe as LCD Soundsystem Someone Great is playing. And now All My Friends. We just can't escape this. Then over to the next door pub, where Crazy is playing, and I go to the PG playlist. I switch to Rabbit Heart for tweaking the end, for obvious reasons. Finished after One More Time, Paparazzi and playing Cowboy off Youtube to conclude.
26.11.15 — PG3.4 playlist. Finish at 13.20, to Total Eclipse. And then, hilariously, One More Time comes on next in the shuffle. No. Definitely not.
20.12.15 — Tom Humberstone's Phono Mood completed to Babies at 2:33.

CEEFAX MAILS

Methodology and craft approaches are pretty common material to stick in the back of a Trade. We've done it quite a few times ourselves. The rhythm is pretty common — script, pencils, inks, flats, finished colours. Except, especially with how we do things, that's only part of the system. In a real way, a lot of work is done in a fluid conversation, trying to get exactly what we want. Here's an example of our e-mail chains trying to sort out the Ceefax lettering, made even worse by editor Chrissy being out at the pub with a bunch of poets...

* * *

Jamie (23:08):
How does the caption in page 1 panel 3 look at the top of the panel?

Clayton (00:17):
It looks like this!

SO WHILE FOR MY PEERS, MUSIC VIDEOS WOULD REMAIN EXOTIC AND ELUSIVE FOR ANOTHER DECADE, I GORGED ON THE FUTURE.

Kieron (00:28):
I need to talk it over tomorrow morning with C. I suspect this is actually the "right" way we're going — I think what I called for in the script is impossible.

Jamie (00:30):
Oh right you wanted it as closed captions didn't you

Clayton (00:30):
Oh! I'm sorry! I can do that too, give me a couple of minutes! I think we can swing that!

Clayton (00:35):
Okay, here's a new page 1 with subtitles. How do they look to you?

1980-SOMETHING.
SOUTH LONDON-ISH
WE HAD SATELLITE TELEVISION FOR SIX MONTHS.
SO WHILE FOR MY PEERS, MUSIC VIDEOS WOULD REMAIN EXOTIC AND ELUSIVE FOR ANOTHER DECADE, I GORGED ON THE FUTURE.
BUT IT WAS ALSO TOO LATE.
THE KING BEHIND THE SCREEN HAD COME TO ME. HE MADE THE OFFER.

Clayton (00:37):
I can also try this with a bolder version of Futura, if you all want.

Jamie (00:39):
I think the intention was 1980s british style ones, sorry — which were like this: https://www.flickr.com/photos/bbccouk/2297959741/ i don't know what you'd do to approximate that though. Kieron?

Kieron (00:42):
Hmm. Trying to do a Ceefax version (as in, Jamie's last caption) is certainly something I'd love to see, but the version of the one pager is closer to the intent. I mean, the thing is to separate the first two pages from the rest of the story. Page 3 is "Phonogram" as we know it, and the first two pages are odd, this weird TV-retro-thing.
... think I like the version you've done, Clayton. I dunno what a bolder version of Futura would do to it though — Clayton, willing to follow advice.

Clayton (00:44):
'll try them both and we'll go with whichever you prefer. ust a sec.

Kieron (00:45):
Sorry, Clayton. Welcome to Phonogram, where nothing s ever easy.

Clayton (00:49):
Here you are! I think I prefer the Ceefax version.
What do you all think?

SO WHILE FOR MY PEERS, MUSIC VIDEOS WOULD REMAIN EXOTIC AND ELUSIVE FOR ANOTHER DECADE, I GORGED ON THE FUTURE.

We had satellite television for six months.

amie (00:51):
LOVE the ceefax version.

Matt (00:52):
like the one with the black field behind the text.

Kieron (00:52):
think I do too. Strong. (Seriously — who's ever seen that in comic lettering before?)
How do the longer captions fit?

Clayton (00:52):
They're probably fine. I think the black field will let me get away with shrinking the text a little more. I'll knock out the rest of the captions right now.

Chrissy (11:04):
Sorry to have been awol last night. The Ceefax lettering looks AMAZING!

Photo © Rantz Hoseley

San Diego, 2006, a week before the first issue of *Phonogram* ever dropped.

On the left is **KIERON GILLEN**, who has since lost the rest of his hair and remaining integrity.
@kierongillen

In the middle is **JAMIE MCKELVIE**, who has since failed to escape working with Kieron.
@mckelvie

On the right isn't **MATTHEW WILSON**. It's **Kelly Sue DeConnick**.
Matt hadn't met Kieron and Jamie by 2006. His life was so much better.
@COLORnMATT

CLAYTON COWLES probably wasn't born in 2006.
@ClaytonCowles

ALSO BY THE CREATORS

PHONOGRAM

VOLUME 1:
RUE BRITANNIA

VOLUME 2:
THE SINGLES CLUB

PHONOGRAM
RUE BRITANNIA
Kieron GILLEN Jamie McKELVIE

PHONOGRAM
THE SINGLES CLUB
KIERON GILLEN & JAMIE McKELVIE

THE WICKED + THE DIVINE

VOL. 1: THE FAUST ACT
#1–5 COLLECTED

VOL. 2: FANDEMONIUM
#6–11 COLLECTED

VOL. 3: COMMERCIAL SUICIDE
#12–17 COLLECTED

WWW.WICDIV.COM

GILLEN McKELVIE WILSON COWLES
THE WICKED +
THE FAUST ACT

GILLEN McKELVIE WILSON COWLES
THE WICKED +
FANDEMONIUM

GILLEN McKELVIE WILSON COWLES
THE
COMMERCIAL SUICIDE

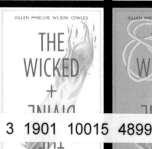